Right as Rain

Right as Rain

TRICIA STRINGER

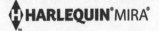

First Published 2013
Second Australian Paperback Edition 2014
ISBN 978 174356945 0

Published by
Harlequin Mira
An imprint of Harlequin Enterprises (Australia) Pty Ltd.
Level 19
201 Elizabeth St
SYDNEY NSW 2000
AUSTRALIA

Printed and bound in Australia by McPhersons Printing Group

MIX
Paper from
responsible sources
FSC® C001695

ACKNOWLEDGEMENTS

During my travels to research Right as Rain, I met many people and visited many wonderful places in South Australia's beautiful South East. In particular, I would like to thank Di & Graham Jenke and Erin & Pete Ballantyne for their generous hospitality and for their patient answering of my many questions about farming in their regions.

My thanks to editor Glenda Downing for her skill and sense of humour and to Sue Brockhoff and the fantastic team at Harlequin Australia. There's so much to do in bringing forth a book and I take my hat off to you all. What a team! Thank you.

To fellow writers who encourage along the way – from the CB group, to Fiona McIntosh and her first group of Sunflowers and my new writing buddies amongst the Romance Writers of Australia – a big thank you for your collegiate support and friendship.

I am so lucky for the love of friends and family, near and far, who understand and encourage my writing life. Margie Arnold who is the quiet voice of reassurance, Sue Barlow and Kathy Snodgrass for some great road trips and Joy & Andrew Hilder who once again have the best spot for a writer to write. Thanks guys.

To my children and their wonderful partners who buoy me up with their love and are so proud for me – as I am for them – and to my rock, Daryl, thank you.

For Jared

CHAPTER
1

A motorbike revved, rousing Mackenna from the deep fug of a dreamless sleep. She rolled over to the other side of the bed. It was empty but she knew she hadn't dreamt the events of the previous night. Adam Walker was a real man, and she was in love. Her heart skipped a beat and she smiled and stretched across the bed. The sheet settled around her as she became aware of the silence of the room.

She prised her eyes open enough to squint through the open bathroom door. It was empty. It was only a small motel room and even through sleepy eyes she could see his clothes were missing from the couch and both bike helmets were no longer on the table by the door. Adam was gone.

The bike revved again, the sound reverberated in the early morning quiet of a slumbering Queenstown. New Zealand's adventure capital was catching its breath in the brief pause between the last of the revellers finally finding their beds and the workers not yet ready to face the new day. Wide awake now, Mackenna flung back the sheet sending assorted tourist brochures and papers from the bed-side cupboard to the floor. She gave only a quick glance to the mess before turning her attention to the window. On the street below, the motorbike burbled and the helmeted rider leant forward, glanced over his shoulder and roared down the street out of sight.

Her heart raced, but not like it had last night when she'd given in to Adam's caresses and taken him to her bed. Last night he'd been an attentive lover. She glanced at the clock by the bed. It was only just six o'clock. Why would he leave without saying anything? She chewed her lip. Surely her judgement wasn't that off? She'd rushed into relationships in the past and this time she'd been determined to take things more slowly and get to know Adam before leaping into bed with him. She'd kept her resolve for a few days. They'd spent the best part of a week together, being tourists and exploring the sights and activities on offer in Queenstown.

She pressed her forehead against the glass. The noise of the bike softened, as if the rider hesitated. She held her breath. The bike revved and revved again then roared away. She listened until the last burble of its engine faded and the street was quiet once again, then she flopped back onto the bed. Just because her past encounters had turned out to be with losers didn't mean Adam was one as well. She sat up quickly. Maybe he'd just gone to get something for breakfast to surprise her.

She dragged the bedclothes back from their pile on the floor and leant down to search for the skydiving brochures. Papers were scattered in all directions but she eventually found the one she was looking for and settled back against the pillows. Adam hadn't planned to skydive and it wasn't on Mackenna's list of must do's either, but they'd talked each other into it. That was the plan for today if the weather was okay.

By seven o'clock she'd studied the skydiving brochure for so long she knew every word on it. She dug her prepaid mobile phone from her bag. It was out of credit again. Because of its unreliability they'd always made set plans and hadn't used their phones, and Adam hadn't given her his number. She tossed the useless phone into a shopping bag along with all the brochures and made herself a coffee. At eight o'clock she had a shower and dressed and had another cup of coffee.

By the time nine o'clock came she realised there was no need for Adam to take both helmets for a trip to the shops. There was nothing of his left in the motel room. He wasn't coming back. The pain of rejection stabbed her like a knife and tears brimmed. In just one short week she had really believed he was the kind of man she could spend her life with. How that would work with him living in New Zealand and her in Australia she hadn't thought through yet.

She picked up her camera and found the picture she'd taken of them yesterday, the two of them leaning in. They both looked so happy. Another stab of pain jabbed her chest. He was just another guy having some fun. What an idiot she'd been to think it would amount to anything more than a holiday romance.

At least no-one else knew about Adam. What happened on holiday stayed on holiday. It was never said exactly, but her parents expected her to find a bloke and get married. Up until now she'd not had much luck with that. No-one had measured up, until Adam. He was a chef on holiday, a kind of busman's holiday, and had been filling in a couple of shifts for a mate. She'd been mesmerised by his deep brown eyes, his tight dark curls and his ready smile. His quirky New Zealand accent, softened by the influence of his Australian mother, was warm and charming. Their attraction had been instant.

What a fool she was. She didn't know much about him at all. She didn't even know where it was he had been cooking. The tears threatened again. She dashed to the bathroom and doused her face in cold water. It was time to move on. She had other things to do, rather than mope over another loser of a guy. She hesitated, reluctant even with his desertion to think of Adam so harshly. At the sight of her puffy-faced reflection in the mirror, she drew in a breath and pulled back her shoulders.

"Time to get back to work, Mackenna," she told herself and began to pack her bags.

"Your husband is out of theatre, Mrs Birch."

Louise dragged her gaze away from the window looking out over the hospital roof and turned to the nurse.

"How . . . how is he?" Her mouth was dry, making her tongue stick as she forced the words out.

"He's doing fine. Doctor will be in to see you as soon as he's finished in theatre."

Left alone, Louise sank onto the one chair in the room as her legs went to jelly under her. No matter how many times they told her angiograms were routine, she knew things could go wrong. She put on a brave face for her husband's sake but, left alone, her thoughts terrorised her.

She looked down at the large white envelope protruding from the handbag she gripped with both hands. While Lyle had been in theatre she'd gone to collect the papers they'd signed the day before. She opened the envelope and slid out the crisp white sheets. They'd had plenty of thinking time over the last month and a new will had been necessary. The previous one had been done before they'd had children, so an update was long overdue. Something they should have attended to before this. Somehow life was always too busy.

She flicked some stray hairs behind her ear. They'd argued over the wording and it had left them both uncomfortable. Arguments were a rare thing in their married life. Lyle had always been in charge of the farm and her domain was the house. In difficult situations one acquiesced to the other, depending on the circumstance, and they'd made a good partnership.

This was quite different, of course. Making decisions about property and livelihoods in the event of someone's death wasn't an easy thing. Lyle hadn't wanted it set out in the way Louise had demanded, but he had wavered and she'd taken advantage of his weakened health to press home her point. A pang of guilt coursed through her. She pushed it away. This was for the best. Lyle would be on his feet again soon and everything would return to normal . . . but just in case.

She dropped the papers onto the bedside cupboard and began to pace the small room. The first lot of stents were meant to fix the problem but Lyle kept getting pains. She'd thought it was the anxiety the doctor had said was natural after a heart attack, but Lyle had insisted it was more than that. Perhaps there was something the doctor was keeping from them. Why was Lyle still getting pain? Would the doctor be able to fix it this time? She stopped as the door opened and her husband was wheeled back into the room.

He gave her a small thumbs-up, and she kept out of the way while the nurses settled him in his bed.

"Doc reckons he's fixed it this time, Lou," Lyle said as soon as the nurses had gone.

"That's a relief."

"He'll be in to see us later."

Louise picked up his hand and squeezed it. "You'll be much better soon."

He cleared his throat. "I'm as dry as a chip."

She reached for his glass and he spotted the envelope.

"That our wills?" he asked.

"I went out while you were in theatre."

Lyle sighed. "I'm still not – "

"I don't want you to worry about it." Louise cut him off. "We're doing the right thing."

"I'm not so sure, love," he mumbled and licked his lips.

Louise offered him a sip of water. He closed his eyes.

"The angio wasn't a very pleasant experience. Hope they won't need to do it again in a hurry."

She brushed gently at his cheek. He lifted a hand to pat hers but kept his eyes closed. He looked like he'd been through the wringer. She slipped the envelope back into her bag. There was no need to worry him about them now. What was done was done.

Hugh hesitated at the back door. After the big noise of his homecoming dinner last night the house was very quiet. Three older brothers, their wives and children made for a rowdy assembly when they all got together. His mum loved it. She was in her element with them all seated around the family table, but not Hugh. He was often the butt of his brothers' jokes and no longer at ease with his father. For Hugh a family gathering wasn't a scene of enjoyment, more one of endurance but he did it for his mother. He'd been home two months earlier for Christmas and had barely stayed for twenty-four hours on that visit.

Now he was home for a couple of months. It was just temporary but he already knew it was a mistake to have taken on the agriculture consultant's job. He'd agreed only because he had some time up his sleeve before his new challenge and he owed it to his mother. His rare visits home were always too short for her.

He turned at the sound of a vehicle.

"What the . . .!"

He retraced his steps to the garden gate. The old farm ute, driven by his mother, grumbled to a stuttering halt with a big log attached to the tow bar. He looked from the lump of wood to the gouge marks in the dust and back to his mother.

"Hello, love," she said brightly as she scrambled out of the driver's seat. "You're just in time to help me."

"What are you doing, Mum?"

"I'm working on the side garden," she said. "This log is going to be a seat."

The side garden was a misleading name for the wild expanse of trees and weeds that his mother had tried to tame. Despite several attempts over the years, she'd never managed to change the garden to the vision she imagined. She was always so busy helping around the property, raising children and now grandchildren. It had become a standard family joke that Mum would get a bee in her bonnet from time to time and try to cultivate the jungle her husband had named Mary's Folly. Of course none of them ever offered to help her, and she would run out of steam. A few months or a year would pass before she'd tackle it again.

They stood either side of the log and she reached across and patted his cheek. "It's so good to have you home, love. Now that you're here a bit longer, you can settle in for a while. If you find a nice local girl, you might like to stay." She winked at him from under her broad hat.

"Don't go down that path, Mum. I've already told you this is just a temporary visit."

"Temporary can be made permanent."

"Mum . . ."

"Help me get this off." She cut him short to deflect what she didn't want to hear and began grappling with the huge log.

Hugh reached across and helped her undo the rope.

"Hell!" he said as the weight of the wood wrenched free from their hands and hit the ground with a thud, forcing them both to jump clear. "How did you get this hooked up by yourself?"

"It was sticking up at one end," his mother said as she inspected her find. "It fell in the strong wind we had a few weeks back. I just lassoed it with the rope and dragged it with the ute."

"Where do you think you're going to put it?"

"I told you, in the side garden." She put her hands to her broad hips and glared at him. She wasn't a very tall woman and at that moment she resembled some kind of mythical woodland creature in her wide hat and a dress that hugged every roll, down to her feet in thick socks and a pair of boots she'd have taken from the assortment at the back door. Hugh didn't dare smile. Instead, he turned and began to walk. He knew there was no point arguing with her, just as he knew she would use every possible chance over the next couple of months to entice him to stay.

"Show me where you want it," he said over his shoulder as he led the way around the side of the house.

CHAPTER
2

"Oh, look at that view," the Australian voice gushed. "Stop darling, take a picture."

Adam felt rather than saw the couple beside him taking their holiday snaps. He knew what they were looking at and he'd purposefully chosen a seat with his back to it.

At the end of the street behind him, the lake stretched out to be met by the greens, browns and greys of the rugged mountains rising out of it. He'd been to Queenstown several times but he'd never really taken a lot of notice of the views. Most of his trips had been for work and to try all the activities on offer. This last week had been different. Mackenna had made it different. They'd wandered the streets hand in hand, eaten at restaurants, had impromptu picnics, enjoyed various tourist activities and yesterday they had planned to skydive together. Instead, he'd spent the afternoon looking for her. Once darkness descended he'd been forced to accept that she was gone.

He put his head in his hands.

"Hey, Ads." A hand slapped him on the back and he sat up. He watched as Jeff slipped into the chair opposite him.

"Has something happened with your grandfather?" Jeff asked.

"Still holding his own."

"I thought that long face might have meant bad news. Have you ordered? I haven't got long." Jeff glanced around. "Where is she?"

Adam picked up the menu. He'd been dreading this moment. He'd wanted to text Jeff and cancel but his need for a friend had stopped him. "I don't know."

"What do you mean you don't know?" Jeff placed his big hand over the list of lunchtime snacks.

Adam forced his eyes to meet his best mate's gaze. "She's gone."

"Gone? As in off to the shops or as in disappeared?" Jeff chuckled.

"Disappeared." Once again the pain of her loss stabbed at him. He watched the smile fade from Jeff's face.

"Have you called the police?"

"She left on purpose," Adam said quickly, before Jeff took things into his own hands. "When I got back to the motel yesterday the woman at reception said she'd checked out."

"Where did she go?"

"I don't know." He rubbed at his chest. "She took a taxi but the woman didn't know where to. She's just . . . disappeared."

Adam studied the menu through watery eyes. Damn, Jeff would think him a fool. Adam was shocked himself. He'd never thought this emotion possible over a woman, but Mackenna wasn't like any woman he'd ever known. He loved her.

"Did you try ringing her?"

Adam shook his head. "Her phone doesn't work and . . . well, I didn't get her number. We were always together. We didn't need . . ." He sucked in a breath and stared at the menu but his eyes weren't reading it.

"Mate, I'm sorry." Jeff reached across the table and gripped his shoulder. "I know you really liked her but maybe you read it wrong."

Adam shook his head. "I couldn't have."

"Sometimes women . . . well, maybe she didn't feel the same way. Aussie girl on holiday meets good-looking New Zealand bloke." Jeff dropped his hand. His voice trailed away leaving the rest unsaid.

Adam frowned. Was Mackenna that kind of girl? He hadn't thought so. They were meant for each other, he'd known that within the first few hours they'd spent together. She'd felt it too. He'd seen it in her vibrant green eyes.

"Well, on the bright side," Jeff said, "if you're here without a woman you can spend more time with me."

Adam looked into Jeff's big round grinning face. They'd been best friends since they started as apprentices in Auckland. Both chefs, Jeff now had his own restaurant here in Queenstown while Adam had always worked for other people, learning and moving on. He had no desire to own his own place.

"Slave labour you mean?" It came out sharper than Adam had intended but if he hadn't responded to Jeff's desperate call yesterday morning, he might still be with Mackenna.

"I didn't plan a flat battery and my sous chef to be sick." Jeff sat back in his chair. He spoke softly. "Giving me a ride and covering a shift was good of you. I do appreciate your help you know, Ads."

Adam instantly regretted his words. "I know, mate. It's not your fault. I should have woken her up, told her what I was doing . . ." They lapsed into silence.

The lunchtime crowd ebbed and flowed around them. A waitress appeared, pen and paper in hand. Adam ordered a bowl of wedges. It was at the top of the menu. Jeff ordered them both a beer.

"So will you hang around a bit longer?" he asked. "You're between jobs and I really could do with the help."

Adam glanced at his mate.

"I'd pay you," Jeff added.

"I don't know what I'm going to do. There was a job I was going to apply for in Wellington but now . . . I don't know. Call me an idiot but I hadn't thought past being with Mackenna."

"Idiot," Jeff said and gave him a pretend slap to the side of his head. "Was she flying back to Australia from here?"

"No, Christchurch."

A sudden thought hit Adam. He jumped up then steadied the table as beer slopped from his glass.

"What are you doing?" Jeff grabbed his own glass.

"Her flight home is still a week away." Adam reached under the table for his bike helmet. He didn't know her number but he knew the airline and the time of her flight.

"What are you going to do?" Jeff was standing now; a good head taller than Adam, he frowned down at him.

"I'm going to Christchurch."

"What about lunch?"

"Sorry, mate."

Adam hurried up the street weaving in and out of the crowd. Suddenly he could see the leafy green trees, hear the birds and smell the food wafting from the eateries.

"Please wait for me, Mackenna," he murmured.

CHAPTER

3

The sun reflected back from the sign announcing Woolly Swamp Farm. Even wearing sunglasses Mackenna had to squint her eyes against the brightness. The sky was cloudless, which was unusual for April.

She braked the car to a stop at the entrance to the driveway and gave herself a moment. Ahead of her the track wound up the slight rise of a hill to the house nestled amongst the gums and assorted sheds scattered across the yard. She let out a sigh. Six weeks ago she'd been anxious to escape but now she was glad to be home again. Surely all travellers felt that way but they didn't necessarily cut their trips short by several days. It didn't bother Mackenna, she was more than happy to be here – in fact she was relieved. Her last few days in New Zealand had been full of turmoil. She thought briefly of her hurried departure. Did that mean Woolly Swamp was home or another escape? She buried that thought and cast her eyes left.

Rising up amongst the recently planted tea-trees, the original stone homestead faced back towards the main road. Signs of restoration were all around the old house and fresh timber beams crisscrossed its gaping top. The iron roof should have been on by now. A small ripple of excitement coursed through her; this building factored large in her plans for Woolly Swamp. Now that she was home she wanted to forge ahead.

She looked right. A mob of sheep grazed in the distance with a couple of lambs amongst them. That was weird. It was too early for lambs. Closer, she watched a crow cruise to the ground and then hop to a lump in the paddock. It was too far away for her to see what had attracted its attention.

She edged her car through the gate and immediately noticed the newspapers lying in the dry grass of the verge, where the bus driver would have tossed them. She frowned. That was odd as well. She pushed open the car door and reached out to retrieve them. Her mother walked to the gate every day to pick up the paper; called it her morning constitutional.

Mackenna glanced back across the paddock. Two crows were busy picking now. She lifted her hand against the midday sun and peered at them. The lump looked like the body of a lamb. She tossed the papers onto the seat beside her and sped down the track. Instead of continuing to the house she turned right and followed the fence to the gate, marking the entrance to the paddock with the sheep.

Judging by the low level of pasture the mob of Corriedale Dorset ewes must have been in here a while. Mackenna cast her eyes about and frowned. There was no sign of top-up feeds either. She drove across the paddock. Several sheep lifted their heads to watch as she advanced and the crows took to the air. The lamb was small, only a few days old. The scavenging birds had already started on its eyes but otherwise it looked perfect. She rolled it over. There was blood on its nose and a hole in its side.

"A bloody fox."

Mackenna gritted her teeth at the waste and scooped up the pathetic animal. She slipped it into an old shopping bag and dumped it in the boot of her car, beside her case. Then she scanned the paddock for Alfie the alpaca, but he was nowhere to be seen. Alfie was always with lambing ewes, an ever-vigilant protector against foxes. Something was definitely not right. These sheep were low on food and normally her father would have been out at first light to check a paddock of lambing ewes. He wouldn't have missed the dead lamb.

She scrutinised the house yard as she pulled up beside the back gate. The garage door was open and there was no car inside it. Nor was there any sign of the two farm dogs that usually greeted any approaching vehicle. As soon as she stepped out of the car she heard them. The kennels were under the stand of gums behind the garage. Mackenna ignored their barking and made her way inside.

Her grandparents had built the house and she stepped into it like she would a pair of comfy boots. Once more she sighed. There really was no place like home – unless home was turned on its head. She stood in the doorway to her mother's kitchen and surveyed the mess. There were dirty dishes on the benches, newspapers and unopened mail scattered across the table amongst empty beer cans and a pizza box, and clothes draped on the backs of chairs. She was beginning to worry. There had been many busy times over the years and sometimes emergencies but her mother somehow managed to maintain a tidy house, even when she was sick.

Mackenna spun at the sound of boots on the verandah. The bloke opening the screen door paused and pulled back his shoulders, drawing him to a height that forced her to look up to meet his deep brown eyes. Wavy black hair escaped from under his cap. By anyone's standards he was a good-looking guy.

"Who are you?" she stammered.

"More to the point, who are you?" He stepped into the house.

"Mackenna Birch."

"The prodigal daughter." His broad face swept into a seductive smile. "You've returned."

Mackenna didn't like the way he looked her up and down. She flicked her eyes down at his huge boots. "My mother doesn't allow boots in the house."

"She's not here and I was just dropping a docket." He waved a piece of paper back and forth in front of her. "In and out."

His casual manner raised Mackenna's ire further. Who was this guy in their family home acting like he owned it?

He moved past her into the kitchen, paused at the mess on the table then went to the fridge and stuck the paper to it with a magnet. It was between the postcard she'd sent first from New York and the one she'd sent next from Hawaii.

"It's the fuel docket," he said. "Should be safe there till Louise gets back."

"So you've delivered the diesel?" Mackenna scratched her forehead. Things had really changed if the new fuel driver was already on first name terms with her mother and was allowed access to their home. Normally the docket would be taped to the tank.

"Kind of." He made his way back to where she still hovered in the kitchen doorway. "You haven't spoken to your parents?"

"I would if I knew where they were."

"Did you try ringing?"

"I was going to surprise them. I'm home earlier than expected."

"Guess it's you with the surprise then." He pushed open the screen door. "Ask Patrick. He's meant to be keeping an eye on things."

"My brother's here?"

"Probably still in bed, but that's not my business." He tapped his hand to the brim of his cap and gave her a smile. "Be seeing ya."

The door swung shut and she remained where she was, listening to the sound of his boots retreating along the verandah.

"Not if I can help it," she muttered. He hadn't even told her his name. "Arrogant . . ."

"Sis!"

Mackenna turned. Her brother, Patrick, stood before her, blinking bleary eyes into the light. He was eight years younger than her but in his unshaven, dishevelled state he looked older.

"I'm glad it's only you. I thought Mum must be home." He swept his fingers through his hair making the short dark tufts stand on end. "There's a bit to do before she gets back."

"What's going on, Patrick? Why are you here?" Her brother rarely spent time at the farm these days. In fact, while she'd been away, he was supposedly working in Sydney.

"It's my home too." He shoved some cups out of the way and flicked on the kettle.

Mackenna ignored the jibe. "Where are Mum and Dad?"

"Haven't you spoken with Mum?" Patrick rummaged in the freezer and pulled out a container of their mother's slice. He sat it in a patch of sunlight on the bench.

"Obviously not. I got an earlier flight. Thought I'd jump in the car and come straight home."

"They're in Adelaide."

"Both of them? Together?" Her mother went to the city from time to time but her father rarely went further than the local community and the odd trip to Mount Gambier.

"Cup of tea?" Patrick waved a mug at her.

Mackenna glanced longingly at the coffee machine gleaming on the bench. It had probably been idle since she'd left six weeks ago.

"Yes, thanks, but tell me what's going on?"

"Dad had a heart attack."

"What!" Mackenna had been half seated but she jumped up, bumping the table and making the scattered papers slide and a can rattle to the floor.

"Settle down," Patrick said. "No need for you to have one too. He's okay now."

"When . . . why didn't . . ." Questions whirled through Mackenna's head. She didn't know which to ask first.

"Dad had the first attack not long after you left." He plonked a mug in front of her.

"First!"

"Well I don't understand these things. They put a couple of stents in and sent him home to take it easy."

"Why didn't they ring me to come home?"

"I reckon Dad was planning to but Mum wouldn't let him. Said it was the first proper holiday you'd had. She asked me to come."

"What about your work?" Patrick had left the farm as soon as he finished school, went to university and was working in marketing for a national company.

"They've been very understanding."

Mackenna gaped at her brother. He wasn't one for farm life and rarely came back to visit.

"My boss said family comes first," he said.

"So why are Mum and Dad in Adelaide now? You said first attack. Has he had another?"

"I don't think so."

"What do you mean?" Mackenna banged her hands on the table. That's what irked her about Patrick, he was always so vague.

"Take it easy. Dad had been complaining of pain so he had to go back for another angiogram. Mum rang last night and I think they've put in another stent."

"You think!" Mackenna slammed her hands on the table again. "Why on earth didn't anyone tell me?" She'd made a couple of phone calls home while she'd been away and sent a few emails but that damned mobile had been so unreliable. Now that she thought about it, she hadn't spoken to her father. Each time she'd been able to get through, her mother had said he was off doing things.

"Like I said, Mum wouldn't let us."

"How've you managed?"

Mackenna saw the anger flare in Patrick's eyes. He pushed away from the table and started dropping cans into the recycle bin. "Dad's been able to direct traffic, and I can follow instructions."

"I know Patch, but there's so much to do even with you here." Mackenna slumped in the chair. She'd sounded harsh and hoped the use of his pet name would calm the situation. "Are the neighbours helping?"

"Of course. And Dad's hired Cam Martin to do the truck work. I never got my heavy vehicle licence." Patrick looked around. "I thought I heard his voice when I got up."

"Really tall, dark wavy hair?"

"Sounds like him."

"Damn," Mackenna muttered. That would explain the confidence of the guy to walk into the kitchen, but she still felt he was taking a liberty.

"When did Dad put this Cam guy on?"

"About two weeks ago."

"So, let me get this straight." Mackenna stood up and paced the kitchen. "While I've been away, Dad's had a heart attack and ongoing treatment, you've given up your job to look after the place – "

"Well, not given up, exactly. I . . ." Patrick stopped talking as Mackenna locked eyes with him.

"And Dad's employed a working man." She stood in front of Patrick. "I've only been gone six weeks. And for the last three I've been in New Zealand for goodness sake. It's not as if I was in outer space." She swept her hair back and held it in a ponytail while she dug in her pocket for a band. "Why didn't someone tell me?"

"Stop bellowing at your brother."

Patrick leapt to his feet and Mackenna swivelled her head to see her mother standing in the doorway.

"Mum, I didn't hear the car. Where's Dad?"

"Letting the dogs out."

"Should he . . .?" Mackenna faltered as the weariness on her mother's face changed to anger.

"He shouldn't be doing anything but try telling him that, especially when his two grown children seem incapable of such a simple job."

"I'll go." Patrick shot out the door.

"How is he?" Mackenna asked. "I wish I'd known, Mum."

"He's tired but okay. It was my decision not to tell you." Her mother gave her a quick hug, then sighed and cast her eyes around the room. "Not quite the welcome home I would have planned."

Mackenna wasn't sure if she meant for herself or her daughter.

"I said I'd put the kettle on."

"It's not long boiled," Mackenna said.

"Good. Do you think you can start on this mess? Then we can all sit down for a chat when your dad comes in." Her mother stepped around the can that had rolled to the floor and reached for the kettle. She peered inside and began to refill it. "You're home early."

"I did most of the things I'd intended. The weather turned bad and there was a seat on an earlier flight." Mackenna had told herself that so often on the journey home, she believed it. She tried again to tug her hair into the band. It was a pity she hadn't taken the time to get it cut before she'd come home, but she didn't trust anyone except the local hairdresser to keep her unruly curls in line. "I didn't stay in Adelaide – came straight from the airport. If only I'd known . . ."

"Your hair looks pretty." Her mother started wiping down the table as Mackenna cleared off the assorted debris. "I like it when you don't colour it. Some people would kill for your auburn curls."

Once again the subject of her father had been redirected. And once again, even though she was thirty-two, Mackenna could still be made to feel guilty about colouring her hair. Dying hair was disapproved of. Some of her friends went to the hairdresser with their mothers and had pamper days together. Her mother would never see the necessity for that. Mackenna pursed her lips to hold in the questions she wanted to ask and instead, flew around the room setting it back in order and trying to keep her annoyance at Patrick in check. This was his mess that she was cleaning up – nothing had changed.

She looked up at the sound of the screen door and bit her lip as her father stepped into the kitchen. His face had lost its ruddy glow and the polo shirt she'd given him for Christmas hung loosely from his shoulders. Patrick appeared in the doorway close behind. For a moment there was silence as they all froze like pieces on a chessboard, then Mackenna flew across the room.

"Dad." She kissed his cheek and wrapped his frail frame in a careful embrace. They were matched in height and when she stepped back she could see tears welling in his eyes. It shocked her. She'd left him strong and healthy, physically tackling all the jobs the farm threw at him, now he looked barely fit enough to wrestle a kitten. She twisted her lips quickly into a grin and slipped an arm through his, leading him to a chair. "You've taken to visiting the city while I've been away."

"Couldn't let you be the only one to have a holiday."

"How'd you find it?"

"Got myself some four star accommodation. Room service was pretty good."

Mackenna laughed as she saw him give a glimmer of a grin. The tension eased and they all sat down. Louise put cups of tea in front of them and the thawed chocolate slice, although her father got dry biscuits Mackenna noted.

"What's been happening, Dad?" she asked.

"I've had a bloody heart attack. Who'd have guessed it?" He began to pat the table.

"Lyle." Louise put a hand on his.

"One of my arteries has required spare parts. They didn't get it right the first time so they've just done some more. Sent me home with a pile of pills and instructions to stay on light duties for a few weeks. Then I'll be right as rain."

"I wish I'd known." Mackenna looked into her father's weary eyes but he avoided her unspoken words and turned to Patrick.

"Your brother's here and I've hired a bloke to do some driving and heavy work."

"Something we should have done years ago," Louise piped in.

"Let's not talk about me for the moment. I've had enough of that while you've been gone." He paused and shifted in his seat. Pain etched in his face. "I want to hear all about your trip."

"Perhaps you should be resting first, Dad."

"Remember what the doctor said, Lyle. You've got to take it easy." Louise stood up and coaxed him to his feet. "You need a sleep. We can hear all about the holiday over dinner tonight."

"I am a bit tired, love." He gave Mackenna an apologetic look.

Once again she was shocked at his frailty and how easily he complied with Louise's instructions.

He stopped at the door. "Did you organise that drench, Patrick?"

"All done, Dad."

"And the rams need to be shifted back to the ram paddock."

"I know."

"Those ewes in the front paddock need more silage."

"Bed, Lyle," Louise said.

"Going."

"Can you bring in our bags, Patrick?" Louise called over her shoulder.

"Sure."

Mackenna was left alone in the kitchen. Her earlier relief at being home was gone. She'd only been away a few weeks but in that short time many things had changed. It was as if she'd stepped back into a different world.

CHAPTER

4

Mackenna's eyes flew open with a start. She was hot and her heart pounded in her chest. Adam had been kissing her, his quirky smile dancing before her eyes, but the grey early morning light brought her back to reality. She'd been dreaming. The warmth of his imagined embrace ebbed away and once again she felt the ache of his loss and rejection. She lay still, listening to the dawn bird calls, telling herself to breathe slowly and push Adam from her mind. That worked okay during the day, but she had no control over wayward dreams at night.

She rolled over and peered at the clock. It was only five thirty. She groaned and flopped back on her pillow. A deep rumbling snore reached her ears. Surely that couldn't be her father or Patrick? Her bedroom was at the top end of the house, away from theirs. It had originally been her parents' room with the corner window looking down towards the swamp; the only bedroom on this side of the house. They'd moved to the room closest to the bathroom and kitchen at the other end of the long passage when she'd left school and gone to Adelaide. Opposite her was the empty guestroom and Patrick's room was next, sandwiched between it and their parents'.

Going back to sleep was no longer an option. Mackenna tossed off the sheet and went to her door. The snoring was so loud she understood why she'd woken. She made her way down the passage to the guestroom door, which was ajar. The noise was loud enough to shake the walls. Perhaps her father had taken up residence in the spare room since his attack.

She peered around the door. There was a shape sprawled across the bed. Mackenna took a step forward, caught her toe on something, lost her balance and toppled to the floor.

The snoring stopped instantly and the bedside light snapped on. She gaped in horror as the new working man sat up on the bed and propped there, blinking back at her.

"What the . . .?" he yelped.

"Sorry, I . . ." Mackenna lost her voice as he swung to his feet and she was confronted with a pair of Mickey Mouse boxers hanging loosely from his hips. She picked herself up from the tangle of clothing on the floor. His naked chest was a solid sixpack and with the stubble on his chin and the hair loosely swept to one side, he could have been a model – except for the ridiculous boxers.

"Lucky Gran gave me these boxers for my birthday. I usually sleep naked."

Once again Mackenna was forced to look up at his face. A smile twitched on his lips – full plump lips. She focused on his crooked front teeth. She hadn't noticed them yesterday.

"Did you want something or is this a social call?" He was really grinning now.

"What are you doing here?"

"I work here."

"In this bedroom?" She flicked a hand at the room. "It's for guests."

"I guess that's another thing your parents haven't told you. Until the old house is fixed I use this room if I need to stay over. I've got a place in town but I got back late last night and was too tired to . . ."

"What old house?"

"The old stone place by the road."

"That's mine," Mackenna snapped.

"Whoa!" Cam put his hands in the air. "You'll need to take it up with them. Now since you've woken me up, I might as well get going."

He reached past her for a towel that was slung over an open wardrobe door, his bare arms just centimetres from her.

"Mind if I go first in the shower?" he said.

He grinned and without waiting for an answer, stepped around her and out the door. His unwashed male scent wafted in the air. She wrinkled her nose. There was no way he was having her house. She turned on her heel and marched back to her bedroom. It appeared there were a lot of things her parents hadn't told her yet.

Yesterday there'd been little time for discussion. She'd tried to go over the stock logbook with her father but her mother had sent her to town on errands. When she got back she'd spent the rest of the afternoon checking sheep. Patrick may think he could follow directions but she'd found a gate not secure, more stock that needed top-up feed and a water trough not working properly. With this unseasonal burst of heat, that could be disastrous. She'd gone to look at the old place while she'd been out and about. Nothing more could be done to it until the roof went on. By the time she'd come inside, Patrick had headed into town, her mother had the evening meal ready and her father was full of questions about her trip. Now that she thought about it, they'd changed the subject when she'd asked why the old house wasn't finished.

She dressed quickly then paused to listen for sounds beyond her door. There was no way she wanted to run into a half-naked Cam in the passage. She made it to the kitchen, where her mother was cooking poached eggs for breakfast.

"What's going on with the old house, Mum?"

"Good morning to you too," her mother said. "Can you get the juice and some glasses?"

She did as she was asked while keeping an eye on her mother. Louise wore one of Mackenna's old black aprons over a light shirt and three-quarter pants, prepared for housework and any jobs she may be called to assist with outside.

"That Cam guy seems to think he's going to live in it," Mackenna said.

"We need a working man."

"I agree. The job's been bigger than us for a while and with our plans for expansion – "

"They've been put on hold."

"I can understand that while I was away but now that I'm back – "

"Mackenna!" Her mother's sharp tone cut her off again. "Your father's had a heart attack. We can't go back to how things were. Everything's changed."

Mackenna frowned. "In what way?" She studied her mother's face as she waited for an answer.

Louise's eyes were bright. The weariness of yesterday was gone. Her hair with its neat strips of salt-and-pepper grey was brushed into the bob style she always wore and a touch of lipstick coloured her lips. All appeared normal. She turned away to check on the eggs.

"Mum?" Mackenna gripped the back of a chair in frustration. "Dad's doing okay isn't he, and I'm fit. Why do our plans for the future of Woolly Swamp have to change?"

Sounds of movement came from the passage.

"Not now," her mother said as Patrick and then Cam arrived.

"Good morning, Louise," Cam said. He turned to Mackenna. "And good morning to you . . . officially."

She nodded her head and busied herself making toast. She didn't want him telling the rest of the family about her blundering into his bedroom.

"How's Lyle today?" Cam asked.

"Tired," Louise said.

Mackenna felt a pang of guilt. She hadn't asked after her father.

"I'll take him some breakfast," she said.

"No." Louise wagged the spatula at her. "He's probably gone back to sleep. I'll make him something later. You don't need to ask him anything do you, Cam?"

"No. The roof iron is on the truck. I'll unload it this morning. Then we've got those rams to shift, Patrick."

Mackenna watched in amazement as the hired help gave directions in the family kitchen. Her mother was right. Lots of things had changed but Mackenna would soon set that straight.

"Has Ted been out to test for worms?" she asked.

"Yes . . . well no," Patrick said. "Dad asked me to call him last week but he was away. His replacement came out, your old friend from Morning Star Station, Hugh McDonald."

"I didn't know he was back." Mackenna hadn't seen Hugh in a long time. They'd been very close once, doing everything together with their mutual friend Carol – a formidable gang of three for many years. She gave a wistful thought to those carefree days before focusing back on Patrick. "What did he say?"

"They've got worms."

"What kind of worms?" she asked, aware that both the men had been served eggs and toast while nothing had been set before her.

"What difference does it make?" Patrick asked.

"There's an extra test to tell what kind of worms so we get the specific drench."

"Drench is drench." Cam chuckled and rolled his eyes at Patrick.

"No, it's not," Mackenna persisted.

"It costs more for that test," Patrick said. "Dad didn't say, so I didn't ask for it."

"It will cost a lot more if the drench you got isn't the right one." Mackenna was annoyed. Between Patrick and Cam, things were obviously not being done properly. "I'll give Hugh a call."

"I can do it," Patrick said. The colour was rising in his cheeks.

"Why don't you leave it to the blokes, Mackenna?" Her mother patted her on the shoulder. "You still haven't shown me your holiday pictures."

"I will later. My camera's in the car." Mackenna had been so busy yesterday, her car was still by the gate where she'd left it. She hadn't unpacked a thing. "Bloody hell, my car!" She jumped up from the table.

"Mackenna!" her mother rebuked. "I won't tolerate bad language in the house."

"What's the matter?" Patrick asked.

"I found a dead lamb in the paddock on my way in yesterday," she snapped. "I put it in my boot."

She turned away from their inquiring eyes and lurched across the kitchen. The smirk she'd seen on Cam's face only deepened her sour mood. She stopped as another thought came to her. She turned to her brother. "Where's Alfie?"

"Who's Alfie?"

"Our alpaca," she said. "If he'd been with the ewes a fox wouldn't have killed one in the first place."

"Dad didn't say anything about an alpaca." Patrick looked to his mother. "I thought he was dead."

"Don't get on your high horse, Mackenna," Louise said. "We haven't been home, and Patrick didn't know about Alfie."

"We've had him over a year," Mackenna said. "I'd better go and shift him in. And hold off on that drench until I can find out more."

Conscious of three sets of eyes glaring at her, she swept out the door.

Mackenna lathered her hands a second time with soap and scrubbed them in the warm water. Not many things made her squeamish but the smell of that lamb after a day in the heat had made her gag. It had taken several attempts to remove the foul mess from her boot. Thank goodness she'd put it in the plastic bag. She'd moved her car to the shade of a tree and left the boot and doors open to air it.

While she'd been busy outside, she'd noticed the truck moving down the track towards the old place. She rubbed her hands dry on a towel and headed back to the kitchen with more confidence. At least Cam would be out of the house. Maybe she'd be able to pin her mother down.

She was surprised to find her father the only occupant. He was sitting at the table with a bowl of cereal. He looked up from the pile of mail he was reading and smiled.

"Morning, Mack."

She moved swiftly to give him a kiss on the cheek. It was a relief to see him looking more like the father she knew. It was only the gaunt face and the small dish of assorted pills beside his glass of juice that was a reminder of his ill health.

"The eggs are in the oven," he said. "Your mother's gone to feed the dogs and the chooks."

"Patrick should be doing that."

"He's helping Cam unload the roofing iron."

Mackenna put her plate of eggs on the table and sat down beside him. "That was all supposed to happen the week after I left." She spoke casually, wanting to know all that had or apparently hadn't happened in her absence but not wanting to push him.

"I took sick and didn't chase them. You know what these tradies are like. They're juggling several jobs and it's the squeaky wheel that gets the work done first. At least the bathroom's finished. We just need the roof back on the rest so we can finish the painting."

"Well now I'm home they'd better get on with it." She took a mouthful of egg. It was rubbery and barely warm. She ate the soggy toast instead.

"You don't mind staying in your old room?" her dad asked. "The old house will make a perfect working man's quarters. We'll leave the kitchen for now. It's fairly basic but Cam can eat most of his meals with us."

Mackenna's heart sank. "I've been working on a plan for the old place while I've been away. There's so much I want to talk over with you."

"I know."

"Like why we've got lambs a month early."

"That was a surprise for me too. I think I've . . ." He stopped at the sound of boots dropping outside the back door then leaned in closer and lowered his voice. "Your mother's taking my heart trouble pretty hard. I took on Cam as much to keep her happy as anything. I'll be back on my feet soon. Just go with things as they are for the moment."

That was rich coming from him. Her father was always busy and in control. It had taken several years of working together before he listened and took some of her suggestions for their property seriously.

"I'm not sure what to do," she said. "Everything's out of whack."

"I know, love." He patted her hand. "Officially you're still on holidays. Relax."

"Mackenna, I hope you're not bothering your father with work talk." Louise eyed them both closely as she came in the door carrying a bowl of eggs.

"Just hearing about her holiday, Lou. The jetboat ride and white-water rafting in New Zealand sound great."

Mackenna looked at her father wondering how he'd come up with that. He gave her a wink and then she noticed the postcard she'd sent from Queenstown was on the top of his pile of mail.

"It was fantastic. There was so much to do there." She let out a sigh. Her sadness over Adam's rejection had made her head for home. In light of all this, perhaps she should have stayed away longer.

CHAPTER

5

Louise returned from her walk to collect the paper and stepped back into the cool of the house. She paused for a moment letting the air settle around her and listened. She couldn't hear any movement from within. She stuck her head around the kitchen door but there was no-one there. The mail Lyle had been reading was still on the table. He'd had another restless night, and his tossing and turning had kept her awake too. Perhaps he'd gone back to bed. Louise felt a pang of envy. Wouldn't she love to sleep in, have someone wait on her and no responsibilities – just for a while?

She moved quietly along the passage to the first bedroom door and peered in. The bed was the rumpled mess he'd left behind when he'd got up this morning but there was no Lyle. Nor was he in his favourite chair in the lounge. Her heart began to thump. Ever since the day she'd found him slumped in that chair, clutching his chest, she imagined it would happen again, but next time he'd be dead. Sometimes, when he'd been dozing there, she'd crept up to him and watched for the rise and fall of his chest. The doctor had been reassuring after this last stent had been put in, but it made no difference to Louise. She was terrified of losing her husband and watched him like a hawk.

She hurried along the passage checking all the rooms. The three other bedrooms were in various forms of disarray. Neither of her children had learnt to make a bed once they got out of it and apparently neither had Cam. The rarely used dining room was empty and Lyle wasn't in the bathroom. He must have gone outside.

She went through the back door and looked across the garden towards the sheds. The air shimmered in the heat. Summer was officially over but this week had been another hot one and the pattern seemed set to continue for a while.

Louise was about to pull on her boots again when she heard a vehicle. Shielding her eyes with her hand she watched as their battered tray-top ute pulled up at the back gate. She could see Mackenna behind the wheel and Lyle beside her. They were laughing together. Louise sucked in a deep breath and went back inside the house. The screen door snapped shut behind her and she closed the wooden door firmly to keep out the heat. She should have known Mackenna would take him off to look at something as soon as her back was turned. Those two were thick as thieves again already, even though she'd worked hard to discourage it.

Thankfully there were plenty of jobs outside to keep Mackenna busy, but she and Lyle had spent an hour or so yesterday afternoon at the computer going over the stock logbook. Louise had encouraged Patrick to join them and he'd been quite involved until Mackenna had teased him about not knowing a wether from a ram. Louise had put her foot down then and made them stop. Lyle needed a rest and she'd sent Mackenna into town for groceries.

Louise gathered up the pile of mail and frowned as she discovered one of Lyle's pills had rolled underneath. It was so important he take them all, and at the right time, but he seemed blasé about them. She knew one of them caused him headaches, but rather a headache than be dead. She sat the pill back in the dish and busied herself at the sink. The breakfast dishes had been stacked in the dishwasher but the pots and pans remained.

The back door opened and the sound of her husband and daughter in conversation drifted in. She shoved the frying pan under the frothy water. It wasn't that she didn't want them to have a close relationship, but for them it wasn't the usual father-daughter bond. They had the farm in common and over the last few years Mackenna had become more and more involved in the decision-making – as if the farm was as much hers as her parents. She forgot she had a brother and he had rights to the property. He was the male, after all.

"I'll do those, Mum."

Louise kept scrubbing. "I've nearly finished."

"Patrick rang," Lyle said. "The roofing contractor's turned up and it's all go."

"I wondered where you were." Louise didn't look back. She was still nursing her anger and fright from Lyle's disappearance. She'd heard all the activity at the old house as she'd walked down the track and back but she hadn't given the place more than a glance. Too many other things to think about.

"I wanted to have a look so Mackenna drove me down."

"Just as well," Louise said. "You know you're not allowed to drive for a few days."

"Really?" Mackenna sounded surprised. "Why, Dad?"

Louise spun around and glared at the two of them. "He's had a heart attack and just had a second angiogram and another stent put in. I know from the outside there's little to show for it but he has to be careful."

"Steady up, Lou."

Lyle smiled but she could see how tired he was. She softened her voice.

"You should go back to bed," she said. "I'll bring you a cup of tea and the pill you forgot to take." She nodded towards the table. The three of them stood staring at the little dish with the coloured pill.

The phone rang, breaking the tension.

"Get that will you, Mackenna?" Louise galvanised into action again. "Lyle, I really think you should rest."

"I'll be in the lounge," he said.

She watched him amble from the room as Mackenna picked up the phone.

"Oh yes, Hugh." Mackenna's voice was warm.

Lyle paused to listen then caught Louise's eye. His shoulders slumped and he ambled off.

Mackenna chatted to her old schoolfriend and Louise turned back to the sink. She felt a wave of remorse. It was as if she was his warden rather than his wife, but Lyle was his own worst enemy. Used to being fit and in control of every situation, he was not so good at taking care of himself. He'd never had to with Louise by his side, and now her job of homemaker and wife had been burdened with that of carer. She didn't like how it had changed her.

"Hugh's following up on the worm test." Mackenna hung up the phone as Louise pulled off her rubber gloves.

"Is that what your father wanted?"

A puzzled look crossed Mackenna's face. "He always has in the past."

"That's fine. It's just that Patrick has to learn these things."

Louise began to lay out a tray with the newspaper and a cup of tea. "Why?"

Mackenna's question made her look up at her daughter. She hadn't moved from her spot beside the phone.

"Why what?"

"Why would Patrick want to learn about worms in sheep poo now when he's never been the slightest bit interested before?"

Louise smothered the urge to defend her son. "He's grown up. Had some time away like you did. It's changed him."

"It was good he could come home to help out."

"You could explain things to him. If he'd understood why the test was necessary . . ."

"I don't blame him." Mackenna chuckled. "Who would want to know about worms if you didn't have to? He doesn't need it with his marketing work."

"What do you think of Cam?" Louise changed the subject. No need for Mackenna to think Patrick was doing any more than help-ing out at this stage.

"I've only just met him."

"There weren't many applicants. He's from Victoria and he's worked on farms before. That was a bonus."

"Hmmm." Mackenna was staring out the window.

"Don't you like him?"

"Well, I wouldn't say that. He's just a bit sure of himself. Comes into the house like he owns it."

"He's not here very often. Mostly he stays in town. It will be easier once the old place is finished."

There was a pause before Mackenna replied.

"I wish there was some other way," she said. "I had a different idea for that house."

She turned back from the window and folded her arms. Louise could see there was going to be trouble. If only Mackenna had stayed away one more week like she'd planned. The house would have been finished enough for Cam to be in it and Patrick would have had another week of learning the ropes.

"Don't go pushing your father. He needs time to recover."

"I understand that Mum, and I haven't said much at all. It's just . . . disappointing."

"Disappointing isn't a word I'd use for a heart attack."

"I didn't mean . . ."

"For once this isn't about you, Mackenna." Louise put some dry biscuits on the tray beside the tea and the pill dish. "We've all got to pull together. That means involving Patrick and taking on extra help."

Mackenna fiddled with her ponytail. Louise could see the hurt on her face.

"There's plenty of room for you in the house." She spoke gently this time. "You don't need the old place and it's perfect for Cam."

Mackenna opened her mouth but the ringing of the phone cut her off.

"Get that will you, love. Drives me crazy ringing all day."

Louise picked up the tray to carry in to Lyle. Behind her she heard her daughter answer the phone. She felt bad about not telling Mackenna the truth. She loved her daughter but she would be taken care of. Louise would make sure of that. There was money put aside. Getting Patrick up to speed was her main concern now – after Lyle of course.

CHAPTER
6

Hugh stepped out of the four-wheel drive and Mackenna rushed forward. She threw her arms around her old friend and hugged him close. He was tense beneath her arms and there was a slight pause before he responded.

"How are you, Mack?" He pushed his hat onto his head.

"I'm fine." She moved back a pace. They were a similar height and she looked directly into his pale blue eyes. The wariness was still there even after all this time and his face had a gaunt look.

"I was surprised to hear from you." Hugh turned away and fiddled with something in the cab before he finally shut the door and turned back to her. "The way Patrick spoke I thought you were away from the place for a lot longer."

"This has been a week of surprises. You're just one more person I didn't expect to see either but I'm glad you're here."

"I'm between jobs so I said I'd fill in while Ted's away."

"Oh." Mackenna tried not to sound disappointed. Hugh had been gone from the district several years but he was a great mate and she missed him. She'd hoped he may have returned for good.

"You and my mother make a good pair. Each time I come back she wants me to stay." He smiled but his lips barely turned up. "Nothing's changed, Mack. There's nothing for me here."

Mackenna slipped her arm through his and they started walking towards the sheep yards. "Ag consultants are always in demand."

Hugh stopped and Mackenna pulled up beside him.

"You know that's not what I mean."

She did know and there was no point in dredging up the past, but she had hoped time would mend some broken bridges. She nudged him with her shoulder. "Come on Mr Ag Consultant. Come and check out these rams. When I left they were in peak condition but with Dad sick and Patrick in charge something's gone astray."

They moved off again.

"I must admit I was surprised to get the call from Patch about the drench."

"That could have been a stuff-up." Mackenna flicked a stone with her boot.

"I feel a bit responsible. I thought Ted had done the preliminaries."

"Patrick doesn't understand the importance of getting the right drench."

"I never thought he was interested in the farm?"

"He's not." This time Mackenna stopped and turned to look at Hugh. "At least he wasn't. I've been away, Dad's had heart trouble, Mum's acting weird, and they've employed a working man along with bringing Patrick home. We've even got sheep dropping lambs that shouldn't be born for another month. It's as if I've stepped back into someone else's life."

"I know what that's like."

"I know," she said gently, "but this isn't quite the same."

"No." He grimaced and they started walking again. "This property has improved heaps since the old days."

"Before I came back to work here, you mean."

"Mum says you've had a lot to do with it. Says you should have been born a boy."

Mackenna ignored Mary McDonald's sexist comment. There were still those around the district who thought a woman's place was in the farmhouse, not out on the farm. Mackenna was glad her father wasn't one of them. "Dad was set in his ways, doing things as he'd always done, but I've worked really hard studying up best practice and he's been gradually seeing things my way. Changing nearly exclusively to Corriedales was a big shift. We're making improvements in our returns already."

"It's a big job for – "

Mackenna pulled her arm from his. "Now don't you go sounding like your mother, Hugh McDonald. I'm more than capable of doing what needs to be done around here."

"Settle, Mack." They'd reached the pen that enclosed the rams and he put a foot on the bottom rail. "I was going to say it's a big job for two. Didn't you buy Murphy's place?"

Mackenna nodded.

"So, you've increased your land and stock and taken on a sheep stud that requires more hands-on practices. I also hear you've started selling direct to a local restaurant."

Mackenna studied her friend. His mother certainly had filled him in.

"It just seems to me that taking on a working man makes sense," he continued, "if you want to manage such a large investment well."

"I know. Dad and I had discussed hiring someone a few times before I went away. I would like to have been consulted, that's all."

"And when I think about it, I can understand why they called Patrick home. Your parents needed help in a hurry and Patch isn't totally useless, even if he can't tell one sheep from another."

He chuckled and Mackenna was pleased to see his face light up, even if it was at her brother's expense.

"We usually drench pre-lambing, but I've got a paddock of ewes dropping full-term lambs a month early. They only started a few days ago, while Dad was having his last angio. I don't think Patrick even realised."

"It can happen," Hugh said. "Is it possible last year's lambs were left with their mothers longer than usual?"

Mackenna thought back. "I don't think . . ." Then she remembered. "Shearing was delayed. We were busy. Dad was helping the neighbours and I was late shifting them, but the lambs would only have been four months."

"Old enough with these fellas."

Mackenna's mouth dropped open and Hugh laughed.

"The little devils," she said then laughed with him. "At least that explains it."

She threw an arm around his shoulder and squeezed.

"I'm so glad you're here, old buddy. Things make sense when you're around."

He removed her arm and climbed up on the railing. "Just don't get used to it," he said and dropped to the other side.

She followed him over. Hugh used to be so bright and full of fun. Mackenna's and Carol's parents were always happy to let them go to parties if Hugh was with them. He was meant to be the responsible, older brother influence. Little did their parents know what the three of them got up to. Mackenna watched him now as he inspected the rams. Not for the first time, she wished she could turn back the hands of time.

"What are you two doing?"

Lost in thought she jumped at the sharp tone of her brother's voice. She spun around to see Patrick on the other side of the railings, wiping his hands on a rag. His face was purple as a beetroot.

"Where did you come from?" she said.

"Hello, Patrick," Hugh murmured and turned back to the rams.

"I've been looking for some pipe Dad said was in the shed." He flicked his head towards the small storage shed beside the yards. "He didn't say anything about bringing the rams in."

"I asked Hugh to come and take a look. They've lost condition."

Patrick climbed onto the railing and watched Hugh. "What's wrong with them?"

"What have they been eating?" Hugh asked.

"They've been in the top paddock for a while."

"That was already low-grade pasture," Mackenna said.

"I've been top-up feeding. I moved them back to the ram paddock yesterday." Patrick turned to Mackenna. "As per Dad's instructions."

She was surprised by the way he snapped the words at her.

"No need to get antsy," she said. "With Dad unwell – "

Patrick stopped her. "I've been doing as instructed. You've only been home a – "

"I think they've got barber's pole worm." This time Hugh cut in and behind him one of the rams stamped its foot in defiance.

"What's that?" Patrick asked.

"A couple of them have swollen necks and their gums are pale." Hugh strolled back to the railing. "That's a sign of a severe infestation but we won't know for sure until the faeces tests are back. I'll follow them up straight away."

"I've not seen it before," Mackenna said.

"Well, be amazed," Patrick said. "Something Mackenna doesn't know."

"I've heard of it." She glared at Patrick then turned back to Hugh. "We've never had it here that I know of. Are they in any danger?"

"A couple of them, maybe."

"How could this happen?" Mackenna's thoughts were in a whirl. These were Woolly Swamp's prize stud rams they were talking about.

"You've got normally healthy sheep and good management. They've probably been doing some intensive grazing in small patches." Hugh looked at Patrick. "Any clover in the paddock they've come from?"

"I don't know," Patrick muttered.

"Yes," Mackenna said turning to Hugh. "There're a few patches of strawberry clover in that top paddock. They'd go for it more than anything else at this time of year."

Patrick stuck his hands on his hips. "I suppose this means it's my fault."

"No need to blame anyone," Hugh said as he climbed back over the rail. "It's happened. Hopefully we've discovered it in time but it could get nasty if you don't treat it properly. I'll head back and find out exactly what we're dealing with before we make any decisions."

Mackenna jumped to the ground beside him. "Thanks, Hugh," she said and they walked back towards his vehicle. She didn't bother to see if Patrick was following them. There was more at stake than his dented ego.

CHAPTER
7

"I'm feeling a lot better today, Lou."

Louise turned from the quiche mixture she was stirring to look at her husband. Even though she knew he'd tossed and turned half the night again, he had better colour. "That's good," she said, "but the trick will be not to do too much. Remember what the doctor said."

"I know, I know." Lyle held his hands in the air and she could see the frustration on his face. "All I've done this morning is look at the pivot irrigator. Patrick's gone to get some pipe to see if he can fix it."

"Why don't you go over the stock program with him when he comes back? At least you can do it sitting down and he'll get a better understanding."

"The pivot needs fixing and I want to know what Hugh says about those rams."

"What's Hugh doing back here?" Louise let go of the wooden spoon and gave Lyle her full attention.

"There's something wrong with the rams."

"Patrick didn't mention it."

"Mackenna called Hugh back again."

Louise felt a pang of annoyance. "She's only been home five minutes and already she's taking over."

"What do you expect, Lou? I'm confined to quarters and she knows this place and the animals nearly as well as I do."

"Well, she shouldn't." Louise turned back to her mixture and began spooning it into the pastry bases. "I want her to have a better life. She shouldn't be tied to this place."

"She doesn't have to stay."

"I told you when we made out the wills. I want her to have the chance to move on, have a life of her own, a husband . . ." Louise sucked in a breath and looked at Lyle. "I want her to have her own babies . . . our grandchildren."

She spun back to her quiches, not wanting Lyle to see the emotion she knew would be showing on her face.

They were both silent for a moment.

Finally he spoke and she could hear the teasing in his tone. "You know, Lou, sometimes I wonder if we haven't raised two children that bat for the other side."

"That's nonsense!"

"We shouldn't presume opposites attract. There's a lot more of that same-sex stuff these days."

"Don't be ridiculous, Lyle, Mackenna has had numerous boyfriends . . ."

"None that have lasted."

"And Patrick's just a bit shy with women. There've been several girls he's been keen on over the years. Anyway, what's that got to do with anything?" Louise slid the quiches into the oven and shut the door firmly. She wasn't going to be distracted by Lyle's attempt to change the subject.

"I'm just saying we mustn't pigeonhole them, Lou. Whatever they do, they must do it because it's what they want, not what we want for them."

"You've changed your tune. You were the one who didn't want Mackenna to be a chef. You were the one who tried to get Patrick to take an ag course at uni rather than management and marketing."

"And I was wrong to do it. They have to make their own way."

The screen door banged and Louise could tell by the footfall it was Patrick. She lowered her voice.

"We've been over this already. We can't tie our daughter to this place, Lyle. It's not fair."

"Is it fair to Patrick?"

"Shush!" She started cleaning down the bench as Patrick stomped into the kitchen.

"Is what fair to Patrick?" he said.

Louise thought fast. "Another trip into town," she said. "I've got some food to deliver for the church trading table."

"I may as well. I'm only the errand boy," he snapped and moved to the sink. He filled a glass with water, drank it down and thumped the glass back on the bench.

"What's up, Patch?" Louise said. Underneath the spiked thatch of died black hair his face was mottled red. He had a bee in his bonnet about something.

"Did you find the pipe?" Lyle asked.

Louise glanced from Patrick to her husband. Lyle had no idea something was bothering his son.

"I found all sorts of things," Patrick said.

Louise focused back on him. "What things?"

"We need to fix that pivot," Lyle said. "Where's Mackenna?"

"Smooching up to Hugh."

"What?" Louise gasped. Hugh McDonald had been a close childhood friend who happened to be male. Mackenna had always made that clear. Had something changed?

"The two of them are sorting out the rams," Patrick said as he slumped into a chair. "Hugh thinks they may have barber's pole worm, whatever that is."

"How could that happen?" Lyle stood up. "Is it bad?"

"He thinks it may have been caught early. Reckons he needs to check the test results."

"Damn!" Lyle punched the flat of one hand with the fist of the other. "We can't afford to lose those rams."

"Hugh also said those early crossbreed lambs are probably the result of Mackenna not shifting last year's lambs out soon enough. The little buggers bonked their mothers."

"Patrick!" Louise found that kind of talk distasteful.

"I thought we must have left them too long," Lyle said and sat down again. "It's the only explanation."

More footsteps at the back door announced Mackenna's arrival. Patrick stood up as she entered the kitchen.

"I'll go and fix the pivot," he said.

"Do you want help?" Mackenna turned to follow him.

"I can manage a bit of pipe."

"I know, but I want to check where it broke. There might be an underlying problem."

"I reckon there must be a bow in it somewhere," Lyle said. "Perhaps I should take a look."

"Lyle." The exasperation in Louise's voice made them all stop and look at her. She spoke more gently. "You've done quite a bit outside already today. Let Patrick handle it."

"I'll take a look, Dad," Mackenna said.

Patrick shrugged. "Suit yourself."

Louise listened to the sound of her two children making their way out of the house. When they were little, Patrick had followed his big sister everywhere hanging on her every word. He was a grown-up now but Mackenna still treated him the same.

"Patrick should head back to the city soon."

Lyle's voice brought her back to the present.

"Why?"

"I don't think he wants to be here."

"He and Mackenna are just testing each other. They'll settle down."

Lyle sighed. "It doesn't come naturally to him."

"You can't blame him for that worm infestation."

"I don't. Just like I don't blame Mackenna for not shifting the lambs early enough. Things happen."

"What then?" she asked.

"He's done his best but this isn't where he wants to be. We really shouldn't hold him here now that Mackenna's back and we've employed Cam."

"There's plenty of work to do."

Lyle sniffed the air. "Is something burning?"

"Damnation!" Louise whipped around and pulled open the oven door.

"I won't have that language in the house," Lyle said.

She raised an eyebrow in his direction.

"Think I'll retire to the lounge and read the *Stock Journal*," he said.

"If you can't stand the heat . . ." she called to his back as he left the room.

She turned her attention back to the quiches. One was dark on top but the rest were simply well done. They could eat the dark one for lunch and the rest would still be fine for the trading table. She was rostered to go on the stall at two o'clock for an hour or so. Hopefully Patrick would forget she'd mentioned taking in the food.

Louise busied herself cleaning up the kitchen and pondered his earlier moodiness. Mackenna had probably said something to upset him. She still saw him as her baby brother instead of the man he'd become. The mention of Mackenna and Hugh was interesting. When they were teenagers Louise had always thought they'd make the perfect couple, but there was also Carol. The three of them had started school together and they were inseparable. After school they'd all left for Adelaide at the same time to take on their respective courses: Mackenna as an apprentice chef with a big hotel in the city, Carol to study nursing and Hugh science. They were all doing so well and it had become apparent that Hugh and Carol had feelings for each other. Then just as they were finishing their respective courses, Carol had been tragically killed. Her vehicle had hit a tree as she returned home to the South East late one night.

Along with Carol's family, the community had been devastated and for a while Louise felt that a part of Mackenna had also died. Something had gone on between Carol's father and Hugh as well. There were rumours that he blamed Hugh for not being with Carol that night. Whatever had happened, her death had impacted them all and Hugh had hardly returned to his home since.

Not long after the accident, Mackenna took up a job in Victoria but only lasted at it a few months before she returned, wanting to spend some time on the property. Louise had thought it would be temporary. Mackenna needed time to grieve and being home on the farm seemed the right place to do it.

Now, life had moved on and somehow Mackenna had become an integral part of the farm. Lyle's sudden heart attack was a timely reminder for Louise that her daughter needed to get on with her life. Being tied to a farm that she may one day have to manage alone was not the future Louise wanted for her. The will would make legally sure it couldn't happen, but Louise knew there was a lot more to be done to get Mackenna to change her views.

Hugh McDonald might be the catalyst that was needed. When they'd hired Cam, Louise had thought it hadn't hurt that he was charming and good-looking. There was a chance he might have been right for Mackenna, but Hugh was much more suitable as a potential husband. Louise decided she could suss out the lay of the land by inviting him over for a meal. See for herself if there was any spark between her daughter and the eligible bachelor. She flicked on the radio and began to sing along. For the first time since Lyle's heart attack she felt the weight lift a little from her shoulders.

CHAPTER

8

Hugh pulled up outside his family home. It was nearly time for dinner but instead of going inside he turned off the ignition, laid back his head and closed his eyes. There was no sound bar the ticking of the engine as it cooled and the last birds singing in the diminishing light. He took in a deep breath and slowly let it out. After he'd left the Birches' property he hadn't had a moment to himself, which was probably just as well. He wanted to keep his head clear of the past and work was good for that.

Now he was home and in no rush to go inside, where his mother would fuss and his father would offer up only the barest of greetings. He thought over his visit to Woolly Swamp and meeting Mackenna after so long. It had been a while since he'd had a panic attack but when she'd thrown her arms around him, his chest had tightened and his heart had begun to race. It had been all he could do to stop himself pulling away from her and jumping back in his vehicle to drive off. He'd made it look like he was rummaging for something in the cab and taken some slow steadying breaths. The attack had faded but the suddenness of it had left him shaken. He hadn't expected the sight of Mackenna to have such an impact on him.

It had only been her rock-like friendship that had kept him going those few weeks after Carol's death. Hugh leaned his head against the steering wheel. He'd been over and over the past with the doctor so many times. The guilt over the night Carol had her accident had driven him to cut the ties with his home. He'd taken up ag consultant work, first on Eyre Peninsula then Victoria and New South Wales. Distance made it easy for him to avoid coming home.

The outside light flicked on. Hugh turned to look but the back door remained closed. He sat back and cast his eyes along the verandah to the end, where its roof was propped up with a couple of posts. They protruded at angles like tent ropes. It had been like that for several years. His father was always going to fix it but never got around to it. His mother commented once that it could fall down around her and no-one would care. The properties always came first. With four sons they'd bought up land in several places. Hugh's three brothers lived on the other properties, all within close distance of the home place. If Hugh wanted to stay, this dilapidated house would eventually become his. He shook his head. That was definitely not going to happen.

A series of taps made him jump. He looked to the passenger-side window, where his father was peering in through the glass.

"You coming inside?" Allan McDonald moved his big frame around the front of the four-wheel drive towards the house without waiting for an answer.

Once again Hugh took in a deep breath and let it out slowly. He only had to sit through the meal. After dinner his father would be on the phone to Hugh's brothers or watching the television. Hugh would help his mother clean up and then he would make an excuse for an early night. This would be the pattern of his existence while he did the fill-in ag consultant work.

Slowly, he made his way to the back door. He left his boots on the verandah and his hat on a hook just inside the door. Molly, their old black and white cat, was immediately weaving between his legs, butting her head against his shins. He reached down and picked her up, carrying her with him into the kitchen.

"Hello, love." His mother greeted him with a smile and took the cat from his hands. "Go and wash up. Tea's ready."

When he returned from the bathroom his father was already seated at the head of the large table and Molly was tucking in to some tasty morsel his mother had put on a plate on the floor for her. Hugh sat at the place set for him beside his father. Since he'd been home, at least one of his brothers and or some of their family had been here at dinnertime, but tonight it was just the three of them.

"Something simple tonight," Mary said as she put steaming plates of savoury mince in front of them. "I've been in the garden all day. Lost track of time."

His father made a low snorting sound that annoyed Hugh, but his mother wasn't fazed.

"Wait till you see what I've done, Allan." She sat down opposite Hugh and offered them bread. "Hugh helped me get my garden seat in place and I've finished digging the bed the boys started for me. They're such willing helpers, my grandsons."

Once again Allan snorted. "Make the most of it, I say. Once they're a bit older there'll be more than enough work for them around the properties. You can always encourage the girls."

"They're a little bit young yet to lift a shovel."

Hugh ate as his parents bantered back and forth discussing the events of their day. He had almost tuned out and was startled when his father spoke directly to him.

"How're things looking over Birches' way?"

"Good." Hugh swallowed his food as they both looked at him expectantly. "Still fairly dry but they're doing okay."

"What about the general area? Have you had much of a look around?"

"Woolly Swamp way?" Hugh wasn't sure what his father meant.

"Yes, there's a place for sale there. I wondered how it was looking after the summer."

Hugh frowned. Then he remembered seeing a For Sale sign along the highway not far from the Birches' home.

"You mean the Suttons' place? They've turned half of it into vineyards." Surely his father wasn't planning on buying more land? If he was, Hugh couldn't imagine his interest in a place that was producing grapes for wine. Allan was strictly a sheep and cattle man. He was a sceptic when it came to plantations of anything but crops for feed.

"I know what they've been doing there," Allan said. "Seems the grapes have been made into drinkable wine."

Hugh put the last forkful of food into his mouth and Mary scooped up the plates. "I've made chocolate pudding for dessert."

"Don't serve any for me, Mum," Hugh said. "The savoury mince was enough."

"It's your favourite." Mary bustled about at the bench. "You need fattening up, love."

"You'll have me the size of a whale before I leave."

The noise from the dishes ceased. Mary turned to look at her husband.

"Tell him, Allan," she said. Her eyes sparkled.

His father wore that funny look he'd had the time he'd given Hugh the ultimatum about coming home to work on the property.

"Tell me what?" Hugh said. Unease churned the food in his stomach.

"We're thinking of buying the Suttons' place," Allan said.

Mary put bowls of pudding and ice-cream on the table and stood between her husband and her son. "For you," she said.

Hugh looked from the excitement on his mother's face to his father's, where he recognised the look of expectation. The weight of their suggestion locked him to the chair, while inside, his body was in turmoil.

"We want you to have a part in the family business," Mary said.

Hugh looked from one to the other again before he found his voice. "We've talked about this before. I'm happy doing what I do."

"But that's only a job, working for someone else," Allan said with a sweep of his hand. "This would be for yourself."

Hugh didn't point out that he'd still be working for someone else, only this time it would be the family.

"I don't know much about growing grapes and winemaking."

"You spent years at uni getting that fancy degree." Allan thrummed the table with his fingers.

"I have a bachelor in agricultural science."

"You used to work at that cellar door during your uni days," Mary said.

"It was a part-time job."

"You were always interested in wine."

"I like to drink it. That's a bit different from making it."

"Someone with your background could easily find out more," Allan said. "Your brothers are keen to help."

"So you've all discussed this?" Hugh could feel his chest tightening.

"We're a family business, one in, all in," his father said and shovelled a large spoonful of dessert into his mouth.

"We want you to come home to stay, love." Mary patted his hand. "It's not right you don't have a part to play here. You're such a clever lad. I'm sure you'd make a go of it."

Hugh opened his mouth to tell her about the fantastic research opportunity he'd accepted in Canada but the anticipation glowing on her face made him stop.

"The auction's a couple of months away," Allan said. "You don't have to make a decision yet."

"Just think on it." Mary patted his arm again. "That's all we ask."

"With you around I might get pudding more often." Allan's face pulled into a small grin and he took another mouthful.

"Your tummy doesn't need it," Mary teased and she went to get her own plate. Hugh pushed his pudding and melting ice-cream around his bowl. This was all strange and unexpected, not only the offer but also his father's attempt at congeniality.

After Carol's accident, Hugh had been made an offer to join the family business. He'd turned it down and after the ruckus that had caused, he thought there would never be another opportunity. Back then Allan had been aggressive and demanding. This time was different, perhaps tempered by Mary's presence. No doubt she'd been in her husband's ear about it. And this was an entirely different proposition, but it was strange all the same.

His mother returned to the table and proceeded to tell them all about her garden exploits, punctuated by silence as she ate her food. Finally Allan cut in, saying he had to make some phone calls and despite Hugh's offers to help with the cleaning up, his mother refused to let him do anything. He hovered in the kitchen.

"Go and relax," she said. "Watch some television."

Hugh headed to the shower instead. Perhaps under the water he could find some solitude and have a chance to mull over this offer – not that he thought for one minute he would accept it. What he had to work out was how to tell his parents he already had plans for the future, and they didn't involve moving back to the family business.

CHAPTER
9

The first mob of sheep moved restlessly in the yard as Mackenna finished mixing the drench. She lifted her head at the sound of the ute approaching. It came to a stop on the other side of the fence and Patrick jumped down from the back. Through the front window she could see her mother behind the wheel and her father in the passenger seat. He would hate that. He was allowed to drive now but evidently he'd had another restless night and was feeling a bit flat. He'd insisted on helping bring in the sheep this morning and Louise had been equally insistent that she would drive. Moving sheep was often something that stirred Mackenna's usually calm father to frustration. She suspected the mood inside the cab would be testy.

She smiled as she watched the two dogs, King and Prince, rush eagerly from side to side on the back of the ute as it moved away again. At least *they* were happy.

"How did the pup go?" she asked.

"All right, I guess," Patrick said.

"Was he a help or a hindrance?"

"He seems to know one end of a sheep from the other – unlike me," Patrick muttered.

Mackenna smiled. "The head's the end with the nose and the ears sticking out."

Patrick scowled at her.

"I'm joking, Patch." She gave him a playful tap. "Lighten up."

"Dad said you need me here. What do you want me to do?"

"You can push them up," Mackenna said, determined to keep cheerful. Patrick turned away from her without a response. He'd been in a touchy mood for days. She wondered if he felt under pressure to stay on at the farm. Maybe his employers were hassling for his return. Their mother was certainly keen for him to stay, but now that Mackenna was home they would manage. Perhaps she'd talk to her dad about it later.

Cam climbed out of the yard, where he'd been pushing up the penned sheep.

"Cam, you can do the marking and I'll do the drenching," she said. "Let's get started."

"Yes, boss." He gave her a mock salute.

Mackenna studied him a moment. It was hard to see his face in the shadow of his cap but his smile seemed genuine enough, then he winked at her. She turned away quickly and busied herself with the drench equipment. He was an employee and she didn't want him thinking there was more to their relationship than that. They'd worked together a few times over the last couple of days and she decided Cam's knowledge was marginally better than Patrick's when it came to farm work.

She picked up the backpack and wobbled as the weight of it caught her off guard. A strong pair of hands grabbed her arms.

"Steady up there, boss." Cam lifted the strap so it sat squarely on her shoulders.

"Thanks." Mackenna pulled away quickly and the drench gun slipped from her hand and swung around her leg. She stumbled and the weight of the backpack full of chemical carried her forward. She shuffled her feet, hooked her toe on a rock and fell in a sprawl onto a pile of loose hay. Her knees hit the ground first, then her hands. The hay did little to soften the impact of the thud that jarred her body. She gasped.

"Are you okay?" Cam was beside her.

Mackenna stretched one arm and then the other, then gingerly rolled and sat back on her bottom.

"Nothing broken," she said then began to giggle. Whether it was from shock or at her own stupidity she didn't know. She rubbed her knees and laughed out loud.

Cam squatted beside her.

"You're going to have to stop this, boss," he said with a grin.

"Laughing is better than crying."

"I meant throwing yourself at my feet. That's the second time you've done it. There are other ways of getting my attention, you know."

He stood up and offered his hand. She ignored it and struggled to her feet. Flirting with Cam had not been on her agenda. Surely he didn't think she'd fallen on purpose?

"You sure you're okay?" he asked.

"I'm fine," she said, feeling the sting in her hands as she brushed bits of straw and dirt from her clothes.

"I could do the drenching . . ."

"I'm fine," she repeated. Then, with as much dignity as she could muster, she snatched up the gun, held it firmly in her hand and made her way to the yard. She kept her back to Cam so he wouldn't see the colour she knew was flooding her face.

"Send them up, Patch," she called, hoping he hadn't witnessed that debacle.

The first sheep moved up the narrow space and she grabbed it, shot the liquid into the corner of its mouth, made sure it swallowed and let it go. It was difficult at first with Cam working right beside her. Every bump of an elbow or knock of a hand had her on high alert, but gradually she relaxed and they got into a rhythm, her awkward stumble confined to history and her mind focused on the job.

They'd drenched the rams as soon as Hugh had confirmed barber's pole worm but there'd been no sign of it in the rest of the sheep. This was just the usual pre-lambing drenching. They'd do all the sheep except the mob of Corriedale Dorset crossbreeds that had jumped the gun. They were busy dropping lambs so they'd have to be dealt with later.

By the time Louise arrived with morning tea they'd made good progress.

"Dad not with you?" Mackenna looked past her mother to the ute.

"I've sent him back to bed," Louise said. "He's okay. Just didn't sleep well so he's tired."

Mackenna noticed the worry on her mother's face. "I'm sure he'll be alright, Mum."

"He shouldn't have come out this morning, but he won't listen to me."

Mackenna was silenced by the bitterness in her mother's voice. Louise began to snap lids off cake tins and Mackenna walked away to wash up. By the time she got back Patrick and Cam were tucking in to cake and tea. Their light banter about their shared musical interests had dispelled the tension and Mackenna relaxed a little but still kept a wary eye on her mother. Between her and Patrick she never knew if what was said would reignite their moodiness.

"We'd better get back to it," she said finally. "This next lot will need drafting. I have to select a couple for the restaurant."

"You'd better do that," Patrick said.

"You could have a go at the drenching, Patrick," their mother said. "Get your hand in again."

Mackenna opened her mouth but Cam cut her off.

"I'll keep an eye on things," he said and gave Patrick a pretend punch in the arm. "Come on, mate, let's show her how blokes drench sheep."

"It has to be done properly or we're wasting our time and money." Mackenna knew her words sounded petty but drenching wasn't a game.

"I know, Mackenna," Patrick snapped and turned on his heel to follow Cam.

She sensed her mother's tension as the cups and food were packed back into the box. She picked up a stray lid, trying to help.

Finally Louise stilled and looked at her. Mackenna could see the telltale flash of anger in her eyes. Now what was wrong?

"You should include your brother in the work," Louise growled.

"I do." Mackenna felt like she had plunged back in time. Patrick had been the nuisance little brother tagging along when she wanted to be with her friends. She'd often evaded him and then got a telling-off from their mother.

"He won't learn what to do unless he's shown," Louise said.

"He can't make up for the years in a few weeks."

"He's trying."

Mackenna thought her mother looked desperate. Somehow her worry for her husband was engulfing Patrick as well.

"I know he is, Mum. It's been great to have his help but – "

They both looked up at Cam's whistle.

"Hey, boss, no time for chitchat," he called. "We're ready to go."

Louise walked to the ute. Mackenna shrugged her shoulders and felt an ache up her arms. No doubt she'd be a bit stiff from the fall followed by a day of drenching. It was probably good that Patrick took over for a while, giving her a chance to move some different muscles.

Patrick had his back to her and as she approached she saw Cam jump as liquid shot from the drench gun. They both laughed and another squirt of liquid splattered in the dust.

"What are you doing?" she snapped.

"I'm testing the gun." Patrick smirked at her.

"Don't waste it." Mackenna stuck her hands to her hips.

"A few shots won't amount to much in the scheme of things," her brother said. "I've seen the books, Mackenna. At least I know how the money works."

"Then you'll know not to waste it."

"A few squirts." He waved the nozzle at her. "Not a bucketful. Lighten up, will you?"

She pursed her lips. That was rich considering how he'd been acting over the last few days.

"You go and send up the sheep," Patrick said and turned his back on her.

"She'll be right, boss." Cam's murmur startled her. He was standing so close.

She turned and looked directly into his eyes. He lifted a hand towards her face and plucked a piece of straw from her hair. His face creased in that cheeky crooked grin of his. She spun around and hurried away, not sure if her wobbly knees were the result of her anger at Patrick or her dislike of Cam's close attention. Whatever the reason, she deliberately steadied her stride. It really would be the last straw if she tripped over again.

They worked in unison, Mackenna assessing the sheep as she herded them forward with Cam and Patrick drenching. A few times there were delays as Patrick got a sheep into position. Cam was right there helping so Mackenna kept out of it, but progress was slower than she wanted.

It was nearly time for lunch as she sent up the last of the mob, but the sheep came to a halt. Patrick dropped the drench gun and fiddled with his mobile phone. Next thing he was shrugging himself out of the drench harness and handing it to Cam. She swore as the sheep pushed back and a couple escaped into the yard behind her. King was an experienced dog and soon had them rounded up. By the time she looked forward again, Cam had taken on the drenching. Patrick was walking away, his mobile phone pressed to his ear.

"Typical," Mackenna muttered. Patrick's mind was elsewhere. It really was time for him to go back to the city.

With only Cam at the other end, the final few took even longer but at last they were finished. She cast her eye over the sheep. The next mob should be in the yard waiting by now. Her dad was obviously still resting or maybe Louise had locked him up.

Mackenna was pleased to see him at the lunch table looking relaxed. He asked her about the progress of the drenching.

Patrick came in late, his mobile phone clutched in his hand.

"You've had lots of calls this morning," Louise said. "Everything alright?"

Patrick glanced at his mother. "Just a bit of work stuff," he said. "It's fine."

Mackenna thought his words didn't match his worried expression. She noticed Louise gave him a second look. Whatever was bothering him would have to wait. She stood up from the table.

"We need to bring in the next mob."

Patrick groaned.

"Give everyone a chance to finish their lunch," Louise said.

"We're running way behind," Mackenna replied. "It's taken longer to do the first few mobs than it should have."

"I suppose that's my fault," Patrick said.

"If the cap fits . . ."

"Mackenna, that's enough," Louise warned.

Lyle stood up. "Cam, you take the last mob back and Patrick and I will bring in the next lot."

"Onto it," Cam said.

"Lyle, you need to rest," Louise said.

"I've slept half the morning, Lou. Patrick can drive."

Patrick took a handful of sandwiches and snatched up his cap.

Mackenna drove with Cam back to the yards. The last mob of sheep they'd drenched were huddled in the outer yard. The heavily pregnant ewes were some of their prime stock. They shuffled uneasily as Mackenna and Cam approached.

Mackenna scanned the yard. There was a sheep down.

"Damn!"

She climbed the fence and noticed two more. From the way they were sprawled she knew immediately they were dead.

"What's happened?" Cam's question floated behind her but she was too concerned to answer.

Mackenna went to each sheep in turn. Their pupils were dilated, their bodies rigid and vomit dribbled from their mouths.

"What's happened?" Cam asked again.

"I'm not sure but I suspect they've had too much drench." Mackenna squatted beside the third sheep and ran her hand over its woolly belly. "Not a nice way to die."

"How?" Cam said. "We . . . I was very careful."

"It's a specially measured dose. Two squirts make them sick. Three's enough to kill them. I thought you'd know that."

"Well, yeah. I do." Cam shuffled his feet.

Mackenna looked up at him and realisation hit her. "Patrick," she said and followed with a string of expletives as she rose to her feet.

"Steady up, boss." Cam held up his hands. "I kept a good eye on him but I couldn't watch him every second. He was a bit distracted at the end."

"Distracted! I'll give him distracted. Three good ewes and their lambs, possibly twins from the size of them – that's nine animals we've lost to distraction."

"He's learning fast. Everyone makes mistakes."

Mackenna took in the worried look on Cam's face. Blokes always stuck together.

"He's your brother and he's doing his best to help. In spite of us taking a bit longer, it would have been twice as long if it had been just you and me." Cam took a step closer and put a gentle hand on her shoulder. "Let's cut Patrick some slack. We'll clean up here before they get back."

Mackenna looked into Cam's concerned eyes. Suddenly she felt like such a bitch. If it had been Cam who was responsible, would she have reacted quite so harshly?

"I know they're good breeding ewes but they are only animals," Cam said.

She stiffened and slipped out from under his hand. She couldn't feel that casual over the death of animals in her care.

"I have to record it in the stock book," she said. "But I won't say anything for now."

"I'll bring up the ute."

"And we don't let Patrick near that drench gun again."

"You're the boss," Cam said and hurried away.

Mackenna was left to study the dead sheep. She squatted and ran her hand over one of the rounded bellies. "I'm sorry," she murmured and she turned to the next one with a heavy heart. Cam was wrong, they might be only animals but she couldn't bear for them to have died this way. At some point she would have to make Patrick understand that his carelessness could cause the death of an animal. But she was still too angry. She'd tackle it later, or maybe their father could. Patrick might understand better coming from Lyle or at least listen. Something she was pretty sure he wouldn't do with her right now.

CHAPTER
10

Laughter erupted around the table and Louise felt the tension ease from her shoulders. She had hoped this dinner would be relaxing but when they'd all first sat down, the conversation had been stilted. Perhaps eating in the kitchen would have helped the mood but she so rarely entertained these days. It was the perfect excuse to use the dining room and the good dinner set. She'd invited Hugh, and Cam was there as well, but it was Mackenna and Patrick who were the problem. They'd been having digs at each other for days and they'd started again as soon as everyone sat down. Lyle changed the subject as usual, oblivious of the tension. Hugh remained quiet but thankfully it was Cam who had broken the ice, telling them stories about his exploits growing up in a large family.

Finally, by the end of the main course, everyone appeared to be enjoying themselves. She started to collect the plates.

"Let me do that," Hugh said.

"I'll help," Mackenna added. "Would you like me to serve dessert?"

"That'd be great, thanks," Louise said, happy to sit down again. "It's cheesecake and berries. There's ice-cream in the big freezer."

"Sounds good," Lyle said, winking at her from the other end of the table. He'd all but given up alcohol since his heart attack, so he was ticking over happily now after a couple of glasses of wine. Perhaps it would help him sleep.

Patrick and Cam took his attention and Louise rested back in her chair. Underneath the table she slipped her shoes from her feet. She wasn't fond of heels and had only put them on to dress up a bit for dinner. Now her legs ached.

In the background she could hear the sound of dishes and laughter. Mackenna and Hugh were getting along okay in the kitchen. She'd watched them during the meal and they'd hardly spoken to each other. Hugh had been through some tough times but he had always seemed dependable to Louise. He came from a good local family. Allan McDonald had some different views on things and was often vocal about them but he was basically a good bloke. There had been talk in the past about Hugh settling back in the area and being part of the family business. Maybe that was still on the cards. Mackenna would be a good partner for a man like him.

They returned to the dining room and shared out the plates of cheesecake. Everyone complimented Louise on her cooking. It was rather good even if she did say so herself. The cheesecake baked with berry juice swirled through it and topped with whole berries was a golden oldie recipe she hadn't used for a long time. It didn't hurt that Mackenna had made some kind of sauce with the extra berries and drizzled that over the ice-cream. Louise considered herself a good cook but her daughter created more interesting food. She'd learnt so much during her years as a chef. If only she'd gone on with that instead of burying herself in the farm. Still, she'd never lost her talent and she'd make someone a good wife.

Mackenna laughed at something Hugh said and gave him a playful tap on the shoulder. Louise focused on the conversation and in particular on the body language of her daughter and her childhood friend.

Lyle raised his near empty glass. "Thanks everyone for all your help over the last few months."

"Here's to you feeling much better, Dad," Mackenna added.

"I'm feeling no pain at the moment." Lyle drained his glass and grinned down the table at Louise.

He might not be so chipper in the morning but she was pleased to see him relaxed and enjoying himself.

"You've been a big help with our worm problems, Hugh," Lyle said. "Following up that faeces test promptly, I really appreciate that."

"Glad we all know what you're talking about, Dad." Mackenna chuckled.

"Do we have to discuss it over the dinner table?" Louise asked.

"Sheep are our bread and butter, Lou. They've got to be in good condition."

"You've made some improvements since you took on the stud," Hugh said.

Louise was thankful for his attempt to divert the conversation.

"That's Mackenna's influence." Lyle smiled at his daughter and Louise flicked a glance in Patrick's direction. She could see no sign of annoyance on his face. She knew Mackenna deserved her father's praise but somehow Patrick needed to be included.

"She's put a lot of time into the research," Lyle continued, "and we've started seeing the rewards. Healthy animals are our aim. That's why this barber's pole worm outbreak with the rams has been such a blow."

"From what I've seen, I'd say it's only a hiccup," Hugh said. "We'll keep an eye on them."

Lyle winced. "I thought we were managing our animals well."

"You are, but you could do more."

Hugh looked set to go on and Louise thought it was time to change the subject.

"They're already spending so much time managing the sheep," she said. "Anyone for tea or coffee?"

"Yes, thanks, Mrs Birch," Hugh said then continued the conversation with Lyle. "You already document growth rate and fertility, you could add in resistance to worms."

"I talked to you about it before I went on holiday, Dad," Mackenna said.

"Don't tell me you'd have to do daily sheep poo checks." Patrick groaned.

"Not quite to that extent," Hugh said.

"I'm heading in to the pub." Cam stood up. "Thanks for the meal, Louise."

"I'll come with you," Patrick said and leapt to his feet.

"Why don't you stay and find out more?" Louise didn't mind if Cam left but she wanted Patrick to be a part of these conversations.

"No offence, Mum, but when it comes to a night at the pub or talking about worms, I'll take the pub."

"I'll introduce you to a couple of chicks I met on the weekend," Cam said. "A couple of lively ladies."

"Not sure if I trust your judgement after the last time." Patrick gave Cam a playful punch on the arm.

"It wasn't my fault she had that jealous ex. Anyway, these two are backpacking. Only around for a few more days."

"I'll see how it pans out when we get there." Patrick waved from the door and they were gone.

Louise looked down the table at her husband and he gave her a lopsided grin before turning back to Hugh.

"You can use genetics to breed worm resistant sheep."

"I know it's being done from what Mackenna told me but it's still experimental, isn't it?" Lyle asked.

"The Corriedale stud I visited near Queenstown was right into it," Mackenna said. "We haven't had much chance to discuss it yet."

"I'd be interested to hear as well," Hugh said. "It's what I've been studying in the last year and I'm about to . . . at least I hope to get involved in some research."

"Where? Maybe we could be part of it," Mackenna said, her eyes bright.

"Possibly." Hugh looked startled. "I don't know . . . it's not my project exactly."

"What was this place you visited, Mack?" Lyle asked.

Louise let the conversation wash over her. The other two hadn't noticed that Hugh had suddenly started tripping over his words. There was something he wasn't saying. Still, if he was involved in research that kind of thing was often hush-hush until the results were clear. Mackenna, on the other hand, was animated. She'd left her thick auburn curls loose and they fell around her shoulders and framed her face. Louise wouldn't describe her daughter as pretty, more a classic beauty that shone from within, especially when she was engrossed in something she was passionate about, like she was now. Louise tuned back in to Mackenna's words.

"With their selective breeding program, the worm resistance comes from the dame and the sire side. The livestock manager shopped around for good genes."

"Sounds like they are a much bigger operation than us," Lyle said.

"Yes, but they started out small, Dad. Just like us."

"Are there any places closer to home doing this?"

"Yes." Mackenna and Hugh both spoke at once.

"I know of a couple in New South Wales," Mackenna said.

"There's another even closer," Hugh added. "Not far over the border in Victoria. I've been to have a look at what they're doing."

"Is it worth us paying them a visit?" Lyle asked.

"Definitely!" Mackenna and Hugh chorused together then laughed.

Louise smiled. There was certainly a connection between the two of them. She was glad she'd invited Hugh for dinner. They were both animated now. Taking turns to tell Lyle all they knew about this selective breeding program. She collected up the dessert dishes and remembered the offer of tea and coffee she'd never fulfilled. Never mind. They were so busy talking they hadn't missed it.

In the kitchen she was relieved to see everything was tidy. Mackenna and Hugh must have cleaned up when they served the dessert. All that was needed was to stack the last things into the dishwasher and turn it on. Louise sighed. She'd missed Mackenna's support around the house. While she'd trained Lyle and Patrick to at least carry their dishes to the bench, they rarely did more than that.

She gave a last glance around her neat kitchen and switched off the light. Suddenly she felt bone weary and it was the latest Lyle had stayed up in a long while. Time for them all to turn in.

At the dining room door she paused.

"I think it could work here, Dad." Mackenna's voice was low but filled with enthusiasm.

Louise entered the room and the three at the table turned as one to look at her.

"What could work here?"

She glanced from one to the other. Hugh gave her a polite smile but it was the fleeting look between father and daughter that bothered her. What ideas was Mackenna filling Lyle's head with now?

"The Corriedale stud that Mackenna visited in New Zealand sounds interesting. Maybe we should go for a look," Lyle said.

"To New Zealand!"

"It's not far, Lou."

"I know that, but you've always got a reason why we can't go."

She had tried on several occasions to convince her husband to take an overseas holiday. He'd always had some excuse about why they couldn't go. They had passports that had never been used.

"I've got a reason now."

"I don't think you'd be allowed to travel too far for a while."

"It's just an idea."

Louise felt a pang of regret as the sparkle left his eyes.

"We can certainly look into it," she said. "We could both do with a holiday. Maybe while we've got all these helpers a short break would be good."

"Thank you for the meal, Mrs Birch." Hugh stood up. "I'd best be off."

Mackenna leapt to her feet. "I'll walk you out."

Louise watched them go. They made a good-looking couple. She turned back to find Lyle studying her.

"What are you up to, Lou? I know that look. I hope you're not thinking Mack and Hugh are an item."

"Of course not," Louise said quickly. "But now that you mention it, they would be a good match."

"He's not staying."

"He might if he had a reason."

"Lou." Lyle's voice was soft and he shook his head.

Louise could see how tired he was.

"Bedtime for us," she said.

As they entered the passage the murmur of voices carried on the tranquil night air. Mackenna and Hugh were still talking.

Louise smiled to herself. Lyle didn't understand these things. Hugh had never had a reason to put down roots but it was just possible he might discover a reason here.

CHAPTER
11

"Would you at least think about it?" Mackenna asked.

She swept a loose curl back into the band holding her ponytail and studied her father closely. The two of them were standing in the kitchen of the original homestead. All the other rooms had been done up except this one. She had asked for this room to be left until she returned from holidays.

"I can't see your mother going for it," he said. "It will be a lot of work."

"Not for Mum. I'll be doing the cooking. The kitchen has to be replaced anyway. It won't take much more to make it restaurant standard."

"Who'd come all the way here to dine out?"

"We're only just off the main road. We'd start out small with tasting and other local produce. Just on weekends, when there are more tourists about."

"It'd be a tie."

"The farm is already a tie."

"But it takes all our time and then some. How will you have time to manage this?"

"You've employed Cam and Patrick's around now." Mackenna saw a small frown flit across her father's face. "I know he's not here to stay," she said, "but it sounds like he plans to hang around for a while. Might give me the time to give it a crack."

"Spending more than is necessary on this old place would be wasted if you don't succeed."

"You were happy to do it up as a working man's quarters."

"There's another point. Your mother's already offered the place to Cam."

"He seems happy enough in the house and he's not here all the time anyway. If we set this place up as a farm gate tasting stop, I'd sleep in the back room so there'd be even more room in the big house." Mackenna stepped into the passage that ran from the kitchen to the front door, pointing as she spoke. "The front room would be the tasting room and the big side room we created by knocking down that internal wall could be a special dining room later down the track."

"Whoa! Steady up, girl." Lyle stood in the doorway shaking his head. "What 'special dining room'?"

"It's another way of building the reputation of our meat. We can do tasting but we can also offer a special dining experience for those who want to book."

He held her gaze and Mackenna could see the doubt in his eyes. Perhaps her enthusiasm had pushed him too far. She so badly wanted to get the kitchen done while the old house was still empty.

Her father pursed his lips and shook his head again. "Maybe your mother was right," he said. "You would be better back in the restaurant game."

"The restaurant game?"

"We're either running a farm or running a restaurant. Which is it?"

Mackenna was confused. It was the first she'd gone into detail about her plans for the old house and she certainly hadn't said anything to her mother about it.

"Why would Mum want me to go back to being a chef? She knows how much I love working here on the farm."

"She worries you're burying yourself in the work."

A feeling of unease niggled in Mackenna's chest. "I love Woolly Swamp, Dad. I've devoted my life to the place for the last nine years. I thought you were happy with what we're doing?"

"I am, love, I am." Lyle's lips turned up into a smile and he placed a hand gently on her arm. "So much has happened in the last few months and your mother worries. Your idea for a farm gate sounds good, but we've so much else on the go at the moment and I'm still not firing on all cylinders. We can do up the kitchen if you want but keep it simple, and I wouldn't go mentioning restaurants and fine dining to your mother. We've got to get the meat right first."

"We are getting it right." Mackenna waved her arms as she spoke. "The restaurant in Robe says customers rave over it. Our reputation is excellent."

"One local restaurant isn't an empire."

"But there will be others."

Lyle rubbed his forehead. "Let's get our head around this genetic stuff first. I like the sound of what we talked about with Hugh the other night."

He gave her another pat then lifted his head at the sound of a vehicle. "That will be your mother home. Time to go in for some lunch."

"I'll be there in a minute." Mackenna waited for him go then walked slowly through the rooms of the old house. With not a curtain or a stitch of furniture, her footsteps echoed on the polished wooden floors. Nonetheless she felt comfortable in this house. It settled around her like a soft shawl. Maybe her great-grandparents were smiling down, happy to see their home come to life again. She stopped in the big room they'd created out of the two on the right side of the passage. Its walls had been painted in the same cream as they'd used in the other rooms and the old skirting boards had been redone in white.

In her mind she could see the tasting room across the passage decked out like a cellar door. In this room she pictured a grand dining table laid out with a linen tablecloth and napkins. She wanted to do it all. The stud she'd visited near Queenstown had been doing a great trade and had extended their markets through their farm gate dining.

Woolly Swamp lambs were delivered to the abattoir and processed the same day. The seaside restaurant that served the meat was happy with the quality and the local butcher was selling it. Before she'd left she'd got some interest from an Adelaide connection. The chef was a guy she'd worked with while she was still an apprentice. He was now head chef at a small restaurant in the city and looking for unique influences for his menu. Getting a couple of restaurants to use their meat would be a good step. Then she wanted to find some city butchers who would stock Woolly Swamp meat. Once people experienced it at a restaurant, she hoped they'd be keen to try cooking it for themselves.

Mackenna poked her head back into the kitchen. The cupboards had rotted away and been removed. The only things remaining were the taps under the window and the old electric oven that had replaced the original wood stove at some point in the past. Her parents had lived here when they were first married but it had been empty since.

She wished she could get them to understand the future she saw for Woolly Swamp. Suddenly, an image of Adam's smiling face came to mind and the ache she'd been hiding surged through her. What had gone wrong? She really believed he loved her but he'd left without a word.

She dropped to a crouch, her back against the wall and put her head in her hands.

"Adam, Adam, Adam," she murmured.

Other than her father just now, Adam was the only person she'd talked to about her farm gate concept for Woolly Swamp. His ideas for tasting dishes and his enthusiasm for her vision had strengthened their bond. Or so she'd thought. A wave of longing swept over her as she recalled the week they'd spent together. How could she have been so wrong?

"Why did you leave?" she asked the empty room. "Why?" she called a little louder.

"Hello." Cam's voice echoed.

Mackenna stifled a groan and rose to her feet. That's all she needed, for Cam to find her wallowing in self-pity.

"Mackenna?"

She pulled back her shoulders.

"Yes, in here."

She turned to face him as he stepped through the back lobby into the kitchen. Her smile faded as he let forth with some foul language.

He took his cap from his head and dragged his fingers through his hair. "This place isn't habitable yet," he said. "I thought your dad said it was nearly finished."

Mackenna felt defensive of her little project. "The rest of the rooms are ready to use. Just the kitchen needs doing now."

"I'll take your word for it." Cam looked around then raised his eyebrows at her. "I thought I heard a voice? You talking to yourself, boss?"

Mackenna turned away from his enquiring eyes and bent down to brush dust from her jeans. "You must be hearing the ghosts."

"Ghosts! No-one told me this place was haunted." Cam glanced around then back at her.

"Only friendly old family ancestors." So the big tough guy was frightened of ghosts. Who'd have thought it? "I've never experienced nasty spirits here but I'm family . . ." She let her words hang in the air.

He shifted from foot to foot. The floorboards creaked beneath his weight. Mackenna held her palms up towards the ceiling. "Not everyone can sense them, you know, but I've always had an affinity with this place."

Cam straightened up and took a few steps backwards. "I said I'd tell you lunch was ready."

"You didn't have to bother."

"No bother. I've eaten. I'm on my way to town to get a load of timber to fix a shed. Said I'd call in on my way past. Your mum has the food on the table so I'd get moving if I was you."

He pushed his cap back onto his head and muttered under his breath before turning around and retracing his steps outside.

Mackenna felt some small satisfaction at Cam's unease, but she wasn't pleased her mother had sent him to call her to lunch as if she were a child. That was another reason why she'd like to move in here. She was tired of living at home. She seemed to ruffle her mother's feathers even more since her return and trying to avoid Cam in the bathroom was a pain. It would be good to have a place to call her own, even if it was only a few hundred metres from home. She hadn't been lying when she said she had an affinity with this old house. It had always felt like it was welcoming her and had been her childhood hiding place when she'd been in trouble.

Maybe Cam's reluctance would work to her advantage. If she got a chance to talk to the carpenter she'd see about getting a kitchen put in. Her father had given her the go-ahead. She closed the door firmly behind her. If Cam wasn't keen to move in she was, and the sooner the better.

CHAPTER
12

It was a quiet Friday afternoon and the shop staff at the stock and station agency were packing up ready to leave on the dot of five. Hugh gave them a wave as he left his office in the back of the building. He'd finished for the week but he wasn't in a rush to go home. With nothing planned, he wasn't looking forward to a full weekend with his parents. A pang of regret rose in him for feeling that way, especially where his mother was concerned but when he was with her he felt the unspoken pressure of her desire for him to stay in the area. He should have made plans to go away, but the local friends he'd kept in touch with were now married and had families. They weren't looking for a blokes' weekend.

He made his way into the main street and strolled along in the general direction of the pubs. There was one on either side of the main road and they would both be filling up with drinkers at this time of the day. He was bound to run into someone he knew.

The shopfronts along this stretch were the old originals and most of them were deserted, but he stopped in front of one that had been given a new lease of life. The paint had been stripped from the door and window frames and the golden brown of the original timber gleamed with a fresh coat of varnish. The glass windows had been cleaned and beyond them Hugh could see metal sculptures. There was a corrugated-iron kangaroo standing tall with a smaller kangaroo at its feet, body bent as if it were just about to eat a mouthful of grass. The metal frame of a windmill rose out of a collection of smaller animals.

Looking at the sculptures gave him an idea. He'd spend the weekend working on his mum's side garden. If he could get it set up properly, she might be able to maintain it after he was gone. He was so lost in his thoughts he didn't notice someone leaving the shop.

"Hello, Hugh."

"Mackenna."

Her smile lit up her face.

"I didn't realise this was here," he said. "I thought all these shops were empty."

They both looked back at the shop Mackenna had just left. He couldn't believe he'd not noticed it before. It clearly stood out from the derelict fronts either side of it.

"Do you remember Rory Heinrich?" she asked.

"Vaguely."

"He was several years older than us. Left the district as soon as he finished high school. Anyway, his folks are still here and he's moved back, done up this shop and makes all kinds of sculptures. Sells a lot of stuff online," Mackenna said. "He's very creative. Makes things from recycled metal. He's going to make me some bronze sheep."

"I'll have to check it out. He might have something for Mum's garden."

"So what are you up to now?"

"Heading to the pub."

"Mind if I join you?"

"Happy to have some company."

They continued on together and Mackenna chatted about Rory and the things he made. For the first time since his return Hugh felt relaxed. Coming back to work in the district he grew up in had been a test. He'd been running from his demons long enough. He wanted to banish them and start his new job in a new country without wondering if he was still running from the past.

"Haven't seen you in a while."

Both Hugh and Mackenna halted. Neither of them had noticed the man getting out of a ute parked near the corner. Even though his tone was low there was no mistaking the contempt in it.

"Hello, Mr Thompson," Mackenna replied, but the man wasn't looking at her.

Hugh met the eyes that glowered at him. Carol's father hadn't mellowed over the years since their last encounter.

"I'm working as a consultant," Hugh said. "Only filling in till Ted's back."

"I heard," Mr Thompson said. "Nice that the two of you can enjoy each other's company." Once again his words had a cynical ring to them.

Sid Thompson's arms were firmly folded over his chest. No handshake looked like it was forthcoming.

"How's Mrs Thompson?" Mackenna asked.

She either didn't notice Sid's stance and tone or she was ignoring it.

"Well, thanks, Mackenna. All things considered."

"That's good to hear."

"What about Lyle?" he asked. "I heard he'd had a heart attack."

"Yes, but the doctors have patched him up. He's on the mend as well."

Sid turned his eyes back to Hugh. "And your parents? I haven't seen them in a long while. How are they and your *three* brothers?"

The older man's eyes bored into him, the emphasis on the word three a reminder that the McDonalds still had all four children. Hugh could feel the familiar tightness in his chest. He willed himself to breathe slowly and speak calmly. "All well, thanks."

Sid stood firm. His arms remained folded.

"Well, it's been nice to see you, Mr Thompson." Mackenna smiled. "I'll tell Mum and Dad I ran into you. Sorry to rush but I have to get to the chemist before it closes."

"You're in a rush too, I s'pose." Sid Thompson met Hugh's eyes again.

"Yes . . . well no. I was just heading to the pub," Hugh said.

"Hmmph!" Sid snorted.

Mackenna had already begun to move on. Hugh nodded at Sid and stepped around him to follow her. Outside the chemist, Mackenna came to a stop and turned back to Hugh.

"That was awkward." She glanced over his shoulder. "He's still standing there, watching us."

Hugh resisted the urge to look, despite a prickling in the back of his head that spread down his neck.

"I haven't seen him in a long time but Mrs Thompson's been quite sick," Mackenna continued. "Some kind of motor neuron disease, I think."

"Somehow I hoped time would have helped . . ." Hugh's voice petered out as he felt his chest tighten. He closed his mouth and took a long slow breath through his nose.

"Are you okay?"

He nodded.

Mackenna's eyes widened. "Surely he's not still blaming you for Carol?"

"I went away. We haven't seen each other for years." Hugh shrugged his shoulders. "Nothing's changed for him."

"That's ridiculous. You weren't to blame any more than I was. He's got to let it go."

"She was his only child."

"I know." Mackenna's voice faltered. "And my best friend and the love of your life, but we had to keep living."

"He still wishes it was me not her."

"It was ten years ago."

Once again Hugh fought back the urge to gasp in air. What had he been thinking? That he could erase all the pain by arriving back in town and starting afresh? Somehow he'd thought he could find a chance to talk to Mackenna about Carol, but that wasn't going to work. Mack was a good friend. He couldn't bear to disillusion her.

He jumped as she put a gentle hand on his arm. "Look, I've got to collect a script for Dad," she said. "Why don't you head next door to the pub and I'll meet you there? I think we should talk about this."

She gave him an encouraging smile then moved swiftly into the shop. He glanced at his watch. It was nearly five thirty. Maybe a couple of drinks with Mackenna would be okay. He just needed to steer the conversation away from Carol.

Around the bar he recognised a couple of faces, blokes he'd been to school with, but the rest were strangers. He bought the drinks and was talking with a local farmer when Mackenna rejoined him. She seemed to know everyone and as the evening wore on he was introduced to most of the people in the bar. Apart from a few questions about what he'd been doing before his return to the district and a couple of work-related discussions, the talk was all light-hearted. No-one cared about the distant past.

Mackenna had become immersed in a conversation with a bloke she introduced as a local winemaker, Chris someone from Bunyip Wines. Hugh got caught up with a guy keen to talk about his new stud bull, but when the bloke went to get another drink Hugh decided to head for home. He gave Mackenna a wave.

"Hugh, we're going to the other pub for a meal. Come with us." Chris nodded in agreement.

"Thanks but I've got an early start tomorrow."

Mackenna leaned in close and gave him a kiss on the cheek. Her eyes were bright.

"We've still got to have that conversation," she said softly.

He gave a vague nod and headed out into the cool night. He was glad there had been no chance to talk with Mackenna alone. His earlier panic was gone. He'd run into Sid Thompson and survived. Even though he thought he'd finally allowed himself to come to terms with Carol's death, her father obviously hadn't reached that conclusion.

Hugh sighed. He wasn't in Sid's shoes but at last he felt as if he could understand the man's anger. He had hoped after all this time it may have dissipated a little but that obviously wasn't to be.

Hugh made his way back along the dark street. At Rory's shop he paused. A couple of lights illuminated the sculptures in the windows. At least bumping into Mackenna had given him the garden idea. Fixing that up would keep him busy when he wasn't working and it would be something good he could do for his mother before he left.

CHAPTER
13

Louise waved to her two sisters as she walked past the window of the seaside café. They'd had to drive further than she but as is often the way, the person with the least distance to travel arrived last. She wove her way between the other lunchtime diners to reach the corner table. Marion, the eldest of the three, rose to her feet and threw her arms around Louise in a perfumed hug.

"How are you, darling?" Marion rested her hands on Louise's shoulders and looked at her closely. "You look a bit tired but that's only to be expected after what you've been through. Perhaps Alfred could make you a tonic. How's Lyle?"

"Let her sit and catch her breath." Caroline, their middle sibling, leaned across and gave Louise a kiss on the cheek as she sat.

Caroline looked smart and well groomed as always. She and Louise liked the same kind of clothes. Marion dressed in layers with beads and bracelets, which were fine for city living but not practical for chasing sheep or pruning vines.

Louise relaxed back into the chair. It was so good to be here with her sisters, even if it had been a rush. Caroline lived closer and had come to visit after Lyle's first stay in hospital, but she'd only spoken to Marion on the phone. Usually they lunched together once a month, but the last two lunches had been cancelled due to Marion's urgent dash to babysit grandchildren in Melbourne and then Lyle's illness.

A waitress appeared at their table.

"I ordered us a pot of tea to share," Caroline said as the young woman set out cups. "They make such delicate brews here."

Once the tea was poured Marion asked after Lyle again.

"He's been improving every day since they put in another stent. It seems to have done the trick." Louise could think about her husband's brush with death calmly now. Although she did still panic easily if he wasn't where she expected him to be. "This morning he wanted to draft some lambs for market, that's why I'm late. He needed a hand."

"I thought Mackenna and Patrick were home?" Caroline said.

"And didn't you employ a working man?" Marion added.

"Even with all of them, we have days when there's not enough people for the jobs to be done," Louise said. "I'm sure the sheep could have been shifted later when one of the others returned but you know men, they want everything done yesterday. It's a sign Lyle's feeling better, though. A week ago he would have left them to it."

"Alfred was like that after his gall bladder op." Marion tapped her neatly manicured nails on the table. "Nothing to show for it on the outside and after a week I had the devil of a job to keep him resting."

Louise and Caroline smiled at each other. Alfred was a chemist and these days only worked a couple of days a week. The most physical work he did was swinging a golf club or tending his rose garden.

"You've been so brave, Lou." Marion patted her hand. "I am sure I'd go to pieces if I'd found Alfred having a heart attack. How did you know what to do?"

"Somehow my first aid kicked in and the ambulance crew were fantastic."

"It took them a while to reach you, though," Marion said. "It must have been terrible on your own."

Flashbacks of that evening flitted through Louise's mind. It didn't seem real now that Lyle was on the mend. "Yes," she said quietly. "I was terrified."

Her sisters took a hand each and gripped firmly. Tears threatened and she had to pull away to rummage for a hanky.

"Sorry," she said. "I try not to think about it too much."

"Don't be sorry." Marion gave her back a gentle pat. "It's been a tough time. We've all been so worried about you both."

Louise took a sip of her tea. "Let's talk about something else," she said.

"I have some exciting news," Caroline said. "Jade is having another baby."

"That's wonderful," Louise said. "When is she due?"

"Not till October."

"You'll be catching me in the grandmother stakes," Marion said. "It'll be lovely to have another baby in the family. We've had a bit of a gap."

Marion gave Louise a quick smile then picked up her phone to show the latest pictures of her grandchildren. The smile wasn't pitying, but that was the message it conveyed. Poor little sister Louise was missing out on grandchildren. Marion had two sons and then a daughter who was Mackenna's age. The three of them had two children each. Caroline had Jade, who was now expecting baby number three and a son younger than Mackenna, who had two children.

Louise looked at the sweet little faces smiling from the screens as her sisters flicked through their photos and felt a pang of envy. Neither of her children had partners. She was unlikely to be a grandmother anytime in the foreseeable future, and how she longed to be part of this wonderful club her siblings so obviously enjoyed.

"You're lucky your grandchildren are so close," Marion said as she put her phone down. "Mine are all in Victoria and I don't see them as often as I'd like."

"I'm glad my children and their partners are all part of our wine business, but it does have its drawbacks." Caroline grimaced. "I get asked to babysit a lot."

"How terrible for you." Marion winked at Louise and patted Caroline's arm.

"Oh, you two." Caroline batted at Marion's hand. "I don't mean it like that. I love to have them but I have a life too, you know. You drop everything to run to your kids, Marion."

"Not everything. I don't miss my golf or tennis but I do go whenever I can. I love being with them. They grow and change so quickly. There's nothing like being called Granny. It's the sweetest sound in the world."

"I have to agree with you there." Caroline laughed. "You'll never guess what the youngest said the other day. She's been hanging around the work sheds too much."

Louise listened as Caroline and Marion one-upped each other with the funniest or cutest grandchild story.

"Let's order," she suggested once she could get a word in. It had been a long time since breakfast. They perused the menu, placed their orders and Caroline started on the grandchildren again. Louise was keen to tell them about her coup in getting a travelling art exhibition for the town. It would be a great event with a lavish supper and fine wine to raise money for the district hospital. She'd always been involved in the fight to keep it, but it was more important to her than ever since Lyle's heart attack. He may not have made the journey to Adelaide if he hadn't received local treatment first. She shuddered at the thought.

"Are you okay?"

Both her sisters had stopped talking and were staring at her.

"You do look a bit peaky," Marion said.

"I'm fine," Louise said. "Just hungry. I could eat a horse and chase the rider."

"Did Mackenna enjoy her time away?" Caroline asked.

"Yes, she did. Got up to all sorts in New Zealand. It's full of great scenery and lots of activities."

"New Zealand's got everything from beaches to glaciers," Caroline said. "Jim and I enjoyed the scenery very much. We spent a lot of our time checking out their wine, of course. It was another working holiday for us."

"It was the first overseas trip we did when the children were all teenagers." Marion chuckled. "We had to come home for a holiday."

"Not quite the same as slumming it on a Greek island," Caroline said.

"Oh, wasn't that the best holiday." Marion clasped her hands together. "Our little apartment looked out over the bay and the water was the most divine blue."

Caroline rolled her eyes. "I loved it because it was the only overseas trip we've had that wasn't to do with business."

She and Marion continued to reminisce about their shared holiday. Two years ago, after they'd both been travelling in different parts of Europe with their husbands, the four of them met in Greece and stayed on a small island for two weeks. Louise had heard about it over and over, and looked at all the photos. It certainly sounded wonderful but she wasn't a beach person. If she went to Europe she'd spend her time in the museums and churches. Not that she thought about it much, only when her sisters prattled on, like they were now.

"Where else did Mackenna go?"

Caroline's question pulled Louise back into the conversation.

"New York."

"What did she think?"

Louise paused. What did Mackenna think? She kept raving on about the sheep stud she'd visited in New Zealand. They'd hardly talked about the rest of her travels. The fridge was adorned with postcards of glowing reports. "She loved it." Louise tried to recall Mackenna's travel itinerary, which was also still clipped to the fridge. "She went to Los Angeles and Hawaii as well."

"That's great," Marion said. "It's all very well to go to New Zealand but it's really only another state of Australia. Hardly even need your passport. It's good she decided to go further afield. See something different."

Louise had been planning to tell them about Lyle's suggestion of a trip to New Zealand but she bit her tongue. Marion wouldn't have meant to be pompous but the comments hurt all the same.

"I remember Mackenna always talked about going to New York when she left school," Caroline said.

The food arrived and Louise was glad to have something to distract them all. She'd been looking forward to this lunch with her sisters but the conversations had left her feeling on the outer and, to her discontent, a little guilty. She'd been so fixated on Lyle and Patrick she'd barely spoken with Mackenna about her holiday. And yet she had been excited for her daughter before she left.

Since Lyle's heart attack life had changed and Louise looked at things differently. But in her determination to find a better future for Mackenna she'd put a distance between them. If nothing else, this lunch had made her realise she needed to spend talking time with her daughter. Louise tucked into her chicken salad. It was delicious and the conversation turned to food. That was something she was comfortable contributing to.

CHAPTER
14

"Yes, yes, I understand." Mackenna paced the verandah with her mobile pressed to her ear. The guy on the other end was hard to hear and she wasn't happy with what he was telling her. She looked up as Patrick's car rumbled to a stop near the gate. It was making a terrible racket.

"Perhaps another time." The voice in her ear was fading.

"You have my mobile number now," she said but the line had either dropped out or disconnected.

"Damn!" She stuffed her mobile into her pocket.

Patrick was coming towards her along the path. "What's the matter?"

"I just wish we had better mobile service out here. No-one noticed the message on the answering machine."

"Was it important?"

Mackenna resisted the urge to snap at him. It wasn't Patrick's fault. He'd been in Adelaide for three days. "We missed some potential customers," she said. "It was a possible opportunity to get a go at a Melbourne restaurant."

"I know they're not reliable but I don't know why people don't try the mobile numbers, at least they could leave voicemail."

"I guess they would if they had them. Mum changed the message on the answering machine before she went to Adelaide last. It doesn't give mobile alternatives."

Patrick frowned. "That's not good business practice."

"I'm aware of that." She shook her head. "And our website wasn't any help to them either."

"What website?"

"I got a high school student to make us one a couple of years back but I rarely update it. Anyway, what have you been up to?" She smiled at him. "How did you score a three-day weekend? We missed you yesterday."

"I rang Mum and told her I was staying an extra day. A few things came up that I had to attend to." Patrick swung his backpack over his shoulder and stepped ahead of her into the house.

Mackenna followed. Was he being evasive or prickly?

"Did you run out of errand boys?" he called over his shoulder.

There was a scornful ring to his voice. Mackenna watched as he disappeared up the passage. She sighed – definitely prickly. What was up with him these days? Maybe Lyle had spoken to him about the dead sheep after drenching. She'd had to tell their father about it and had left it with him to speak with Patrick.

In the kitchen she switched on the computer. While she waited for it to come to life she thought about her little brother. It had to be something more than the drenching business. He'd been touchy before that, ever since she'd returned from her holiday. She was sure it was because he resented being here. He had a life and work in Adelaide. There really was no need for him to stay on even though he'd been a big help. They had actually missed him yesterday but they would have to manage without him eventually.

Mackenna felt a little guilty about being gone most of the day herself. She'd left home early to deliver sheep to the abattoir then instead of coming straight home, she'd gone to see a carpenter about getting a kitchen put in the old house. It had been a fruitful visit. He knew of a second-hand kitchen that had just been removed from a place in Mount Gambier. It was available at a good price if they collected it themselves. She'd only need to buy a new oven, cooktop and microwave. On a roll, she'd put in an order. She had some money leftover from her holiday and hoped her father would be happy for the farm to pay the difference. He had given her the go-ahead. Second-hand cupboards and a near new dishwasher from Mount Gambier meant they could install at a fraction of the cost of new, but commercial cooking equipment was expensive.

She opened up the web page for Woolly Swamp Farm. That would be another thing she'd need, a till and some kind of computer.

"Is that it?"

Mackenna jumped at the sound of Patrick's voice behind her.

"That's it," she said. "I know nothing about making web pages and young Sam Martin did it as part of his school research project."

Patrick leaned in over her shoulder and they both studied the screen. The page was nearly all white with black writing reminiscent of an old typewriter. The only colour came from the bold name *Woolly Swamp Corriedales* across the top and an old photo of their father standing beside their first prize-winning ram.

"Certainly doesn't fill me with confidence as a potential customer," Patrick said.

"I looked into getting a professional site done but Mum and Dad baulked at the cost."

"Move over." Patrick gave her a nudge, his eyes glued to the screen.

Mackenna vacated the seat and he slid into it. Her mobile rang and she moved away from him to answer it.

The woman selling the kitchen was happy with her offer but she wanted Mackenna to collect it as soon as possible. They agreed on a time the next day. Mackenna hoped she'd get a chance to run it all past her dad before her mum came home. Louise was attending committee meetings in two different towns, so she should be gone most of the day. Lyle had gone with Cam in the truck to pick up the new irrigator. They'd hoped to put it off until next summer but the dry was dragging on. Everyone in the district was casting their eyes to the sky, waiting on the first good autumn rains.

Before Mackenna had gone overseas, they'd purchased two more paddocks from their neighbours. They still owed some on the small place they'd bought across the road, but she and her father had both agreed it was the right thing to do. Opportunities to expand didn't come along often and to be able to extend their boundaries rather than buy a totally separate property was too good an opportunity to miss.

Mackenna flicked her eyes from Patrick to the family portrait on the wall above his head. It had been taken the year he left to go to uni. They all looked younger but it shocked her to realise how much her father had aged since the photo was taken. He was fifty-seven, not young but not old either. Mackenna had thought of them as a team, but maybe he was doing it all for her. There would come a time when he would want to retire, or so she assumed. The distant future had never been discussed. Perhaps she was pushing him too hard.

"This is the kind of site you should be looking at."

Patrick's voice brought her eyes back to the computer. She moved closer. A page with colour and a crisp modern font with constantly changing pictures filled the screen. It was for a sheep stud interstate.

"They're not Corriedales but it's just to give you an idea."

Patrick flicked through the menu. There were several pages with information about the history of the owners and the stud, genetics and a map with contact details. Everything looked very smart.

"It's exactly the kind of site I'd love us to have, but it costs a lot to set up." Mackenna went to the fridge for a drink. "It's just not a high priority."

"In today's world it should be." Patrick spun on the chair to look at her. "Trust me, I don't know as much about sheep farming as you do but I do know a bit about marketing. Not only should you have a web presence, you should be using social media."

"Someone has to create it and manage it. I can't see Mum doing it, and she'd be the only one with a small window of opportunity. We can't afford the time or money."

"Maybe we can."

"How?"

"I've got a few connections." Patrick had a strange look on his face. "Bartering works well for some people. Leave it with me."

Mackenna opened her mouth to speak and he grinned at her.

"No point badgering me. That's all I can say for now. Any chance of some lunch?" He spun back to the computer and started typing. "I didn't get any breakfast this morning."

She watched the back of his head a moment longer then pursed her lips. She looked at her watch. It was late for lunch but she hadn't eaten either. She tugged open the fridge door. There were a few bits and pieces she'd noticed earlier that would make a good pasta dish.

By the time she'd finished preparing lunch her father and Cam were back. She made the bacon and mushroom carbonara stretch to four.

"Is the truck being used tomorrow?" she asked after they'd all tucked in.

"Don't think so, why?"

She ignored Cam's response and looked at her father.

"I've managed to get a second-hand kitchen at a really low cost. Only drawback is it's in Mount Gambier and I have to collect it tomorrow."

"Should be okay," her father said. "Does it include everything?"

"Not all the cooking items."

"What's it for?" Patrick asked.

"The kitchen in the old house," Lyle said, and scraped up the last of the sauce with his fork. "That was delicious. Thanks, Mackenna."

"I can rearrange my day to drive you," Cam said and lazed back in his chair with his arms behind his head.

"No need," Mackenna said as she collected the plates. "I have a truck licence." She was pleased to see the smug grin falter on Cam's face.

"Cam should go," Lyle said. "You'll need help to load up."

The grin was back as she carried the plates to the sink.

"There'll be someone there to help me," she said. The last thing she wanted was to be cooped up in a cab with him all the way to Mount Gambier and back.

"I'll go," Patrick said.

Mackenna shot a grateful glance at her brother but his face was turned towards Lyle and she could see colour spreading across his cheek.

"I want to look at cars." Patrick paused and tapped the table with his fingers. "I might need some help funding a new one."

"Really?" Lyle said. "What's wrong with the old one?"

"I'm afraid it's on its last legs."

Mackenna wanted to say it had been that way when he bought it but she thought better of it. She and Patrick were sharing some rare moments of harmony and she didn't want to spoil it. His car was an ancient BMW, probably about fifth-hand when he took it on.

Not practical at all, but it had been his childhood dream to own a BMW. Still, she thought, her car was old as well and it got used for farm business more often than not. She'd been hoping to trade it for a ute in the near future. There'd be no chance with the renovations to the old house and Patrick needing a car.

"There seems to be a lot of money going out for non farm-related expenses at the moment." Lyle looked from Patrick to Mackenna. There was a brief silence before they heard Louise at the back door. "Your mother's the one to speak to," he said.

Mackenna looked at her father. He was such a dodger when he didn't want to make a decision, but surely he didn't mean the kitchen. He'd already said to go ahead. Louise wouldn't know anything about it till the bills arrived.

"Speak to me about what?" Louise asked.

"Money matters," Lyle said.

"I wouldn't mind a cup of tea first," Louise said.

Mackenna flicked on the kettle. She really didn't think they should be discussing finances with Cam here. He wasn't family. But he looked settled in his chair with his ears flapping.

"Thank goodness my afternoon meeting was cancelled. That first meeting dragged out past lunch. Mavis Pritchard asks the most irritating questions." Louise let out a large sigh then looked around. "Have you all eaten? I filled up on sandwiches."

"Mackenna looked after us," Lyle said.

"Oh, that's good." Louise turned to look at Cam and Mackenna thought her smile was so sweet it was almost sickly. "Cam, I've brought home a couple of bags of chook pellets and one of urea. They're in the back of the car. Would you be a dear and take them to the shed for me please?"

"Sure, Louise," he said but didn't move from his position.

Mackenna kept an eye on her mother between pouring cups of tea. Louise held Cam's gaze. Finally he sat forward.

"Would you like me to do it now?" he said.

"That'd be good, thanks. We don't want to forget and have another smelly boot."

Once the screen door shut Louise turned to her husband. "I know Cam is almost like one of the family already but I do think we should keep our finances between ourselves."

Mackenna settled at the table with a grin. At least she and her mother agreed on something.

"You're probably right, love," Lyle said. "Patch says his car's on the way out and he needs some help financing a new one."

"I'm sure we can work something out. He's been such a help these last months and Mackenna's had some funds for holidays. I think it's only fair."

Mackenna opened her mouth and closed it again. She'd saved her wages for her holiday. The farm had contributed to some of her New Zealand expenses but that was because she was there on business. It was a tax deduction.

Her parents focused on Patrick who had brightened up and started talking replacement cars. At least what he was suggesting were more practical than the old BMW had ever been. Mackenna seethed quietly until she couldn't sit still any longer. She got up to start stacking the dishwasher. She didn't care if the farm paid for Patrick's bloody car but she resented her mother suggesting her holiday had been covered by the business. She should have asked Patrick to suggest the kitchen for the old house. If he'd made the request she was sure their mother would have been happy to go along with it.

"Excuse me folks, but I need to get on with what you're paying me for."

They all turned to see Cam with his head stuck around the door. His face was serious, rather than the grin he usually had in place.

"Which paddock are we putting this irrigator in?" he asked.

"The shorter one at Murphy's place," Lyle said and pushed back from the table.

"Let one of the kids go," Louise said. "Remember not to overdo it."

"I've been sitting in a truck half the day and now lunch. If I keep going like this I'll be overweight and have a heart attack from lack of exercise."

There was a note of irritation in his voice. He tugged on his hat and followed Cam out. Louise turned back to Patrick.

"When will you need the money by?" she asked.

Mackenna shoved the dishwasher shut and pushed the start button.

"And would you like cream or ice-cream with that?" she muttered under the roar of the machine starting its work.

CHAPTER
15

"One hundred and fifty per cent lambing." Mackenna high-fived her dad. "That's not a bad result considering we weren't expecting them for another month."

"Corriedale Dorset crosses have always done well for us," he replied. "Of course they're not at the market yet so we can't get too far ahead of ourselves, but we should do well from them."

They were sitting in the cab of the tray-top looking out over the paddock of ewes with lambs frolicking in all directions. Alfie the alpaca was standing guard under the shade of a tree.

"Now that we've got more space we should consider staggering two mobs on purpose," Lyle said and drove the vehicle forward to follow the fence line. "That way they're not all going to market at the same time."

"I was thinking the same thing."

"Sometimes mistakes are just opportunities to try something new."

Mackenna studied her dad's profile. They'd had a good morning, just the two of them doing paddock inspections. Lyle was looking well and he was pleased with the way things were going on the property, in spite of the lack of rain. Mackenna thought it an ideal opportunity to suggest another of her ideas.

"Dad, now that we've got Murphy's place across the road, I think we should keep all the crosses there."

"That property was in a bad way when we bought it. It's taken some work but the pasture there is much improved. That new irrigator's made a difference already. We must plant those replacement trees soon," Lyle said.

"It's crazy we have to plant five trees to replace one spindly gum."

"That spindly gum had five branches coming out from its stump. That's classed as five trees we've removed to put in the pivot irrigator. Anyway, once we get some good rain I was thinking we should shift our best Corriedale ewes over there."

"We have more Corriedales than we do crosses." Mackenna tried to keep her voice level but she was excited by the prospect of taking Woolly Swamp one step closer to a top class business. "It makes sense to keep them all here and now that we've got the two extra paddocks adjoining, we can utilise them easily."

Lyle eased the vehicle to a stop at the gate and gave Mackenna his full attention. "So you think Woolly Swamp should be exclusively Corriedales?"

"It's a good marketing ploy." She flicked her hand back towards the sheep. "And we can be guaranteed there won't be any future little accidents to interfere with the bloodlines we're building."

"We'd still have to bring the crosses back here for shearing."

"Yes, but we can control what sheep are where."

Lyle stared off into the distance, thinking. Mackenna decided she'd said enough for the time being and jumped out to open the gate.

He drove through and she joined him again. His face was creased in a frown.

The ute moved forward and she waited anxiously for him to speak. They drove all the way to the next closed gate before he did.

"I like the idea," he said.

"But?"

"But what?"

"It sounded like there was going to be a but." Mackenna smiled at him but his face was still creased in the frown.

"Don't get too far ahead. It's just that . . ." He paused.

Mackenna watched him closely. He looked like he was struggling for the right words.

"Is there a problem, Dad?"

He tapped his hands on the steering wheel. "We've been spending a lot of money buying land, doing up the old place, employing a working man. We need to take stock before we go any further."

"Shifting some sheep won't cost us money. In fact it should only improve things." Mackenna was surprised by his talk of expenditure. They had stretched their finances but they were set to see good returns.

"I know love, it's just that . . . well . . . your mother . . ."

Mackenna waited for him to continue but his silence stretched on. What was going on with Mum? She'd been acting strangely but Mackenna had put it down to concern over Lyle. Could there be more to it?

"What about – "

"Your mother – "

They both spoke at once and then stopped and looked at the other.

Lyle pulled his lips into a grin. "I think your idea is a good one. We'll give it a go."

"What were you going to say about Mum?"

"Mum?" He shook his head. "No, nothing, it doesn't matter."

"Are you sure?"

"What I am sure of is, if we shift these beggars to Murphy's place we'll have to do regular fence checks. One's dug out again."

Mackenna looked over the closed gate to the next mob of cross-breds. She could see one standing on the wrong side of the fence.

"Damn it," she muttered. That meant there'd be a hole under the fence somewhere. "I'll fix it but I'll be marking her for a trip to the abattoir."

As she opened the gate Mackenna could see where the sheep had dug. The bottom wire was bent and there was wool caught on it.

Lyle drove through and called from the window. "I'll go round the perimeter in case there's any more damage then I'll open the other gate."

Before he drove off Mackenna took a shovel and let King off the back. The pup gave an excited bark.

"Not you this time, Prince."

The young dog sank to its haunches and cocked its head to one side giving her a soulful look. That's all she'd need, to have the sheep scared off by him.

"You bring her in, King," Mackenna indicated to the older dog. He was on the job straight away, moving the sheep up to where Lyle would soon have the gate open. She turned her attention to filling the hole.

Her father's disjointed conversation replayed in her head as she worked. It almost seemed as if he was worried about Louise. Mackenna thought over the recent conversations she'd had with her mother. They'd been few and far between, and were mostly something to do with another member of the family or Cam. She hadn't really had a long personal conversation with her mother since she'd returned from holiday. The household was busier with Patrick and

Cam around. Mackenna hadn't thought about it till now, but she hadn't got around to showing her parents her holiday snaps. They were still on the camera.

Maybe her dad was concerned about the expense of renovating the old place. The kitchen was ready to be installed. They were just waiting on the new oven and cooktop. The freight company had already collected them so they should arrive any day.

A tingle of excitement bubbled up as she thought of the farm gate outlet she was so close to creating. She was determined it would be successful and her parents would have nothing to worry about other than turning customers away. Of course once things started happening there, Louise would soon know all about it. Maybe that's what was worrying Lyle. He hadn't explained the current plan for the old house.

Mackenna had spoken to Cam about it this morning. He hadn't been at all concerned about staying in the main house. Quite liked running into her in the mornings, he'd quipped. She hadn't bothered to tell him she was planning to move to the old place. In fact now that she thought about it there was nothing to stop her moving in straight away.

The tray-top pulled up behind her.

"No more holes," her father called.

Mackenna whistled up King and then climbed into the passenger seat.

"I'd better get you back to the house," Lyle said. "Aren't you supposed to be helping your mother?"

Mackenna looked at her watch. "Damn it, yes. I have to make sausage rolls for her fundraiser tomorrow." Mackenna was beginning to feel weary but instead of knocking off she had to wash up and start cooking.

They pulled up near the back gate and Lyle gave her a pat on the knee. "Your mother appreciates your help, love. Just like I do." He gave her an apologetic smile.

"Farming's what I love, Dad," she said. "And I don't mind doing the odd bit of cooking now and then. I just forgot about the sausage rolls."

"Make sure some of them stay in our fridge," he said before he drove away.

Mackenna rushed inside to wash up, calling out to her mother as she passed the kitchen. The aroma of warm chocolate cake wafted after her.

"Smells good," she said as she returned. All around the kitchen, baked items were lined up in varying stages of production. The cause of the delicious aroma was the tray of little cakes her mother had just pulled from the oven.

"Is that the time?" Louise said. "No wonder I'm bushed. I've been going at this since lunch."

"The reason you're bushed, Mum, is you've cooked enough to feed a small army. Isn't anyone else doing anything?"

"Yes, but we're expecting a big crowd at the luncheon. All our efforts are going to the hospital fund and people all over the place are doing things."

"We don't want *you* ending up in the hospital."

"I'm alright," Louise said and slipped her apron over her head. "I think I'll sit down for a while, though, and have a cuppa. Your pork and chicken mince has defrosted. I put it back in the fridge."

"Okay." Mackenna began pulling out bowls and the other ingredients she would need.

"You know, we haven't had a chance to have a proper talk about your holiday."

Mackenna glanced at her mother. She was sitting with her feet up, resting on a second chair.

"I'd particularly like to hear about New Zealand."

"I'll have to transfer my photos."

"I'd like to see them."

Mackenna remembered the bag of brochures and leaflets she'd brought back with her. They were still in her backpack on the bedroom floor. "I've got a pile of tourist stuff you could look at."

She whipped up to her room and dug out the white plastic bag. It was quite heavy. Silly to have lugged it all home, but at least her parents might find it useful.

The next hour passed quickly as Mackenna cooked and her mother flicked through the brochures asking questions as she came to things that interested her. Finally she packed them back into the bag.

"I haven't made it through half of the pile yet," she said.

"Some of the brochures are from my American trip," Mackenna said. "Not sure what I'm going to do with it all."

"Oh well," Louise said, slipping her apron back on, "they're a kind of memento. I'd like to keep them to look at later if that's okay."

"Of course."

"Thanks, love. And thanks for all this." Louise waved her hand over the sausage rolls, some cooling and more waiting to go in the oven. She reached up and kissed Mackenna on the cheek. "You're a great cook. I really appreciate your help."

"I don't mind helping," Mackenna said as a wave of happiness swept over her. This was more like the mother she knew.

CHAPTER
16

Hugh drove up the Birches' driveway and stopped near the back door. Both dogs came running at the sound of his vehicle. He hoped Mackenna would be around somewhere. This wasn't a work visit, although he could check on the rams while he was here. It was more about avoiding going home. His last client had only been a short distance away, and on a whim he'd driven to Woolly Swamp instead of in the opposite direction to Morning Star. His mother was out for the evening and Hugh wasn't in the mood for a stilted conversation with his father.

He got out and patted the dogs.

"Hello, Hugh." Louise Birch came towards him along the path from the house. "I thought I heard a vehicle. Lyle's not here at the moment, can I make you a cup of tea?"

"It's really a social call," he said. "I was hoping to catch Mackenna."

"Oh, of course." Louise beamed at him. "She was up at the sheds but then she did say something about the old house. She's had work-men over there doing something."

"Okay, I'll check it out." He got back into his four-wheel drive.

"If you're not rushing off, I've got a roast cooking. There's plenty if you'd like to stay for dinner." Louise continued to smile at him.

"Oh, thanks, I'm not sure . . ."

"Well, when you find Mackenna let her know I've invited you." She patted his hand, which was resting on the open window frame.

"Thanks," he said again as he reversed away.

That was odd. Louise Birch was usually a direct, no-nonsense kind of woman but she'd been almost – what was the word – gushing. Hugh cruised past the sheds and came to a stop beside the Birches' truck. Cam had his head under the bonnet and twisted to look at him.

Hugh raised his hand in recognition. "Just looking for Mackenna."

Cam jabbed a finger in the air. "She went to the old house," he said and stuck his head back under the bonnet before Hugh could say thanks.

What was going on here? The normally straight-up Mrs Birch was being over-the-top effusive and Cam, who was always joking, was barely civil. He wondered in what mood he'd find Mackenna.

There was no vehicle or sign of anyone when he pulled up at the old house. The sun was low in the sky and the light was almost yellow, reflecting off the old stonework and giving it a golden glow.

The front door opened and Mackenna stepped out.

"I hope you've brought champagne," she called as she rushed towards him. He was barely out of the vehicle when she flung her arms around his neck and kissed his cheek. "I'm so glad it's you, Hugh. I can't think of anyone else I'd rather share this moment with. Come in and see."

She danced ahead of him through the door. Hugh took a hesitant step forward. His heart was pounding and the burning tingle began to deepen in his wrists. He took slow deep breaths in through his nose, out through his mouth. Why was this happening? Mackenna was being her usual friendly self and yet twice now her enthusiastic welcome had triggered panic attacks. They hadn't bothered him in a long time.

She stuck her head back through the door. "Come on," she beckoned.

Hugh forced himself to follow. His footsteps echoed on the polished wooden floor.

"In here." Mackenna's call came from the room to his left.

In the doorway he paused. Across from him, along the opposite wall, was a corrugated-iron bar with a polished wood top. Mackenna stood behind it beaming at him. She flung out her arms.

"Welcome to the tasting room."

Hugh looked around. The room was furnished with several small tables of varying designs and an eclectic mix of old wooden chairs. The freshly painted walls were unadorned except for a large canvas print hanging above the fireplace. It was a picture of a mob of Corriedales looking in prime condition. They were standing up to their knees in the lush green of Woolly Swamp pastures with a line of gum trees behind.

"What do you think?" she asked.

"I like it."

"We couldn't run to new furniture so I've scoured our sheds and second-hand shops for the tables and chairs. They don't match but I think that adds character. Rory made the bar for me. Mates' rates. I owe him some meat."

"What will happen in here?"

Mackenna came around the counter and pulled out a seat for him.

"It's like a cellar door for wine, only in this case people will taste Woolly Swamp lamb – everything from roast to sausages. It will be a serving platter with an assortment of local cheese and seasonal salad vegetables."

"Sounds good." Hugh wasn't sure how she would manage everything but he didn't want to dampen her enthusiasm.

"But there's more." Mackenna grabbed his hand, pulled him to his feet and drew him across the passage.

The big room was empty except for a large patterned mat in front of the restored fireplace.

"This will be a bit longer coming but it will eventually be the dining room. I want to put a big long table in here with matching chairs." She cast her arm up the centre of the room. "People can book in advance for a private dinner. We can include local wines and a four or five course meal featuring our meat."

She turned back to him, took both his hands in hers and jigged them up and down. Hugh's heart thumped but not in panic this time.

"What do you think?" Mackenna's face was lit up in a smile and her eyes sparkled. "I know it hasn't been done around here with sheep before." She didn't give him time to answer. "But the beef people have made a go of it locally and in New Zealand I went to a place where they had a tasting room for their Corriedale meat. It was just one part of the marketing they did."

Hugh's head was spinning, partly from Mackenna's close proximity and partly from her explanation. She'd hardly drawn breath since he arrived.

"It sounds impressive."

"You don't look convinced. Oh, Hugh." She dropped his hands and her eyes, now serious, locked with his. "If I can't convince you what hope will I have with Mum?"

"You know me, Mackenna, slow and cautious. I have to take things in before I come to a decision."

"You never used to be like that. You were the one always leading the charge."

Tension sparked through Hugh's body. He hadn't expected that.

"I'm sorry." Mackenna bit her lip in the way she'd always done when she was bothered about something. "That was out of my mouth before I changed gears. I didn't mean it the way it sounded. I'm really looking for support here. Dad's wavering, where once I'm sure he would have been right behind me, and I don't dare tell Mum about it for fear she'll put a stop to the whole venture. I don't know what's going on with those two. Dad was always a tower of strength and confident in his decisions about the property. Now he seems to defer to Mum on everything."

"Events change people."

Mackenna drooped. He wanted to wrap her in his arms and tell her it would all work out okay but he couldn't mislead her.

"Maybe having the heart attack has changed how your dad looks at life," he said gently.

"I don't know how to cope with that." Mackenna slumped against the wall. "I came back from overseas refreshed and ready to get stuck into work but it's almost as if . . . as if they don't want me here."

That made Hugh smile. "Now come on. I'm sure that's not true. Your parents love you and you are your dad's right hand. Maybe you need to slow down and give them a bit more time to see the picture you're painting."

"Maybe." Mackenna straightened up with a sigh. "I really want to move in here and put this place to use, or Mum will be renting it out to someone else now that Cam's not so keen."

"Why would she do that?"

"Mum had plans to use this as a workman's house. Cam was all set to move in once it was finished."

"That would be tricky if you're running it as a farm gate outlet."

"He's happy to stay at the house now." A satisfied grin spread across Mackenna's face.

"What did you do?"

"Just mentioned the ancestors who keep this place cosy."

"How would that deter him?"

"You should have seen his face." Mackenna laughed. "Big tough Cam couldn't get out of here fast enough."

"You're a wicked woman."

"Ah, but you love me." She grabbed his hand again. "Come and see the rest of the place. The kitchen has turned out really well."

Hugh let her lead him along the passage. This time his hand completely relaxed in hers.

The last of the sun's rays were fading fast. Mackenna flicked on the light. While she waited for Hugh to finish washing up in the bathroom, she took the opportunity to once more survey her gleaming kitchen. It was ready to go and she was keen to start, but he was probably right. Her dad may be looking at things differently after his life-threatening experience. Perhaps she needed to rethink how she tackled him with her own ideas. Thank goodness for Hugh being here. He might not be the old carefree guy he once was but the same Hugh was still there underneath, she was sure of it. He'd been changed by circumstances as well.

She heard the bathroom door open and turned as he entered the kitchen.

He smiled at her. "You really have done a fantastic job with the house. Even that old bathroom looks new again."

"I've enjoyed the challenge."

"Look, Mack." He hesitated a moment. "I've been a bit of a wet blanket. I don't want to dampen your enthusiasm. Just because something hasn't been done around here before doesn't mean it can't succeed. This sort of thing is out of my range of expertise."

Mackenna clapped her hands together. "We both know life's too short to not give it your best shot."

"You're right."

"I don't have champagne but I've got a bottle of a good local sauv blanc." She opened the fridge that had been delivered only yesterday. "Have a glass with me."

"Your mum invited me to stay for roast dinner."

"Even better. We can have a pre-dinner drink and nibbles here. You can be my first guest. I have an antipasto tasting plate prepared." She lifted out the small platter of meat and vegetables she'd been playing with earlier and offered it to Hugh.

"You'll do well, Mack." Hugh raised the glass she'd given him. "Here's to Woolly Swamp farm gate."

"And to good friends." Mackenna took a sip.

In the silence that followed they both put down their glasses and reached for something from the platter. She was suddenly very hungry.

"This is good." Hugh mumbled through a mouthful of spiced lamb and cauliflower. Some sauce trickled down his chin. She laughed and dabbed at it with a serviette. His hand brushed hers and she felt a quiver in the pit of her stomach.

Her eyes locked with his and she could see the yearning there. Suddenly their arms were around each other and he pulled her in close. Her lips searched for his and the strength of his response surprised her. She held him tight as his hands roamed down her back.

Then he let her go and stepped back. She opened her eyes wide in surprise.

"What are we doing, Mack?" he groaned.

"I don't . . . I don't know." She put her fingers to her lips where she could still feel the tingle of their kiss.

A knock at the back door made them both jump.

"Hello."

Mackenna tucked in the tail of her shirt that had come loose in their embrace.

"Hello, anyone home?" The voice called again.

She turned as Hugh picked up his hat. Surely she was mistaken? The bright tone and the funny vowels, it sounded like Adam but her ears must be playing tricks. What would the guy who had run out and left her in New Zealand be doing here at Woolly Swamp?

CHAPTER
17

Louise glanced around the table at everyone eating her roast lamb. Within the space of three weeks they were using the dining room again. Two extra for dinner, well three if you counted Cam, made it a tight squeeze in the kitchen. The dining room table was much better for seven.

The conversation was sporadic. This time Cam didn't come to the rescue. He'd been a bit quiet for days now, only coming in for meals. Mackenna's friend, Adam, was the one doing most of the talking, answering questions from everyone it seemed but Mackenna. She wasn't saying much at all. Louise wondered if something had happened between them. Adam certainly looked and talked like a decent young man but his presence could complicate things. She had set her cap on Hugh being the right man for Mackenna. They'd seen a bit of each other lately and Mack was always chirpy when Hugh was around. But even he was quiet tonight. Adam had changed the dynamics somehow.

"Have you done any bungee jumping, Adam?" Patrick asked.

"Several times," Adam said, "years ago now. What about you?"

"No," Patrick said, "I would have liked to."

"Would have?"

"Patrick," Louise exclaimed. "Why would you want to do that?"

"You'll have to come to New Zealand someday." Adam grinned. "Give it a go."

"Mug's game," Cam muttered.

"It's a real adrenalin rush," Hugh said.

"Not you too." Louise was amazed. Why people would throw themselves off a bridge with a little piece of rope to yank them up and down and scare themselves witless was beyond her.

"Sure is," Adam said.

He glanced across at Mackenna but Louise noticed she lowered her eyes.

"That will be on the back burner for a while now." Patrick pushed the last of his vegetables around his plate.

He looked decidedly glum. Louise was puzzled by the strange atmosphere around her table.

"Lyle and I are planning a trip to New Zealand," she chirped.

"When?" Both Patrick and Mackenna exclaimed in unison. Everyone looked at her and Lyle raised his eyebrows.

"Not for a while," he said.

Louise locked eyes with him. "You only have to get the doctor's go-ahead."

"There's a lot to do here."

Louise gripped her hands together under the table. "If we don't start planning we'll never get there."

She was annoyed that Lyle was making excuses. They'd discussed the trip several times since he'd first mentioned the idea. That was back when Hugh was last here for dinner. After the last lunch with her sisters she'd been all the more determined to go. She'd talked with Lyle about it as soon as she arrived home and he assured her they would do it.

"We can manage, Dad," Mackenna said. "It's no different from when I was away and you were sick. In fact, we've got more help now. With Cam and Patrick we can manage."

"Yeah," Patrick said. "I'll soon have a car to pay back."

Louise looked from one of her children to the other. Mackenna's expression was one of excitement and Patrick's was brooding.

"You know that's not necessary, Patch," Louise said, "but we are grateful you're here. We'd love you to stay on, wouldn't we Lyle."

"Whatever Patrick wants," Lyle said. "Work must be wondering where you are."

"I'm between projects at the moment and the rest I can do online."

Once again the conversation faltered. Louise began stacking the plates. Both Hugh and Mackenna had eaten very little.

"I'll get dessert," she said.

"Not for me thanks, Louise." Cam pushed back from the table. "I'm heading into town. I'll stay at my mate's place tonight. I'll be back here first thing." He barely glanced at the others and left.

"I should be going too," Hugh said. "I have an early start tomorrow as well."

"I've made trifle," Louise said giving him an encouraging smile.

"The roast was delicious, thanks Mrs Birch, and more than enough." Hugh patted his stomach. "Mum's been making desserts as well. I think I've stacked on a couple of kilos since I've been back."

"I can't see where." He'd hardly eaten any of the roast but Louise wouldn't point that out. "Anyway, you're always welcome here, isn't he Mackenna." She looked at her daughter who suddenly leapt to her feet.

"Yes," she said. "I'll see you out."

"No need. You stay with your guest." Hugh reached a hand across the table. "Nice to meet you, Adam."

"You too."

Adam rose to his feet and Louise saw the look of confusion on Mackenna's face as she turned from the departing Hugh to look at Adam.

"I must go as well," he said. "I should have followed Cam. Can you give me directions back to town? I'm not sure I can find my way in the dark."

"You can stay here," Lyle said.

Louise pursed her lips. What was he thinking, encouraging this stranger?

"There must be a place in town to stay," Adam said. "I don't want to impose."

"You'll have trouble at this hour on a week night," Lyle said. "There's a spare bed in Cam's room."

"It's not made up." Louise baulked at the severity of her own voice. "At least . . . well Cam's been using that room. I don't know the state of it, I haven't been in there for a while."

"If you don't mind sharing an empty room," Lyle chuckled, "I'm sure Mack will be happy to find you some sheets."

Louise looked from her husband to Adam who was giving Mackenna a soulful look.

"I'll get them," Mack said.

Louise was right. There was something going on. She had seen the anguish on Mackenna's face as she'd rushed out the door.

"I'm off too," Patrick said and brushed his lips across Louise's cheek.

Lyle was still focused on their visitor. "You planning on staying around here long?"

"I'm not sure." Adam ran a hand back and forth along the top of the dining chair. "I came to Australia with my mother. Her dad lives in Melbourne and his health hasn't been good. I'll need to head back there soon but I couldn't come all this way and not look Mackenna up."

"Where did you meet?" Louise wanted to find out the lay of the land between the two of them.

"We . . . we did a bit of sightseeing together."

"Where was that?" Louise asked. "We haven't heard much about Mackenna's trip yet."

"That's because we've been working her to the bone since she's been home." Lyle put an arm around Louise. "I had some heart trouble while Mack was away and it's taken a while to get myself back up to speed. By this hour I've run out of puff. If you'll excuse us we'll head to bed, won't we Lou?"

He winked at her and Louise felt the gentle pressure of his arm around her waist, guiding her to the door.

"Yes, well I'd better show Adam to his room first," she said.

Lyle kept his arm locked around her. "Bathroom's back opposite the kitchen and your room's at the top of the passage on the right. I'm sure Mack will show you anything else you need."

"Thanks."

"Goodnight." Lyle said. Louise managed a quick smile in Adam's direction before Lyle propelled her out of the room.

"What are you doing?" she hissed at him.

"Giving them some space." Lyle said as he shut their bedroom door.

"Why?"

"Haven't you seen how edgy Mack's been all night?" He snorted. "You tell me I don't notice the vibes but you couldn't miss them tonight. There's definitely history between those two."

"We don't know anything about him." Louise stripped off her clothes. Why of all times would Lyle choose tonight to notice body language?

"I'm just saying you're trying to match Mack to Hugh but maybe she's already found someone."

"Oh for goodness sake, Lyle, we shouldn't encourage . . ."

"I'm not expecting him to propose marriage," Lyle said. "All I'm saying is let's give them a chance to catch up without us old fogies being around."

Louise opened her mouth then thought better of it. There was no point in further discussion. Poor Hugh had looked rather devastated when he left but Lyle wouldn't have noticed that. She really thought something was simmering between Hugh and Mackenna and she wasn't going to let some foreigner spoil it. No, Adam was here for the night but she would be doing her best to make sure he was gone tomorrow.

"Louise," Lyle warned as she opened the door.

"I'm going to the bathroom," she said.

"Can I help?"

Mackenna jumped at the sound of Adam's voice.

"I've done it," she said and bent to straighten the quilt over the top of the bed.

Adam moved to the other side of the bed and helped her. She could feel his eyes burning into her scalp but she didn't look up.

"I'll get you a towel," she said and turned away.

"Mackenna wait."

She froze. The sound of his husky voice and that quirky accent sent a shiver through her. She couldn't believe how easily her fickle body was letting her down. She'd vowed to forget all about Adam and only a couple of hours ago she was kissing Hugh. What had that been about? They'd been friends since childhood, along with Carol. If Carol hadn't been killed in that car crash she and Hugh would probably have married and had a brood of kids by now. Mackenna didn't know what to think. She didn't trust herself to look at Adam let alone speak to him.

"Can I talk to you?" he persisted.

She clenched her nails into the palms of her hands.

"At least can you tell me why you left me? I thought – "

"Left you!" Mackenna spun to look at him. "You left me."

"I was only gone half a day. I know it was longer than I said but my mate needed me, I couldn't let him down."

"You left without saying anything." Anger and hurt bubbled inside her.

"It was early. I left you a note explaining."

"What note?" Mackenna was trying not to raise her voice but she couldn't help herself. "Explaining what? That I was your holiday fling? And now you're on holiday again and you thought you'd look me up for a good time in Oz."

"Mackenna, you can't believe . . ." He started towards her.

"Keep away."

"Everything sorted in here?" Louise stuck her head around the door.

Mackenna spun around but kept her face averted from her mother as she passed her.

"Yes," she said firmly. "Everything's sorted."

CHAPTER
18

"Good morning."

Louise looked up at the sound of Adam's voice.

"Come and sit down," she said. "Did you sleep well?"

"It's so quiet. I've overslept."

"You've missed everyone, I'm afraid." Louise was glad. Now she'd have a chance to quiz him about his relationship with Mackenna. "They're all off doing jobs. Except Patrick, he's still in bed, I'm assuming. I haven't seen him yet."

"I should go," Adam said.

"Please stay for breakfast."

Louise watched the indecision cross his face. Even with the forlorn expression he was a good-looking young man. She could see why Mackenna might have been attracted to him.

"I'd hoped to see Mackenna before I left," he said.

"She'll be gone most of the day." Louise was happy for him to stay a while but she didn't want him here when Mackenna came back.

She hadn't heard what they were saying in the guestroom last night but Mackenna was obviously upset. She'd been in such a rush to leave this morning she hadn't eaten breakfast. Louise felt pretty sure her daughter was avoiding Adam. But why?

"Mack's not far away, is she?"

They both turned to see Patrick drift in. His hair stood up all over his head and he was still wearing pyjamas – if that's what you could call the ripped t-shirt and threadbare boxers.

"She's got a busy day," Louise said and set another place at the table. "Both of you sit down. Would you like a cooked breakfast, Adam?"

Adam hesitated and then sat next to Patrick. "Cereal will be fine, thank you."

"Yeah but they're only over at the new place, aren't they?" Patrick scratched his head.

"Murphy's?" Louise said.

"Yeah. It's not like they're far away."

She put bowls and cereal boxes on the table. "Adam's probably got other things planned."

"I could take you over there," Patrick said. "I'm supposed to go over and plant some trees or something."

"I'd like to see your property," Adam said. "I went with Mackenna to a Corriedale stud outside of Queenstown. I'm a chef but it was really interesting to find out the whole process before the meat reaches the restaurant."

"Yeah, Mackenna's into all that." Patrick slurped a big spoonful of cereal into his mouth and milk ran down his chin.

"Really, Patrick," Louise said and passed him a serviette.

"She said she was hoping to open some kind of farm gate outlet here," Adam said.

Louise stopped pouring the tea. She had thought that idea had been squashed.

"We've done up the old house at the front gate," Patrick said.

"Oh yes," Adam replied. "I went there last night but I didn't go in."

"It will be the working man's quarters," Louise said as she handed round the cups.

"But Mack's done all that work." Patrick turned to her. "The new kitchen is ready to go."

"What new kitchen?"

"Where have you been the last few weeks, Mum? Mack has put every spare minute into getting the place shipshape. It's looking really good over there."

Louise gathered up their empty bowls. She hadn't been over to the old place since it was decided Cam would use it. Her life had been confined to keeping an eye on Lyle, the housework and trips to town for her committees and fundraisers. She walked past the old house nearly every day to collect the paper but she hadn't gone in.

"I'll just throw on some clothes," Patrick said, "then I'll take you over to where Dad and Mack are working. I'll leave the guided tour of the farm to her, though. I'm sure she'll want to show you around, especially her farm gate outlet."

Louise glared at Patrick's back as he disappeared out the door. How was it possible all this was going on and she didn't know about it? Lyle would have to be in the loop. Surely Mackenna wouldn't have kept it from him as well.

"Can I help with the dishes?" Adam's question brought her back.

"No," she said, "thank you. We have a dishwasher."

"Thanks for your hospitality, Mrs Birch." He held out his hand and Louise accepted his firm shake.

"Will you be heading back to Melbourne today?" she asked.

"No," Adam said. "I'm not really sure what I'll do next. I've got a bit of time to wander unless I get a call from my mother."

"Is your grandfather very sick?"

"I think it's only a matter of time but he was looking quite good when I was there."

"Ready to go?" Patrick called brightly from the passage.

"Thanks again," Adam said and followed Patrick out.

Louise cleared the table in a flash, whipped off her apron and set off to the old house. She needed to see for herself what was going on there.

Mackenna and her father both stopped at the sound of Patrick's old bomb approaching. Thank goodness, Mackenna thought, and risked a quick glance at her father. He straightened up and arched his back. He looked okay but he wasn't moving at his usual speed.

They were putting a new gate between the two paddocks they'd bought and it was taking more work than they'd anticipated. The ground was hard. She was worried her father was overdoing it. She should have brought Cam to help her, but he'd gone to get a load of hay. Maybe Patrick could take over.

She shielded her eyes from the morning sun as the car drew to a stop and Patrick bounced out.

"I've brought you a visitor," he said.

Mackenna stiffened as Adam got out of the passenger side. He looked so good. She'd noticed last night he wasn't clean-shaven like he had been in New Zealand and the dark stubble, along with his tight, closely cropped curls, made him look so rugged.

"Hello, Adam," Lyle said. "What are you like at mixing cement?"

"Not bad actually." Adam grinned. "I've helped my cuz lay a few paths recently. It's just like mixing a cake."

He gave Mackenna a nod and a smile, which she didn't return. The look of him and the sound of his voice was making her body react even though her head was trying to remain aloof.

"We can't make a visitor work," she said.

"Why not?" her father and brother said in unison. The three men chuckled together. Lyle gave some instructions and they were soon all working.

Mackenna tried not to look when Adam stripped off his shirt and bent over the cement mixer. He wasn't bulky but his trim body was firm. She shuddered as she remembered their nights together.

"Stop gawping, sis," Patrick murmured in her ear.

She spun around and glared. Patrick was grinning at her with that smug smile of his.

"Where am I supposed to put these trees?" he asked.

"This way," she said and moved off to a double-fenced stretch along from the gate. Instead of the five replacement trees they'd decided to plant a stand and some other natives to create some shelter. The paddocks here had been all but stripped of vegetation. She helped Patrick get started.

"I can manage," Patrick said after she'd hovered over him while he planted the first two trees. "You get back to Dad and Adam."

"Mack," her father called, "can you hold this post while I add the cement?"

Adam was manoeuvring the wheelbarrow in place as Mackenna took the post from her father. It was heavy and she didn't get a good grip on it. Suddenly Adam was opposite her, his hands on the post and his face only a short distance away.

"I don't want to leave without talking to you, Mackenna, please." His deep brown eyes bored into her.

"Watch your feet." Lyle started shovelling cement into the hole and she was saved from replying.

Somehow she managed to avoid getting too close to Adam again all morning, until finally Lyle called it quits.

"We're finished for now," he said. "Thanks for your help, Adam. Patrick and I can load up here. Why don't you take Adam for a look around before lunch, Mack?"

"I wasn't expecting lunch," Adam said.

"Of course you must." Lyle patted his back. "You've earned it. Go for a drive and we'll see you back at the house."

There was no escaping him this time. Mackenna picked up her hat that had fallen off when she'd been wrestling with the last piece of wire and led the way to her car. Once Adam was in, she started the motor and drove back towards the main property. Alongside the boundary fence she pulled into the shade of some gum trees and nosed the car in so that they had a view across the paddocks towards the house. Normally it was picturesque with lush green pasture but at the moment it was looking dry. They really needed some decent rain. She turned off the engine and they both sat, looking ahead in the silence that followed.

Yesterday she'd been kissing her old friend Hugh. Today she was sitting a metre away from Adam, the man she loved in New Zealand and who she'd thought had loved her. Her emotions were all over the place and she didn't trust her judgement at all.

"This is a nice place," Adam said at last.

Mackenna kept her eyes fixed on the distant house while the silence stretched between them again.

"I had trouble tracking you down," he said. "I had your name, Corriedales and South East to go with. Australia's a big place."

Finally Mackenna spoke. "I wasn't hiding." What did he want, a medal? She gave him only a quick glance, still not trusting herself to look into those deep brown eyes.

"We didn't even exchange addresses."

Mackenna flicked her eyes his way again. He was grinning for goodness sake.

"You've found me now," she said and waved a hand at the view. "This is where I live."

"Sounds like you've got your dream happening."

"My dream?" Mackenna frowned. There was no hint of sarcasm in his voice.

"Your brother was telling us over breakfast about the work you've done in the old farmhouse, the kitchen and – "

"Breakfast!" Mackenna's heart thumped. "Was Mum there?"

"Yes." Adam put his head to one side, a puzzled expression on his face. "She got our breakfast."

"Damn!" Mackenna started the car. "I need to get back to the house. You can have a tour of the old place later if you like."

The car bounced back over the verge of the road and slid in the gravel as Mackenna put her foot down. She gritted her teeth. That's if I've still got access to it, she thought.

CHAPTER
19

Hugh pulled over at the crossroads and looked again at the directions he'd been given. He was a long way from town in an area he didn't know so well and he wasn't sure if he should have taken the turn-off before this one. He bent forward to look up at the post but someone had removed the sign. The clock on his dash showed he was still on time. He'd left early in case of this very event, but he'd have to ring the bloke and get new directions. No point doing it from here though, without being able to name the crossroad. He'd have to go back a few kilometres to the previous one.

He did a U-turn and immediately his phone rang. A farmer he was visiting later in the day had some questions. Hugh pulled over to check his paperwork. He was about to start out again but waited to give way to a truck coming along behind him. He watched its approach in his side mirror then as it passed him, he realised it was the Birches' truck. He couldn't see who was driving, but they were going like the clappers with the empty truck. It could have been either Lyle or Mackenna, but somehow he thought it more likely to be Cam.

Hugh wondered what he'd be doing out this way but the thought was quickly replaced by a vision of Mackenna and that kiss. Damn! He put his four-wheel drive in gear and moved out onto the road, following the trail of dust left by the truck. Half the night he'd tossed and turned replaying their encounter. They were good mates. He'd kissed her without thinking.

Thank goodness her friend from New Zealand had turned up, or who knows what would have happened next. Hugh would have done a runner then but Mackenna had been insistent he stay and so had Louise, but the meal had been a nightmare. The tightness had returned to his chest, he'd had trouble focusing on the conversation and his stomach had shut down. All he could do was push the food around his plate and try to make it look as if he'd eaten some of it. The drive home had been slow. He'd practised every one of the strategies his psychologist had given him to calm himself.

This wasn't good. He'd only agreed to come back to the district thinking he'd put all the demons well and truly behind him, but they seemed to resurface at every turn and it was Mackenna who set them off. Hugh pulled up at the next crossroad. Going to Canada was the easy solution. He could make a new start but somehow the thought of that didn't excite him like it had before.

He sighed. At least his appetite had returned and he reached for the roll his mother had prepared for him this morning. He never wanted to lose all the weight he had back in the dark days. None of his family ever saw him that thin. Even though he'd never put all the bulk back on, at least his appetite had returned – up until last night.

Hugh brushed the crumbs off his clothes. He was alright, he told himself, coming home to live would either make him or break him, he decided. A chill went through him. He never wanted to feel that bad again.

He took a drink from his water bottle then twisted back and forth in his seat to stretch. He reached for his phone – time to ring this farmer and get directions.

Louise sat in one of the chairs in the front room of the old house. She'd spent the morning wandering from room to room. Her emotions had ranged from amazement to anger and even admiration. Mackenna had changed the place completely since Louise had last been over. The kitchen was refurbished and decked out with brand new equipment. No doubt this room where she now sat was where the food would be served.

None of it could have happened without Lyle's knowledge and it sounded like Patrick was in on it as well, perhaps even Cam. Louise was the only one who'd been oblivious of the goings on here, and that annoyed her. She shared everything with Lyle and she always believed he did with her. Well, perhaps not everything about the farm. He shared the intricacies of the day to day with Mackenna but Louise helped whenever she was needed, paid the bills and kept the paperwork up to date. She had a fair idea of how things went. She and Lyle always started the day with a cuddle and a chat about the work to be done.

She squirmed in her chair making it creak. It made her sad to think they'd lost some of that closeness since his heart attack. He was sleeping better now. Not so many restless nights but these days she often got up before he was awake. And their sex life was non-existent. The doctor had told Lyle he was fine to resume his normal activities, but Louise was still anxious that any over-exertion might cause problems and Lyle hadn't shown any interest in being that intimate until the other night.

Louise got up from the seat and wandered the room as she recalled their first attempt at love-making since his heart attack. It had been a disaster. She'd been anxious and he'd been frustrated by his lack of ability. It wasn't a problem they'd experienced before. She'd suggested it was probably due to all the treatment he'd had and the medication. He didn't want to talk about it then and there hadn't been an opportunity since. Besides, how did you bring up the subject of impotence? It was probably normal, but would things ever go back to the way they'd been?

She straightened a chair, tucked it further under the table and kept walking. She couldn't imagine talking to her sisters or her friends about it, nor the young GP who was their local doctor. She came to a stop in front of the large print on the wall above the fireplace. The photo had been taken at a good time of year, with everything looking so green and the sheep looking like prize specimens. It was the only thing on the walls and it drew the eye straight to it as soon as you entered the room. Mackenna was clever, Louise conceded that.

The room across the hall was a blank canvas. Louise had no idea what Mackenna's intentions were for it but the room would easily accommodate antique furniture. No doubt there was a plan. Louise wandered up the passage again. The room between the table area and the kitchen was going to be a bedroom. It should have been Cam's but some of Mackenna's things were draped across a chair, and a couple of framed prints that had been taken down when she'd made the shift into the top bedroom of the new house were propped against a wall. A piece of lace curtain had been hooked across the window and there was a swag laid out on the floor. Perhaps Mackenna had slept here already.

Hugh had come looking for her yesterday and Louise assumed he'd found her here. They were still not back at the house when Adam had turned up and Louise had sent him in this direction.

She pulled the door shut on the bedroom, then paused and pushed it open again. She studied the swag. She didn't like to think of her daughter in that situation but maybe Adam had interrupted something between Hugh and Mackenna.

Of course! How silly of her not to have seen it. She wanted Mackenna and Hugh to get together but maybe it had already happened. That would explain Mackenna's early arrival back from her holiday and Hugh's return to the area after so long away.

Louise almost skipped through the kitchen and out the back door. That's what this was all about. Mackenna needed space. She lived on the family property and it was hard to get privacy, especially with Patrick at home now and Cam living with them. No wonder Mackenna had been so disappointed when she thought Cam would be living there. If turning the old house into a farm gate outlet was the space Mackenna needed to pursue Hugh then Louise wouldn't stand in her way. In fact, it might work out quite well. Patrick could step up and be more involved in the property, Hugh and Mackenna could live in the old place and it would give her something to do until babies came along. Louise was sure the McDonalds would come up with a place for them to live eventually. They had for their other three sons.

She looked at her watch as she hurried through the back door. She'd been over at the old place so long they'd all be in soon and she had nothing prepared for lunch. They could make their own sandwiches today. Louise hummed a tune as she took salad items from the fridge. It seemed as though things were falling into place where Mackenna was concerned. If only Patrick would follow suit.

Mackenna burst into the kitchen and her mother looked up from the table she was setting and smiled.

"Hello. Is everyone coming in for lunch? I see Adam's hire car is still here."

"No . . . well, yes." Mackenna watched her mother for any sign of anger but Louise was smiling at her.

"Which is it?"

"What?"

"You're not making sense, Mackenna. How many am I expecting for lunch?"

"Dad, Patrick and me." Mackenna put her hand to her forehead. "Oh, and Adam."

She'd left him behind in the car when she ran inside. She stared at her mother for a moment longer but Louise turned away and started slicing tomatoes. Behind her Mackenna could hear male voices. Dad and Patrick must have arrived. Patrick was talking about the trees he'd planted. She flew into the bathroom to wash up before they got there first.

Last night she'd taken her swag over to the old house and slept in the bedroom there. She hadn't planned to move in until she'd worked out a proper bed and some cupboards but she hadn't wanted to risk being under the same roof with Adam. Besides, everything was ready at the old house, she just needed to move in.

Back in the kitchen, she boiled the kettle.

"I went over to the old house this morning," Louise said. She had her back to Mackenna so there was no way to predict what she was going to say.

She turned around holding a plate of sliced tomatoes and cucumber. "You've done a great job with the place." She put the plate on the table with the other sandwich items. "At least I'm assuming it's all your work? I can't see Dad and Patrick managing such a tasteful makeover."

Mackenna tried to smile. "I'm happy with it. I was planning on having you all over for a meal as a surprise to christen it, but now you know."

"Yes, I do."

The men came into the kitchen still talking about trees.

"There are a few things that need doing," Louise said quietly in Mackenna's ear. "You should have a decent bed for starters." She winked and turned away.

Mackenna studied her mother's profile as she got the men to sit down. What had just happened? She'd expected Louise to go off about the farm gate idea, the expense and the lack of quarters for Cam. Instead, her mother seemed to have taken the whole thing in her stride. Mackenna wondered why she'd worried so much about telling Louise. She should have just included her all along.

The blokes were already putting together their sandwiches. Mackenna sat as far from Adam as she could. He was beside Patrick, on the other side of the table.

Louise reached over to put salt and pepper on the table and behind Adam's head she winked again.

Mackenna looked down. What was with all this winking business? Adam laughed at something Patrick said and she looked at him in horror. Oh no! All this smiling and winking and comments about the old house and needing a bed – her mother must think Adam's her boyfriend.

Patrick kicked Mackenna under the table. "Earth to Mars," he said. "I asked you how come you didn't take Adam to show him the swamp?"

"Oh, sorry." Mackenna looked from Patrick to Adam then down at her empty plate. "We ran out of time."

"It's a very special part of our property," Lyle explained. "My grandparents built their house to look out over it. We're a bit dry at the moment but the birdlife can be magnificent."

"I've spent most of my life in cities," Adam said. "Going to the farm out of Queenstown with Mackenna was my first experience of rural life since I was a kid. And now I'm seeing where she lives. It's great."

"You'll have to take him later," Patrick said and gave her another gentle tap under the table.

"Yes, later," Mackenna mumbled, not lifting her eyes to look at anyone.

CHAPTER
20

"Three weeks, Lyle, that's all I'm asking." Louise looked across the car seat at him.

"You said two."

"Two and a half or it won't be worth going."

Lyle didn't respond and she remained silent for a moment letting him mull it over. They'd been in town for his check-up. The doctor had given him the all clear and Louise had left the room hoping Lyle might talk about personal issues, man to man, without her there. She'd taken the opportunity to call in at the travel agent. They could leave for New Zealand in a couple of weeks and she was keen to get Lyle to commit.

Raindrops began to spot the window. With any luck it would be a decent rain and that would improve his mood.

"So much has happened, Lyle." Louise kept her eyes on the windscreen where dust was turning to mud streaks. "We both deserve a break. Getting right away from here would do us good and it wouldn't be for long."

"We'll see." Lyle switched on the windscreen wipers and leaned forward in his seat to glance at the grey sky. "I hope this rain sets in."

"How about I get out the brochures and the suggestions from Effie at the travel agent and come up with an itinerary?" Louise wanted to get some assurance from him while they were in the car. It was harder for him to evade her in the confines of the vehicle. "Mackenna will probably add some good ideas and she'll have the farm contacts."

"We'll see," he said again. "Right now I want to get this mattress home before it gets ruined."

Louise watched him flick his eyes to the rear-view mirror. She turned her head and looked at the trailer.

"It's encased in plastic and you've got the tarp over it. I'm sure it will be fine and we can't go any quicker than we are now." She put a gentle hand on his forearm. "We need this holiday, Lyle."

"I want to be home for lambing."

"We've got lambs now."

"They were unexpected. May and June will be very busy."

"We've still got time and if a few start lambing before we get back what will it matter? You've said yourself Mackenna can manage."

"Of course she can."

"Well then." Louise folded her arms and waited.

They drove on in silence. The rain got heavier and Lyle continued to cast the odd glance in the rear-view mirror. They'd bought a new mattress for the old brass double bed they had stored in one of the sheds. It was perfect for Mackenna's bedroom in the old farmhouse. Louise had even bought a new quilt cover and sheets. She hoped with all her might that Mackenna and Hugh would pair up. Not that she wanted to be seen as condoning her daughter sleeping with Hugh before they were married, but she wasn't naïve enough to think Mackenna was still a virgin. Young people had a different view of life from the way Louise had been brought up.

Lyle thought there was something between Mackenna and Adam but Louise couldn't see it. He was smart and easy on the eye, but Mack had kept her distance from him since his arrival. Something may have happened between them in New Zealand and he'd decided to look her up. Friends – that was all. What would Lyle know about it anyway? He'd never been very observant when it came to relationships between those around him.

Discomfort wormed through her. She wondered if he'd spoken to the doctor after she left. Prior to his heart attack their own relationship had been warm and loving. She'd always thought they had a healthy physical relationship. Not as often didn't worry her, but not at all was a different thing altogether.

She flicked her eyes in his direction again as they turned onto the road that led to their driveway. Somehow she'd find the right moment to discuss what the doctor had said.

"Mackenna will have her work cut out but we're not far off the main road," she said, trying a different tack. "I'm sure she'll get some interest in this farm gate idea of hers. Patrick can take on the farm role."

Lyle sighed. "I think we made a mistake." He glanced her way. "Patrick doesn't want to be here."

"What makes you say that? He's been a big help and he's learning quickly. He shifted that mob of sheep the other day with only old King to help."

"I'm not saying he's not capable, he just wants to go back to Adelaide."

Louise fixed her gaze on him as he manoeuvred through their front gates and pulled up by the old house. "When did he say that?"

"He didn't, but we've had a few general chats and he keeps going back for weekends whenever he gets the chance. His work won't let him stay here indefinitely."

"Woolly Swamp *is* his work." She shifted in her seat and folded her arms.

The re-roofing on the old house had included a back verandah and carport. Lyle backed the trailer under but she kept her eyes focused ahead.

"By the look of these puddles it's been raining here a while," he said.

"Lyle – "

"Someone's here." He cut her off. "The quad bike's at the back door."

Louise glanced in that direction. Mackenna appeared and waved to them from the verandah.

"That's good," Lyle said. "We can unload this mattress and see if any damage has been done." He opened his door then turned back to look at her. "You come up with a plan and some dates."

She smiled.

"I'm not committing," he warned. "We'll talk about it later." He was out of the car before she could say any more.

Under the shelter of the verandah the three of them wrestled the mattress out of its protective covers before they took it inside. Lyle went off to unhook the trailer and Louise stayed to help with the bed.

"These old queen sheets will do the trick until I can get the new ones washed and dried," Louise said as they tucked the extra material under the mattress.

"Thanks, Mum," Mackenna said. "I didn't expect you to go to all this trouble."

"It's no trouble." Louise felt a pang of guilt. She'd almost shut Mackenna out since her return home. This had been a small peace offering. "You know I enjoy doing it. You've made a great start with the decorating. It looks good."

"You think so?"

Louise could see her indecision. "Of course. I just wish I'd known what you were doing."

"I'm sorry, Mum, I didn't – "

"I only meant I would love to have helped." Louise didn't want to spoil the moment.

She studied her daughter across the bed. Her hair was pulled back in a ponytail but loose curls bobbed around her face, evidence of the damp air, and her skin glowed. She was the picture of good health. Surely the men lined up for her attention.

"Adam seems a nice young man."

Mackenna's head came up with a jerk.

"He is."

"Do you think he'll stay much longer?"

"He's tried to leave several times but you keep insisting he stay." Mackenna pulled the quilt straight.

Louise could see her relaxed mood ebbing away. Anyway, it was Lyle who kept saying Adam should stay when he tried to move into town, but Louise wasn't going to labour the point.

"It seems a shame someone comes all that way and we send him to a hotel," she offered.

"He'll probably head off again soon." Mackenna tidied a pile of clothes dumped on the floor.

Louise cast her eyes around the large room. "Why don't we bring over the tallboy from the top bedroom?" she said. "It's not being used and it would suit the bed and the room perfectly."

"That'd be great."

"We'll get the men to wrestle it. It's such a heavy old thing. Might be good that Adam's still here."

Mackenna stood tall and put her hands on her hips.

"Mum, Adam and I met on holiday. He's just a friend. Don't go making more out of it than that."

"I'm not." A flood of relief swept over Louise. Thank goodness Lyle was wrong and there was still a chance for Hugh. "I just meant it will probably take three of them to move it and I'd rather one of them wasn't your father."

Mackenna's frown changed to concern. "He's alright, isn't he? What did the doctor say?"

"Yes, he's fine. I'm trying to convince him to take this New Zealand holiday before lambing but you know what he's like. Won't leave the place."

"Well maybe I can help." Mackenna slipped her arm through Louise's and they walked together. "I think he should go and check out those two farms I visited near Queenstown. Maybe I can convince him it's a business trip."

Louise nudged her daughter. "Thanks, Mack," she said. She hoped Mackenna was right. Once upon a time Mackenna could have convinced Lyle to do anything but in his current mood even she might have trouble.

"We really need a holiday," she said.

They stopped at the edge of the verandah and looked up at the clearing sky.

"Damn!" They said in unison.

CHAPTER
21

"Hopefully there'll be some more rain again soon." Lyle cast his eyes to the sky. "The forecast sounds promising for the weekend."

Mackenna looked back at the paddock they'd just sown. The soil looked dark and rich in spite of the drier than normal summer. With the seed in the ground all they needed was the rain to produce some excellent pasture, but she still had her doubts. Sowing before they had a good rain was her father's idea. The twenty millimetres they got a few days back had galvanised him into action and she'd gone along with it.

"I'll move the seeder over to Murphy's place ready for an early start in the morning," she said.

"Didn't you say you had an appointment in town? I can shift the machinery."

"I've got time," she said. "You head home, Dad. Ask Mum or Patrick to come and pick me up."

"I'd rather not just yet."

"But you look worn out."

"I'm okay. I had a restless night. Didn't sleep much." He moved along the seeder checking the hoses. "Where's Adam today?"

His question took her by surprise. At dinner last night Adam had been asking about the caves. She was up early and out on the tractor and hadn't been up to the house today. "Doing tourist things, I think."

"Shouldn't you be looking after your guest a little better?"

Her father's weary expression had been swapped for a strange half smile.

"Shouldn't you be minding your own business?" she said.

He ran his hand over a hose. "Have we got enough fertiliser ready for tomorrow?"

"We were running a bit low. I asked Cam to pick some up today. He's going to do the first shift in the morning."

"How are you finding him?"

Mack glared at her father. "Is this another personal question?"

"You're being a bit touchy." Lyle leant back against the tractor wheel and folded his arms. "Must be what comes from two blokes making goggle eyes at you."

Mackenna felt a wave of heat flow through her. "What are you talking about?"

"Adam's obviously totally smitten with you."

Mackenna opened her mouth to protest but her father cut her off.

"And Cam's got his eye on you as well."

"Cam!" Mackenna scrunched her face up in a frown. "Dad, you've lost the plot."

"You may have noticed he's not hanging around the house as much since Adam's been here."

"What's that got to do with anything?" Mackenna cast her mind back over the last few weeks. She'd been too busy to give Cam much thought other than the work he did for them. He liked a joke and sometimes he'd been a bit . . . she wasn't sure what. He had good looks and a good body but that didn't mean . . .

"He seems to know what he's doing." Lyle's voice cut into her thoughts.

"Yes," she murmured. "You know, maybe he doesn't like sharing a room with Adam. He wasn't actually given a choice."

"Adam's a nice bloke."

"Yes?" Mackenna drew the word out slowly like a question.

"Is there something you're not telling us about him?"

"I don't believe so." Mackenna opened the tractor cab door and took out her jumper. The air was getting chilly.

"So you reckon Cam will be right to sow those paddocks tomorrow while we organise the crossbreeds for market?"

"I'll be keeping the seed up to him. He says he's done it before and he certainly knows about the machinery."

"I think he's done some work as a diesel mechanic."

"Really?" Mackenna rested her chin on her hand and tapped her lips with a finger. "With his truck licence it makes you wonder why he hasn't taken up the money the mines are offering."

"He's worked with a mechanic. Hasn't got the actual qualification from what I can gather." Lyle pushed himself forward. "Besides, mine work doesn't suit everyone."

"I guess not."

"I've got my second wind now. Hopefully it won't be much longer and I'll be back to my old self — right as rain," Lyle said. "You drive the tractor and I'll follow in the ute and bring you home."

Mackenna thought he looked a bit brighter and it was then that she remembered her suggestion she would try to convince him to go on the New Zealand holiday. The trip home together in the ute might be the best chance she'd get.

Louise turned the parcel over again then placed it on the kitchen table where it covered one end and poked out over the edges. It was a large cylindrical shape but not excessively heavy and it was addressed to Lyle. She didn't want to open it, but to her chagrin she was busting to know what was inside. It wasn't his birthday and he rarely received parcels. The odd incentive from a stock and station company maybe, but they were only ever towels or umbrellas.

She snatched up the bag of New Zealand brochures Mackenna had given her and sat at the other end of the table. The information Effie had provided was good for maps and special features, but she wanted to look at Mackenna's collection again. It was full of brochures that had been collected along the way and held snippets of information not necessarily found in the travel guides. There were other assorted bits and pieces that Mackenna had hoarded in the bag, like receipts for train travel, tickets, food menus and a photo of her aboard a jetboat. Louise glanced at Mackenna's smiling face then stopped to look closely at the man next to her. It was Adam. They were sitting close together and, like the other occupants of the boat, they each held an arm aloft in a group wave for the camera.

Louise put the picture to one side and continued sliding papers and brochures from the bag. It was just one of those travel photos people collected, nothing special about it. Mackenna certainly didn't act like there was anything between them.

A couple of sheets slipped from her hand and slid to the floor. As she bent to retrieve them she noticed handwriting on the back of a menu from a takeaway shop in Queenstown. It was a note that began with 'My dear Aussie princess'. Although it was personal, Louise couldn't stop herself from reading it. Adam had had to go and help a mate, he'd written, but he'd bring back lunch and there was still time for their afternoon jump together. That was the gist of it.

Louise recalled the night Adam had arrived and she'd gone up to the bedroom to make sure he had everything he needed. He and Mackenna had been having words over a note. Louise had heard that much and something about a fling before she'd stepped in to interrupt them.

The words in this note were more than a message – they were intimate. Something a lover might write. And at the very bottom was a mobile phone number. Now she was totally at a loss to understand what was going on. She couldn't believe Mackenna and Adam were close now from the way they acted. It surely must have been only a holiday fling. But why would Adam come all this way to see Mackenna and stay so long? Whatever the reason, he needed to leave soon.

Louise ripped the menu into tiny pieces and pushed it into the bin then she gathered up the pile of brochures she wanted to look at and put the rest back in the bag. Mackenna was seeing quite a lot of Hugh and Louise didn't want anything to stand in the way of that possibility. She could already see a church wedding in her head.

Lyle's parcel attracted her eye again. She ran her hand over the wrapping then turned her back on it. It was time to prepare the evening meal and these days she was never sure how many to expect at her table. She'd gone from cooking for three to cooking for anything up to six if they all turned up, although Cam had let her know he wasn't staying tonight. They'd fallen on their feet employing him. He was able to turn his hand to anything, which helped take the pressure off Lyle, and he was always so polite and helpful around the house – when he was around. That was another reason she'd be glad to see Adam leave. Cam hadn't stayed over as much since Adam had taken up residence.

Louise had the braised steak simmering and was preparing the vegetables when she heard Lyle and Mackenna come in.

"You've got a parcel," Louise said as soon as Lyle stepped through the door.

"What's that, Dad?" Mackenna asked from right behind him.

Lyle picked up one end and looked at the address.

"Have I missed someone's birthday?" Mackenna went to look at it too.

"No," Lyle said with a smug look on his face. "Just something I ordered."

"What is it?" Mackenna asked. Louise wanted to know as well but she was biding her time.

"It's something I ordered for your mother and me." He gave Louise a proud smile. "You can open it, Lou."

Louise wiped her hands on her apron and took a pair of scissors from the drawer.

"Are you sure?"

"Of course," Lyle said. "You do the honours."

"For goodness sake, will someone open it," Mackenna said, glaring from one to the other.

Louise cut the tape binding the package together and slid the paper away.

"What is it?" Mackenna peered over her shoulder.

"I don't know yet," Louise said.

All she could see was something white. She slid the plastic away to reveal some kind of tightly rolled fabric. She squeezed. It felt spongy.

Lyle put his arm around her shoulders. "It's for our bed," he said. "It goes between the mattress and the bottom sheet and is supposed to give you a good night's sleep."

"That's a nice surprise," Mackenna said. A smile hovered at the corners of her mouth. "Perhaps you'd better tell her your other surprise, Dad, while we're on a roll."

Louise was trying to keep the emotion from her face but she wasn't sure she was going to like Lyle's next surprise any more then she had the first.

"Oh yes," he said. His grin spread wider. He guided her to a chair. "You'd better sit down, Lou."

Louise shook herself free of his arm. "I'm not sitting down and you can stop being silly, the pair of you." She'd endured enough suspense for one day. "What's going on?"

"Am I missing something?" Patrick wandered into the kitchen and lifted the lid on the braising steak.

"Leave that be," Louise said.

"What's this?" Patrick asked, picking up one end of the mattress overlay.

"Never mind," Louise snapped.

Patrick gave her a pained look but she ignored him. "What else have you got to tell me?" She locked eyes with Lyle.

"Only that you can book the tickets for New Zealand, but if you don't – "

"When?" She cut him off as her heart did a little leap. Was he teasing?

"In the next few weeks. I want to be back by lambing."

"Does that mean you'll need me longer?" Patrick still bore the injured expression.

"Of course," Louise said eagerly.

"Only if you want to," Mackenna said. "Cam and I can manage."

"We'd love you to stay," Louise said. "I'm sure Mackenna would be grateful for the help."

"Well, yes," Mackenna said, "but it's not necessary. Isn't your boss wanting you back?"

"We can talk about it later." Louise kissed Lyle. "I'm so pleased. We'll both enjoy the break. I've got the fundraiser luncheon next week but the art show is under control for the moment. I can leave it in the hands of the committee until I get back. There's a lot to plan in a short time." Louise was already making lists in her head.

"I'd better get going," Mackenna said.

"Will you be back for dinner?"

"No. By the time I get back from Bunyip Wines it'll be late. I'll make myself a snack at my place." Mackenna threw an arm around her parents and gave them both a squeeze. "Great news," she said and hurried out the door.

Louise turned to Patrick as his mobile rang. He peered at the screen and left the kitchen.

"It might be just you and me for tea," Lyle said.

"Where's Adam?"

"Mackenna thought he'd gone off to visit the caves today."

"Oh yes, I'd forgotten. I suppose he'll be back for the meal."

"Probably." Lyle picked up the overlay and gave it a squeeze.

"When did you order that?" Louise asked as she set to peeling the potatoes.

"I saw it on the television."

"When?"

"Early hours of the morning about a week back. They have a lot of really good stuff on that shopping channel, you know."

She stopped peeling and looked at her husband. "What are you doing watching the shopping channel?"

"Couldn't sleep," he said with a silly grin.

"Well I think that's the sort of thing you should leave to me, Lyle." She nodded at the bundle in his arms. "You haven't ordered anything else, have you?"

"I might have."

"Oh, Lyle."

"Wait till you see it. You'll love it." He moved to the door. "Shall I take this up in the bedroom? You can put it on when you change the sheets."

She opened her mouth but he was already halfway out the door.

"I really think it'll help with our sleeping problems," he said.

"Sleeping problems," she muttered to the empty kitchen. "I wouldn't have any sleeping problems if you didn't." She took a deep breath in through her nose and picked up the next potato. What difference a bit of fancily covered foam was going to make to Lyle's sleep patterns she had no idea.

CHAPTER

22

Hugh dragged the last load of creeper from under the tree and dumped it on the overflowing trailer. He put his hands to his hips and stretched his back. With his weekend work and now a few free hours this afternoon, he and his mother were finally seeing some results in the garden.

He went back into the yard to take another look at the log they'd positioned underneath the large gum. A motley collection of faded gnomes, frogs and garden ornaments were lined up ready for placement. As they'd unearthed each one, Mary had fondly brushed the debris from its surface and recalled who had given it to her.

Propped against the log was a weird little box with holes in its sides. Hugh had been going to throw it on the trailer when his mother had snatched it from him and cradled it in her arms. Apparently it was a bird feeder that had been made by one of her grandsons. It was to be hung from a branch.

He breathed in the smell of freshly dug earth mingled with the sweet smell of the gum and other native trees he'd reclaimed from the ivy and the treacherous bougainvillea. Of all the things Mary had planted over the years and then lost, the bougainvillea wasn't one of them. His arms still bore the marks from his weekend of struggling with the evil plant but he'd won in the end. Another dose of herbicide on the stump should finish it off.

He came out from under the tree just as his mother walked along the verandah carrying a tray laden with afternoon tea things.

"Here you are, love," she said and put the tray on the old wrought-iron table. The table wobbled a moment then settled.

"That area will make the perfect secret garden." Her eyes were bright as she nodded to the trees over his shoulder. "The kids will love it. They can climb the trees now without getting scratched by thorns, they can have tea parties, they can – "

"It's your garden, Mum," he said. They had done all this work and he wanted her to relax in it, not have it destroyed by his horde of nieces and nephews.

"Gardens are meant to be shared," she said. "And there'll be plenty of opportunities for me to enjoy it . . . and your dad."

Hugh couldn't imagine his dad sitting out here with her.

"I still can't believe I'd forgotten all about this old setting," she said as she handed him a cup.

They sat on the two matching chairs that had been cut from the ivy and brushed clean of cobwebs, leaves and loose dirt to reveal dark wrought iron under peeling paint. The whole lot looked like it should have gone on the trailer as well but Hugh had an idea for the garden furniture. He'd already been a couple of times to see Rory Heinrich. Instead of the animal sculpture, Hugh had come up with a different idea for his mother's garden. Now he wondered what Rory could do with the old table and chairs.

"It's been wonderful to have your help, love."

She clasped her cup in two hands and gazed out across the garden.

"I've enjoyed it," Hugh said and he meant it.

Having the garden as a project had been a great way to exercise and clear his mind, although it was hard to keep his thoughts of Mackenna at bay for too long. He hadn't seen her since the dinner. He'd run into Patrick in town and their visitor, Adam, but she hadn't been with them. He was so mixed up by that kiss. And she'd kissed him back, so did that mean she felt they were more than friends?

"Not so bad living at home then?"

His mother's question surprised him.

"What do you mean?"

"It's been years since you've spent so much time at home. It's as if you've been avoiding us."

"I'm sorry, Mum. It's been hard up till now to get the time. I've been living so far away, lots on my plate . . ." His voice trailed off. His excuses sounded weak even to his own ears.

"I'm not blaming you, love." She put down her cup. "It's just that . . . well, you're my baby and I feel as if we've lost touch. A few more phone calls would have been good."

Hugh saw the longing in her eyes and his heart lurched. He loved his mum, but he wouldn't know where to begin to try to fill her in on everything he'd been through and done since he left home.

"Have you given any more thought to your dad's offer?"

He scratched the back of his neck. He hadn't really. When he'd first arrived home joining the family business had been the last thing he'd wanted to do, but the past few weeks had gone well. He didn't see a lot of his dad, but they had civil conversations when they did talk and his dad had even asked his opinion on some seed issues. Nothing more had been said about the offer of the Sutton property since the night it was mentioned over dinner.

"Yes and no," he said.

"It would be a great opportunity."

"I know but . . . well, it came as a surprise. It wasn't the direction I'd imagined I would be taking."

"What were you imagining?" Mary's voice was gentle and she fixed her big round eyes on his. "I always thought I knew you inside out but now . . . I know you're a man, Hugh. I don't mean you have to tell your old mum everything, but it seems to me like you're a bit lost. What is it that you want so badly that you wouldn't jump at an offer like your dad's made?"

Hugh turned away from her searching eyes and studied the towering gum in the corner of the garden. The last remnants of its bright yellow flowers still clung to its lower branches. He wanted to be back under its cover, digging the soil, not having a deep and meaningful conversation with his mum. And anyway, where did he begin? His life was intertwined like the ivy and bougainvillea he'd cut from the trees – Carol's death, his guilt, his panic attacks, the research job in Canada, kissing Mackenna. It was all too complicated to sort through and he didn't have the energy to try.

Instead, he said, "I'm interested in animal genetics. I've done some extra study in the last couple of years, sheep in particular. There's this research project I've been asked to – "

"Why didn't you tell us?" Mary sat forward. "Your brothers and your dad would be keen to find out more. If the property Dad mentioned isn't what interests you, there would be different ways you could be involved in the family business."

"Well the research project is in – "

"'Research project' sounds so important."

"I enjoy it."

"I always knew you had the most brains." She stacked the tray as she spoke. "Don't get me wrong, your brothers are all clever men in their own ways but you were the only one to go to university and you've put that smart brain of yours to good use."

"Mum, I'm not – "

She leapt from her chair and hugged him, cutting off his words.

"Wait till I tell your dad. He'll be as proud as punch." She picked up the tray. "I'm going to cook us a special dinner. I wonder if it's too short notice to get all the family here."

Hugh's heart sank as she gave him a beaming smile and bustled off into the house, the cups and plates rattling as she went. The last thing he wanted was to be the centre of attention, especially at a McDonald family dinner. But what could he do? He couldn't avoid it, his mother would be heartbroken. He needed something more than the general hubbub of a McDonald family get-together to deflect the focus from him.

He paced the verandah. What about Adam? A visitor from New Zealand would give them more to talk about than Hugh's future or even past for that matter. He'd been avoiding Mackenna but right now she was his only hope. He needed a distraction and Adam could do the trick along with Mack who was always chatty. Well, most of the time. Their last dinner together had been a bit stilted but time had passed since then. He tugged his mobile from his pocket and hoped Mack would be able to come.

CHAPTER
23

Mackenna threw an assortment of clothes into her bag, which still lay on the floor where she'd left it on her return from holiday. With everyone else off in different directions this afternoon she had the house to herself. She only had the bare essentials at the old place and had to keep returning home to get clothes. Now that her kitchen was fully stocked and her linen installed in the wooden cupboard her mother had unearthed from another shed, all that was needed were her clothes and personal effects and she wouldn't have to keep popping back home.

Hugh's call had been another reason to collect all her clothes. She needed something suitable to wear to the McDonalds'. So far she only had work clothes over at the other house. She couldn't decide what she would wear tonight. It wasn't a special occasion, just a family dinner Hugh had said, and he needed help deflecting the conversation away from him. Mackenna hadn't asked any questions, but she had to hold her tongue when he asked if she could bring Adam along too. So far she'd had little time alone with Adam. She wouldn't be able to avoid him on the twenty-minute drive to the McDonalds' and then back again.

If only Patrick was here, but his car had finally died and he and their father had gone to Adelaide to buy another one. It was amazing Lyle had agreed to go at all, but when he said he was driving there and back in one day, Louise had hit the roof. Finally, they'd all gone. Louise wasn't going to let Lyle drive back alone and if she decided they needed to stay over somewhere on the way back, they jolly well would. Mackenna was relieved her dad had agreed to stop sowing pasture. They'd done a couple of paddocks and the rest would wait until they got a good season opening rain.

Cam had gone to help a neighbour shift cattle and Adam had gone with him. With any luck they would be back late and she could slip off to Hugh's by herself. She would have an honest excuse for Adam's absence.

Anyway, regardless of who was where, they'd all agreed to be back in time for her special dinner tomorrow night. She was officially opening the Woolly Swamp Gatehouse, as she'd decided to name it, and she was planning a celebration.

She turned back to the wardrobe and studied the assortment of sturdy boxes on top; one of them held her old chef uniforms. When she'd returned home from her last chef's job in Victoria she'd wanted to chuck them out but her mother had insisted they keep them, just in case. Tomorrow, Mackenna decided, she would wear her black jacket again.

She dragged the wobbly bedroom chair over and started lifting lids. Finding the box she wanted, she drew it forward and stepped down at the same time. The chair wobbled and she lost her footing. The box hit the floor with a thud, tipping its contents across the room and she crashed sideways into the wardrobe door.

"Are you okay?"

Mackenna gasped and spun around at the sound of Adam's voice.

"Where are you hurt?"

"I'm not," she stuttered. "You frightened me. I thought I had the house to myself."

"I thought the same," he said. "Are you sure you're not hurt?"

He stepped towards her but Mackenna thrust out her hand.

"I'm fine," she said. "It was just the noise. I'm not hurt."

Adam looked around. "I was expecting to find a burglar but it looks like they've already been."

Mackenna flicked her eyes from the box of spilled clothes, to the unmade bed with more clothes strewn across it, to the heaps she'd made on the floor amongst the boxes and the bags. It certainly was a mess but some of it was going to the charity bin. She hadn't had a good clean-out in years.

"I'm sorting through what to shift and what to throw out."

"It looks very final."

"I'm leaving home."

A smile twitched on Adam's lips and she had to look away.

"Lucky you're not going far. Can I help?"

"No need," Mackenna said as she shovelled the uniforms back in the box. "I've got my car at the front door. I'll drive everything over in that."

"I'll carry this for you." Adam reached for the box as she put its lid on and his hand brushed hers.

She pulled away. The touch of his fingers felt like a caress and she didn't want to be reminded of that. She picked up the case she'd packed full of clothes and led the way through the front door.

"I haven't been out here before," Adam said.

"It's a lovely verandah with a view down to the swamp, but like most farmhouses it rarely gets used." She turned to Adam and couldn't stop her eyes sweeping across his gorgeous face, tight-fitting t-shirt and pale but sturdy arms wrapped around the box. "Why are you here?" she asked.

Adam looked surprised. "I've been trying to tell you. I came to find *you*. You left New Zealand before – "

"No." Mackenna cut him off before he could soften her resolve with his words. "I mean now. I thought you were spending the afternoon with Cam shifting the cattle? He can't be finished yet."

Adam's shoulders drooped as he let the box slide a little further down his body. "He hasn't finished. He said he was heading straight into town once he'd delivered the last load so he offered to drop me back here. I didn't know you were home."

Mackenna frowned. Cam took the truck into town a lot, rather than his own vehicle. He treated the truck like it was his own.

"I'll keep out of your way."

Adam looked so forlorn, Mackenna softened her tone.

"I hadn't planned to be here either but I had a call from Hugh. He's asked me over for dinner tonight . . . both of us actually and I didn't have anything to wear. One thing led to another and I ended up in full throw-out mode."

She hoisted the case into the boot of her car and he placed the box beside it.

"I can manage the rest," she said.

"I'm happy to help."

She flicked him a quick smile and hurried back inside. They made several trips until finally her car was full.

"Thanks, Adam," she said as she slammed the back door on a precarious pile of jackets and hats. "I'll come back and pick you up at six."

"Thanks for the offer," he said, "but I'll stay here. Have a quiet night. It's time for me to think about heading back to Melbourne. Do some touristy things on the way."

"When are you leaving?" Mackenna felt a pang of regret. She didn't want him here and yet she didn't want him to go.

"I'll pack up tonight, maybe get going in the morning."

There was sadness in his eyes.

"Is your grandfather worse?"

"No, he's holding his own, but I need to move on. It's been great seeing where you live but I think it's time for me to let you all get back to normal without having to entertain the Kiwi. Say thanks and goodbye to Hugh for me."

He climbed the steps to the verandah. Mackenna took two paces to follow. She suddenly felt very bad about her offhand manner. She'd been behaving like a callous bitch.

"Please stay a bit longer, Adam."

He paused but didn't turn.

"Hugh especially invited you tonight and I'd like you to stay for my celebratory dinner tomorrow night," she babbled. "You've come all this way."

She watched his shoulders rise and fall as he took a long breath in then out. Finally he looked over his shoulder.

"All right, I'll stay two more nights. Thanks," he said and walked inside the house.

Mackenna watched the door close behind him. A mixture of emotions tumbled around inside her. Cam, a complete stranger, and Adam, her ex-lover, had infiltrated her family and taken up residence in her family home, the home that she'd just evicted herself from. Her oldest friend Hugh was behaving strangely and had kissed her, a kiss that she hadn't rejected. She'd always thought her life was ordinary but right now she'd trade it for something far simpler.

Her mobile rang and she plucked it from her pocket to peer at the screen. It was Chris from Bunyip Wines, no doubt wanting to know something about tomorrow night's dinner. She slid her finger across the screen to answer but the call dropped out. She tossed the phone on the car seat and drove back to the old house. The reception was much better there and talking to Chris about the dinner was a topic she was comfortable with.

It was well after six by the time she went back to collect Adam. He was waiting for her at the gate.

"Sorry," she said as he climbed in. "Had a few phone calls then I had to find something to wear out of that mess I'd created."

"It was worth the wait," Adam said. "You look good."

Mackenna turned quickly from his gaze and put the car into gear. She hadn't meant to sound like she was fishing for a compliment. "It had to be something that didn't require ironing." She chuckled. "My little place doesn't have an iron yet."

She'd put the black and red wrap tunic dress over a black three-quarter t-shirt and black leggings. She'd bought the tunic in New Zealand after Adam left her. The girl in the shop had filled the cramped change room with options for her to try and Mackenna ended up buying a couple of outfits. They'd been spur-of-the-moment purchases, a new look to build her confidence, but there'd been no opportunity to wear any of it until now.

"Did you enjoy the cattle work today?" she asked in an attempt to divert the conversation from anything personal.

"It was different," Adam said. "They've got some prime cattle there but they're worried they are losing condition. Looks like everyone wants some rain."

"Yes, doesn't matter if you've got sheep, cattle or wine in this area, at the moment we're all expecting rain." Mackenna gripped the steering wheel and watched the road, not wanting to look at Adam in his green checked shirt that complemented the healthy glow of his skin.

By the time they arrived at the McDonalds' her arms were tired and her head hurt from the strain of keeping the conversation neutral. There were several cars in the yard already as they pulled up.

"Hope you're not overwhelmed by large family gatherings," Mackenna said as she got out of the car. The sound of children's squeals and several voices talking at once wafted from the house. "The McDonalds can be a lively bunch when they're all together."

"Hello."

Hugh came down the path to meet them.

"Sorry we're late," she said. "My fault."

"You haven't missed anything. Mum's giving the kids their meal so we can eat with some semblance of calm."

A shriek of laughter echoed from the house.

Hugh laughed and shook Adam's hand. "Welcome to bedlam," he said and turned to kiss Mackenna on the cheek. She thrust the bottle of wine she'd brought into his hands.

"Dinner at your house was always entertaining," she said.

"Hello, Mackenna."

They all turned at Mary's welcome bellow. She gave a beckoning wave.

"Bring them in, Hugh. The food's ready."

Inside the house chaos reigned. Mackenna introduced Adam as best she could to Hugh's three brothers and their wives. She rarely saw them and always muddled up their names. The older children were watching television in another room but two of Hugh's brothers had babies and another a toddler, so their noise added to the voices of the eleven adults.

They all squeezed around the huge kitchen table. Mackenna found herself seated between Hugh and his oldest brother, while Adam was seated opposite her between Mary and one of the sisters-in-law. They all had mountainous plates of roast lamb and vegetables in front of them, not a fancy meal but hearty. The smell of it set Mackenna's mouth watering.

"What's this research stuff Mum's been babbling on about?" Hugh's brother spoke through a mouthful of food.

There was a momentary lull around the table and Mackenna looked up to see all eyes turned to Hugh. She glanced sideways, took in his startled expression and put her cutlery down with a clatter. She presumed this was her queue to distract their attention, as Hugh had asked.

"It's similar to what Adam and I saw at the Corriedale stud we visited in New Zealand. They've used the latest research to help them map out which rams to use, which ewes to keep. It was really interesting, wasn't it Adam?" She smiled at his puzzled expression across the table.

"Yes . . . well, I don't know much about farming but I found it . . ." His voice petered out.

"Interesting," Mackenna finished for him.

"What do you do for a living, Adam?" the sister-in-law beside him asked.

"I'm a chef," he said, finding his voice again. "I'm very interested in the farm-to-table experience."

"Which part of New Zealand do you come from?" Another of Hugh's brothers joined the conversation and soon they were discussing popular spots in New Zealand, poking fun at Adam's accent and Kiwis in general.

Somehow the conversation never got back to Hugh and his research project. Mackenna noticed he ate very little of his dinner and when his mother put a huge serving of apple crumble and ice-cream in front of him, Hugh sat back from the table.

"Are you okay?" She kept her voice low.

"Yes," he said. "Mum serves up too much. I'm not used to these big meals anymore."

"You could still eat a bit more, you know." She leaned in closer. "Why can't you tell them about the research project you're involved with? Is it a secret?"

"No." Hugh inclined his head towards hers. "It's just that it's overseas, in Canada, and Mum is so keen on me staying here. I don't want to burst her bubble."

Mackenna tried to keep her own surprise from her voice. "You're going to have to tell her sometime if you're planning on leaving the country."

"It's still to be finalised and I'd rather not discuss it while we've got a crowd."

So he wasn't a hundred per cent committed. She wondered why.

Mackenna took a mouthful of the crumble. It melted in her mouth. "I'd forgotten how good your mum's apple crumble is," she said. "You really should try and eat a little."

She gave him an encouraging smile and nudged his plate closer. Hugh picked up his spoon and took a small taste.

"You could tell them about the study you've already done," she said.

"What are you two whispering about?" The question came from one of Hugh's brothers further down the table and all eyes were directed their way.

Hugh's spoon clattered to his bowl.

"Not whispering," Mackenna said with a chuckle. "Do you guys know how hard it is to get a word in when you're all together?"

"They're a noisy bunch," Mary said and beamed at her family around the table. Immediately the chatter began again.

Mackenna spoke up. "Hugh was telling me about his study," she said and gave him a wink.

"Let's have a bit of quiet for a moment so he can tell us." Allan McDonald's voice wasn't loud but he achieved instant silence. Even the babies seemed to understand that their grandfather was not a man to be trifled with.

Hugh looked like a startled rabbit. Mackenna felt for his hand under the table and gave it a gentle squeeze. He coughed and pushed his bowl away a little.

"Tell us, Hugh," Mary said, her face full of pride.

"The course was all about animal breeding management," Hugh said.

"Sounds like what we do already," muttered the brother next to Mackenna.

"Let him finish." Once again Allan's tone commanded respect.

Mackenna heard Hugh draw in a breath before he began again.

"Besides studying genetics we went into biotechnology and designed specific breeding programs."

The confidence grew in his voice as he spoke. She turned to look at the others and found Adam staring at her. His face was expressionless but those deep brown eyes of his looked sad again.

Allan fired a question down the table at Hugh and she directed her attention to him. She had been on her best behaviour tonight, making conversation. Whatever was upsetting Adam couldn't be her doing this time. Maybe he hadn't taken the McDonalds' rowdy teasing very well.

Hugh continued to elaborate on his study and Mackenna couldn't help but be impressed by his depth of knowledge. She would definitely have to pick his brain further.

When Mary began gathering the bowls, Mackenna noticed how late it was. She had a big day tomorrow and another dinner, but this time she would be doing the cooking and serving. She caught Adam between conversations.

"Ready to go?"

He nodded and they made their farewells. Once again the voices became rowdy. Mackenna leant in to kiss Hugh's cheek. "That wasn't so terrible, was it?" she murmured in his ear.

He gave her a thankful smile.

"See you tomorrow night at Woolly Swamp Gatehouse," she said.

Outside, the still night was a welcome release from the noise in the kitchen but Mackenna wasn't looking forward to trying to make conversation all the way home. As it turned out, she needn't have worried. Adam settled back in his seat and hardly said a word. When they arrived at the house he jumped out of the car with a quick goodnight. She watched for a moment until she saw the glow of an inside light then headed back to the old house.

She was getting used to Adam being around even if she didn't see him all that often. She had to admit she'd be sorry when he left. Still, she had no time to worry about him tonight. There was a big day ahead of her tomorrow. She pulled in at her back door mentally ticking off the list of jobs.

CHAPTER
24

Mackenna cast her eyes around the dining room one more time. Everything was ready. She'd shifted a couple of the tables in from the tasting room, joined them and covered them with one of her mother's large white damask tablecloths. The table was set with silver cutlery and white napkins, also her mother's, and she'd put a small bunch of flowers in the centre and a larger arrangement on the mantelpiece.

In the pit of her stomach, she had a strange sensation. Nerves! She hadn't felt that since her early days as an apprentice chef. So much was riding on tonight. She wanted her family to see the possibilities of the farm gate tasting room. She wiped her palms down the sides of her jacket and went back to the kitchen.

Once again she looked around. She was happy with the way everything had come together. She'd been working all day and things were where they should be. Her food prep was complete, all she needed now were her guests. She looked at the clock on the wall. There was time for a glass of Bunyip sparkling before everyone arrived. She got out one of the crystal glasses she'd found when she'd cleaned out her bedroom; a twenty-first gift that had never been used. She popped the cork on the bottle.

"Celebrating already?"

The bottle nearly slipped from her grasp as she spun around.

Adam was leaning against the doorframe watching her. He was wearing a deep red check shirt, a sleeveless jacket and dark denim jeans.

"You've been shopping," she said.

"Thought I'd try some Aussie clothing. This R.M. Williams gear seems to be the thing."

"Would you like a glass?" Mackenna turned away and willed her trembling hands to be steady as she took another piece of long-stemmed crystal from the cupboard. She remembered every detail of the body underneath those clothes.

"Thanks," he said. He took the glass she offered and nodded at her jacket. "You look the part."

She brushed her hands quickly down her black chef's. coat. "I haven't worn it in years but I thought it would add to the atmosphere for tonight."

"This really is what you want to do," Adam said.

"Not just the tasting room." Mackenna waved her hand at the land beyond the window. "I want the running of our stud and the management of our animals to be top class. Not so much guesswork, making use of research and up-to-date genetic mapping. I want the people who buy our sheep to know they're getting the best and to ask for it in restaurants."

She turned back to Adam and felt the tiniest niggle of self-doubt. Maybe she was expecting too much and maybe she was doing the wrong thing pushing away this gorgeous man standing before her.

Why was he still here when she'd done her best to keep the distance between them?

Adam raised his glass. "Here's to you, Mackenna. A woman who knows what she wants."

She clinked her glass against his and gave him a wry smile. If only you knew the turmoil below the surface, she thought.

His eyes held hers as they both sipped their drinks.

The sound of an approaching vehicle drew Mackenna's eyes to the clock. "Time to get started," she said.

Adam leaned in. "Yes, chef," he murmured. "You look delicious by the way." He kissed her cheek. A shiver ran through her. She breathed in the scent of him. Then he was gone. From the front of the house she could hear his deep voice mixing with those of her parents'. There was no time to waste. She took the first tasting platter from the fridge, added the brie she'd had sitting out then whipped into the bathroom.

The face that stared back at her from the mirror could have been a stranger's. The young woman with bright eyes and glowing cheeks didn't match the emotions that battled within her. Self-doubt and indecision were not common feelings for Mackenna. If only Adam wasn't here, she thought. He was distracting her from her purpose.

She snatched up a lipstick and applied the subtle red to her lips, then patted her hair with her hands. She'd taken time earlier to braid her long locks then pulled them up and back and pinned them to her head. A few shorter curls floated loose around her face but she couldn't do anything about them. She went to meet her guests.

"Mackenna, you look gorgeous," her mother said as she hugged her. "I love it when you wear your hair up like that."

"How did your trip to Adelaide go?" Mackenna asked, conscious of Adam's eyes studying her.

"Busy."

"Your mother made me stay in the city last night." Lyle said as he took his turn to hug Mackenna.

"It was so late by the time we'd done all the paperwork for Patrick's car," Louise said.

"Where is Patrick?" Mackenna looked through the open front door to the darkening sky.

"We haven't heard from him today," Lyle said. "But he's definitely coming."

"And he's bringing a friend." Louise's smile grew.

"Now don't go reading anything into it," Lyle said. "It's probably just a mate."

Mackenna thought of the table she'd set. She had plenty of food but she'd need to set another place. Mate or not, she hoped Patrick's friend was female. They had males galore at the table but Mackenna, her mother and Chris's wife, Ginnie, were the only women. Another female would help balance the numbers.

Hugh arrived with a bunch of flowers from his mother's garden, closely followed by Cam, and then Chris and Ginnie with two bottles of a new dessert wine. The entrance was crowded and footsteps and voices echoed loudly. She'd need to get a carpet runner for the passage. Mackenna ushered them all into the tasting room, where she put Chris in charge of pouring everyone a glass of his Bunyip sparkling while she returned to the kitchen.

She had no vase for the flowers but an empty jar did the trick. They'd been held together with a piece of brown and white striped ribbon, which she tied around the jar. They would look perfect on the bar in the tasting room.

Then she turned her attention to the first of her tasting plates. It was a simple platter of cheeses, nuts, some dried bush tomatoes, her green pesto dip and cured lamb. Satisfied, she picked up the plate and the flowers.

Ginnie was the first to greet her when she returned. "Mackenna, you've done a wonderful job with the decorating. The room looks great and the little touches of the wool in the basket and the corrugated-iron bar – I love it."

"Thanks. Would you like to try something?"

"It all looks delicious," Ginnie said and she picked some food from the plate.

"Can I put those somewhere?" Hugh took the jar of flowers from her hand.

"On the bar." Mackenna was relieved to have two hands to support the heavy platter. "Thanks Hugh, they're lovely."

"Mum's doing, of course." Hugh smiled. "But I had the original thought."

Everyone took turns to select something from the platter.

"Where did this come from?" Her father waved a piece of cured meat at her.

"It's our lamb," Mackenna replied, watching her father closely as he took a bite. "What do you think?"

Lyle frowned and inspected the meat left in his fingers. "How can it be our lamb?"

"Don't you like it?" Mackenna was worried. This was one of her surprises.

He took another bite. "The flavour is strong." He chewed some more and swallowed. "Perfect for a lamb lover," he said with a grin. "Did you do this?"

"The first part, preparing and flavouring, then I took it to a butcher in Mount Gambier for the curing part."

"Try this, Lou," he said, tapping Louise on the arm.

Louise murmured her approval and the others crowded round again.

"I hope you've got more," Hugh said.

Mackenna was excited by the enthusiastic reaction to the cured lamb and thankful she'd made a second platter. The food was disappearing at a rate of knots and Patrick hadn't arrived yet.

"Let me offer this one," Adam said, taking the plate from her hands.

"Thanks."

She turned just as Patrick appeared in the doorway with a young woman by his side. She was what could only be described as striking, with straight jet-black hair cut in a sharp fringe above her eyebrows and curving into the nape of her pale neck where it almost touched. Her clothes were all different layers but each layer was black. In fact the only contrast was the bright red of her lips and the paleness of her skin.

Conversation halted around the room as all eyes turned to the newcomers.

"Hope we're not too late." Patrick's vibrant tone broke the silence. "Everyone, this is Yasmine."

Yasmine gave a shy smile and lifted her hand to flutter long fingers ending with fingernails painted in black nail polish.

"Just started." Mackenna was the first to find her voice. She couldn't help staring at Yasmine who had enough black around her eyes to make up several people. "I'm Patrick's sister, Mackenna."

"I've seen pictures of you," Yasmine said.

"Really?" Mackenna looked at her brother and the protective arm he draped around Yasmine. He really was secretive. He hadn't mentioned a girlfriend.

"Welcome, Jasmine," Lyle said and offered his hand.

"It's Yasmine, Dad," Patrick said.

"Call me, Yassie." She flicked her large brown eyes around the group. "A lot of people have trouble with the Y and the J."

"Hello, Yassie. I'm Louise, Patrick's mother." Louise took Yassie by the arm. "Let me introduce the others."

"Aren't you the dark horse," Mackenna said to Patrick who had remained by her side.

"Yas and I've been together a long time. I haven't been ready to bring her home until now."

Mackenna was surprised and then had a sudden flood of sibling protection for her brother. She understood what he meant. She never brought anyone home either. She looked again at Yasmine being introduced to the rest of the party. Patrick must be really serious about her to risk bringing her home.

"I can't understand why," Mackenna joked as they both watched their mother gushing over his girlfriend. "You'd better go rescue her before Mum whips out your baby photos. I've got the next course to prepare."

"Yeah, I need to talk to you about the food." Patrick's eyes darted from Yasmine to Mackenna.

"What about it?"

"Yasmine can't eat meat."

"You're kidding?"

"Patrick." Louise beckoned him.

"The mother calls. You'll rustle something up for her, won't you? She doesn't eat much." He gave Mackenna a peck on the cheek then headed off to Yasmine's side, leaving Mackenna stewing.

Adam had drifted from the edge of the crowd and raised his eyebrow. Her heart skipped and she turned away quickly. She didn't have time to think about him. She had to come up with food without meat for a meal that featured lamb as the main ingredient.

In the kitchen she looked at the second tasting platter. There was enough on that for a non-meat eater but entrée was tricky. She had prepared to serve a trilogy of lamb – lamb sausage on buttered potatoes, lamb fillet wrapped in vine leaves, and lamb with feta and spinach in sausage roll bites. Nothing meat free there.

"How's it going?"

Adam's voice startled her.

"Fine," she said and turned on the oven. There was a lot to do before she could serve.

"Can I help?"

He wouldn't go away.

"I can manage," she said.

"I'm sure you can, but I could tell by the look on your face you weren't expecting a vegetarian."

"We're a sheep farm," Mackenna snapped and wiped the back of her hand across her forehead. "What was Patrick thinking?"

"I guess he can't help the eating choices of his girlfriend."

"I know, but he might have given me some warning. Tonight is all about celebrating our lamb. It's the main ingredient." Mackenna flicked a hand at the menu she had stuck to the board on the wall.

Adam studied it. "Have you put all these dishes together?"

"Most of it." Mackenna opened the fridge and began pulling out the food she'd prepped during the day.

He looked over her shoulder. "You've got haloumi."

"Yes." She sidestepped around him.

"It's not on your menu?"

"Not tonight."

"I could wrap some in vine leaves. It's delicious deep fried."

"I know that but tonight – "

"Is all about the lamb, I know, but we need something for a vegetarian." He poked in the fridge. "You've got plenty of pastry, I could do a couple of feta and spinach bites minus the lamb."

Mackenna's hands flew to her hips. Finally it registered that he was suggesting he could help.

"Everything going okay?"

Hugh was standing in the doorway. What was with all these men in her kitchen?

"Fine," she declared.

"Small problem," Adam said at the same time.

Hugh looked from one to the other. "Can I help?"

Laughter echoed up the passage behind him.

"Take that platter and make sure they eat it." Mackenna gave him a weak smile. It was hardly his fault things were going awry. "I need to get the next course cooking before they're all too drunk to enjoy it."

"Sure thing." Hugh picked up the plate. "Let me know if I can do anything else."

Mackenna was already at the cooktop igniting the gas. From the corner of her eye she saw Adam don the apron she'd hung on the back of the door. She was happy to let him cook for Yasmine. It was one less thing to worry about.

When the sausages were cooking she put the bites in the oven and checked her potatoes. She was aware of Adam moving around her asking the odd question about where to find things. They worked independently but didn't get in each other's way. That was good at least. She glanced up at her menu. It was ready to go.

"Damn!" she muttered.

"What's up?"

"I need to set an extra place for Yasmine."

"I can do it while you plate up."

"Thanks. There's a space at the end of the table and the cutlery's on the side cupboard in the dining room."

"No problem." He gave her a big smile.

Mackenna turned back to her food and her plates. Adam was leaving tomorrow and there was no way she was going to fall for him again.

"That was a fantastic meal, Mackenna." Chris raised his glass to her. "Congratulations."

All around the table voices echoed his words. Mackenna was exhausted. It had been a long time since she'd spent so long in the kitchen.

"You must be very pleased," Ginnie said. "So many ways to eat lamb and each of them divine."

"The spiced lamb on the cauliflower and pine nut salad was so light and tasty," Louise said. "You'll have to share that recipe with me."

"My favourite was the seared lamb rump." Lyle beamed at her along the table. "I know our lamb has good flavour but you really brought it out with that one."

There were more murmurs of agreement and then a brief moment of silence.

"The berry dessert was very refreshing." Yasmine's voice was low but everyone heard her and nodded in agreement.

At least she ate that, Mackenna thought. She looked down the table to Yasmine at the other end. After all Adam's work to make sure there was a vegetarian option for every course, Yasmine had hardly eaten any of it. Still, she'd taken lots of photos. If any of them turned out alright, Mackenna might be able to use them for publicity.

Hugh got to his feet and raised his glass.

"I'd like to propose a toast to Mackenna. Not only is she a talented farmer but also a fantastic chef and I want to wish her every success with the Gatehouse."

Mackenna glanced around the table as her guests echoed his sentiments and finally her eyes came back to Hugh, her good friend. Although they'd been apart for many years, their friendship was as strong as ever. She stood up and he leant in and kissed her on the cheek. Then Chris and Ginnie were doing the same.

"We must be off," Chris said. "Congratulations again."

"This will be a popular place," Ginnie said.

Mackenna saw them out and returned to the dining room to find Cam with an arm around Adam's shoulder.

"I'll be staying at the farm tonight, my Kiwi friend." Cam's words tumbled out. Mackenna noticed he'd tipped back a few extra glasses of red wine after the main course. "Sounds like it will be our last night together – unless you get a better offer."

Cam winked at Mackenna and she glanced away. Her parents were in conversation with Patrick and Yasmine. Only Adam and Hugh heard his innuendo, but she had no idea why Cam would say that now even if he was drunk. She'd given no-one any cause to think there was anything more than a holiday friendship between them. Had Adam said something? She risked a look in his direction but his face was a mask as he extricated himself from Cam's hold.

Hugh hugged Mackenna and gave her another kiss on the cheek. She was beginning to think he may have had too much wine as well, but his murmur in her ear was steady and reassuring.

"You've done a great job, Mack. I'm sure this will be a successful venture for you."

She glowed in his praise. "Thanks, Hugh."

He shook Adam's hand. "Hope our paths will cross again one day."

"Yes," Adam said. "Maybe."

"Night all," Hugh called and let himself out.

"We've a busy day ahead," Louise said. "We'd best be off."

"Are you staying a while, Yasmine?" Mackenna asked. "We've hardly had a chance to chat."

"She's staying all week," Louise crowed, her face a beacon of delight. "Then she and Patrick are driving us to the airport on Friday."

"Friday?" Mackenna gasped.

"Yes, they've got things on in Adelaide next weekend, so it works out perfectly," Louise said.

"But you weren't going until the following week?" Mackenna's brain whirled with the amount of things that needed to be done over the next few days.

"We hadn't had a chance to tell you." Louise grabbed Lyle's arm and gave it a squeeze. "The travel agent rang while we were in Adelaide. Our flights have been brought forward. It will put us in Christchurch at a better time to fit in with some tours we want to take."

"You can manage the sheep," Lyle said. "Cam will be here."

"I'll be here," Cam echoed.

"Patrick can come back next week to help," Louise added.

Mackenna swished at the loose curls tickling her face. "I've got a bus group booked in here for next Saturday night."

"This wasn't meant to take you away from farm work." Louise glared at Mackenna. "We've talked about this."

"It's only a small group." Mackenna backtracked quickly. There was no way she wanted her mother to put the kybosh on the Gatehouse before it had begun. "I'll be fine."

Her family left and Cam grabbed Adam in another shoulder grip. "Come on Kiwi, off to bed."

Cam wobbled and they both stumbled. Adam put a steadying arm over Cam's. "Bye, Mackenna," he called over his shoulder.

"Bye, Mackenna," Cam mimicked.

She listened to their footsteps and Cam's slurry voice as they disappeared into the night.

She shivered. Suddenly she was cold. The house was totally silent. She went back to the dining room. She paused and studied the remains of her beautifully set table now in disarray. Then it hit her. Adam was leaving in the morning and she hadn't even thanked him for his help tonight. She'd have to get up early to make sure she caught him before he left. The lightness and excitement she'd felt evaporated, replaced by exhaustion tinged with sadness. In her heart she knew she didn't want him to go but she couldn't tell him that. She sucked in a breath and stood tall. She wouldn't tell him that. Slowly the breath slipped past her lips and she began to clear up the mess.

CHAPTER
25

"Damn!" Mackenna muttered as she tried to find some clothes from the piles dotted around her floor. There'd been no chance to unpack properly. Each time she'd needed something she'd rummaged through bags and boxes and now her room looked like a clothes sorting room at St Vinnies.

She'd slept in. Adam had probably left already. She ran out to the carport and jumped into her car.

"Damn!" she said again as the only sound the car made was a click when she turned the ignition. "Flat battery," she muttered and dashed back to the house for her jumper. The sun was shining but the wind was chilly. She pushed her hat firmly on her head, pressed her arms to her sides and hurried up the track to the house. Adam's car was gone from beside the garage where he usually parked it.

Mackenna scanned the yard but his car was definitely nowhere to be seen. Inside the house, all was quiet. There were signs that some-one had eaten breakfast. Her parents would have gone to church.

She took a few steps up the passage thinking she might peep into Adam's room but she was greeted by the rumble of snoring. Cam. There was no way she was sticking her head in that room again. No other sound reached her. Patrick and Yassie must still be asleep.

She set the coffee machine going and made toast. It was cold this morning and the air felt damp even in the house.

"Is there tea?"

Mackenna turned at the sound of Yasmine's voice. The younger woman looked even paler than she had last night and she'd wrapped herself in the thick blue dressing-gown that hung behind Mackenna's old bedroom door.

"Yes, of course. Come in and take a seat. Would you like toast?" Mackenna waved the piece she'd been biting into.

"Yes, thanks." Yasmine slipped onto a chair. "Just one piece. No butter."

No wonder the girl was so thin and pale, thought Mackenna.

"Did you sleep well?" she asked.

"Yes, really well thanks. I think I'm in your old room. I hope you don't mind me wearing this. I'm guessing it's yours?"

"Not at all," Mackenna said. "I don't wear a dressing-gown much. Usually I'm up and dressed and outside early, but I slept in this morning."

Yasmine covered her mouth with a hand to stifle a yawn. "I'm usually late to bed, so this is my normal get-up time."

"Really? What do you do?" Mackenna's sleep patterns had been different in her chef days, depending on her shift but today's sleep-in was unusual for her now.

"I work in IT."

"Hello. You're up early." Patrick came in and wrapped Yasmine in a tight embrace, kissing her on the lips. "You should have come and got me."

Mackenna turned away to the kettle. It felt odd watching her brother being intimate with someone. It made her feel the loss of Adam more keenly, no matter that she kept telling herself there was no longer anything between them.

"I don't suppose you saw Adam before he left?" she said as she put toast and tea on the table.

"I've been out to it since my head hit the pillow," Patrick said.

"Me too." Yassie picked up the teacup and wrapped her fingers around it. "Thanks for this."

"I thought he was going this morning?" Patrick said.

"He was . . . did," Mackenna said. "I just hoped to catch him, that's all. I didn't thank him properly for his help last night."

"I'm sorry about that. Patrick should have warned you I was coming." Yasmine gave Patrick a playful tap and he immediately wrapped his arms around her again.

"Mack didn't mind. She's a whiz in the kitchen."

Mackenna smiled. No point in telling Patrick off. He just didn't get it.

"Your food was wonderful," Yasmine said. "And you have a talent for decorating. Patrick said the old house was very run down. You've transformed it."

"Thanks," Mackenna said. Yasmine's words were warm and genuine.

"Our Mack's good at everything," Patrick said as he stood up to make himself a coffee. "She can even run the farm single-handed. She's a marvel."

Mackenna heard the teasing in his voice.

"I gather Adam's a friend of yours from New Zealand?" Yasmine said, turning her back on Patrick.

"Yes, we met while I was on holiday recently."

"Why'd you let him get away?" Patrick asked as he drew his chair in close to Yasmine's.

Mackenna frowned at him. "I wasn't trying to catch him."

"He seemed like a good bloke and he'd come all this way to see you. You acted like it hardly mattered. Does he have bad breath or a hidden evil streak?"

"No."

"Ah-ha!" Patrick pointed a finger at Mackenna. "So you do know him quite well."

"I didn't say that."

"You really like him, don't you? I thought you were trying too hard to avoid him. Did you two hook up in New Zealand? What happened?"

"Patrick," Yasmine chided. "Leave your sister alone. It's her business not yours."

Mackenna's emotions were in turmoil. She was angry with Patrick but only because he was partly right. She spun away from them. "I've got work to do."

"Of course you do," Patrick said. "There's always work to do around here."

Mackenna stopped in the doorway and turned. There was no way she wanted to have a blazing row with Patrick in front of his girlfriend.

"That's farming," she said with a tight smile. "Always something to be done."

"Damn it Mackenna, you're such a martyr. Surely things can wait while you eat some breakfast and make conversation. Even Mum and Dad have taken the morning off."

"Because they know I'll check the sheep."

"They don't need checking every five seconds."

"No, but it's been warm and now we've had a bit of rain." Mackenna nodded towards the window. "Besides keeping feed and water up to them we need to check for flies – and I've got a flat car battery to charge."

"Perhaps we could help," Yasmine said in a gentle tone.

"No," Mackenna said. "You stay and eat some breakfast. We'll go for a drive later."

"I'll show Yasmine around. You're so busy." He waved his arms at her. "Off you go."

Mackenna opened her mouth but thought better of it and turned on her heel. Her anger was gone, replaced by embarrassment. She shouldn't have been in such a rush. There was plenty of time for her to eat with them. She wanted to get to know Yasmine better, but Patrick's digging for information about Adam had unsettled her. She hadn't meant for it to turn into a fight. Now it was best to keep out of their way.

The dogs were waiting for her at the gate. She gave them both a pat and the pup jumped around in excitement.

"Evidently I'm not much company guys but I guess you won't mind."

The chilly wind was still blowing strong as she crossed the yard to the sheds with the dogs close by. It added to her unease. If this wind kept up, the bit of moisture in the topsoil from the rain the other day would soon be gone and their early pasture sowing would be in jeopardy.

The distant sound of a vehicle travelling along the main road made her think of Adam again. She pulled back her shoulders, whistled the dogs onto the tray-top and backed out of the shed. She wasn't making up the work that needed doing. They really did have to keep a close eye on the stock in these conditions.

An hour later she was back at the shed. She'd found two flyblown sheep in a paddock they hadn't checked for a couple of days. The sheep were treatable but she needed to get on to it straight away.

"What's the rush?"

She looked up to see her dad approaching.

"A couple of sheep need cleaning up. They've got flies."

"I'll come with you."

"There's no need, Dad."

"I'll come with you," he repeated. "I want to look at those couple of paddocks we've sown as well."

"Okay," she said, and she loaded the things she'd need to treat the sheep in the back of the ute. "You stay here this time, boys," she said as the two dogs milled about her feet.

King sunk to his belly straight away but the pup continued to dance.

"Get out of it," Lyle commanded and the pup took a few steps back, a bewildered look on its face.

Lyle stepped out of the shed and looked up at the cloudless sky. "We can't afford to lose anymore sheep or that pasture," he said. "Perhaps this holiday of your mother's isn't such good timing."

Mackenna climbed back into the driver's seat. There was no need for her to say anything. Empty reassurances would be useless. The weather conditions were out of their control and if things did go pear-shaped, the cost of an overseas holiday would be an extra burden they didn't need.

CHAPTER
26

Louise hung up the phone and hummed to herself as she went back to folding the washing. She'd just had a long chat with Mary McDonald and although they both danced around the topic, Louise felt that Hugh's mother was of a similar opinion when it came to Mackenna and Hugh.

Mary had rung about the art show fundraiser and as soon as they covered that topic Louise started fishing for information on Hugh. Without saying too much, Mary eluded to the possibility of Hugh settling into the family business. Louise said how much they were enjoying his visits and Mary said they felt the same about Mackenna. Mary had babbled on about the two of them being such good friends in their earlier days and how it was so nice to see them getting on well again now. Louise had agreed, of course.

Patrick seemed smitten with Yasmine. Louise liked her apart from her being such a city girl. If Patrick married her, she would have to adapt to farm life. It was too early to expect a wedding but Louise was glad Patrick had found such a nice young woman. Now all they needed was for Mackenna and Hugh to officially pair up. That would be both her children on their way to settling down.

Louise paused midway through folding one of Cam's t-shirts. Thankfully he was turning out to be a good addition. When they'd advertised the job, Lyle had preferred an older bloke who'd done more stock work but he didn't have a truck licence. Cam had less experience but was a mechanic, and the licence tipped the scales in his favour. It didn't hurt that he was around the right age, well mannered and good-looking to boot. Funny she'd even considered him as a possibility for Mackenna when they were first employing him, but now that Hugh was on the scene Louise was glad there'd been no spark between her daughter and Cam.

She felt a small pang of guilt when it came to Adam. He'd given Louise his mobile number before he left and asked her to tell Mackenna to call him if she needed help with the bus group on the weekend. Louise had got rid of the number. She'd passed on Adam's farewell message without the part about his coming back to help. He was a nice bloke, but he only complicated things. Hugh and Mackenna needed space to work things out together without anyone distracting them.

Louise started to imagine babies but pulled herself up. "Bit early for that yet," she muttered, but she longed for the time when she could fill her days with grandchildren. And if everything worked out, they'd all be living close enough for her to see them all regularly.

She held up a dress wondering if she should add it to the pile of clothes she'd set aside to pack for New Zealand. It was a good wash-and-wear fabric that didn't require ironing. She put it to one side. If she took it she'd take a cardigan that matched, then she'd have all bases covered.

The sound of murmuring voices and a soft giggle let her know Patrick and Yasmine had returned from their trip to the coast. Louise stacked the folded clothes back in the basket and shifted it to the desk alongside the parcel that had arrived for Lyle. At least this one was in a plastic postbag and didn't feel very heavy, but after the mattress overlay she wasn't looking forward to finding out what was in it.

A pile of unopened mail sat beside the parcel. Most of the letters had windows and she hadn't wanted to spoil her day by opening them. Their cash flow was very tight at the moment with the land payments, extra feed and Lyle's medical bills on top of everything else. Mackenna was spending money on the old house like there was no tomorrow and they'd helped Patrick get his car. Louise knew the New Zealand holiday was adding pressure but they'd survived tight times before and she wasn't going to give up her holiday.

The sound of Patrick's teasing voice brought a squealed response from Yasmine.

Louise flicked on the kettle and got out some plates. She'd discovered Yasmine had a sweet tooth so she'd made a moist chocolate cake and added shards of chocolate to the top for afternoon tea. The young woman needed fattening up, she was so thin.

"Hello, you two," she said as she placed the cake on the table. "How was the beach?"

"It was beautiful along the coast," Yasmine said. "Such rugged coastline and then those beaches. The colours were fantastic. I'm hoping I got some good shots."

"Cake." Patrick groaned and patted his stomach. "We just ate ice-cream."

"That was an hour ago," Yasmine said. "You're mum's been baking, Patrick."

"Come and sit down," Louise said. "I love to cook for people who appreciate it." She gave her son a playful tap on the back.

Yasmine wriggled onto a chair.

"Your scarf looks good," Louise said. "I never have much luck with getting them to sit right." Yasmine wore so many layers but they suited her. At least today the vest and the scarf were a gentle shade of grey that softened the black of the rest of her clothes.

"I love scarves. There are so many ways to wear them," Yasmine said and took a bite of the cake.

"She has a million of them," Patrick said.

"That's an exaggeration." Yasmine chuckled. "I do have quite a few, though. This cake is delicious, Mrs Birch."

"Please call me Louise."

"Okay . . . Louise." Yasmine's face was pale but her brown eyes flashed with life. "And thank you for making this cake. It's to die for. Can I have the recipe?"

"It's an old favourite from a recipe book our church ladies put together years ago. I'll copy it for you."

"Yassie makes a mean zucchini and banana cake," Patrick said.

"That sounds interesting." Louise smiled, not sure she liked the idea of that combination.

"It's easy to make and always works out," Yasmine said. "We can swap recipes."

"Do I get an invite to this party?" Lyle was standing in the doorway. He smiled but Louise could tell he was tired. He'd been putting in longer days at work since they made the decision to go on holiday.

"I'll make you a cup of tea," she said, "but you'll have to stick with nut loaf."

"Surely a little sliver wouldn't hurt." Lyle pulled off his hat and a grubby line from its brim marked his forehead.

Louise felt sorry for him. He looked worn out and he had such a sweet tooth.

"Just a sliver," she said.

"What have you been doing, Mr Birch?" Yasmine asked.

"Not a very pleasant job, I'm afraid." Lyle slipped into his chair and pushed his hair back from his face. "We've been getting a few flyblown sheep."

"We will not have a discussion about that while we're eating," Louise said with a shudder. A vivid childhood memory of her father cutting away the rotten maggoty wool and flesh from an infected sheep leapt into her mind.

"I'll explain later," Patrick murmured.

Louise liked the way her son cared for Yasmine. He was a doting partner and there was obviously a deep bond between them. It was so nice to see.

"Has anyone seen Mackenna today?"

"She and Cam have been with me," Lyle said. "They've gone over to feed sheep and check the water across the road."

"I asked her to come and eat with us one night before we go," Louise said. She'd hardly seen Mackenna since the Gatehouse dinner. It felt strange not having her at the table for every meal.

"She'll be in later." Lyle sat back in his chair. "We've got some paperwork to go through and I really think we'll have to bring crutching forward, although how it can be managed with me away I don't know."

"Can't it wait? You look bushed." Louise was worried Lyle wouldn't be up to overseas travel with all the work he was doing.

"You know it can't," he said.

"Why don't you go and have a shower and a lie down till she gets here? I'll give you a call."

"I think I might," he said. He passed the pile of mail and stopped. "This is for you." He held out the postbag. "Open it."

Louise slit the bag open. The contents slid onto the table – something black with splashes of bright colour encased in a clear plastic bag.

"What is it?" Patrick asked.

"Take it out, Lou," Lyle said. "It's a travel bag. It's got one of those across the shoulder straps and compartments for everything."

"What a great idea," Yasmine said.

Louise pulled the garish bag from its plastic cover and unfolded it.

"See how many pockets it has." Lyle took it from her then slid the strap over her head so the bag rested against her hip.

Louise looked down at the monstrosity. Why would he pick such a thing?

"Did it come in other colours?" Patrick asked.

"Patrick," Yasmine chided. "They're fabulous colours. That's a great travel bag. It's got splashes of so many colours it will go with whatever you're wearing."

"Don't you like it?" Lyle's face was full of concern.

She leaned in and kissed him. "It's a very thoughtful gift," she said. "Thank you. Now I really want you to have a rest. You look done in."

"On my way."

Louise watched him go. That he went without a fight worried her even more.

"Dad's doing okay, isn't he?"

She saw the concern on Patrick's face.

"Yes," she said with a brightness she didn't feel. "He's just got to remember to pace himself. The doctors are happy with him."

"What's crutching?" Yasmine asked. "Is it something we can help with?"

"That's very kind of you, Yasmine, but we get contractors to do the work. It just means a busy time with getting sheep in, helping around the shed, feeding everyone."

"I can help with feeding," Yasmine said brightly.

Louise smiled at this young woman who barely ate enough herself to keep a flea alive.

"Mackenna's back," Patrick said, looking out the kitchen window.

"I hope she doesn't need Lyle for a while," Louise said.

The screen door squeaked but Mackenna's tread was soundless and she suddenly popped her head around the door. "Good, you're here," she said to the room in general. "Where's Dad?"

"He's having a bit of a rest. I don't want – "

"It's okay, Mum." Mackenna cut her off. "I wanted to talk to you on my own. I'll just wash up."

"Have a seat." Louise pulled out a chair as soon as Mackenna returned. She'd washed her hands but her clothes were dirty and she looked as weary as her father. "Patrick, can you make a coffee for your sister?"

Patrick moved in the direction of the coffee machine.

"Hi, Yasmine," Mackenna said. "Sorry we haven't caught up."

"You look as if you've had a busy day," Yasmine smiled and reached for a plate. "Let me cut you some of your mother's delicious cake."

"Thanks," Mackenna replied but Louise could tell she was distracted.

"What's this?" Mackenna picked up the bag Lyle had ordered.

"A travel bag," Louise said.

"Your dad bought it for your mum. Isn't it great?" Yasmine ran her hand down the side of the bag.

Louise met Mackenna's look and saw the hint of a smile on her lips. She gave a gentle shake of her head. She could tell her daughter thought it as ghastly as she did but there was no need to hurt anyone's feelings.

"What did you want to talk about?" she asked, steering the conversation away from the bag.

"We're getting a lot of flyblown sheep. Dad and I both agree we need to bring crutching forward but he's worried he won't be here to help and . . ."

Louise saw Mackenna's eyes flick to Yasmine and back.

"I think Yasmine knows a fair bit about us already," Louise said. "Spit it out."

Mackenna continued to hesitate.

"Would you like me to leave?" Yasmine asked.

Louise held up her hand. "Stay where you are," she said and nodded at Mackenna. "Go on."

"He's worried about the cash flow," Mackenna said, "and so am I."

Louise felt anger begin to bubble inside her. The first overseas holiday they'd ever tried to take was constantly in jeopardy and she wouldn't allow it.

"We'll manage."

"You're the one who knows," Mackenna replied quietly.

"We'll be fine," Louise said. "Besides, most of our holiday is booked and paid for. We just won't be dining out on caviar or bringing back expensive presents." She tried to make light of it but she suddenly worried about the mail that still lay unopened on the desk.

"Don't say anything to Dad," Mackenna said. "I'll organise the crutching."

"When will you do it?" They all turned in response to Yasmine's cheerful voice.

"Next week," Mackenna said. "If I can get the crutching team here."

"We could come back and help, couldn't we Patrick?"

"I've already said so." Patrick put a coffee in front of Mackenna and moved away to stand behind Yasmine's chair.

"I'd appreciate that," Mackenna said.

Louise was relieved to see her smile at her brother and that he nodded in reply.

"There are a few containers of sausage rolls in the freezer for morning and afternoon teas," she said.

"I can cook." Yasmine jumped up from her chair, nearly knocking Patrick over. "Well, sweet things anyway," she said with a quirky giggle.

CHAPTER
27

Hugh made a mental list as he drove away from the office. He only had to throw a few things in a bag for his weekend trip to Adelaide. He had to meet the agent and there was still paperwork to finish if he was to leave for Canada on time.

He glanced in the direction of Rory's shop and his attention was drawn by the sight of Mackenna, struggling with two sheep on the back of her ute. He pulled his four-wheel drive in beside her.

"I wouldn't have thought these two would give you any trouble," he chuckled.

Mackenna let the rope she'd been holding drop and laughed with him.

"You wouldn't think so would you, but a bronze cut-out is heavier than it looks."

"Is this what Rory was making for the Gatehouse?"

"Yes, they're going out the front of the old house amongst the tea-trees with the tasting room sign."

"Very clever." Hugh nodded at the rope. "Can I help?"

"Thanks," Mackenna said. "Rory helped me lift them on but he had to get to the bank before it closed. I didn't realise tying them down would give me such trouble."

They worked together and soon had the two sheep firmly secured in the back of the tray-top.

"Are you heading home?" Mackenna asked.

Hugh nodded.

"I owe you a drink," she said. "Fancy one now?"

He hesitated.

"It's only a drink," she said quickly. "My place isn't far out of your way."

Hugh should go home but he wasn't leaving till morning. Besides, he wanted to let Mackenna know what was happening. "Sure," he said.

They stepped apart and ahead of them a truck slowed and crossed the intersection. Hugh noticed the frown on Mackenna's face as she continued to stare after it.

"Isn't that your truck?" he asked. He'd noticed a few bags on the back of the otherwise empty tray as the truck disappeared from sight.

"Yes. I didn't think we needed it for any jobs at the moment," she said. "Cam drives it more than he does his ute some weeks."

"Where does he stay when he's in town?"

"I don't know," Mackenna said. "Well at least I don't know exactly. At a mate's place. Anyway," she grinned at Hugh, "see you at the Gatehouse."

Hugh followed Mackenna out of town and as they reached the dirt road he recalled the day the Birches' truck had passed him a long way from home. Perhaps he should mention it, but it seemed liked telling tales. He hadn't seen who was driving it but he remembered thinking it was Cam. Hugh wasn't as taken with him as the Birches seemed to be, but if they were happy with their working man then it wasn't his place to rock the boat, especially while Lyle wasn't operating at full strength.

Just before the Birches' driveway Mackenna turned right instead of left. She stopped at a paddock gate and he pulled in beside her. She jumped out of the ute and leaned in the passenger window as he lowered it. A frown creased her brow.

"What's up?" he said.

"Looks like the internal gate's been left open," she said. "Instead of two mobs of sheep I've got one. Sorry, but I need to separate them."

"I'll give you a hand." Hugh opened the gate and closed it again behind Mackenna's ute then joined her in the cab.

"Bloody Patrick," she muttered. "He came over here this morning to check the water. He mustn't have closed the gate properly."

Hugh felt a bit sorry for Patrick. As the youngest he could empathise with being an easy target when things went wrong.

"Are you sure it was Patrick?" he asked.

"Well it wasn't me and Dad wouldn't be so careless. Who else?"

"Cam."

Mackenna glanced at him as they pulled up at the internal gate.

"It could be, except he was doing other jobs on the main property today. Why are you defending Patrick all of a sudden? It had to be him."

"No reason." Hugh gave her a grin. He didn't want to argue. "Tell me what you want me to do."

"Can you push them up to the gate and I'll draft them through?"

"Sure thing," he said. "I'll be the dog."

She raised an eyebrow at him before she jumped out, and he slid across into the driver's seat.

They worked together well. Hugh found himself imagining himself and Mackenna doing this permanently, working as a team, sharing their lives. What would life be like if he stayed here? He could easily talk his father out of the property he had his eye on for something more suitable. His parents would be happy but doubt gnawed at him. He'd misread the difference between friends and lovers once in his life. He didn't want to make that mistake again.

Finally the last sheep was through and Mackenna shut the gate. As he pulled up beside her she burst out laughing.

"What's so funny?" he asked as she jumped into the passenger seat.

"Those sheep." She jerked her finger over her shoulder.

He looked back to the two bronze sculptures.

"It looked bizarre. This ute rounding up sheep, whizzing around with two statues on the back."

He chuckled. Life with Mackenna was never dull. He got back into his own car at the road and she already had the tops off two beers by the time he walked into her kitchen. She handed him one and they sat either side of the old laminex table.

"This will be my last chance to sit down for a while," Mackenna said as they touched glasses. "With Mum and Dad away it will be full-on. Add to the mix the busload of tourists I'm feeding on Saturday night with another possible group the following Saturday. I don't know when I'll be able to start the weekend tasting room idea. The dinners are taking over at the moment."

"I might be able to help once I get back."

"Patrick is coming back at some stage and Cam will be around." Mackenna took another swig from her beer. "Where are you off to?" she asked.

"Only to Adelaide," Hugh said. "I'll be back Monday afternoon."

"Everyone's deserting me."

Hugh thought about the amount of work she was taking on. It was a big responsibility. He admired her courage.

"I'm sure you'll manage," he said. He looked into her eyes and then down at his beer. "I'm wavering over my Canadian trip."

"Why?"

Hugh fiddled with the label on the bottle. Why was the million dollar question. "I never imagined I'd settle back here," he said, "but it hasn't been as bad as I thought."

"Oh, Hugh." Mackenna leant forward and placed a hand over his. "It would be fantastic if you stayed . . ."

His heart gave an extra thud and he relished the comforting touch of her hand.

She studied him closely. "What's changed?"

"Changed?"

"You were so excited about this opportunity in Canada. What happened to that?"

Hugh sighed. Canada had been the beacon that had got him through the first few weeks here. It was something he still wanted to do but was it also just running away again? Could Mackenna be more than a friend?

"I still want to go," he said. "It's the kind of research that has the potential to improve the way we do things here."

"Then what's stopping you? Has your father put the hard word on you again about joining the family business?"

"No," Hugh said. He took a deep breath and looked into her eyes. He saw her puzzled expression change to realisation and she gripped his hand tighter.

"Don't you change your plans for me, Hugh," she said. "We're friends, good mates and that's never going to go away. Mates don't stop each other from following their dreams. They support them. I don't know how I would have got through the last few weeks here without you." She reached across with her other hand and gave both his hands a firm shake. "I'm following my dream, you must follow yours. Otherwise, what's the point of anything?"

Hugh sat back. He withdrew his hand and lifted the beer in the air. "Here's to dreams," he said.

"To dreams," she echoed and they tapped bottles.

Hugh stood up. "I'll help you unload those sheep before I go."

Mackenna frowned at him then she laughed. "Oh yes. I wondered what you were talking about for a moment. That would be great. I'll need help to get them into position."

Mackenna threw her arm around Hugh's shoulders and gave him a squeeze. "Thanks for your help," she said. They were both puffing from their exertions but at last the sheep were exactly where she wanted them.

"They look good," he said. "You have an eye for putting things in the right spot."

"Thanks." Mackenna dropped her arm.

"I'll be off." He kissed her on the cheek.

She remained where she was and lifted a hand to wave as he drove away. She had the sense there would have been more to that kiss if she'd responded.

"Well, well, love is in the air."

Mackenna spun at the sound of her brother's voice. She was already confused about her feelings without Patrick muddying the waters.

"What are you sneaking around here for?" Her voice had a hard edge and she watched the smile slip from his face.

"Mum wants you to come for dinner tonight," he said. "We're leaving early in the morning."

"She could have phoned."

"She tried but you didn't answer."

Mackenna patted her pocket. There was no phone. She must have left it in the car.

"I didn't realise you were going early."

"I have to touch base at work." Patrick put his hands on his hips. "It hasn't been easy staying here so long, you know. I've had to juggle my job."

"What about the crutching next week?" She hadn't thought much about Patrick's real job but if he wasn't able to be here she'd have to get help from somewhere else.

"I'll be back. That's if you think I can be useful," he growled.

"For goodness sake, Patrick, I've already wasted time this afternoon fixing up one of your mistakes." Mackenna hadn't intended to say anything but the words were out before she could stop them.

"Oh really?" he spat. "What have I supposedly done this time?"

"You didn't shut the gate properly over at the new paddocks."

"I didn't – "

She cut him off. "I had to sort sheep on my way home."

"Well poor you."

"Take some responsibility, Patrick. I haven't got time to do everything."

He took a step towards her. "I'm sick of your patronising, Mackenna. I'm not an idiot."

"I never said you were," she snapped.

"Really?" he sneered. "I heard you and Hugh that day checking the rams and laughing about me not knowing one sheep from another. 'Totally useless', Hugh said."

Mackenna had a vague recollection of Hugh's first visit and Patrick appearing all hot and flustered from the shed.

"You're such a Miss High and Mighty I never got a look in. You and Dad would pat me on the head and send me off to do other things. The only time I'm useful is to be the lackey, shifting sheep, checking water, then you want me to help. Well this is my place too, you know. I've as much right to work this property as you have.

Mum wants me to stay and get more involved. She said I should have a share of it all and maybe I will."

Mackenna opened her mouth but nothing came out.

"Nothing to say now? You usually have an answer for everything." He shook his head at her. "Will I tell Mum you're on your way, or will you be too busy to join us?"

"Of course I'll be there. I just have to wash up." Mackenna turned away quickly and walked back inside on wobbly legs. Her stomach felt weak as if she'd been punched. She splashed water on her face. Patrick had obviously been nursing hurt feelings. And what had he meant by 'staying on and having a share'? She hadn't thought his visit anything more than that – a visit to help out.

Her dad had never mentioned including Patrick in the running of the property. In fact, there'd never been any discussion about who did what. She'd worked alongside her dad for a long time. They had plans for the future but what if his heart attack had killed him? Mackenna slid onto the old kitchen chair. What happened to Woolly Swamp if something happened to her dad? She'd never thought about it, but older people made wills. She assumed her parents had. It was something she should talk over with her dad, just the two of them.

She went back to the bathroom to finish tidying herself up. Dinner would be ready and her mother would be getting impatient. Talking to her dad alone wouldn't be easy. Everyone would be at dinner then they had an early start in the morning. She didn't like her chances. Besides, it probably wasn't the time to bring up wills just as he was about to set off on his first overseas holiday.

CHAPTER
28

Mackenna zipped up and down the supermarket aisles, marking off her list as quickly as she could. Cam was tackling a problem with one of the irrigators. A part was needed and she'd come to town for it so she could grocery shop at the same time.

Patrick and Yasmine had left very early this morning taking Louise and Lyle with them. She'd heard the vehicle from her bed and felt miserable on two counts. Her argument with Patrick had come out of the blue. There'd been no chance to patch it up and no opportunity to speak with her father alone last night. She gripped the shopping trolley tightly. She had to push away thoughts of Patrick and wills and concentrate on the here and now. There were sheep succumbing to flies and now an irrigator not working. She had the tourists arriving at the Gatehouse tomorrow night and this was her only window of opportunity to shop.

She'd just loaded everything into her car when her phone rang. She glanced at the screen but no name showed.

"Hello."

"Mackenna? It's Simon from Sparks Restaurant."

Mackenna rolled the name around in her head. It sounded familiar.

"I spoke to you a while back about your tasting room," he said. "How's that going?"

Realisation struck. This was the guy from the Melbourne restaurant who'd tried to make contact when he'd been passing through the area a month or so ago.

"I've just got it up and running," she said.

"That's great. A group of us are on our way to Adelaide tomorrow. I was thinking we might stay over somewhere and come out and try this lamb of yours."

Mackenna's heart gave a skip of excitement, then reality hit. "Tomorrow night? How many are in your group?"

"Five of us," he said. "Is that a problem?"

"No." Mackenna was doing the maths in her head. There were twelve coming in the mini bus. She'd planned to put them at small tables in the tasting room but she might need to rethink that and set everything up in the dining room. "I've got another party booked in but I can accommodate your group as well."

She suggested places to stay at the nearest town and gave him directions to Woolly Swamp from there before he disconnected. Mackenna leant against her car. There was so much to do without the tasting room, and only her and Cam to do it. Tomorrow she'd need to spend a lot of time prepping in the kitchen and Cam would have to do the farm work.

She thought briefly about having Adam at her side again, or Hugh, or even Patrick, but there was no-one. It had been her idea and now she was left to carry it out. She slipped the scrunched paper from her pocket and rechecked her list. She'd have to get more of some items if she was to have extras in the tasting room.

She grabbed the empty shopping bags from the back seat and hurried into the supermarket.

Back at the Gatehouse she threw everything onto the kitchen bench, shoved a bag of perishables into the fridge then hightailed it back to where Cam was waiting for the part. She was much later than she'd meant to be. As she got closer she could see no sign of a vehicle or Cam. She drove closer, the ground was wet and water glistened from all the nozzles. He must have got it working. She sighed. Keeping water up to sheep and pastures was a full-time job.

Mackenna drove on to the next paddock. The rams lifted their heads to give her a quick look, dismissed her and went back to munching the pasture. She cruised quietly around them. After the worm scare they'd made a good recovery and, with care, had picked up condition. Their water trough was full.

She headed for the house yard. Maybe Cam was at the sheds. She drove up just as the truck pulled away from the diesel tank. What was he doing now? There were no jobs requiring the truck in the next few days that she knew of.

She got out of her car as the truck rumbled forward. Cam pulled up beside her and lowered the window.

"You've been a while," he said before she had a chance to speak. "I've fiddled it up for now but I'll still need to replace the O ring next week."

"Next week?" She stepped closer to the truck so she could hear him better over the rumble of the idling engine.

"It should work like it is," Cam said, "but just to be sure I'll replace it anyway."

"It's getting a bit late today but surely you could do it tomorrow?"

"Won't be here." Cam tapped the steering wheel.

"Why not?" Cam usually had the weekends off unless there were urgent jobs to be done, but with everyone away he must have realised he was needed.

"Your dad said I could borrow the truck to help out a mate this weekend." Cam took his sunglasses from their perch on his cap and slid them onto his face. "It's all organised. I can't let him down."

She could no longer see his eyes and his mouth was straight. Mackenna had the sense he was smirking at her.

"Woolly Swamp is where your job is," she said.

"With weekends off, boss."

She glared up at him. He liked to call her "boss" but each time he did it was more like he was letting her know she wasn't in charge.

"Look, Mackenna," he leant out the window, his voice soothing. "I've checked the last few mobs in the back paddocks and that pivot will hold now for ages. You'll be right till I get back." He tapped the door with the flat of his hand and moved the truck forward. She stepped back from the fine dust that rose around it and watched as he drove away.

"Damn it," she muttered. She was alone, with a farm to run as well as the tasting room. With no time to feel sorry for herself she jumped back into her car. There was only a soft click in response to her turn of the key. She hit the steering wheel in annoyance. She'd recharged the battery but it had obviously been on its way out. The farm ute was close by in the shed. She left her car where it was and climbed into the other vehicle. The fuel gauge barely moved when she started it up.

She sighed in frustration. Who puts a vehicle away with no fuel? Certainly not her father. It was more likely to have been Patrick, he'd been using it to take Yasmine around the place rather than his new car. She drove over to the diesel tank and filled up. The marker on the tank was low as well. She tapped it with her finger but it didn't budge. She frowned at the gauge. It had been filled not that long ago. In fact, twice since she'd come home from holiday.

The air temperature was dropping and Mackenna suddenly felt cold. She rubbed at her arms and whistled up the dogs. She shut them up and hurried back to the Gatehouse. There was plenty for her to do if she was going to be ready to serve dinner tomorrow night.

Mackenna took her coffee cup from the machine and slid onto one of the chairs in her kitchen. Just the smell of the coffee was enough to lift her spirits. She'd been up since five o'clock, checking irrigators and sheep, making phone calls, prepping food for tonight. Now it was mid-afternoon. She'd run out of puff and fancied a real coffee. Instead of making it in her mother's kitchen, she shifted the machine to the Gatehouse. She was usually the only one who made coffee with it anyway.

She glanced at her menu for tonight's meal. With only a few changes she was sticking to the menu she'd prepared for her family. The bus company was a small one doing short tours between Melbourne and Adelaide. The guy running it had been prepared to test her out on this trip but said he wasn't sure his customers were the type to pay the prices she was asking. She'd had to make some cuts but Simon and his group from Melbourne were a different proposition altogether. She wanted them to fully explore the potential of Woolly Swamp lamb for their restaurant.

She rested her head in her hands a moment. She'd decided to set the two groups up in separate rooms but hadn't finished rearranging the furniture yet. There was still food to be prepped and there was one last paddock of sheep she wanted to check.

A footfall made her whizz around, spilling her coffee as she went. Cam was standing behind her and she hadn't heard him come in.

"How did you get here?"

"A mate dropped me off. My ute's still here." He jerked his finger over his shoulder.

"I didn't hear a vehicle. Where's the truck?"

"Still in town with his gear on it. I left them to unload. Thought you could use some help." His mouth opened in a wide grin revealing his crooked tooth.

A shiver ran through Mackenna. She pushed back her chair and went to the sink for a cloth to mop up the spilt coffee.

"The sheep in the swamp paddock need checking," she said. "No-one's been there for a couple of days."

"I meant here with your bus group." Cam opened the fridge and peered in. "I'm not a chef." He closed the fridge and turned back to her. "But I can take orders."

His eyes swept over her. She wanted to turn away from him but she forced herself to meet his look. If it were orders he was wanting he'd get them.

"That's good," she said. "I've got everything under control here but I do need you to check the sheep."

"One more day wouldn't hurt." He took a step towards her. "I'm handy at more than farm work, you know."

Mackenna resisted the urge to step back. She'd never felt lonely on the farm but she suddenly felt very alone. It was still several hours till her guests arrived and she didn't like the way Cam was acting. She wanted him gone from her kitchen.

The sound of a motorbike grew louder and she realised it was coming their way. They both listened as it roared closer then stopped near the house.

A frown flitted across Cam's face. "You've got a visitor."

Neither of them moved as the crunch of footsteps approached the back door.

"Mackenna?" The sound of the familiar voice was a welcome surprise.

She stepped around Cam and opened the door.

"Adam," she smiled. "What are you doing here?"

"I told your mum to let you know I'd be back to help tonight. I'd have been here earlier but I got delayed by an accident not far out of Melbourne."

Mackenna was so pleased to see him she barely listened to his explanation. Whatever reason had brought him back, she was glad of it.

"How are things going?" he asked as he stepped into the kitchen. He paused at the sight of Cam. "Looks like you've got help already."

"Adam," Cam said with a nod of his head.

"Cam just called in to see what else needed doing on the property," Mackenna said quickly. She tossed her head back and looked Cam firmly in the eye. "If you could check those sheep for me that would be great. Then you don't need to be back until Monday. You can finish helping your friend shift house."

Mackenna spoke with a brightness she didn't feel. Cam had been acting almost predatory. What might have happened if Adam hadn't turned up?

"You're the boss," Cam said, but once again Mackenna felt his tone mocked her. "I'll leave you to it."

He passed her to get to the door, brushing her shoulder with his as he went. She followed and watched him leave.

"Everything okay?" Adam asked.

"Yes." She tugged at her ponytail and turned to her menu. "Except that I'm way behind with the prep. I don't know why you're here but I hope you've come to work."

"Yes, chef," he said.

Adam's quip reminded her of Cam and the way he called her boss, but there was a difference. Adam was laughing with her.

She focused on the menu. There was no time to waste on thinking about Cam. She had a big night ahead and plenty of jobs for Adam. She started listing them.

It was midnight when she waved off Simon and his mates. The bus group had enjoyed their meal, had a few drinks and were gone by nine thirty, but Simon's group had settled in, enjoying her food and wine. Just before they left he had cornered her and, exhausted as she was, Mackenna managed to strike a deal with him to get their lamb to his Melbourne restaurant. The excitement of that put a spring in her step as she made her way through the house, turning off lights on her way to the kitchen.

Adam was wiping the last of the pans. Everything was cleaned up and the work surface gleamed. While she'd been chatting, he had been cleaning.

"Thank you," she said. "I really appreciate your help."

"No problem. I've got time to kill. I've run out of interest in the touristy stuff for now and Mum's at the hospital a lot."

"I'm sorry," Mackenna said. "I haven't asked you how your grandfather is."

"Deteriorating, but he's getting good care. There's nothing I can do for him."

"You're not close?"

"I've never really known him. We sometimes came to Melbourne for Christmas when I was a kid. I remember him as a grumpy old man. He worked away from home a lot and didn't visit us. I really only made this trip to support Mum. I've been driving her to the hospital and making an evening meal for her."

"You shouldn't have worried about me," Mackenna said. "You should be with your mum."

"My uncle's come from Sydney now and the flat's only small. I thought I'd keep away for a while. She'll call me if anything happens, but the doctors say it could be weeks. He's a tough old coot."

"Well, I wasn't expecting you but I have to say you were a sight for sore eyes when you turned up."

"Didn't your mum tell you I was coming back?"

"No."

"I left my phone number with her in case . . ." His voice trailed off.

Mackenna was immediately back in the motel room in Queenstown. He said he'd left his number then too.

"Mum's been in a tizz getting ready for their trip. She probably forgot."

"I'll be off then." Adam backed towards the door.

"Where are you going at this hour?"

"Up to the house." He turned his deep brown eyes to her. "I'm pretty bushed. I'm assuming I can use my old bed again for a while?"

"Oh, of course." Mackenna stumbled over her words. She hadn't given a thought to where he might sleep. "The back door's not locked. I don't know if the bed's made up."

"That's okay. I know my way around. I'll fix it."

Mackenna followed him outside.

"Where'd you get the bike?"

"I found a company that hires them. Mum's got a hire car in Melbourne. This suits me better."

He strapped on his helmet and kicked the bike into life. Mackenna closed the door and leaned her back against it as he roared away up the track. The sound once again transported her back to Queenstown, to another time when Adam had ridden out of her life.

It was good of him to come back to help. She couldn't have managed tonight without him, she knew that. Once again they had worked well as a team in the kitchen. Adam was a good chef with an eye for detail. She hadn't needed to check anything. They'd had a few jokes and the kitchen had been a busy but happy scene.

She dragged herself to the bathroom and stripped off her clothes. Her mixed emotions were having a field day in her exhausted state. It was time for a shower and sleep. In the morning she'd think about Adam.

CHAPTER

29

Mackenna inhaled the sweet smell of the wet grass at her feet. She'd come to inspect the irrigator that had given them trouble yesterday and it was apparent that it had done its job, watering the pasture overnight. She cast her eyes over the long, gangly arm of the pivot then slowly turned in a circle. The green of the irrigated pasture was a vivid contrast to the brown of the surrounding landscape. They needed a good rain but in the meantime she hoped Cam was right and the irrigator would continue to work until he could replace the O ring.

She thought back over his visit yesterday afternoon. Had it been as creepy as she'd perceived or was it that he'd just caught her off guard? She brushed hair from her face and turned the ute around. With the crutching team arriving on Tuesday she had plenty to do. She'd allowed herself a sleep-in this morning after the big day and night she'd had. She assumed Adam was doing the same. His bike was by the house gate when she'd gone past to let the dogs out but there was no sign of him. She hadn't stopped.

Now she made her way back there. She couldn't very well leave him on his own with no-one else at the house. Besides, it would be downright rude after all the help he'd given her last night. She just wasn't sure what to say to him.

Mackenna stopped the ute next to his bike. That's what she'd been doing the whole time he'd stayed before, hiding from him, from her feelings for him. Her phone vibrated in her pocket. Simon's name came up on the screen. She leaned against the ute and answered the call.

He and his friends were about to leave for Adelaide but he'd been in touch with some other friends who were travelling through today and they were keen to try the Gatehouse tonight. There'd be six of them. Mackenna had agreed to open before she'd had time to think about what was left in her fridge. Once again she was compiling lists in her head as she entered her family home. The smell of cooking greeted her before she reached the kitchen.

"Scrambled eggs?" Adam asked as he ran a spatula around the pan.

"Smells divine," Mackenna said, eying off the mixture. "Could you find everything you need?"

"I hope you don't mind but I have, yes. It seems a bit rude to be poking about in someone else's kitchen when they're not here, but I was feeling hungry this morning."

Mackenna clasped her hand to her mouth. "I'm so sorry," she mumbled between her fingers. Neither of them had time to eat last night except for a few tastings as dishes were served. "How terrible of me, making you work and not feeding you."

"You didn't make me and as you can see, I'm perfectly capable of feeding myself."

Mackenna took the toast as it popped and buttered it while Adam lifted the eggs from the cook top.

"I've just had a call," she said. "Six more guests for the Gatehouse tonight."

"That's fantastic. It's a brilliant concept, and your food selections are a perfect showcase for your lamb."

Adam smiled at her. Her stomach did a flip and she turned her attention to the food in front of her.

"Mmm," she murmured after the first mouthful. "Delicious."

"Glad you like it. I've owed you for a long time."

"Owed me?"

Once again Mackenna gazed into those deep brown eyes. She felt as if she could leap into his arms and kiss him, forget all about the eggs and drag him off to bed.

"I was going to make you a special breakfast the day you . . . the day I cooked for my mate . . . the day you left," he finished.

"I didn't leave," she said.

She realised how silly that sounded.

"What I meant was . . ."

"It was a misunderstanding by both of us. I came to Australia looking for you because I needed to know why you left."

"I thought you came for your grandfather."

"I would have come anyway. I needed to know what happened."

Mackenna studied his face, searching for the man she'd fallen in love with in Queenstown. She didn't have to search long, he was there – she just wouldn't let him back into her heart. Her bruised and battered, mixed-up and confused heart.

"Now I get it," he said. "Staying here with your family, watching you work, you were born to life on the land. It suits you. I understand Queenstown . . . us . . . it was just a holiday."

"Adam – "

"No." He cut her off. "It's okay, Mackenna. You don't have to explain. I got the picture last time I was here. I'm only back now because I had time to spare and I thought you could use the help."

"Got what picture?" He was talking in riddles now.

"You and Hugh. You're so close. A lovely couple with your fond kisses and caresses. He's a nice bloke and you've known him a long time – "

"Hugh?" This time Mackenna chopped Adam off. How could he think there was something between her and Hugh when she didn't understand it herself? What kisses and caresses?

Adam's mobile rang.

They both stared at it in amazement. "I bought a new one," Adam said. "The guy told me it had good coverage." He glanced down at the screen. The phone stopped ringing and he shook his head.

"It's Mum, but it's dropped out. Can I use your landline?"

"Sure."

He dialled the number then took the cordless handpiece and left the room as he started speaking.

Mackenna poked the last of the scrambled eggs with her fork. She'd lost her appetite. What had Adam thought he'd seen? The only time she and Hugh had been close was the day he'd kissed her. While it had been Adam who had interrupted them, he couldn't have seen them.

Adam was back at the door. "I have to go."

"Has something happened?"

"My grandfather died this morning."

Mackenna rose to her feet. "I'm so sorry."

"His time had come. Mum's taking it pretty hard. I need to get back to her."

"Of course."

"Are you going to be okay on your own?"

"Of course," she said again. "Don't worry about me. I appreciated your help last night but I've only got six at the table tonight."

"I might come back," he said. "After . . ."

"You don't have to Adam, really. Patrick will be back next week, and Cam. I'll have plenty of help. You be with your family."

He hesitated in the doorway then rushed forward, pulled her towards him and kissed her firmly on the lips. Before she could respond, he was gone. Mackenna stood fixed to the spot, wondering if she'd just conjured up that kiss. Then the motorbike started, revved a few times and roared off. At the main road it paused, revved, then roared away. It was taking Adam away from her once again. Why had she said he didn't have to come back when that was what she wanted? She waited until she couldn't hear the bike any longer then she sank onto a chair.

"You fool, Mackenna," she said to the empty room. Once again his loss overwhelmed her. She put her head in her hands and let the tears fall. Her body shuddered with the strength of her sobs until finally they stopped. She pushed Adam to the back of her mind. There was no time for self-pity and plenty of work to keep her busy. She lurched to her feet, cleaned up her mother's kitchen and drove back to the Gatehouse to collect last night's scraps for the chooks.

When she got there her phone rang and she eagerly scooped it from her pocket. Her heart sank when she saw Rory's name on the screen. She let it ring and then realised it couldn't have been Adam anyway. She'd never given him her number, but hadn't he said he'd left his with Louise?

She flew out to the ute and drove the short distance back to her family home like a madwoman. She didn't even bother to shut the door when she jumped out and ran into the house. She wasn't sure what she'd do with his number when she found it. She just wanted to have it. Her mother always pinned important things on the board above the computer but there was nothing there. Nothing on the fridge, except her postcards. Mackenna sifted through every piece of paper clipped in piles in trays ready for filing. She rummaged through the desk drawers and finally thumped the desktop in frustration. Maybe she'd misunderstood. Maybe he said he'd meant to leave Louise his number.

Finally she gave up. Her phone beeped a reminder that she had a message. She tapped the screen and put the phone to her ear. Rory wanted to know how the tasting room was going and whether he and his wife and his parents could come out for a meal tonight. Why not, she thought, just as easy to cook for ten as six. She rang him back then went to the Gatehouse.

She meant to check her supplies but instead she wandered the kitchen replaying last night in her head. All she could see was Adam. Adam at the bench wrapping lamb in vine leaves and joking about people eating leaves. Adam rinsing dishes and flicking her with water as she passed with an instruction. Adam searing the lamb on her gleaming cook top, his face creased in concentration. And there on her menu was the big star he'd drawn next to her spiced lamb on the cauliflower and pine nut salad. That had been his favourite.

"This is what I wanted," she said aloud to the empty kitchen.

How long had she been planning this? Now it was a reality – a tasting room where people could come and enjoy the produce of her hands. She gathered food from the fridge, pulled some bowls from the cupboard and made a start on the prep. She worked methodically but the joy of yesterday was gone, replaced by an aching loss she had no idea how to fill.

CHAPTER
30

Hugh was home earlier than anticipated. He'd planned to catch up with some mates today and drive back to the South East on Monday, but the other blokes' plans had changed and he'd decided to head home.

The drive had given him good thinking time but he was no closer to a decision. He'd met with the Canadian agent as planned and applied for his visa. He'd fitted a lot into his one day interstate. He hadn't said anything to the agent but there would be no need for a visa if he decided not to go to Canada.

Two months ago he couldn't wait to get there. Now he was undecided about going at all. He pulled up outside his family home, got out of his vehicle and stretched. He paused to take in the house with its wonky verandah post, cracked back window, assorted pots and the old cat, Molly, curled up on the chair at the back door. This was home. A home he'd been avoiding for years but today felt like the place of his childhood, where he belonged. He wouldn't describe himself as content but at least more comfortable. Somehow he'd laid the demons to rest during his stay.

He gave Molly a pat and went inside. The house was quiet. His parents were out somewhere. This would be a good chance to bring out the replacement verandah post he'd stashed in the shed.

He changed into work clothes and set off to tackle the verandah. At one stage the whole corner threatened to give way on top of him but he managed to keep it in place while he got the new post in. He worked hard until finally, it was done. He stepped back, taking in the new post and the nearly straight roof. Molly came to weave between his legs.

"Now you offer to help," he said. He reached down to pat her and received a head butt to his leg in response.

There was still no sign of his parents and with nothing else immediate to do, he relaxed on the side verandah. With inactivity his thoughts to strayed to Mackenna. His new-found ease at being home wasn't the only reason he might stay. They were good friends but could they be lovers, partners? Did they have a future together? She'd told him to follow his dreams but he knew he'd stay if she wanted him too. She hadn't avoided him after their kiss at the Gatehouse, but she hadn't encouraged him to repeat it either.

Rather than sit alone pondering, he decided to head over to Woolly Swamp. Sunday afternoon was as good a time as any to catch Mackenna. If he was going to test their possible relationship, it needed to be soon.

When he pulled up at the back door of the Gatehouse Mackenna came straight out, as if she'd been watching for him.

"Hi," she called and wrapped her arms around him in a close hug.

He pulled back and studied her. Her lips were turned up in a smile that didn't reach her tired eyes, and her face was pale.

"Are you feeling okay?" he asked.

"Much better now you're here," she said. She stepped away from him quickly, her face creased in a puzzled look. "I thought you weren't coming back till Monday."

"A change of plans, so I thought I might as well come home. There's no-one there, so here I am begging a meal maybe."

"You could be in luck, but you'll have to earn it," she said. "Come with me."

He followed her inside, feeling like a puppy bouncing adoringly behind its mistress. Inside the kitchen, benches were loaded with dishes and food in different degrees of preparation.

"I've got ten coming for dinner tonight, I'm on my own and I'm up to my ears in prep. I need more wine from Bunyip and Chris can't leave because he's also on his own, and there are dogs and chooks to feed and shut up." She swept an arm in an arc. "Take your pick. Whatever it is you can do to help, I'd be grateful."

Hugh looked at the benches and back at Mackenna. "I'll leave the cooking to you," he said. "Deliveries and animals I can deal with."

"Thanks, Hugh." This time the smile was stronger. "I wasn't planning on people for a meal here tonight but I don't want to say no now that word's getting out. With everyone else away it's a bit more than I can handle on my own."

"Where's Cam?"

"Helping a mate shift house."

Hugh raised his eyebrows. Cam Martin was on a pretty good wicket. He worked for the Birches but appeared to come and go when it suited him and had free use of their vehicles.

"He'll be back tonight." Mackenna glanced at the clock. "Or maybe in the morning."

"Okay," Hugh said. "Drinks or animals first?"

"Drinks please. The animals will be fine till you get back."

"Right."

"Thanks, errand boy." She laughed. "And there will be a meal in it for you," she said. "I promise."

He waved a hand over his shoulder as he walked out the door, happy to be the person she could depend on to help out when needed.

A couple of hours later he was back at her kitchen table tucking into a delicious serve of her Trio of Lamb. He'd help set up tables and serve wine and Mackenna had made sure there was something of everything she'd cooked set aside for him. She'd offered to make a place for him with the guests but he was happy to eat in the kitchen, watching her work and washing up for her.

Now she was throwing together a dessert. She muttered about not enough berries but the concoction she was arranging, ice-cream drizzled with berries and toffee, looked fantastic. Finally she put her hands to her hips and stood back.

"I'm sorry I haven't got a skerrick left to make one for you," she said.

He patted his stomach.

"I don't need any. The lamb's been enough."

She ferried the desserts down to her guests but didn't return. He could hear her voice amongst the others, drifting along the passage. He stacked what dishes he could in the dishwasher and tackled the last of the pots and pans.

He was making such a racket and lost in his own thoughts that he got a shock when she spoke close behind him.

"Just what every chef needs,' she chuckled. "A dish pig."

"Charming," he said. "I'm quite the animal. A gopher and a pig all in one day."

"Oh, don't be upset." She laughed at him. "I've done my time, you know. Besides, if you weren't here I would be doing them myself now that my guests have gone."

"Are you going to eat?" he asked.

"I'll just pick at the last of the tasting plate. But I'm going to have a small drink." She went to the fridge, pulled out a bottle of the Bunyip sauvignon blanc and wiggled it at him. "Want to join me?"

"Sure," he said.

He accepted the glass she offered then watched as she poured the wine.

"Here's to the Gatehouse," he said as they touched glasses.

"To the Gatehouse," she repeated.

Mackenna took a plate of food from the fridge and put it on the table. The two of them sat opposite each other and sipped their wine while she picked at the food and told him all about Simon, the restaurant owner from Melbourne and his mates. She was animated in her excitement, in spite of her busy weekend and the lateness of the hour. Hugh listened, asking the odd question, and then Adam's name popped up.

"Is Adam back?" he asked. The Kiwi was a good bloke. Instinct told Hugh there was a connection between him and Mackenna.

"No," she said quickly. "At least he was. Just for last night. Thank goodness, or I would have gone under. He's back in Melbourne again now. His grandfather died this morning."

"Oh." Hugh felt guilty over his little pang of jealousy.

Mackenna stifled a yawn with the back of her hand. She looked done in.

"Sorry," she mumbled. "It's been a big weekend."

"I should go."

She stood up quicker than he did.

"I'm glad you called in, Hugh. I hope it wasn't too boring for you?"

"No." He smiled. He wanted to kiss her but she'd already started moving ahead of him to the door. "I'm glad I could help out."

She walked him to his car then stepped back as he hesitated, one hand on the open door. There was no opportunity for a kiss, not even one on the cheek without it being awkward.

"I probably won't see you much this week," she said. "We'll be crutching."

"I don't have anything on my books tomorrow if I can be of any help."

"No," she said, "but thanks. You've already helped so much. I'm sure your mum would like to see a bit more of you. It must be getting close to your heading overseas."

He got into his four-wheel drive and lowered the window. "A bit longer yet. I have to wait for my visa."

"Goodnight then," she said and stepped back even further.

He gave her a wave and backed out, totally bamboozled now about his feelings and with no idea of hers. He'd never had much success working out women.

CHAPTER
31

Mackenna pushed the large bristle broom over the rough cement floor of the shearing shed with great vigour. A cloud of dust rose around her. She'd risen early after a restless night and with no-one to help her prepare for crutching, she'd come straight to the shed. It had taken a while to fix the grinding wheel and a hinge had been half off one of the doors. After that she'd picked up the broom. Physical work was a good way to banish the melancholy thoughts that had plagued her half the night.

When she flung her arms around Hugh yesterday in welcome, it had suddenly dawned on her what Adam had seen, or thought he had seen. She often kissed Hugh on the cheek, patted his arm, gave him a hug. And if someone like Adam got the wrong idea, what were others thinking? What was Hugh thinking for that matter?

She gave the broom a final shove to push the pile of dirt out the shed door and burst into a fit of sneezing. The dogs barked but it was the sound of a vehicle that had attracted their attention. She raised bleary eyes and peered through the swirling dust. She expected to see Cam. It was ten o'clock and he was late. To her surprise it was Patrick's car that rolled into view and even more surprising was the relief she felt. She hadn't been looking forward to working alone with Cam after his odd behaviour on Saturday, and another pair of hands for crutching would be useful.

She propped the broom against the wall and made her way to the house. Patrick and Yasmine were both getting out of the car as she reached it.

"Hello," Mackenna called. "Did Mum and Dad get away okay?"

"Hi." Yassie greeted her with a wave. "Yes, they're off on their big holiday."

As usual Yasmine looked like she'd just stepped out of a fashion magazine with her boots and layers of clothing. Today the black was teemed with shades of grey and splashes of mauve. Vivid purple lip-stick glistened on her lips.

"I wasn't expecting you so soon," Mackenna said.

"I told you I'd be back." Patrick unloaded the bags with a thump.

"I know. I just wasn't sure when. It's great to see you," Mackenna said brightly. She didn't want to put Patrick offside. "There's a lot to be done."

"I've brought food," Yasmine said and rushed to the boot of the car.

She raised it to reveal eskys and boxes.

"Oh, what . . .?" Mackenna was gobsmacked.

"Your mum said there were sausage rolls in the freezer and I've picked up loaves of bread and all sorts of fillings for sandwiches. My mum helped me cook on the weekend. We've made little quiches . . . I hope that's alright. Patrick said it wasn't working men's food, but hot sausage rolls and quiches usually disappear off the plate. Then there are cakes and – "

"Let's get them inside, Yas," Patrick said. "You can show off your cakes."

He met Mackenna's eyes over the top of Yasmine's head and winked.

"Don't tease, Patrick." Yasmine handed one of the boxes to Mackenna. "Mum and I are into cake decorating. We thought this was a good chance to practise. After looking at computer screens all day I find it very therapeutic."

Mackenna led the way inside with Yasmine's bubbly voice following along behind. By the time they'd finished unloading, Mackenna decided it would be fine to leave the responsibility of the food to Yasmine. There was enough to feed several crutching teams.

Barking announced the arrival of another vehicle.

"I hope that's Cam," Mackenna said, and made her way to the door. "Will you be right to give us a hand with the stock, Patrick?"

"That's why I'm here." He pulled at his shirt. "I'll change and be right with you."

Mackenna hurried outside, already mapping who would shift what where. Cam had pulled up in his ute near the shearing shed. She strode across the yard towards him.

"What time do you call this?" she said as he unfolded himself from his ute.

"Sorry, boss. Had a flat tyre."

Cam looked bleary-eyed and dishevelled. Somehow she thought there was more to his lateness than a troublesome tyre.

"Where's the truck?"

"Still got gear on it. We don't need it, do we? I'll have it back tomorrow."

He gave her one of his big smiles but she didn't respond.

"I'll expect it tomorrow then," she said. "I need you to bring in the first mob from the back paddock. Patrick's here now so he can help."

Mackenna thought she saw a slight roll of his eyes. He and Patrick had appeared to be thick as thieves when she first came home. She'd rather they worked together. She preferred the company of King and Prince to Cam.

"I'll take the dogs and bring in the mob from the swamp paddock. I'll bring them in here." She waved at the pens beside the shearing shed. The dozen pregnant ewes Lyle had brought in were already there. "You can put the other mob in the holding paddock."

Patrick turned up and greeted Cam. The two of them started talking about football before Mackenna could get a word in. She left them to it a minute while she cast her eyes over the ewes. They'd all had dirty wool around their backsides and her dad had tidied them up before he'd gone. She could see no sign of flies.

Patrick and Cam joined her at the rails. "They're in good condition," Patrick said.

"I'm a bit worried about that dirty wool," she said.

"Isn't that why we're crutching them?"

"Nothing like a good crutch," Cam said and nudged Patrick.

Mackenna saw the glow on Patrick's cheeks. They'd both been raised by a mother who found smutty jokes distasteful.

"You go with Cam," she said to change the subject. She whistled the dogs to follow her to the ute. Hopefully between the two men they could bring in a mob of sheep without any problems.

An hour later, Mackenna's mood had turned from irritation to anger. She'd found two flyblown sheep amongst the mob she'd brought in. They were too sick to walk so she'd had to tie their legs and get them on the back of the ute. There were quite a few dirty bottoms amongst the rest. They could wait for tomorrow's crutching, but if she didn't do something about the sheep in the ute it would be too late. If it wasn't already.

She was wrestling them into the shearing shed when Yasmine appeared.

"Can I help?" she asked.

Mackenna swept her eyes down Yasmine's clothes to her boots. At least the heels were flat but she wasn't dressed for sheep work.

"I'll be right, thanks," she said. She grabbed the first sheep by its legs and dragged it backwards into a pen then retuned for the other one.

"Is something wrong with them?" Yasmine followed her as she hauled the second sheep in.

"They've got flies."

"Flies?"

Mackenna glanced from her bent position to study Yasmine's puzzled face.

"They've got faeces around their hindquarters. Flies lay eggs in it and the maggots hatch out and burrow into the wool."

"The poor things," Yasmine wailed. "How can that happen?"

"That's what I want to know," Mackenna said. She took up the hand shears and began snipping away the rotten wool. "In the case of these two I'm afraid the maggots have gone further. We've been keeping an eye on the sheep regularly because conditions are conducive to flystrike. We only checked these sheep on Saturday. I can't understand how they got so bad so quickly."

She gritted her teeth as she saw the extent of the damage. It wasn't good.

"You might want to clear out before I go any further."

"I'm alright," Yasmine said. "I want to learn more about what you do."

Mackenna shook her head. "Last chance."

"Go ahead," Yasmine said.

Yasmine couldn't say she hadn't been warned. Mackenna held her breath, closed her mouth and poured the flystrike liquid over the clipped hind area of the sheep. Her stomach lurched as the maggots began wriggling out of the flesh. As she'd suspected, this sheep was in a bad way and the other would probably be the same.

Beside her she heard a gasp and a gurgling sound. She glanced around to see Yasmine wide-eyed with her hand clamped over her mouth. The gurgling sound came again and Mackenna watched as Yasmine's chest heaved. Suddenly the younger woman spun around and dashed outside. The groans she made as she vomited reached Mackenna's ears but there was no time to see if she was alright, the sheep needed attention. Mackenna concentrated on the task at hand, trying to control the turmoil in her own belly. By the time she'd finished her gruesome job there was no sign of Yasmine outside except for the cloud of flies on a pool of liquid.

Mackenna felt miserable – for herself, the poor sheep and also for Yasmine. She'd had a similar experience as a young girl when she'd witnessed her father dealing with a badly flyblown sheep. Suddenly she felt the need for a drink and to wash her hands. She'd check on Yasmine at the same time. She made her way to the house and called out as she went inside.

"Yasmine?"

There was no answer. Mackenna paused and listened. Then she heard the sound of running water from the direction of the bathroom.

"Yasmine?" she called again and slowly pushed the door open. The sight that greeted her stopped her in her tracks. Yasmine, wearing only a bra and knickers was bending over the handbasin. "I'm sorry," Mackenna gasped and stepped back.

"It's okay." Yasmine splashed water on her face. "I got vomit all over me. I had to strip off."

"I'll . . ." Mackenna turned away not knowing what to say. It wasn't the sight of Yasmine stripped to her underwear that surprised her – it was the round bulge of her belly protruding from her reedy body, as if she'd swallowed a basketball.

"Stay," Yasmine said, "please."

Mackenna remained stuck to the spot, not knowing what to say or do. Yasmine was pregnant and obviously well advanced, and Mackenna had never realised. She felt even guiltier about the poor girl witnessing that horrible scene in the shed.

"You must be shocked." Yasmine turned her face to Mackenna. Mascara was smudged around her eyes and the beautiful purple lipstick was smeared down her chin. She looked like a sad clown. "I wanted to tell you all sooner," she said.

Mackenna offered her a towel. "Mum and Dad don't know?" she asked.

"No."

"What about Patrick?"

"Of course I know."

They both spun at the sound of his voice.

Patrick pushed past Mackenna and put his arm around Yasmine. "What's happened?"

The bathroom was suddenly very crowded. Mackenna shuffled back to the door.

"The sheep . . ." Yasmine began but petered out.

"I had to clean up some flyblown sheep," Mackenna explained.

"It turned my stomach. I'm all right now."

"You should never have been there." Patrick glared past her to Mackenna.

"Oh, Patrick, those poor animals." Yasmine covered her mouth with her hand again.

"Try not to think about it," Mackenna said. "Give me your clothes. I'll put them in the machine then I'll make you a cup of tea."

"I'll wash them," Yasmine said quickly. "They're handwash only." She gave Mackenna a little smile. "I'll do it later, but I would love a cup of tea, thanks."

"I'll make the tea," Patrick said. "Cam wants you. We've brought in the mob you asked for. There's a problem with a fence and he wants to know if you want us to bring in more sheep. I'll come back out once Yasmine's settled."

"You go Patrick, I'm fine," Yasmine said. "It was just a bit of a shock."

Mackenna gave Patrick an apologetic look and left them to it. There was still so much to do to get ready for crutching tomorrow and she was annoyed at Cam. He said he'd checked those sheep she'd treated but he couldn't have. Then there was her guilt about Yasmine being so physically upset but overriding it all, she felt a wave of excitement. She was going to be an aunty. Her excitement waned a little when she thought of her mother. Louise could be very old fashioned when it came to moral issues like children out of wedlock.

"You've got a spring in your step," Cam said as she approached.

"Lucky for you," Mackenna snapped.

"Why?"

"I've just had to deal with flyblown sheep because you didn't do your job properly."

"Hang on a minute, boss." Cam held up two dirty palms to Mackenna. "What's this about?"

"Saturday. I asked you to check the sheep in the swamp paddock."

He shrugged his shoulders. "I checked them," he said. "They were all fine."

"You had a good look?"

"Yeah."

"Every single one of them?" Mackenna watched his face closely.

He glared back. "I checked them," he said emphatically and bent to pick up a roll of wire at his feet. "I just fixed the fence leading up to the yards. You might want to check that. Make sure I've done it properly."

Mackenna opened her mouth but he didn't wait for her to speak. He tossed the wire over his shoulder and headed to the shed.

"Damn it," Mackenna muttered. Patrick was often prickly to deal with and now Cam was as well. Why were men so tricky to get along with?

CHAPTER
32

The early morning air was crisp but there was still no sign of rain. Mackenna hugged her jacket close and quickened her steps. It wasn't very often she and her father disagreed but she wished now she'd fought harder to stop him from sowing those early paddocks.

The light was on in the kitchen as she approached. She hoped that meant Patrick and Yassie were up. They'd both gone to bed early last night and there hadn't been a chance to go over today's plans or talk much about the bombshell discovery of their baby.

Patrick was standing at the sink with a mug in his hand when she stepped inside. There was no sign of Yasmine.

"Good morning," Mackenna said brightly.

"Morning," said Patrick. "Want one?" He lifted the mug.

"No thanks. I've had breakfast."

"I'm ready to get started but I let Yassie sleep in."

"Is she okay?"

"She worked late last night." He nodded towards the desk where a laptop and a bag sat beside the family computer.

"I thought you were getting an early night?"

"We did. At least I did. Yassie can be a bit nocturnal. She says she does her best work at night. She'll be up later and she'll make sure the food is done."

"Are you sure? Food just doesn't seem her thing."

"That's only since she's been pregnant. Savoury food turns her stomach and the smell of meat cooking really sets her off, but she's been craving sweet things. Half the grannies at work say it means she's having a boy and the other half say it means a girl. She'd been feeling better these last few days."

Mackenna still couldn't believe Yasmine was pregnant. It seemed strange to hear her little brother talk about a baby – his and Yasmine's baby. Even stranger to think so many other people knew but not his family.

"It's such exciting news, Patch," she said. "When is Yasmine due?"

"Mid-August."

"I can't believe you kept it from us all this time."

"It was more about keeping it from Mum and Dad . . . Mum really. I wasn't sure how she'd react."

"It will be a shock but she'll get over it." Mackenna spoke with a certainty she didn't feel. She understood Patrick's reluctance. "She's always hinting about weddings and grandchildren."

"I guess one out of two will be okay." Patrick had a wry smile on his face.

"You're not planning to marry?"

"The baby was a surprise to us, too. I wanted to get married straight away but Yasmine thought I only asked her because of the baby."

"Is she right?"

Patrick wrapped both hands around his mug. "Partly. We've been together a long time and . . . I love her. I can't imagine being with anyone else and the baby is a surprise – a wonderful surprise. I'm sure I would have asked her eventually, baby or no baby."

"Maybe Yasmine's a bit overwhelmed. A baby and marriage are both big steps."

"I know."

His voice was so mature. Mackenna found it hard to equate the man who stood before her with the weight of the world on his shoulders, to her carefree baby brother. He'd grown up and she hadn't noticed. The silence stretched between them.

Finally she spoke. "I've made a list for Yasmine of what we need and when." She pulled it from her pocket.

"That's a good idea. Yassie likes lists."

They both stared at the paper on the table between them. Once again there was nothing more to say.

The rumble of a truck broke the silence.

"That will be Cam," Mackenna said. She was relieved. After their words yesterday she had been almost afraid he wouldn't turn up this morning.

"How do you know?" Patrick asked.

"I asked him to bring the truck back. He's been using it a lot lately."

"He is the working man."

"For his own use, I mean." Mackenna studied Patrick a moment. "What do you think of him?" she asked.

"Haven't given him any thought."

"You two have spent a bit of time together. What kind of bloke do you think he is?"

"Hadn't really thought about it." Patrick put his cup and plate in the dishwasher. "He's easy to get on with. He does the work. What more is there?"

"Nothing, I guess," Mackenna said. Nothing except, more and more, she had the feeling that Cam was easy to get on with because it suited him. He did the work but she wasn't convinced he always did it well.

"Sometimes I get the feeling he's taking the micky." Patrick looked her in the eye. "But I'm used to that around here."

Mackenna saw a brief look of hurt cross his face before he moved away. She assumed his words were aimed at her but she wasn't buying into an argument this morning. She pushed her hat firmly onto her head and was about to pat him on the back when she thought better of it.

"Time to get this show on the road," she said and led the way outside.

They had everything ready to go by the time the crutching team arrived. Mackenna shook hands with Garry Finn. He'd brought the men together to do the job.

"Thanks for fitting us in, Garry," she said.

"You were lucky," he replied. "We've had a few calls from this area to come earlier. You got in first. We've just finished a big job way out the other side of Naracoorte. Saw that guy picking up sheep at the last place and now he's here. He gets around."

"What guy?" Mackenna followed Garry's gaze to the open shed window. Cam was pushing up sheep in the yard. "You mean Cam?"

"Don't know his name but it looks like him, and the truck's the same as the one out in your yard. There was another bloke with him. They were carting sheep for the farmer where we worked last."

Mackenna looked from Garry back to Cam. Surely Garry was mistaken. Cam had been helping a mate shift house over the weekend.

"Time to start," Garry called and the shed burst into life.

Mackenna forgot about Cam in the business of the next few hours, and it wasn't until smoko time approached that she gave any thought to Yasmine either and how she was managing with the food. Mackenna was about to ask Patrick to go and check when Yasmine appeared at the shed door, her arms laden with containers.

Mackenna went to help.

She was surprised by Yasmine's very different look. The hair and make-up were immaculate as usual and she wore the same flat black boots as she'd had on yesterday, but her clothes were in total contrast to her usual layered outfits. She was wearing a long red jumper over skinny-legged black jeans that were tucked into her boots. A black and grey scarf was knotted loosely around her neck. The loose jumper didn't give away her pregnancy.

Mackenna showed her where to put everything beside the kettle and the mugs that had been set up yesterday. The noise of the crutching ceased and the blokes gathered round to take their morning tea break.

Patrick lifted a couple of pieces of slice from a container and waved at Mackenna. "Cam's waiting for me outside. We'll shift this lot back and bring in the next mob."

"Okay," Mackenna replied. Cam hadn't come into the shed at all. Was he avoiding her, or maybe someone else? She glanced over at Garry but was distracted by the look of total surprise on his face. One of the other blokes whistled and another gave a sharp laugh.

Yasmine had lifted the lids on the other containers. There was a log cake that looked vaguely like a train and a container of little cakes decorated as farm animals with bright icing, lollies and sprinkles.

"I hope you men don't mind," Yasmine said shyly, "but I've been practising my decorating skills. You're the guinea pigs."

There was a moment of silence where the only sound was the shuffling of sheep in the pens behind them. Then Garry reached forward.

"Don't mind at all," he said and picked up a pink cake decorated as a pig.

The others quickly followed suit and soon cakes decorated as cows and sheep were also being consumed. Mackenna chose a chicken. Not only did it look cute but it tasted great too. Yasmine was suddenly the centre of a discussion about cakes. Mackenna couldn't believe her ears. She'd heard all kinds of conversations at smoko in the shearing shed over the years but never one like this. Now she knew why Patrick had given her the funny look and teased his girlfriend about her cakes. Life was certainly entertaining with Yasmine around. Mackenna was beginning to enjoy the idea of having a sister.

CHAPTER
33

"Your chooks look in fine shape to me, Mr Johnstone." Hugh climbed out of the rickety yard, trying not to get hooked up in the loops of chicken wire. "Maybe a bit too well fed."

"It was good of you to call in, lad," George Johnstone said. "Only, your mother was saying how well you'd done with your studies and my girls have gone off the lay a bit lately. It's not the usual time and I was worried."

Hugh smiled. Old George had to be ninety if he was a day. "It's no trouble," he said. Goodness knows what stories his mother had been telling about him around town. She'd be setting him up as a vet next.

"I was worried it might have been the bags of grain I bought from the young fella at the pub that had upset them," George said.

"What kind of grain?"

"Looks like good wheat to me but I'm no expert."

Hugh followed the old man as he walked on wobbly legs to his equally unsteady feed shed.

"I got it at a good price."

George pointed at three bags stacked against the wall. One was open with an old tin sitting in it. Hugh stuck his hand in and sniffed the grain then let it run between his fingers back into the bag.

"It's good quality wheat. Where'd you say you got it?"

"Young bloke at the pub. As you know I go every Friday night for my weekly constitutional. Seen this chap in there a few times with odds and sods for sale. Last week it was bags of wheat. Nice bloke. Even dropped it off and put it in the shed for me. Does your mum need some? I can ask him if he's got anymore if you reckon it's okay."

"Mum's got plenty, thanks Mr Johnstone." Hugh wondered about this bloke selling stuff at the pub. Occasionally there'd be some not so honest types moving gear that fell off the back of a truck.

"This guy's not a local then?" Hugh asked.

Mr Johnstone had lived in town most of his life. He used to work in the post office but he'd been retired for as long as Hugh could remember. There weren't too many people in town he didn't know.

"Seen him around a bit but not for all that long. Very tall with hair that needs cutting. What's he call himself?" The old man tapped his forehead with a crooked finger. "It's a short name, something like Sam but that's not it."

"Cam?"

"By jingoes that's it. Do you know him?"

"Maybe." Hugh didn't know what made him mention Cam's name but if it was Cam Martin and he was selling gear from his boot at the pub, it was just one more piece in a puzzle about the bloke that left Hugh with a bad taste in his mouth. "Look, I'd better get going, Mr Johnstone."

"Righto lad, and say hello to your lovely mother."

"Will do." Hugh followed George up the overgrown path to his back door.

"She drops in with some baked goodies from time to time. Such a kind-hearted woman, your mother. She's just delighted to have you home at last."

Hugh once again felt that niggle of guilt when he was reminded how he'd shut his family out of his life.

George stooped under a vine to step up on his verandah. "Last time she called in she was telling me all about your study. Education's a good thing. I didn't get past grade seven but I can read. Learned about the world through books."

He pointed to a rickety old table beside an equally ancient chair. The chair was padded with assorted cushions and the table was piled with books. A couple of empty mugs perched amongst the books and a plate with a half-eaten orange. This was obviously a favourite spot for George.

"Don't know how to work those computers," George continued, "but I love my books. Would liked to have seen some of those places I've read about but it wasn't to be. Reading about them gives me great pleasure." George turned his steel grey eyes on Hugh. "Have you travelled, lad?"

"Not much."

"Ah."

Hugh stuck his hands in his pockets and watched George whose eyes were focused somewhere in the distance.

"I'd better get going, Mr Johnstone."

George held up a hand. "Wait a minute, lad. There's something I'd like you to have."

Before Hugh could protest, George disappeared into his house. Hugh listened to the sounds of a search in progress.

"Got it."

George came back clutching a small brown object a bit larger than a wallet.

"This came with one of my book sets. It's no good to me but maybe you could use it."

Hugh looked at the item George pressed into his hands. It was a small compendium. *Travel Diary* was etched in black lettering on the front cover. He opened it to reveal a blank notebook, a pen and tiny calculator which included currency conversions according to the plastic sticker. A sudden sense of longing swept over him. Hugh closed the cover. He had no idea what he'd do with it but knew he couldn't refuse the gift.

"Thanks, Mr Johnstone."

"You've a kind heart like your mother, lad."

Hugh extricated himself from the old man's grip and returned to his vehicle. What a strange visit that had turned out to be. George was a funny old bloke, but his words had shaken something awake in Hugh. He glanced at the travel diary he'd tossed on the passenger seat. Old George could just have easily poked him in the chest and told him to stop marking time, because Hugh now realised that's what he was doing. Life here had become comfortable but what would he be giving up if he stayed? What would he lose if he went? Mackenna's smile danced before his eyes.

Mackenna! Should he tell her what he'd found out about Cam? It may be nothing. Cam could just be making some money from a perk the Birches allowed him, but Hugh kept playing the thought over in his head. It just didn't sit right.

He was still thinking about it as he drove to Rory's shop. He stopped at an intersection and a familiar ute crossed the road in front of him. It was loaded up with drums, treated pine posts, wire and several other items. Of all people, it was Cam. He could have been doing anything, but he was driving in the opposite direction to the road leading to the Birches' farm.

On a whim Hugh decided to follow him, glad he was in his father's ute rather than the work four-wheel drive with signage all over it. Near the edge of town Cam stopped and backed into a driveway. Hugh hung back a while then cruised slowly past. Surveillance looked simple when people did it on TV shows but he felt as conspicuous as if he had flashing lights and a siren wailing.

Hugh glanced down the driveway. Cam had backed up to a dilapidated shed. One door was partly open and he was carrying a post into the shed. Hugh drove on. The far end of the street marked the edge of town and was a dead end bounded by paddocks. He turned the ute around and drove back along the street. This time he saw Cam take a small drum into the shed. Hugh kept driving. He turned back the way he'd come and pulled over.

After about ten minutes Cam drove past, heading in the opposite direction, probably to the Birches'. The back of the ute still had most of the earlier contents Hugh had seen. He sat a little longer. He had an uneasy feeling and yet it all could be quite legitimate. There's nothing wrong with buying extra stuff for a friend or yourself and dropping it off before taking the boss's supplies to the farm.

He'd wasted half an hour playing super sleuth and was no closer to getting any answers. Better to mind his own business and do what he'd come to town to do, and that was to collect the things he'd organised for his mother from Rory.

It didn't take him long to get them loaded. Rory had breathed new life into the old garden setting and he'd made a fantastic birdbath. Hugh knew his mother was going to love it. Heading out of town with the load tied on the back reminded him of Mackenna and the day he'd helped her put in the sheep sculptures. Just like old times, they'd laughed and enjoyed each other's company. Just like old times . . . Hugh gripped the steering wheel a little tighter. He knew what he had to do.

Mackenna looked around at the sound of a ute. It was Cam, and he was late again. She watched as he drove to the far side of the yard and disappeared from sight. In the shearing shed behind her Garry and his crew were finished and just cleaning up ready to head off. Lucky for Cam they hadn't needed the extra chemicals she'd sent him into town a couple of hours ago to get. They'd eked out the last of what they had so the crutching could be finished.

"Thanks for running such a good operation, Mack."

She turned to see Garry walking her way with his hand outstretched. She took it and returned his firm shake.

"Thanks for coming at short notice," she said. "It's saved us a lot of work."

"No probs," Garry said. "And don't forget that dead sheep."

One of the crossbreeds had run flat out, headbutted a rail and broken its neck. They'd lifted it over the fence out of the way, but it needed to be disposed of.

"I asked Cam to do it. He's back now and went in that direction, so he's probably dealing with it now."

Mackenna shook the other blokes' hands.

"Mr Finn!"

They all turned to see Yasmine hurrying towards them waving a piece of paper in her hand. "I was worried I'd missed you," she said. She stopped and put her other hand to her chest. "Phew, not fit these days." She offered the paper to Garry. "These are my details if you want those cakes. I'd be happy to make them for you."

"Thanks, Yassie." Garry's face lit up in a big smile. He flapped the paper. "I'll let you know."

Mackenna and Yasmine watched as the men got into their vehicles and waved goodbye.

"Well," Mackenna said, "how about you getting some business from Garry? He'd be the last person I'd expect to want fancy cakes."

"His son's birthday is coming up and his wife doesn't like cooking cakes. I said I'd make some of the farm animals if he wanted. I'm not charging for them."

"You should," Mackenna laughed. "You never know when having another string to your bow will come in handy. You did a great job with the food, Yassie. Thank you. I couldn't have done that and worked the shed."

"Happy to help. Where's Patrick?"

"Returning sheep to the paddock."

"Is there anything more I can do?"

"There's a bit of stuff to take back to the house."

They went inside the shed and filled a couple of boxes with the kettle, cups, tea and coffee.

A slow-moving vehicle was heading their way.

"Maybe it's Patrick," Yasmine said.

She hurried to the door. There was a loud crash as the box of cups hit the floor and she staggered backwards.

"What's wrong?" Mackenna rushed to her side just in time to see Cam pass by in his ute, dragging the dead sheep by a rope tied to the tow bar.

"Oh for heaven's sake! What an idiot he can be." Thank goodness the dogs were with Patrick. Mackenna put an arm around Yasmine who had both hands pressed to her mouth. "Are you okay?"

Yasmine nodded.

"You're not going to be sick?"

Yasmine shook her head, watching Mackenna with big round eyes.

"Do you want to sit down?"

Yasmine lifted her hands away from her mouth. "Was that . . . was that sheep alive?"

"Oh, no. It killed itself earlier."

Yasmine looked at her in surprise and Mackenna realised how flippant that sounded.

"It was an accident," she said. "It hit its head and broke its neck. It died instantly. I asked Cam to get rid of it but I didn't expect him to do it that way. Putting it in the back of his ute would have been a better option."

"The poor thing." Yasmine looked down at the box of crockery. "I'm sorry. I've broken some of your cups."

"Don't worry," Mackenna said as they sank to their heels to pick up a few broken pieces. "It's only old stuff Mum keeps for the shearing shed. There's plenty more." Mackenna was glad Yasmine hadn't thrown up again. Being a pregnant vegetarian on a farm was fraught with danger.

Once she knew Yasmine was safely on her way back to the house, Mackenna went in search of Cam. She found him unloading a container at the chemical shed.

"What do you think you're doing?" she snapped.

"Unloading the chemical. I'm guessing you don't need it at the shed anymore."

"I mean that business with the sheep."

"The sheep?"

"The dead one."

"You told me to get rid of it."

"Yes, but I didn't expect you to drag it across the yard by its feet." Cam shrugged his shoulders. "It was dead."

"It would have been better in the back of the ute."

"Then I would have had to clean out the ute."

Mackenna put her hands to her hips in exasperation.

Cam gave her a grin. He walked right up to her then around to the door of his ute.

"Where are you going now?" she asked.

"To replace that O ring on the pivot. I didn't get to it before crutching."

Damn it, she'd forgotten about the pivot.

He came back and stopped just in front of her again. "Unless there's something else you want me to do?"

She met his look. "No. It needs changing, you'd better do it."

"Then it'll be knock-off time. I'm staying at my mate's again tonight."

Before Mackenna had a chance to speak he was in his ute and driving away. She watched him go, frustration gnawing in her chest. She hadn't found out why he'd been gone so long this afternoon. He'd been elusive the whole time the men were crutching and hadn't eaten with them at all. Not that he hadn't done any work, just opted for all the outside jobs and stayed in town each night. And he hadn't done anything wrong other than being late this afternoon and insensitive in dealing with a dead animal. Mackenna couldn't put her finger on what annoyed her about him but something wasn't right.

CHAPTER
34

"We'll have to head back to Adelaide again tomorrow," Patrick said through a mouthful of pizza.

None of them had felt like cooking once the last of the cleaning up had been done, so Patrick had volunteered to drive into town for pizza.

"So soon?" Mackenna was enjoying having Patrick and Yasmine around. Although it had been a busy time and she hadn't seen a lot of them, they'd played a part in ensuring the crutching ran to schedule.

"We've been here for four days," Patrick said. "I've got work to get ready for Monday. You said things would calm down here for a while."

"You're right," Mackenna said. "At least until Mum and Dad get back."

"Have you heard from them?" Yasmine asked.

"No," Mackenna said.

"Yes," Patrick said.

Both women looked at him.

"I forgot to tell you, they rang last night."

"How are they going?" Mackenna asked.

"Having a great time. I didn't speak to Dad but Mum raved on for ages. They're in Wellington about to head to the South Island."

"You didn't mention crutching?" Mackenna wanted her father to enjoy his holiday. If he knew they were crutching early, he'd be anxious.

"I didn't get a chance. I told Mum everything was fine here. The only question from Dad in the background was whether it had rained."

Yasmine took a bite of the lamb pizza. Mackenna watched her take a second mouthful.

"I thought meat upset your stomach?"

"I'm feeling better now," Yasmine said. "I love meat normally."

"You do?"

"Yes. I'm not a vegetarian. It was just that, right from the early stages of my pregnancy, I was totally turned off the smell of any kind of meat cooking."

Mackenna gaped as Yasmine wiped her fingers and her mouth on a serviette. Just one more surprise to add to the mix.

Yasmine put her arms around Patrick. "You didn't drop the baby into the conversation you had with your parents?" she said playfully.

"Sure Yas, right between Mum saying they were enjoying the sights of Wellington and me saying there was no rain here I slipped in, 'And by the way you're going to be a grandma'."

They all laughed.

"Seriously, Patch, when are you going to tell them?" Mackenna asked.

"Good luck with that," Yasmine said and patted her belly. "I can't hide it much longer but Patrick keeps sticking his head in the sand."

"I'll tell them when they get back," Patrick said. "In my own way." He gave Yasmine a determined look.

"Well, I'm off to have a bath," Yasmine said. "Your lovely deep bath is so luxurious."

Patrick kissed her as she left.

"You've changed a lot over the last couple of months, baby brother," Mackenna said.

"In what way?"

She chose her words carefully. "You're a lot more mature. Maybe it's the responsibility of becoming a father."

"Maybe, or maybe I've always been this way but you haven't noticed."

"We worked well together over crutching."

"I must admit I've never realised until now what a big job that is."

"And I'll admit I was a bit nervous without Dad here but we did it." Mackenna lifted her hand and they high-fived. "And only a few minor mishaps."

"Yeah, I keep forgetting to ask you about that," Patrick said. "Those two mobs that ended up in the same paddock. What was the go there?"

"They weren't meant to be, but Cam said he sorted it before they got too mixed up."

"So he should." Patrick snorted. "It was his mistake in the first place."

"His mistake?"

"I knew there were already sheep in that paddock. I was surprised when he said that was where you wanted the next mob."

"But he said . . ." Mackenna's voice trailed off. Luckily she'd realised straight away they'd put a mob of crossbreeds in with a mob of Corriedales. Cam had said he'd sort it and he did, but not before pointing the blame at Patrick.

"He said what?"

Mackenna looked at her brother. They'd had such a smooth run lately she didn't want to rock the boat.

"He said it was my fault, didn't he?"

She nodded. "It doesn't matter. It's sorted."

"Once again Patrick is the scapegoat." He started collecting the empty pizza boxes then he stopped and leaned in towards Mackenna. "I tried to tell Cam there were sheep in that paddock but he wouldn't listen, said that was where you wanted them and you were the boss. Who was I to disagree? I'm only the silly young brother."

Mackenna stared at him. "That's quite a chip on your shoulder, Patch," she said gently.

"I don't mind being the butt of the jokes when I do something stupid."

Mackenna raised her eyebrows.

"But I'm not taking the blame for everything that goes wrong around here," he snapped.

Here we go. Mackenna could feel her own irritation rising. "Like what?"

"Like gates being left open, sheep in the wrong paddock, water not being checked. Who do you blame when I'm not here?" Patrick's voice was low but his eyes blazed.

Mackenna opened her mouth and closed it. Cam's smirking face came straight to mind. When Patrick wasn't around and things went wrong, Cam always had an explanation to shift the blame. But when she thought about it, if Patrick was around, Cam often managed to point the finger at him. She felt a pang of guilt that she had been so ready to believe the hired help over her brother.

"I know I'm not as up on farming as you and Dad," Patrick said, "but I'm not an idiot."

He held her gaze a moment longer then picked up the stack of pizza boxes and went outside.

Mackenna sat and thought back over the time since she'd returned from her holiday and found Cam installed in the family home. He always had a ready answer for everything. By the time Patrick came back to the kitchen Mackenna had replayed several events, but without the shutters over her eyes.

"Patrick, can you sit a moment?" she asked tentatively.

He paused then came and sat opposite her.

"I want to ask you something and I don't want you to get antsy," Mackenna said. "It's just a question."

He rolled his eyes but remained seated.

"Do you remember when we were drenching sheep?"

"Of course, and you told me off for wasting drench. That was the day I got a call from Yasmine in the hospital."

"I didn't know that. What happened?"

"She couldn't keep anything down and she was dehydrated. They put her in hospital for a couple of days."

"You poor things," Mackenna said. "I wish I'd known about the baby back then."

"Anyway," Patrick said, "back to me wasting drench."

"Yes, well forget that bit. I remember you taking that call now. I was annoyed at the time."

Patrick snorted. "What's new?"

Mackenna ignored him. "When you dosed those sheep, do you remember giving any of them extra?"

"Of course not. I'd already been told off for wasting drench. Anyway, isn't it poisonous if they get too much?"

Mackenna nodded. "Three sheep died that day."

"And I'm to blame, I suppose?"

"That's not what I'm saying." In Mackenna's mind she replayed Cam taking over the drenching from Patrick, then finding the dead sheep, and Cam pointing the blame clearly at Patrick but convincing her not to say anything. She'd been manipulated.

"What are you saying then?" Patrick asked.

"In hindsight I think Cam did it. He's good at bluffing his way through things. I don't think he knew as much about drenching as he made out. When we found those dead sheep he pointed the finger at you but made me feel like a heel if I mentioned it."

"And you went along with it." Patrick shook his head slowly. "What else have I taken the fall for that I didn't do?"

"I don't know," Mackenna replied vaguely.

"What did you say last week about me not shutting the gate over at Murphy's place?"

"I don't want to fight with you, Patrick."

"I'm not looking for a fight, but what you didn't let me tell you when you accused me of not taking responsibility was that Cam ended up doing that job. Dad asked me to help him with a water trough and Cam said he'd check the sheep on his way to town."

Mackenna stared at Patrick and recalled how Hugh had defended him that day. Even Hugh was ready to take Patrick's side. Why did she find it so hard?

"I'm sorry, Patrick. I won't be so easily fooled in the future."

"Don't worry about it. Anyway, he can't blame me if I'm not here." Patrick stood up. "I'm off to bed. Yas and I have to get away early in the morning so we won't see you before we go."

"Thanks for all you've done." Mackenna stood up and gave her little brother a hug. "I have really appreciated your help."

She watched him turn away. She wasn't so sure Cam wouldn't find some way to blame Patrick for things going wrong even in his absence. Then another thought struck her.

"Patrick."

He turned back.

"Did you ever meet this mate that Cam stays with?"

"I've met a few blokes he hangs out with at the pub. He could stay with any of them."

"Do you remember their names?"

"No, I didn't talk to them much, they were more interested in chasing women." Patrick scratched his head. "There was one bloke who Cam hung out with more than the others. I think his name was Trevor but they called him by a nickname . . . Dingo. I remember now, it suited him. He's a lean, sharp-eyed guy with a pointy nose. Ginger hair. Looks like he's been in a fight or two."

"I know him," Mackenna said. "Thanks."

"Goodnight." Patrick raised a hand in a short wave as he left.

Mackenna sat back at the table. "Trevor Dingle," she murmured. He was aptly named Dingo, often on the prowl and up to no good, but always eluding any charges that could stick. If Cam was hanging out with him, that couldn't be good.

CHAPTER
35

Mackenna was at a loose end. She and Cam had spent the day doing the last follow-ups from crutching and getting crossbreeds ready for market. She'd been on edge, watching his every move, trying not to be too obvious. Finally, he'd finished and gone for the weekend. Now she was at the Gatehouse alone and unable to relax. One minute she was wondering about Cam, was he just a sloppy worker who managed to lay blame elsewhere for his mistakes, or was there more to him than that? The next she was thinking of Adam. His grandfather's funeral must be over by now. Would he come back to see her or would he return to New Zealand?

She drifted from room to room in the Gatehouse. The walls glowed pink from the rays of the setting sun. There were no guests booked for the weekend but she'd put an ad in the local paper this week so she had to be organised just in case. She had her menu sorted and she planned to shop for the remaining ingredients in the morning. She'd have to drive her parents' car in and pick up a new battery for her car at the same time. She and Patrick had pushed it down the hill in the hope she might be able to jump-start it but had no luck. The car was still half under the carport, where it had coasted to a silent stop several days ago.

Mackenna flicked on the kitchen light and looked in the fridge for something easy to make a meal with. She gave up and plucked out a beer instead, lifted the top and tilted the bottle to the empty room. "To success," she said and took a sip. A wave of sadness swept over her. What she wanted was someone to share her day with.

Her mobile buzzed with a text message. Hugh was asking if she was home. She replied yes and would he like to come over. Her phone remained silent for a few minutes then she got a response: *on my way*.

Inspired to have someone else to cook for, she threw together a risotto. Good old reliable Hugh. He was a dear friend. For a while there her feelings for him had been confused but she knew now she loved him as a friend, no more than that. She looked forward to sharing a meal with him, with friendly banter and no complications. The food was all but ready to serve by the time he arrived carrying a bottle of wine.

"You're a sight for sore eyes," she said, careful to give him a friendly welcoming peck on the cheek. Nothing that could be construed as anything more.

"Mum and Dad have gone to some event at the school. I wasn't in the mood," he said.

"I hope you haven't eaten?"

He followed her to the kitchen. "Not yet, thank goodness. That smells good."

"It's risotto with bacon and leek. A kind of BLT." She chuckled. "Truthfully, it's made with whatever I could find in the fridge."

She served the risotto and he poured the wine.

"We fit well together, don't we?" Hugh said as he sat in front of the plate she'd set down for him.

Mackenna paused.

He grinned at her and raised his glass. "To good friends."

She relaxed and raised hers. "Couldn't survive without them," she said.

They both tucked into the risotto.

"Mmm!" Hugh said through a mouthful. "This is good. You sure I can't convince you to leave all this and come away with me as my personal chef?"

Mackenna put down her fork and met his eyes across the table. "Is that a proposal?"

He smiled at her. "No."

"So you're going then?"

"Yes."

"I'm happy for you but I'll miss you."

"I think I've made things more complicated than they should have been," Hugh said.

"You think?" Mackenna grinned at him but his face remained serious.

"I mistook our good friendship for something more."

Mackenna took in his solemn expression then burst out laughing. "That's so funny," she said.

"Hardly."

"No, I mean it's the same for me. These last weeks since you've been back, I've been confused as well. But we're good friends. Not like you and Carol."

Hugh sat back in his seat. His face crumpled in pain.

"Oh, Hugh." Mackenna leant forward. "I'm sorry, I didn't mean to stir up old memories, but Carol's been dead a long time now. She'd want you to find someone else."

"It's not that."

"What then?"

"Carol and I were good friends," Hugh began, "and I loved her but . . . as a friend. I should never have taken it further. I was going to tell her the night she died. I drank too much, trying to get up the courage while I waited for her to come home – she never did. I still don't know why she tried to drive back here that night but I must have given her some indication. I keep imagining her upset and driving . . . and it was my fault."

"You can't keep blaming yourself, Hugh. Carol was responsible for her death, not you."

His face filled with alarm. "You can't believe she killed herself?"

"Not on purpose," Mackenna said quickly. "I don't mean that, but I'm pretty sure she had no idea what you were going to tell her."

"How can you know that?"

"Because it would have been a relief for her, not a terrible revelation."

"How?"

Mackenna studied the face of her childhood friend. Would she make things better or worse by telling him what she knew? She inhaled deeply and reached for his hand.

"Remember the night before she died, when we were all out together?"

"We were celebrating my graduation."

"You were drinking with some mates at the bar and Carol was suddenly sad. I asked her what was wrong. She had her nursing degree and you two were facing a bright future together."

Hugh nodded.

Mackenna clutched his hand tighter. "She thought she'd made a big mistake. You two were great friends but she doubted the future. You were mates who should never have become lovers."

"Carol said that?"

Mackenna nodded.

Hugh snatched back his hand. "You're just saying that to ease my guilt."

"No I'm not."

"Why didn't you tell me that when she died then?"

"I didn't know you were feeling guilty because you felt the same way. I wasn't going to tell *you*, Carol's grieving boyfriend, that she didn't really love you. What kind of heartless bitch would that make me?"

They sat in silence, their half-eaten meal going cold.

Mackenna shivered. The air was suddenly chilly. She picked up the bottle of wine.

"I've got the fire set in the dining room. Let's go up there."

Hugh followed her. "This is new." He patted the couch then sat on it.

"Only for me. My aunty, Caroline, didn't need it anymore."

Hugh watched in silence while she lit the fire and coaxed it to life. Mackenna sat down beside him and refilled their glasses. Still he didn't speak and she was beginning to wonder if she'd done the right thing in telling him about Carol.

He took a sip of wine then leant forward staring at the flames. "Why do you think she drove home that night?"

"I don't know."

"Was she running away?"

"Carol was never one to avoid tricky situations. I think she'd been mulling it over for a while and that night she'd finally come to a decision."

"Then why didn't she tell me?"

"On your graduation night? She didn't hate you."

He shrugged his shoulders.

"She was still your friend, you know," Mackenna said. "Whatever made her leave, I don't think running away was the reason."

They both stared at the flames.

"What a sad, mixed-up pair we've become," Mackenna said. "Carol's probably laughing at us right now."

Hugh sat back. "Time to move on?"

"Yes."

He raised his glass again. "To good friends."

"One for all and all for one."

They laughed at their old childhood motto and drank some more wine. It was cosy by the fire and Mackenna opened another bottle. They were easy friends again, relaxed in each other's company.

Finally Hugh stretched and stood up. "I should get going."

"You can't drive," Mackenna said. "Stay the night."

He gave her a cheeky grin.

She wagged her finger at him. "I'll get the swag," she said. "You can sleep in here by the fire."

"Sold."

Mackenna set up the swag and had just cleared away the glasses when her mobile rang. She was relieved to hear Ginnie's voice. She didn't want to be taking bookings this late.

"Chris and I wanted to talk with you," she said. "Have you got time for a chat?"

"That sounds ominous?" Mackenna joked.

"It won't take long. Are you at the Gatehouse?"

Mackenna was surprised by Ginnie's serious tone. "Yes," she said. "We'll be there soon."

She stared at her phone a moment. The abruptness of the call made her feel uneasy. What could they want? Had something gone wrong with the wine they were supplying? Perhaps they weren't happy with the way she was promoting it? She went to the tasting room and looked at her menu, which clearly named the varieties and gave a small history of Bunyip Wines on the back. They had expressed their delight with it when they'd come for dinner.

A vehicle pulled up at the front door. To her surprise it was Chris and Ginnie. They couldn't have been far away when they made the call.

"Visitors?" Hugh was behind her, a towel draped over his shoulder and the buttons of his shirt half undone.

"Chris and Ginnie," she replied.

"Sorry to turn up at short notice," Ginnie said. She gave Mackenna a peck on the cheek. Chris followed her looking very concerned. They both paused at the sight of Hugh doing up his buttons.

"Hello, Hugh," they murmured together.

"What's up?" Mackenna was going to take them into the tasting room but decided on the dining room instead, where they would see the swag laid out on the floor. She didn't want them jumping to the wrong conclusions. Chris hovered in the doorway as if he'd rather be anywhere but here.

"Chris didn't want to say anything," Ginnie said.

Mackenna's heart lurched. "Say what?" she asked. "What's happened?"

"It's a bit awkward really," Ginnie said, glancing at her husband. "But I thought you should know."

Mackenna flicked her eyes from one to the other. "Know what?"

Chris looked down at his boots.

"Tell me," Mackenna said. Her heart was thumping in her chest.

"Oh for goodness sake, Chris," Ginnie said, "tell her what you heard."

"It's a load of rubbish," Chris snapped. "Just gossip."

"But small town gossip can be dangerous. I think Mackenna should know."

"Please, will one of you tell me what's going on?" Mackenna said.

Hugh put a hand on her shoulder.

Ginnie began. "Evidently, Cam – "

"We think it was Cam," Chris interrupted.

"Cam's been suggesting that he's doing more out here than farm work." Ginnie's words came out in a rush.

Mackenna looked at them. Cam and all his comings and goings whirled around in her head. What could he be up to? "Something illegal?" she said.

"Not exactly," Chris said. "Word is he's getting a few extra perks."

"I'd heard he was selling stuff from his ute at the pub," Hugh said.

Mackenna twisted her head to look at him. "You didn't tell me."

"That's not what Chris means," Ginnie said.

Mackenna could see the discomfort on her friend's face.

"What then?"

"Word is you and he . . . that he's been attending to more than your stock."

"The bloody mongrel." Hugh's hand gripped her shoulder tightly.

Mackenna frowned at Chris. "I still don't get – " She sucked in a breath as realisation struck her. "He reckons he's sharing my bed?"

"As I said, I didn't hear it from Cam. It was another bloke. That Dingo guy who's been in all kinds of trouble. He was shooting his mouth off tonight at the bar. I didn't believe him for a minute, but he was spinning a yarn and there were plenty of flapping ears willing to listen. He seemed to think it was only a matter of time before Cam became a permanent part of Woolly Swamp."

Mackenna let fly a mouthful of words about what she'd like to do with Cam Martin, none of them pleasant. When she finished they were all silent.

Finally Chris spoke up. "We shouldn't have come repeating gossip."

"Rubbish. Mackenna should know what's being said. I don't think it's good manners for a bloke to smear a woman's reputation," Ginnie said primly.

Once again there was silence, then Mackenna burst out laughing.

"Normally I don't care about gossip," she spluttered, "but I'll be damned if I'll allow people to think I'd be that desperate I'd sleep with Cam Martin."

"What will you do?" Ginnie asked.

"I don't know yet, but I'm glad you let me know." She patted Chris on the shoulder. "I know it wasn't easy for you but forewarned is forearmed. Besides," she nodded at Hugh, "it sounds like Cam might be stretching his employment terms even more than I thought."

Ginnie said goodnight and Chris followed forlornly behind.

"Poor guy," Mackenna said as she shut the door.

"Poor guy nothing," Hugh snapped. "He should have shut Dingo up there and then."

"What? Punched him on the nose to defend my honour?" Mackenna laughed.

"What will you do?"

"Dingo's a sly dog and I'm beginning to think Cam's following in his footsteps. What's this about him selling stuff at the pub?"

"I know someone who bought three bags of good quality wheat from him. I don't know what else Cam has been selling but I saw him unloading a few posts and a drum of something at a rundown place in town. You know, out the north side along that dead end dirt road."

"I think Dingo lives out there somewhere. Maybe he's the mate Cam stays with when he's in town."

"What are you going to do?"

"What can I do? It's all gossip and innuendo. I have no proof of anything . . . except I know Cam hasn't been in my bed." She shuddered at the sudden vision of Cam in his boxers.

"We can't let him get away with it."

"I'll think on it." She yawned. "All that wine has made me sleepy."

She waved Hugh goodnight, went to her own room and climbed into bed. Feigning sleepiness had been an excuse to be alone. Mackenna was pretty sure she wouldn't sleep much tonight. Her best friend was leaving the country, her parents' working man was a liar and a thief, and she'd driven off the guy she loved. There was plenty to keep her brain working long into the night.

CHAPTER

36

The beep of a text message prised Mackenna's bleary gaze from the coffee cup she clutched in her hand. She picked up her phone and pulled it close to her face. She didn't recognise the number. The message said, *Can I cook you breakfast?*

She glanced towards the passage door. Was it Hugh being silly? It couldn't be. She had his number with his name stored in her phone. There was no name with this message.

A shiver ran down her back. After what she'd heard last night, could it be Cam using someone else's phone? She was glad Hugh had stayed over. She wrapped her cold fingers back around the coffee cup, grateful for the small burst of warmth against the chilly air. Then she stopped to listen. An engine was approaching and it sounded like a motorbike. It slowed and revved. It *was* a bike. She rushed to the back door in time to see the rider pause beside Hugh's company vehicle. He didn't take his helmet off but it was Adam, she was sure of it. She pushed open the screen door. The bike was already turning away.

Her call was lost in the noise of the motor.

She ran back back inside. She wasn't going to let Adam go this time. He would have jumped to the wrong conclusion with Hugh's vehicle parked at her back door, covered in last night's dew. She snatched up her keys then tossed them down in frustration. Her battery was dead.

Hugh wandered in scratching his head.

"Was that . . .?"

"Adam," she said. "Quick, give me your keys."

He swept them off the bench beside him and tossed them to her.

"Thanks," she called over her shoulder as she ran to his vehicle. She had the four-wheel drive started and in reverse before she'd shut her door. At the gate she clicked on her seatbelt to shut off the incessant beeping of the alarm and turned right towards town. She was guessing that was the way Adam had gone.

She peered ahead and could just make out the dark figure on the bike approaching the main road. She tooted the horn. Once he reached the bitumen she knew he'd be hard to catch. She increased her speed and tooted again. Ahead of her, the bike slowed and she saw the rider look back over his shoulder. She flashed her lights. The bike moved to the side of the road and stopped.

Mackenna came to a halt and jumped out of the vehicle as the rider took off his helmet.

"Adam."

Her step faltered as she saw the expression on his face. His brown eyes had lost their sparkle and there was no warm greeting smile for her.

"What are you doing here, Mackenna?"

"Following you."

"Why?"

"I wanted to talk to you," she said. "Explain . . ."

She bit her lip. His expression was grim. Had she made a mistake coming after him?

"How are your family?" she asked.

"Doing okay. Mum and my uncle have got lots of sorting out to do but I've done all I can for now. They don't need me."

"So you thought you'd come back?"

"You didn't call but . . ."

"I don't have your number."

"I left it with your mum."

Mackenna frowned. "She forgot to give it to me."

"Doesn't matter," Adam said. "I didn't trust that you'd ring anyway."

"So you came back."

"Call me an idiot but I couldn't get you out of my head." Adam shuffled his feet. "I shouldn't have come. You and Hugh – "

She cut him off. "I think you may have the wrong idea about Hugh and me."

Adam's eyes searched hers. She'd come this far, she had to make him understand.

"We've been friends since school," she said. "Friends, that's all. When I was with you there was no-one else, still is no-one else but I thought you'd left me. I thought . . ." She faltered. What more could she say? She didn't want to make a fool of herself again but he'd come to the farm. Surely that meant something. Unless he had simply planned to say goodbye?

Adam looked down. When he lifted his face again it was stretched in a smile. "I think," he said and took a step closer, "you should stop thinking so much and let your heart do the talking."

She opened her mouth and he leant forward and covered her lips with his. One arm went around her and she melted against him. She slid her hands under his jacket and felt his heart beating against her chest. He pressed closer, kissing her again until her body tingled all over in response.

The sound of a distant vehicle made them both pause. A car went past along the main road.

Mackenna dropped her arms but gave him one more kiss. "We'd better get home," she said.

"So we can have some privacy?" His eyes smouldered.

"No. You were going to cook me breakfast." She grinned. "I've worked up an appetite."

Hugh was waiting for them as they both pulled up at the back door.

"Well," he said, shaking Adam's hand. "This wasn't quite the start to the day I was expecting."

"Nor me." Mackenna laughed. She was almost light-headed with happiness.

"You two make a good pair," Hugh said.

"I know." Adam and Mackenna spoke as one, then laughed.

"I don't know why you tried so hard to avoid this bloke." Hugh gave Adam a friendly slap on the shoulder.

"It was complicated." Mackenna turned to Adam. "We've got some talking to do but I think we can sort it."

"Good," Hugh said. "I'd be happier leaving if I knew you two had worked things out."

"What about you?" Mackenna asked.

"There could be some wonderful Canadian woman waiting for me."

"I hope so."

"I'd better head off."

"Won't you stay?" Adam said.

"I owe you breakfast at least," Mackenna added.

"No, I'll be on my way." Hugh leant in and gave her a quick kiss on the cheek. "Be happy, Mackenna."

She smiled at him, a little perplexed at the shift in his mood. "You too," she said. "No more looking back."

He waved. She locked arms with Adam and together they watched as Hugh climbed into his vehicle and drove away. As soon as he was out of sight they were kissing again. Mackenna came up for air first and dragged Adam into the house.

CHAPTER
37

Hugh didn't go home. He went back into town instead. So much of what he and Mackenna had talked about yesterday was still raw. He couldn't believe how easily sleep had taken him last night, burrowed in the swag by the fire. It wasn't until he'd heard Mackenna moving about that he'd woken this morning.

If he went home, his mother would be full of questions. He'd left her a message last night to say he was staying at Mackenna's and knowing his mother, she would have already put two and two together to make six. He wasn't ready to face that yet, so he decided to go into the office.

He parked out the back and took the side door into the shop. The Saturday morning staff were stocking shelves and dealing with customers. He gave them a wave, let himself into his office and shut the door. Ted would be back in another week. All Hugh had to do was get the paperwork up to date for handover and he was a free agent.

He sat at the desk. It only seemed a short time ago that he'd arrived full of trepidation about his decision to fill in for Ted. Living at home again hadn't turned out to be so bad and now he felt he would be able to explain his Canadian venture to his parents without fear of their adverse reaction. He and Mackenna were back on a strong friendship basis and he was happy that she had a good bloke like Adam in her life. It was Mackenna's revelation about Carol's feelings the night before she died that bothered him now. Carol hadn't planned to drive back to the South East that night, so why did she do it? It was that question he always came back to.

He went through the paperwork on his desk. Carol played on his mind as keenly as she had after the accident. He'd mourned for her and carried guilt for her death for so long the two were part of his being. Even though the psychologist had helped with strategies, Carol had always been with him but now he was more confused than ever. If they were both doubting their love for each other, what happened? Was it her own guilt that urged her to get in her car and drive home, or something else?

He slapped the folder he'd been holding to the desk in frustration. Mackenna had given him a reason to let go of his guilt but he was still no closer to finding an answer for Carol's trip home. After all these years there was no-one else to ask.

"Carol," he muttered and put his head in his hands. "Why?"

Hugh sat like that for quite a while then it struck him. Maybe the Thompsons knew something he didn't. Sid had blamed him for Carol's return home that night but Hugh hadn't seen Beryl Thompson since the funeral. Carol had been very close to her mother, maybe she knew something.

Hugh thought about Sid. After the funeral he'd physically threatened Hugh to keep away from them. He remembered Sid's face only centimetres from his own. The man had trembled with pent-up rage and Hugh had been afraid of him. But after seeing him in the street a while back, Sid was not the bull of a man he used to be. He'd aged a lot in the ensuing years.

Hugh snatched up his keys. He didn't know how he'd go but he had to try to talk to the Thompsons before he left town.

Their farm wasn't as far out of town as Woolly Swamp or Morning Star. Hugh rolled in over the grid and pulled up near the gate in the house yard. The place was run down. All around were piles of discarded farm junk, the house fence was leaning over and nothing but weeds grew in the dustbowl that had once been a lawn.

There were no dogs and no vehicle parked outside. Hugh walked up the cracked cement path. Near the back door several pairs of dirty boots and shoes littered the verandah and a few old bones attracted the flies. They must still have at least one dog.

Hugh went to knock on the tatty screen door but it opened before he could reach it.

"Hugh?" Beryl Thompson stooped in the doorway. She glanced over his shoulder then her worried eyes met his. "What brings you here?"

Hugh hesitated. He hadn't thought about what he was going to say when he got here.

"I'm going away, Mrs Thompson. I wanted to see you before I left."

"You've already been away for a long time, haven't you?"

"Yes, but this time I'm going to Canada."

She studied him a moment. "Away is away," she said.

"I saw Mr Thompson in town the other day."

"He didn't mention it."

She gave another look over his shoulder. Hugh wanted to turn and look behind him as well, but he resisted the urge.

"How are you?" he asked.

"I have my good days and my bad days but I'm surviving. Would you like a cup of tea?"

"Thank you."

Beryl stepped back to let him inside and looked out over the yard before she pulled the door shut behind them.

"Have a seat," she said.

He looked around the kitchen. Nearly every surface was covered with stacks of papers or boxes or household items, and dirty dishes were piled in the sink. Two chairs were clear of clutter. Hugh sat on one. He wondered where Mr Thompson was. He didn't ask.

Beryl sat opposite him and poured a cup of tea from the pot on the table. He noticed how her hand shook. She topped up her own cup and pulled a tin closer.

"Can you take the lid off please? There are biscuits inside."

Hugh did as he was asked.

"So, what's taking you to Canada?" she asked.

"Work," Hugh said. "A research project, breeding sheep for specific qualities."

"You always liked working with animals. Carol was the same. I was surprised when she wanted to do nursing but she was good at it."

They both sipped their tea staring at the biscuits that neither of them touched. Hugh thought desperately for something to say but Beryl beat him to it.

"You've never . . . you don't have a woman in your life?"

"No."

"You're young, Hugh. Carol wouldn't have wanted you to be alone." She reached a trembling hand to touch his cheek. "You were such good kids, so full of life and adventure." "I still think of her every day and wonder what might have been. Where would her career have taken her? Would you two have married, come back here, had babies?" Her hand dropped to her side and Hugh saw the tears well in her eyes. "Such a waste."

She turned away. "Sid's bringing in some sheep. We're crutching next week."

Hugh thought about the work that took place to make that happen. Although the Thompsons' was a small property, times like crutching and shearing needed extra hands outdoors and food to be supplied. Mrs Thompson didn't look like she had the strength to do much at all.

"That must be difficult for you," he said.

"We manage." She nodded stiffly to the door. "Sid's happiest when he's out working. Since Carol . . . it's been hard on him and my illness has been an extra burden. Some days I can't even get out of bed."

Hugh clutched his cup. Who was he to talk about his pain? He was getting on with his life but Beryl Thompson was trapped in hers.

"I should have come to see you before this," he said.

"Sid would have made it difficult."

Hugh looked at the deep worry lines etched on her face and then into her weary eyes.

"Seeing Carol's friends, especially you and Mackenna, that would have helped me but not Sid. He was angry that you were alive and Carol wasn't."

"He made it clear I wasn't welcome."

"Threatened you, no doubt." Beryl shook her head. "Sid was always a difficult man but Carol's death . . ." She sucked in a breath.

"Do you know why she drove home that night?" Hugh asked the question before his courage failed him.

Once again Beryl turned her tired eyes to his. His chest tightened as he recognised the look in them. He'd seen it in his own reflection in the mirror so many times. Hugh knew what guilt looked like.

Beryl picked up her cup with two hands, took a sip and carefully placed it down again. "I'd been to the doctor that day and received the news about this illness. Sid's never been an easy man to talk to, so I rang Carol. She'd just finished her shift and we talked for ages." Tears seeped from Beryl's eyes. "She was my rock. She was so reassuring, so level-headed when I had gone to pieces." Beryl looked at Hugh. "I didn't ask her to come home but she knew I was upset and worried about telling Sid. I think . . . well, I'm sure she must have decided to come home to support me. I never told Sid about that call and, of course, with the accident it wasn't until later I told him about my diagnosis. He blamed that on Carol's death as well. She didn't tell you she was coming home?"

"No." Hugh shook his head. Carol must have been more upset than she let on to her mother. "She may have tried to call me before she left but I got home late that night. Neither of us had mobile phones back then."

"I blame myself. She was probably tired, if I hadn't called her . . ."

"Carol would have expected you to call her."

"I know that but . . ."

"It was simply an accident." Finally Hugh could say those words and believe them. "Carol hadn't been drinking, she'd made that trip at night a hundred times before. We're never going to know exactly what went wrong, but it *was* an accident."

They both looked up at the distant bark of a dog and once again Beryl stared past him to the door.

"Sid had to blame someone." She fixed her eyes back on Hugh. He could see the sorrow in them. "I'm so sorry it was you. I guessed when you didn't come and see us that it was more than your grief that kept you away, but I couldn't tell him. If he shifted that blame to me . . . please don't despise me. It was easier to let Sid hate someone who wasn't around. He's all I've got now."

Hugh sat back. A mixture of anger and pity surged through him for this woman who he'd once thought of as a friend.

"I'm weak, I know," she said. "I didn't only lose my daughter but also her friends. I've missed you all."

The barking of the dog was getting closer, accompanied by the sound of a horn tooting. Hugh stood up. He wasn't sure how he'd react if he ran into Sid right now.

"I'd better go," he said.

Beryl's eyes were dry when she looked up at him. "Good luck in Canada. Please come back and see me when you come home, and maybe Mackenna would call by."

"I'll ask her."

"Thank you."

Hugh left her sitting at the table and let himself out the door. He couldn't help but wonder how different life might have been for him had he known Carol's true feelings and her reason for driving home that night.

Outside, it had turned into a beautiful day, sunny with clear skies and barely a breath of wind. Not what the farmers wanted but perfect weather to set up the surprise gifts for his mother's garden. That was what he looked forward to as he drove out of the Thompsons' gate.

CHAPTER
38

Mackenna parked the ute behind her car and scooped up the bags of groceries sprawled across the seat beside her. She flew across the space to the back door and into her kitchen. Adam wasn't there. She tiptoed down the passage and peeped around her bedroom door. He was fast asleep where she'd left him, in her bed. Goosebumps prickled down her back. Only a few hours ago they'd been truly reunited in that bed. She smiled at the memory.

She pulled the door closed and went back to the kitchen. As much as she'd love to jump back into bed with him, she had work to do and sleep was probably what he needed after his family's bereavement and his long ride to get here.

She made another trip out to the ute to get the rest of the shopping. She'd picked up a new battery for her car but that would have to wait. She had two bookings for tonight and there was prep work to be done.

She was bent over the cured meat, concentrating on shaving long thin slices when she was startled by an arm slipping around her waist.

"I've got a knife," she said, then felt a shudder roll down her as the stubble of Adam's cheek brushed her neck.

"Best put it down then," he murmured in her ear. "Can't have you hurting yourself."

"You'd better put some clothes on." She laughed. "I wouldn't want to slip."

"I'm going to the shower."

She watched him amble to the door then quickly turned her back on his naked body.

"Damn it," she muttered. There was so much to do but she'd rather be following him to the shower. Her mobile rang. It was her chef friend in Adelaide. She hadn't heard from him for quite a while.

By the time Adam came back wrapped in one of her towels she was dancing around the kitchen. His eyes opened wide as she flew at him and flung her arms around him.

"Whoa! Steady!" he yelped as she caught him off guard.

She ignored his complaints and kissed him.

He quickly responded. Finally, she stepped back.

"I'm so excited."

"I can see that."

"Woolly Swamp lamb will be a feature of my friend's new menu. He's head chef at a swanky restaurant in Adelaide."

"That's great news."

"Great! It's fantastic. Of course there's a bit to organise to get the meat to them but at least we're moving beyond the local area."

Mackenna wrapped her arms around him again. "First you arrive on my doorstep and now this." She kissed him and they were quickly lost in each other's embrace again. The towel he'd been wearing fell to the ground and his hands slid inside her shirt. Mackenna forgot all about the food she'd been preparing.

Adam dug in his bag for some fresh clothes. Making love with Mackenna twice in one morning wasn't something he'd complain about but after his early start and long ride he was feeling weary. Mackenna had told him to stay in bed and get some more rest but he was hungry. He'd missed breakfast and now it was past lunchtime.

There was a loud bang from the kitchen followed by some very expressive words. He went in to see what she was doing.

"Can I help?" he asked.

She brushed a loose curl from her face with the back of her free hand. "I'm way behind with the food prep."

He leaned in and brushed his cheek softly past hers. "I can stay focused if you can."

He chuckled at her sharp intake of breath.

"That's playing dirty," she said. "Just for that you can chop that pumpkin. It's as hard as a rock."

The smell of roasting garlic mingled with that of hot pastry made his stomach grumble loudly.

"Oh, you poor thing," she said. "Have you eaten at all today?"

"A cup of coffee before I left Horsham." That had been very early this morning.

"There are some hot sausage rolls. Would you like some?"

"Anything," he said and his stomach rumbled again in anticipation.

He retrieved the apron from its spot behind the door and attacked the pumpkin in between taking bites from the plate of sausage rolls she'd put beside him. While he chopped, Mackenna took two more calls. They'd have a full house tonight by the sound of it. She was so excited but he was worried how she'd manage the Gatehouse as well as the property. He hadn't realised how much work was involved in farming until his stay at Woolly Swamp. There was plenty to keep Mackenna, Lyle and Cam busy as well as Patrick when he was here.

"Taste this," Mackenna said.

He licked purée from the spoon she held in front of him.

"Mmm. That's good. Parsnip and garlic?"

"I caramelised the garlic first," she said. "It's not too strong?"

"No. What's it for?"

"I'm doing crispy shoulder of lamb. Mum has parsnips in her garden but there's not enough to serve everyone as a vegetable dish."

"I'd add a bit more pepper."

Mackenna was instantly back at her pan. He watched as she added pepper and tasted again. She smiled at him. Adam felt his own face lift in a grin. He turned back to the pumpkin and hacked into it again. He needed the diversion. Mackenna was right. They had a big night ahead of them and working hard would stop his mind from wandering to what he'd much rather be doing with her.

CHAPTER
39

Mackenna crept across the room and gathered her clothes in the moonlight. Adam's gentle snores continued behind her as she slipped into the chilly bathroom. Yesterday had been sheer bliss. They'd slept in after Saturday night's late dinner and welcomed the new day with the gentle rediscovery of each other's bodies. Then they'd had the rest of the day and the whole property, totally to themselves.

She'd taken him with her to feed the dogs and the chooks, to check irrigators and sheep, a perfect day followed by an early night. She smiled, wishing she was still cuddled up next to him but there were sheep to take to market and Cam would be here soon.

Mackenna hadn't given the illusive working man a thought since Adam's return but she needed to get her head around what to do about him. Trouble was, she didn't know. If he was helping himself to small amounts of grain, a roll of wire, a bottle of chemical, it would be hard to prove unless she caught him in the act. Everything she'd heard about Cam was possible, except him being in her bed, and there was no way in hell that would happen.

She pulled her jacket tight against the early morning air. The pup danced around her feet excitedly and King walked steadily at her side as she made her way to the yards where the mob of crossbreeds were beginning to stir. No sign of Cam, so she started the truck and sat watching the gauges while it warmed up.

"Damn it," she muttered. The fuel gauge hardly moved.

She stomped around to keep her circulation moving while the diesel flowed. In the light of her torch she could see the storage tank needed refilling as well – too many people using it and no-one keeping an eye on the levels. She wondered if her mum had booked the tanker to call before she left.

Mackenna climbed back into the truck to shift it to the sheep yards. Something Garry had said during crutching lurked on the edge of her memory. A guy that looked like Cam in a truck that looked like theirs on the other side of Naracoorte and he was carting sheep. That was the weekend Cam had helped his mate shift house and the truck had been gone for several days. She tried to remember what jobs Cam had been doing around that time. So much had happened since then it was too hard to pinpoint what he'd been doing on a particular day.

She backed the truck up to the ramp and looked over the gauges again, her eyes lingering on the odometer. She pulled a notebook from her pocket and scribbled the numbers. What she thought she would do with them she had no idea.

"Hey, boss."

"Bloody hell!" She jumped at Cam's cheery greeting.

"Thought you'd be pleased to see me." His face tilted in that lazy smile.

Mackenna glanced around. "I didn't hear you arrive."

"I got in late last night." He nodded over his shoulder. "Stayed at the house."

She peered past him. The house was a distant shape against the lightening sky. There were no lights on and there hadn't been when she'd let the dogs out. She hadn't noticed Cam's ute anywhere. It felt odd him being in her family home when no-one else was there, but not surprising. He did have a bed there.

"Thought you might have slept there too."

His comment drew her eyes back to his. "I live in the Gatehouse now."

"I know, but to keep an eye on things while your folks are away." His smile stretched wider and he leant closer. "There's only the two of us."

Mackenna stiffened. The gossip Chris had related from the pub no longer seemed funny with Cam looming over her. This wasn't the time or the place to mention it – if she was going to mention it at all.

"And plenty of work to do." She stepped briskly past him and rolled her ankle on a loose stone. The pain was swift and sharp. Well aware he'd be watching, she bit her lip and kept walking as if nothing had happened.

"Let's get these sheep loaded," she said over her shoulder.

They were finished in good time. Cam tried to engage her in conversation but she kept her responses brief. They didn't have time to waste or he wouldn't make the markets, but there was also the part of her that no longer wanted to make idle conversation with him. Mackenna was so glad Adam had come back. She wasn't frightened of Cam, but in light of the things she'd heard in the last few days he gave her the creeps.

She saw him off. He took King with him and she kept Prince. The young dog was proving to be a quick learner but he wasn't ready for the complexity of sheep markets yet.

"Come on, boy," she said. "We've got work to do."

Prince yapped in delight from the tray of the ute as Mackenna made her way around the property. She glanced up at the clear sky. They'd taken a risk with the couple of paddocks they'd seeded early and it seemed it would be money down the drain now.

She gave a quick thought to Adam back at the Gatehouse. He would be up and she was getting hungry. She just wanted to check the pivot irrigator that had been giving them trouble, and even before she got close she could see something was wrong. One end was at a funny angle and water trickled from it. It should have turned itself off.

Mackenna jumped from the ute and squelched through the sodden ground to the machine. A quick glance told her the problem was much more major than the O ring Cam had replaced last week. Expensive as well, she was sure.

She ducked down to take another look at the motor and her hat fell into the mud.

"Damn it!" She whistled up Prince. Breakfast might have to be a piece of toast on the way into town.

Adam was flicking through her pile of rural magazines when she got back.

"Uh-oh!" he said. "I hope that frown's not for me?"

"I didn't realise I was frowning." She reached around him and gave him a hug, nestling into his back and smelling the freshness of his skin. She closed her eyes a moment. Nothing seemed as bad when she was with him.

He pulled her onto his lap.

"What's up?"

"One of the irrigators has broken down. I think it will mean big dollars." She kissed him. "I have to go into town."

"I'll come with you." His eyes sparkled and he rubbed the end of her nose with his finger. "You might want to wash your face first.

Being a Kiwi I like the mud look, but I'm not sure how it goes down around here."

He chuckled and Mackenna had to drag herself away from him. She'd never had any trouble getting on with work but with Adam around it was suddenly proving difficult.

CHAPTER
40

Louise settled herself into the chair, glanced once more at the man behind the reception desk and began to type. She hadn't planned to use a computer while they were away but with some time to herself she decided to email the children and her sisters. Last week she'd posted cards from Wellington but there was little point sending more from Queenstown. They would probably beat them home. She sent an email instead, giving a quick rundown of their South Island travels and a bit about their farm visit to appease Mackenna.

Lyle had been so interested and got on so well with the bloke who ran the place, he'd gone back to see more today but not Louise. She'd come on holiday to get away from the farm.

She peeped around the monitor. The receptionist was talking on the phone. Louise inhaled deeply then opened a new web page. She quickly typed their banking username and password. She hoped these communal computers were safe. She'd only ever done the online banking from home but with time on her hands she wanted to check the accounts. The last payment for their wool should be close. It would make her feel better about what she'd just spent in the shops if she could see a large credit rather than only debits.

She gasped as the list of their farm bank accounts opened on the screen. They had been low when she left but the working account was almost empty. She clicked on the link, fear rising in her throat. It should have plenty of money in it for day-to-day expenses. She'd always calculated how much they needed to live on with accuracy. The backup account was low but that was to be expected with this holiday, Patrick's car and Mackenna's Gatehouse. The working account should have enough to last them another month.

Her eyes flicked down the screen as the detailed account page opened. The figures wobbled and she blinked, forcing her eyes to focus. She looked at the list of payments and it dawned on her.

"Crutching," she muttered.

She glanced down at the shopping bags at her feet. She'd used her personal account, money she'd been saving a long time for this holiday but the excitement of her purchases had soured. They'd be living on the overdraught until the wool cheque arrived, and that would be needed to pay the seeding bills.

She logged out of the site. Why had she looked at their bank accounts today? It was only a few more days until they went home. This holiday was so special, spending time together, just the two of them, away from the farm. Just what the doctor ordered for Lyle – for both of them really.

Louise picked up her bags and headed for the lift. The doors closed and she couldn't help but smile. They'd giggled and kissed like teenagers in this same lift only last night. They'd both had a few drinks but it had been more than the alcohol. For a short time Louise had felt the euphoria of no responsibility – no meals to get, no accounts to keep, no community fundraisers – and a husband who had found his mojo again.

She kept the smile in place as she entered their room with its beautiful view across the lake and she felt her strength return. She wasn't going to let money spoil this holiday, but it was a good opportunity to discuss the future. They'd made a succession plan when Lyle had been sick but they'd done nothing about it. A united front was needed. Lyle had to agree.

By the time she heard his card in the lock she had a strategy all mapped out.

She poured him a beer and greeted him at the door.

"What's this?" he said. "Are you intending to get me drunk again, Lou?"

"I thought we'd have a few drinks for our last night in this pretty spot," she chided, "not an orgy."

"No." He winked. "That was last night."

She smiled and picked up her wine. It was hardly an orgy but last night had certainly been pleasurable.

"I've ordered a meal from room service," she said. "We can enjoy the view, relax, talk . . ." Her voice trailed off.

Lyle was watching her closely. "What's up?"

"Nothing." She stood at the window. The light was fading and the first lights were beginning to glint across the water. "I felt like a quiet night before our last leg back to Christchurch."

"And?"

"And what?"

"I can tell there's something going on in that head of yours."

Louise sighed and slid onto one of the dining chairs. "I checked the bank accounts today."

"Oh?" Lyle came to join her. "What's up?"

"The accounts are nearly in the red."

"There'll be a wool cheque soon."

"I know, but that will be swallowed up."

Lyle draped his arm across her shoulders. "Stop fretting. We've got good credit with the bank. We've been in overdraught plenty of times before."

"I know that." A surge of anger loosened her resolve to keep calm. "We had been steadily staying in the black before Mackenna started having her grand ideas about improvements. Now we owe money for stock, money for land, money everywhere including that Gatehouse idea of hers. We should have insisted it be kept a simple working man's cottage. Then there's Cam's wages. If Mackenna hadn't made all these changes, we wouldn't need a working man and – "

"Whoa! Steady up, Lou." Lyle put both hands in the air. "Where has all this come from?"

"We made our wills but we've done nothing about them."

"Wills are for dead people." He grinned. "We're not dead."

"Be serious, Lyle," she snapped. "We should be taking more time for enjoying life like this, not worrying about money."

He sighed. "What is it that you want?"

"I want our kids to know about our plans so they can decide what to do."

"Haven't you mapped out their future as well?"

Louise regretted her outburst when she saw the anger smouldering in his eyes. This wasn't going as she'd planned. She softened her tone.

"Of course not but if they knew about the future we've planned for, they could factor that into their own plans."

"But they're not getting a choice."

Louise frowned at him. "What do you mean?"

"Even after all that's happened since my heart attack, you want to cut Mackenna out."

"Not cut her out – "

"No matter how you say it, we have cut her out." He thrust back his chair and stood at the window. His back was ramrod straight. His words came out in a murmur. "It's her inheritance, Louise."

"If Mackenna keeps spending like she has been there will be no farm to inherit." Louise stepped up beside him. "We have a son, Lyle. It's his right."

"He doesn't want it. Mackenna's the one who wants to farm."

"We've talked about this. I don't want her to be tied to the property. She works too hard. She should be doing something else – going out with friends, getting married, having babies. The farm is such a tie."

"I don't see it that way."

"Because you're a man."

"So you think Patrick wants this weight around his neck?"

"Men work farms." There. She'd said it. No matter what Lyle said and how much interest Mackenna showed, it was the male's right to inherit.

Lyle shook his head. "How can you choose between our children?"

"You already have. Mackenna gets free reign to do whatever she wants with the farm and all Patrick gets is a car."

"And an education, HECS fees paid, accommodation in the city – which we're still helping with even though he's working now. Anyway, it was their choice. They've both had a chance to do what they want to do."

"Patrick would step up if Mackenna wasn't in his way."

They glared at each other. Louise pressed her lips together. How had her carefully planned discussion turned into this? She looked out the window. Night had fallen and lights glittered in the blackness.

Finally Lyle spoke. "I don't want to argue, Lou."

"I'm sorry," she said taking his hand, "neither do I."

"What will we do?"

"We have to tell them. If Mackenna really wants to stay she can, but Patrick needs to prepare to take it all on when we no longer can."

There was a knock on the door and a voice called, "Room service!"

A bright young man wheeled in a trolley and parked it next to their small table. Lyle made conversation with him and saw him out. Louise poured another glass of wine for herself and opened another beer for Lyle. They sat down and lifted the lid off the food.

"This smells good," he said.

Louise pulled her lips into a smile. She'd ordered lamb. Another reminder of what they'd argued about. She should have asked for the fish.

CHAPTER
41

"Keep your eyes closed." Hugh glanced back at his mother, expecting to see her peeping.

"I am," Mary said. "What are you up to?"

Molly sat at her feet. Her bell tinkled as she licked her paw.

Hugh jumped back to the verandah beside his mother.

"Now you can open them."

She blinked as her eyes adjusted to the light.

"What have you . . . oh, Hugh."

She hurried forward to the table and chairs that Rory had restored. Molly beat her to it, already making circles on one of the seats.

"This is my old setting," Mary cried. "It looks brand new."

"Rory Heinrich did it."

"I thought he made things from corrugated iron."

"He does much more than that." Hugh took his mother's hand. "Come and see."

"What else have you done?"

"You'll see."

He led her off the verandah and under the branches of the secret garden they'd been working on. He watched her face as she glanced around. Her eyes opened wide in surprise and she put her hands to her mouth.

"A birdbath," she murmured through her fingers. She flung her arms around Hugh's neck. "Thank you," she said.

"Do you like it?"

Mary let him go. She ran her hand over the small bronze bird perched on the edge of the old plough disk that Rory had turned into a bowl.

"I love it," she said.

"That stump it's sitting on is from that old tree that fell down. You've got one of its branches for your seat." Hugh nodded at the big log he'd helped her position when he'd first come home.

"It's perfect."

She turned to him and he could see tears brimming in her eyes.

"Thank you," she said.

"You're welcome."

Mary dug in her pocket and pulled out a hanky.

"You're not meant to cry," Hugh said.

She blew her nose and dabbed at her eyes. "It's the most special gift."

Hugh felt a pang of remorse. He'd helped her with the garden because he enjoyed it, but a part of him knew it was also his way of trying to make up for not being home much. He knew that was the gift she wanted most and he couldn't give it to her.

"You go and sit on the verandah," he said brightly, "and I'll make us a cup of tea."

He'd thought she might argue but she didn't. Instead, she called out there were fresh biscuits in the tin and let him go.

When he came back his mother was just coming out of the secret garden with Molly firmly clasped in her arms.

"I'll have to put more bells on her collar." Mary chuckled. "She's already been checking out the birdbath and helping herself to a drink. She probably thinks it's a giant water bowl just for her."

Hugh set the tray on the table and they both sat down. The day had been warm but the wind had dropped out. Grey clouds were spreading across the sky.

"Do you think it will rain?" Mary asked.

"Forecast is saying rain but only one to five millimetres. Even if that does fall it's not enough."

"We'll take any we can get."

They lapsed into silence. Hugh took a deep breath. He needed to tell his mother about his plans and now was the best chance he had.

"Mum – "

Mary cut him off. "You've done so much around here since you've been home. Fixing up that back verandah was such a surprise. It's been propped up for so long we didn't notice it anymore." She paused. "Your father appreciated it as well."

Hugh twisted his lips into a smile. His father would never say it but Hugh got the feeling he was finally seeing his youngest son as doing something useful. A pity that was all going to change.

"Mum . . ."

"You're not going to stay, are you?" she said.

There were no tears in her eyes now. He shook his head.

Her teeth clenched as she looked away.

"I'm sorry, Mum."

"Don't apologise." She stroked the cat on her lap.

"I've really enjoyed being home. I didn't . . ." He faltered and Molly's crackly purr punctuated the air between them.

"You didn't want to be home, did you?"

"Not at first." Hugh decided to be honest. "I've conquered a few demons over these last weeks."

Mary looked up at him with a puzzled expression. "Your father really only wants what's best for you. We both do."

"I know. That's not what I meant."

"Carol?"

Hugh nodded and took a mouthful of tea to hide his surprise. His mother had got it in one.

"You've carried that guilt for too long, love. You weren't to blame."

"I understand that now."

"Good. Maybe you'll come home more often in the future."

Once again they lapsed into silence.

"What about Mackenna?" Mary asked.

"We're good mates again."

"I'm glad, although I have a feeling Louise Birch was lining you up as her future son-in-law."

"Really?" Hugh felt a small pang of sadness for lost possibilities.

"Is there something else?"

He glanced at his mother and looked away.

"This isn't a criticism but you've hardly been home in ten years, love, and when you did come home you were like a shadow. I worried about you. Lately you've been much more like the old Hugh. Was there more to it than grieving for Carol?"

Hugh clasped his hands tightly then let them go. If he didn't tell his mother now, he never would.

Mary reached across and gripped his hand. "What is it, love?"

Hugh lifted his gaze to meet his mother's. "I'm okay now," he said and knew he meant it, "but when I took that job in Victoria I suffered panic attacks."

Mary gripped his hand tighter but didn't say a word.

"It was exactly two years after Carol's death. I'd just shifted to the Gippsland and didn't know a soul except for the bloke who employed me. Thankfully there was an agricultural counsellor working for the business." Hugh would never forget her calm reassurance. "Jenny took me to a GP and a psychologist. Together they got me through it."

When he thought back he could remember little of the first terrible month he was there. All he could recall was the pain and the sensation that his body was constantly on high alert. He'd craved sleep but his mind refused to rest. He'd tried to eat but the lump in his throat wouldn't let him.

Mary let go his hand. Her face was creased in a frown. "Did they tell you why it happened? You'd think if it was Carol's death it would have happened sooner."

He recalled that first anxiety attack like it was yesterday. He'd arrived in town late one afternoon, checked out the office and then the accommodation. The bloke in charge had rounded up a few others and they'd come over with pizza and beer. It had been a big night.

"The psychologist told me when emotions are repressed they can resurface with the simplest connection. There was an old couch in the flat I was renting. It was the same as the one in the flat I shared with Carol. The night she left I'd fallen asleep on the couch in front of the television. I didn't even know she'd gone until the police woke me."

"Oh, love."

"Two years later there I am in a new town having a big night with the blokes from work, and I fell asleep on the couch." Hugh paused. "In the early hours of the morning I jumped awake. My heart was hammering and I felt terrible – like I was going to die. Who'd have thought a tatty old couch would have such power?"

Mary got up from her chair and wrapped her arms around him. "Oh, Hugh."

He stood up so she didn't have to bend and extricated himself from her hug. "I'm fine now. I've been to hell and back but I really am okay now."

"I can't bear the thought that you went through it alone."

"I wasn't alone. I had the right people to help me."

She put a hand gently on his cheek. "But I wasn't there."

"I had to conquer it myself. There was nothing you could do."

"You're wrong, Hugh. You didn't give us a chance. We would have supported you through a terrible time."

Hugh looked into his mother's gentle eyes and thought of his father.

"All of us," she said and kissed him on the cheek. "Let's sit down again. Tell me about this job you're taking."

"It's in Canada."

She paused momentarily then settled herself on her chair.

"It's the research project I was telling you about," Hugh said. "It's a great opportunity."

"When do you go?"

"A few weeks."

Hugh watched his mother's profile as she stared straight ahead.

"I'm so glad we worked on the garden together," she said. "I won't miss you so much when I'm out here." Finally she turned to look at him. "Dad will miss you too."

"What about the Sutton property he was going to buy?"

"We want you to be happy, love. We knew something was wrong, we just didn't know what. Your dad thought offering you a place of your own might be the answer."

"I'm sorry."

"Don't be sorry," she said with a tiny smile. "You're a good, clever man. Your dad and I only want what's best for you. If that's researching in Canada, then you do it." Her smile grew wider. "Maybe we could come and visit you."

"Of course." Hugh wasn't sure that would ever happen but he knew he'd be more than happy if they did.

CHAPTER
42

"I'm good at trussing things up," Adam said.

"I could get Dad's gun," Hugh added.

"Big help you two are." Mackenna laughed. It was a relief after her tense day working with Cam. She wasn't any closer to sorting out what was going on with him. On the surface he seemed to do his job but she no longer trusted him.

At the end of the day he'd taken off to town and she'd come home to find Adam had cooked dinner. They invited Hugh to join them. She told them about Cam and her concerns for all the things he was possibly up to. With a few beers under their belts, they'd started making outrageous suggestions to get rid of him.

"Seriously, your dad will be home soon," Adam said.

"What's that got to do with it?"

"Maybe he should sort it out."

"What's he going to do that I can't?" Mackenna bristled.

"Don't go there, mate," Hugh said and made a silly face.

"I need a plan." Mackenna drummed her fingers on the table.

"What sort of a plan?" Adam asked.

"Some way of catching him in the act. He's too good at covering his tracks."

"So what's he actually done, apart from being a big-noting smart-arse?"

"Tell it like it is, Adam." Hugh chuckled and got them all another beer.

"You hardly know him," Mackenna said. She was surprised at Adam's strong reaction.

"I shared a room with him."

"That would do it," Hugh said and clinked his bottle against Adam's.

"I'd forgotten." Mackenna fell silent. It was her fault Adam had been bunked in with Cam.

"So while you were sharing a room," Hugh went on, "did you find out anything that might be useful?"

"He snores."

"Anything that might be useful in finding out what he's been up to?"

"Not really. I just don't like the guy."

"Ditto," Hugh said.

"I had no idea you both felt that way," Mackenna said. "I must admit my first impression of Cam was he was a bit over-confident but he appeared to be doing the job." She stopped as she recalled her first weeks at home from holiday.

"He made eyes at you, didn't he?" Adam banged his beer on the table and Mackenna jumped.

"I wouldn't say that," she said. "Don't go getting all macho protective over me. I can deal with Cam if I have to. I'm not sucked in by his attempt at charm."

"Your mum is," Adam replied. "He has her wrapped around his little finger."

"He's been misleading people about his relationship with Mackenna too," Hugh said.

"What does that mean?" Adam looked from Hugh to Mackenna.

"It's only gossip," she said.

"It becomes gospel quickly with some people," Hugh said.

"So back to my plan." Mackenna tapped the table again. "Cam's slack with his work but always seems to shift the blame elsewhere. That's annoying but it's not illegal."

"He gossips by the sound of it," Adam said.

Mackenna glanced at him. "Once again not illegal."

"Do you want to get rid of him?" Hugh asked.

"There's no point in having a working man I can't trust."

"Cam has been selling things at the pub but we've no proof they're stolen." Hugh held up a finger. "I saw him dropping things off at his mate's place but we don't know they weren't his." Hugh held up another finger. "He takes your truck on long trips that don't seem to be related to your farm." He raised a third finger. "That's three strikes but none of them can call him out."

Mackenna bolted upright. "Yes," she said. "Garry Finn said he thought he'd seen Cam before. He reckons Cam was carting for the farm where Garry and his team were crutching, out the other side of Naracoorte."

"What does that mean?" Adam asked.

"He's driving our truck to do jobs for other people."

"And I'd be guessing he's charging them cash to do it and filling up at your diesel tank," Hugh said.

"How am I going to catch him out?" Mackenna pushed back her chair and started pacing the floor. "I need a plan." It was all very well to say it but she was no closer to working out what. She thought about the truck. It was the best bet. Everything else was too tricky, but if he was doing jobs for other people in the Woolly Swamp truck . . . She patted her chest with her hand.

"What's the matter?" Adam asked.

"Nothing." She pulled her notebook out of her shirt pocket, flipped through the pages and stared at the numbers she'd scribbled there.

"What is it?" Hugh asked.

"The odometer reading for the truck." She waved the little book at them. "I'll keep jotting it down. Next time he drives it I'll be able to tell if he's done the job we asked him to. If he's doing another job for someone else there will be a whole lot of extra kilometres."

"He'll have an excuse for it," Adam said. "He's got a smooth tongue."

"Not if I've followed him and watched what he's up to," Mackenna said. "Then I can talk to whoever he does the delivery for."

"Hang on a minute." Adam's face was serious. "Cam thinks he's getting away with stuff now. You don't know how he might react if he's cornered."

"Adam's right." Hugh pitched in. "He'll get cagey if he notices you. We need a person he won't recognise if he sees them."

"Who's that going to be?" Mackenna put her hands on her hips.

"And you'll need a vehicle," Hugh said.

"Or a bike."

They both looked at Adam.

"He knows you, though," Hugh said.

"But a guy on a bike under a helmet could be anyone." Mackenna grinned. "And I don't think he even knows you're here."

"Not unless you've mentioned it," Adam said. "I've only been out of the house for our trip to town yesterday."

"He doesn't know you're here." Mackenna said it with such conviction both men studied her.

"It's just a feeling I get." She shrugged her shoulders. "The things he says. He thinks we're alone on the property."

"I don't like the sound of that," Hugh said.

Adam's chair scraped across the floor. "Neither do I."

"Perhaps we should be visible." Hugh stood up, too. "So he knows you're not alone."

Mackenna glanced from one to the other. She covered her unease with a laugh. "For goodness sake, you two, you look like you're about to arrange a shoot-out at high noon."

Adam slipped an arm around her. "I don't like the idea of that creep making eyes at you."

"I can handle Cam." She gave Adam a quick kiss. "Besides, he might not know you're here but I do."

"My cue to leave, I think," Hugh said. He shook Adam's hand. "Thanks for the meal."

Mackenna gave Hugh a hug. "Thanks for coming."

"You take care," he said with a pointed look.

They waved him off and began to clear up the dishes.

"Maybe I should put in an appearance tomorrow," Adam said. "Let Cam know I'm here."

"No," Mackenna said quickly.

Adam's eyebrows shot up.

"I don't want him to know yet. I like coming home to you with no-one else around." She threw her arms around his neck, kissed him then leant back to look into his eyes. "And you can cook."

"That's why you've got me locked up here, as your slave."

She pulled his head closer so their lips were nearly touching.

"There are other benefits," she said.

"Is that so?"

His deep brown eyes smouldered. She felt his arms tighten around her and then she was lost in his kiss.

CHAPTER

43

"You want me to do the abattoir run with those sheep for the restaurants?"

Mackenna was on her knees checking the seeder. She pulled herself upright and turned to face Cam.

"Have you finished all the troughs?" she asked. She glanced at her watch. He hadn't been gone that long.

"I don't waste time," he said. "They're all done."

She held his gaze a moment. His look dared her to call him a liar. She shrugged her shoulders. "I was going to go to the abattoir myself . . ." She hesitated. If Cam was off doing that job, Adam could come with her to shift some sheep without the risk that Cam might see him. "Okay, thanks. They're in the yard behind the shearing shed."

She watched him walk away then returned to checking the seeder hoses. Smiling to herself as she imagined Adam by her side for the afternoon. She forgot all about Cam until she heard the truck. She jumped up to see what he was doing.

The truck was pulling up beside the diesel tank. The very tank she'd just had refilled. She hurried over. Her carefully selected sheep were penned in a corner of the tray.

"Why are you taking the truck?"

Cam lifted his head at the sound of her voice.

"The trailer had a flat tyre." He grinned and flicked his eyes over her. "I'll change it tomorrow."

Mackenna clamped her lips shut. She'd been about to tell him he had plenty of time to change a tyre when she suddenly realised this might be their opportunity to see what else he got up to.

"Okay," she said.

"I might stay in town again tonight." He hooked the fuel hose back on the tank and stepped closer to her. "That's if you think you'll be okay on your own?"

"Of course I am," she snapped.

He smirked and climbed into the truck.

As soon as he started moving she dashed back to the ute and followed him down the drive. She pulled in at the Gatehouse. Adam was already at the door with his helmet.

"I assume Cam's going somewhere in the truck?" he said.

"The abattoirs. It's quite a distance but he may have plans for afterwards. He doesn't normally volunteer to do that run. He should be taking the trailer but he reckons a tyre's flat. There's no rush," she said. "I'll show you a different way to get there. You'll be able to watch from a distance to see where he heads afterwards."

Adam studied her rough map and asked a few questions then they walked out to where they'd stashed his bike out of sight yesterday.

She put a hand on his arm as he threw his leg over the bike. He smiled, leant over and kissed her. "I'll be fine," he said. "If I'm not back by dinnertime you're the chef tonight."

He pulled on his helmet and kicked the bike into life.

She waved as he rode away. Once again she listened as the bike slowed at the gate, revved and then roared out onto the road. Only when she could no longer hear him did she move.

"Not back by dinnertime," she murmured. She hadn't thought past Adam following Cam. What if Cam went somewhere a long way off? Adam could be gone late into the night. He didn't know his way around the district. If he did see Cam doing jobs for other people, what then?

They hadn't really thought this through properly.

She walked back to the sheds. The dogs met her, King keeping a discreet distance but Prince dancing in front of her, eager for attention. She patted them both and glanced towards the crumbling stone shed behind them. It was a leftover from the original days of the farm and full of relics from the past and drums of bits and pieces that often came in handy when something needed fixing. It was her dad's Aladdin's cave, but it also housed the trailer.

Mackenna stepped inside. The pup still played at her feet, stirring up the musty smell of the dirt floor. She waited for her eyes to adjust to the gloom. Sure enough, one tyre was flat as a tack. She poked it with the tip of her boot then bent down to take a good look. It probably had a nail or a bit of wire in it. She stepped back and the pup yelped as she caught his foot under her boot. She jerked away and banged her face into a bit of pipe jutting out from a drum of spare parts. Her teeth jarred together. She groaned and put her hand to her cheek. She shoved the pipe away with her free hand and glared back at the trailer. There was nothing strange about a flat tyre, it was just convenient for him if he had been planning to use the truck all along.

She pressed her hand to her throbbing cheek and went back to the seeder. Prince kept a mindful step away. Mackenna replayed the times Cam had driven the truck and come back late or the next day. None of it had seemed odd until now. If he did work for other people, she'd need proof. Hopefully Adam would get close enough to take a few pictures with his phone. She'd be happier to confront Cam if she had a bit more evidence that he was actually using Woolly Swamp's truck to do cash jobs.

Garry had been sure Cam was the bloke he'd seen driving the truck. She should have thought to find out who that farmer was.

Mackenna snapped her fingers. "Garry! That's it."

King lifted his head to look at her and Prince began dancing in circles again. If she got the name of the bloke Garry had been working for, she could ask him outright. Pretend she was looking for someone to do a carting job for cash and see what he said.

She took her notebook from her pocket.

"Damn!" she muttered. She hadn't made a note of the truck's odometer. Still, it hadn't been used since she jotted the last reading. That would still be a good indication. She took out her phone to ring Garry.

Adam pulled up on the side of the road and watched the trail of dust made by the truck as it turned off the bitumen. Now it would be tricky to follow. While they were on main roads he could have been anyone travelling the same direction but this road was dirt, which would make the bike much more obvious. The sign named it Shaggy Rise Road. The part he could see was straight with very little vegetation.

He wasn't sure what to do. It had been easy to watch Cam as he delivered the sheep to the abattoirs. Another bloke had met him there and they'd gone on together in the truck. Adam had followed them to a town called Penola, where they'd taken a road towards Millicent and then turned off at this point. Where he was in relation to Woolly Swamp he had no idea.

He did have a phone, however. He unzipped his jacket. The new phone had more apps than he knew how to use. At least with a map he might be able to get a rough idea of the area he was in. He reached into his top pocket but his phone wasn't there. He searched his jeans then sank back onto his bike. He remembered exactly where it was. He'd been sitting at Mackenna's table about to call his mother when he'd heard the truck coming. In his hurry to grab his helmet he'd left the phone on the table.

On the side road the dust had cleared and there was no longer any sign of the truck. The sun was getting low on the horizon. It would be dark in a few hours. There was nothing for it but to keep going. He edged forward. With one last look around, he turned on to Shaggy Rise Road.

After a couple of kilometres, what had started out as a straight road changed into a sweeping bend around a rocky outcrop and low bushes, then it swung back the other way. It continued its winding course and every now and then Adam caught sight of some dust in the distance. He assumed he was still following Cam in the truck.

He came to a property entrance. He slowed and peered ahead. Trees blocked his view of the track. To his left the road continued on with its telltale dust cloud. He kept going. After a few more kilometres he came to another tree-lined entrance to a farm. A sign declaring it to be Shaggy Rise was nailed to the rails beside the open gate and underneath in smaller print was the name A. & A. Bennett.

Once again Adam slowed. He looked along the road but there was no dust. Perhaps Shaggy Rise was Cam's destination. There was little vegetation around other than some clumps of trees and bushes along the driveway. Adam rode in, turned off his bike and rolled it behind the thickest of the bushes. It was exposed to the paddock behind but would be out of sight from anyone using the driveway.

He hooked his helmet over the handle and waited. He couldn't see the house, but ahead there were bigger trees and he could see assorted roofs and a television tower poking through. If he walked up the driveway he would be visible for all to see. If he didn't, he wouldn't be able to find out what Cam was doing.

The bleats of sheep and a dog's bark pressed him into motion. If sheep were being loaded on the truck, he guessed there wouldn't be anyone watching the driveway. He decided walking briskly was the best option. That way, if anyone saw him, he could say he was lost and looking for directions.

Before he reached the house, the driveway divided. He took the wider option, edged with thicker bush. It led away from the house towards some sheds. The noise of the sheep was much louder. Adam slowed and peered around a bushy branch. The cab of the truck was ahead of him. He studied it a moment. There was no sign of anyone, only the sounds of sheep, a man's call and occasional whistle as he worked the dogs. The back of the truck was out of sight behind the large shed. That's where all the action was.

He hesitated. He had the property's and its owners' names. He only had to wait and he would see the load Cam was taking and where he went with it.

"Can I help you, mate?"

Adam spun around.

Walking towards him was a lean bloke in a green shirt and dirty red cap, carrying a couple of empty hessian bags. The guy Adam had seen join Cam at the abattoirs had been wearing a green shirt and a red cap.

"I'm visiting the Bennetts," he said, remembering the name on the gate. He took a risk that this bloke didn't know the people who lived here, apart from whoever was working the sheep.

"Is that so?" The man stopped right in front of him. He was about Adam's height. His pointy nose had a bump in it as if it had been broken and he had a scar under his right eye.

"Just checking what was going on up here." Adam nodded towards the shed, deciding honesty was the best policy.

"Come and take a look then." The bloke's beady eyes bored into him.

A prickle ran down Adam's spine. He didn't trust Cam as far as he could throw him and coming face to face with his mate didn't do anything to change his mind. They were both bad news.

"I have." Adam took a chance this bloke had been away from the truck for a few minutes. "I'm on my way back to the house." He nodded and walked steadily back down the track. He could feel the guy's eyes boring into him as he went. There was nothing for it but to take the path that led towards the house.

Through the trees he came to a fence, beyond which was a manicured bed of roses, a trim lawn and the house. There was no sign of anyone so he walked quickly around the outside of the yard and followed the house track to where it joined the main driveway back to the road. There was nowhere to hide along this stretch until he reached the bushes where he'd stashed his bike.

Adam risked a look back towards the sheds. Still no sign of anyone. He hoped the guy had believed his story but there was always the risk he might ask the farmer working the sheep if he had a visitor.

The sound of a vehicle moving slowly in his direction spurred him into action. He sprinted down the driveway to his bike and crouched down beside it as the vehicle approached. He held his breath as it slowed even more, drew level with his hiding place then continued on.

Adam peered out to see a farm ute driving away from him down the track. The arm that rested on the open window was wearing navy but he'd seen the backs of two heads through its rear window. He could only assume the bloke who'd seen him had gone back and asked questions and now they were looking for him. No doubt wondering what a guy on foot was doing hanging around the house saying he knew the Bennetts.

Adam's story had been a risky one but it was the best he could do on the spot. He watched through the trees as the ute went left along the road then did a U-turn and came back, passed the driveway and headed in the opposite direction. He crouched down on the other side of his bike. If they went far enough and looked back, they would be able to see it.

Behind him he heard the rumble of the truck motor coming to life. Cam must have finished loading. Adam held his breath. He watched as the ute continued on to the top of a rise. When they turned they'd surely see him. He'd have to get away now. The sun was dropping fast and it would be dark soon.

He pushed his bike out onto the driveway just as the lights of the truck lit it up. The bike roared to life beneath him and he shot off. There was no way the truck could reach him. He left his own lights off. Visibility was still good enough. Good enough for him to see the ute approaching the gate just as he did. He opened the throttle. He would make the entrance before them and be away down the road. Just as he reached the gate they flicked their lights on high beam, blinding him. He swerved, felt his back tyre clip the solid gatepost and lost control. The bike roared across the road, hit the gravel bank on the other side and then was gone from under him. Adam had the strange sensation he was flying. He pictured Mackenna just as his helmet and shoulder connected with solid earth in a jarring crunch.

CHAPTER

44

Mackenna shut the door on the dog kennel and glanced up at the darkening sky. A thick bank of cloud hugged the western horizon, illuminated by the setting sun. Perhaps the weather forecast would be right this time and they would get some rain.

She walked past her family home and on down the driveway to the Gatehouse. Ever since Adam left she'd kept herself busy trying not to think about what he might be doing. She hadn't tried to ring him but the urge to do so now was overpowering. She rang as she opened the door to the Gatehouse. Her heart skipped a beat as she heard the jingle of his new phone. He was back and she hadn't heard the bike.

Her joy switched to worry again as she saw his phone on the kitchen table. He'd left the damn thing behind. She picked up the phone and turned it over and over in her hands. What could she do? If he was still following Cam he could be anywhere.

She needed to keep busy. She took meat from the fridge. Adam had cooked all sorts since his return so Mackenna hadn't been able to test her lamb shank recipe. It would be a good opportunity to make it tonight. She browned the meat, added stock, carrots and onions then took the torch and went outside to her herb pots. By the time she returned the delicious smell of the shanks and vegetables had filled the kitchen. There was a bottle of Bunyip shiraz open from last night. She poured a good half bottle into the casserole, tossed in the herbs then the rest of the red for good measure. She put the dish in the oven and cleaned up.

Once again she was sitting at the table with Adam's phone in one hand and her own in the other.

"Damn," she muttered. "Now what do I do? Come home, Adam. Come home."

Mackenna put the phones down and paced the floor, stopping in front of the oven to check the lamb shanks. It'd be at least another two hours till they were ready. She went into the bedroom and flicked on the television. The news was all doom and gloom and the bed reminded her of Adam.

She paused as she caught a glimpse of herself in the mirror. She leant closer and turned her head. There was a dark bruise on her cheek with a red graze beneath it. She touched the area gently with her fingers. It was tender. She'd probably end up with a black eye. Great. That would give the weekend's dinner guests something to talk about.

Mackenna went back to the kitchen and stared at her phone again, willing Adam to find some way of calling her. Then she remembered her conversation with Garry. He'd given her the property owner's phone number where he'd been crutching when he'd seen Cam driving the Woolly Swamp truck. She looked at the page in her notebook. Rob Watson was the farmer's name. She'd never heard of him but that wasn't surprising. He lived quite a distance from Woolly Swamp and Garry said he hadn't owned the property long.

She hadn't rung straight away, not sure what to do. A mobile number could easily be rung back. She wanted to sound the bloke out without him knowing who she was.

Mackenna paced the kitchen then clapped her hands together. Her parent's landline! Her mother always kept it as a private number, which meant it didn't leave caller ID. She swept both mobiles up from the table and ran out to her car. She would ring the bloke from her parents' phone and he'd not be able to trace the call if the conversation got tricky.

It was very quiet and cold in the house. Mackenna switched on the verandah, passage and kitchen lights, flicked the reverse cycle air conditioning to warm and turned on the radio before she finally got up the courage to call.

Rob was a friendly chap who was quite happy to tell her about the cash deal he'd made to have his sheep transported.

"There were two blokes. They were recommended to me by someone else but I can't remember who," Rob said.

"Doesn't matter," Mackenna replied. "Do you have a name and phone number for them? I've got a job needs doing and my truck's out of action."

"Sure. I have it written down. I only got the one bloke's first name. I was flat out with the crutching. We didn't waste time chatting. Very efficient, they were. Let's see . . ."

Mackenna could hear rustling as Rob searched for the number.

"Here we are," he said. "The name of the bloke I dealt with was Trev."

Mackenna had to ask Rob to repeat the phone number twice before she hung up. She stared at the name and mobile number she'd written across her mother's notepad. She was pretty sure if she rang that number she'd get Trevor bloody Dingle. Goodness knows how many times Dingo and Cam had used the Woolly Swamp truck to do jobs on the side.

She wondered about the stuff Cam was supposed to be selling at the pub. It would be hard to miss a few bags of grain but it made her wonder what else he might be taking.

She went to the pile of mail she'd stacked up waiting for her mother's return and flicked through it looking for the account from the stock and station agent. There was nothing surprising on the itemised list, except possibly the amounts. If Cam went in to town to collect goods, he could ask for three rolls of wire instead of two or ten posts instead of eight. By the time the account came, small differences like that wouldn't be noticed.

Mackenna tossed the bill beside the pile. She moved around the kitchen straightening chairs, wiping benches, doing anything to keep busy. She reread her holiday postcards on the fridge. It felt like a lifetime ago. Finally, she plucked her phone from her pocket and rang Hugh. If she couldn't talk to Adam, at least Hugh would understand her anxiety.

His phone went to voicemail. She started to speak then thought better of it. She couldn't expect Hugh to drop whatever he was doing. Surely Adam would be home soon. She placed her phone beside his on the table willing one of them to ring, but both remained silent.

She glanced around her mother's kitchen. Only a few days and they'd be home. Mackenna looked again at the family photo on the kitchen wall. Now there was Yassie and soon a baby. They'd have to get a new one taken.

"Hello, boss."

She spun around.

"Cam!" She put a hand to her chest. Her heart was racing. "I didn't hear you come in."

"No boots," he said with a grin.

She glanced down at his feet. He wiggled his toes inside his socks.

"What are you doing here?" she asked. Her thoughts raced in all directions. Did his presence mean Adam was back at the Gatehouse?

"I live here."

"You said you were staying in town tonight."

He took a step inside the kitchen door. "Change of plans. Thought you might like some company." His grin widened, his crooked teeth turning it into a leer. "You looked a bit lonely."

Mackenna glanced towards the window. The blinds were still open. How long had he been watching her? Her skin prickled.

"Not at all," she said firmly.

"You've lost your smile lately, boss. All the worry of running the place with your dad away. I brought us some drinks."

He raised his hand to show a sixpack of beer.

"Where's the truck?" she asked.

"Come on, boss." His grin slipped a little. He took another step forward and placed the beers on the table next to the two phones. "You're always so worried about that truck. I'll bring it back in the morning."

"How did you get here?"

"Borrowed a mate's car."

Mackenna glanced again at the window. Where was Adam?

"You expecting someone?"

"Hugh," she said quickly.

They watched each other across the table. The radio played in the background. Adam's phone began to ring. She reached for it but Cam swept it up. Before he could look at it, her phone began to ring and he grabbed that with his other hand. He looked from one screen to the other then held them in the air.

"You got two phones?" He held Adam's phone up. "Mum's on this one." Then he held hers up. "And Hugh's on this one. Maybe he's not coming after all." He grinned at her again, turned the phones off and put them back on the table. "I really think this is our chance to get to know each other better."

Mackenna's heart was thumping in her chest. Cam was still between her and the doorway. She could try to get past him but he was a big bloke. She couldn't rely on Adam or Hugh to turn up. She reached across the table and he placed his hand over hers.

"Just getting a beer," she said.

He shifted his hand, ripped open the pack and offered her a bottle. They twisted the lids and he leant forward and tapped the neck of his against hers.

"Cheers," he said with the Cam sparkle that gave her the creeps.

She held his gaze. "Cheers."

They both took a mouthful. She put her bottle on the table and reached for the rest of the pack.

"What are you doing?" he asked.

"Putting these in the fridge." She turned her lips up into what she hoped was a smile. "Don't want them getting hot."

He let her take the bottles. She moved to the fridge, relieved to have her back to him for a moment. The fridge was all but empty but she delayed there, pretending she was making space, trying to think of what to do next.

"This is cosy."

Mackenna shut the fridge with a thud and spun around. He had stepped close to her.

"Hell, what happened to you?"

She flinched as he lifted his hand and poked her cheek gently with his finger.

"Bumped into some pipe," she said.

"You're gonna have a shiner." He grinned. "You're one tough cookie, boss, I'll give you that. We should have hooked up a long time ago."

"What are you talking about?" Her mind was racing, playing for time. She could just walk out. Or could she?

"You're always coming on to me," he said.

Did he truly think that? Her father had made some comment about Cam making goggle eyes at her, but she had dismissed it.

"I thought for a while you were going to hook up with Hugh," he said, "but I get it now. You're just old mates. Then that Adam guy showed up."

Mackenna glared at Cam. Did he know Adam was back?

"Sharing a room with him was the pits," Cam said. "Bloody Kiwi thought he was something else. Anyway he's gone now, so it's just you and me."

"Gone?" The word came out as a wail.

"Went back to his travels your mum said . . ." Cam's eyes darkened and his mouth fell open. "He came back, didn't he?"

Mackenna pressed against the fridge. Cam hadn't known Adam was back. She hoped that meant Adam would turn up soon.

Cam took a small step closer. "It was him on the bike at the Bennetts' place."

A chill went through Mackenna.

"You bitch," Cam yelled.

She flinched as spittle sprayed from his mouth.

"You were stringing me along and all the while you had Adam on the side. You pretended he left but you've been shacked up with him in that stupid cottage of yours, haven't you?"

Her mouth was dry. "Where is he?" she croaked.

His eyes widened. "That dumb Kiwi was following us, wasn't he?"

"What have you done to him?"

"I haven't done anything," Cam sneered. "But he's useless to you now."

He pressed his hands to the fridge either side of her head. Magnets and postcards showered to the floor. Mackenna's mind raced from Adam and what could have happened to him to Cam standing centimetres away.

"Might as well make the most of it," Cam said.

He leant forward and she could smell the beer on his breath mingled with something bad.

Her nose wrinkled as his lips reached hers. She used the fridge to brace herself and pushed her knee up with as much force as she could muster, straight into his crotch.

Cam expelled a gasp of rotten breath, doubled over and staggered backwards into the table. Their open bottles wobbled and fell, spilling beer as they went. One rolled off the edge and smashed on the floor. Cam sank to his knees, his face pale and his eyes fluttering.

Mackenna gripped one of the kitchen chairs, picked it up and swung the legs wildly in his direction.

"You're fired," she hissed.

He opened his mouth but no words came out.

"You leave here tonight," she said.

Cam stayed where he was gasping in short breaths. "I'll tell people you attacked me," he puffed.

"In self-defence," she said. "Your word against mine and I've got the bruise."

His eyes widened. "You scheming – "

"Get out," she screamed, jabbing the chair legs at him.

"You're mad, you bitch." Finally Cam was getting some air. He gripped the table and pulled himself to his feet but remained hunched over.

Mackenna glared at him. "And I want my truck back here by eight o'clock tomorrow morning." The strength had returned to her voice. "Or I'll report it stolen."

He backed out of the kitchen. She followed him with the chair and watched him fumble with the back door and struggle to pull on his boots. He staggered to his ute. She stood at the door and watched until its lights had disappeared and the sound of the engine had faded.

The cold night air flooded around her and she began to shake. She flicked the nib on the lock, shut the door and pressed her back against it. Great shuddering sobs racked her body as she slid to the floor.

CHAPTER
45

Hugh squinted as a set of headlights on high beam hit him in the eye. He pulled to one side to let a vehicle out of Mackenna's driveway.

There were no lights on at the Gatehouse. He peered ahead and could make out a glow from the direction on the Birches' farmhouse. Maybe Mackenna and Adam were there. She'd only left half a message but she'd sounded worried. When he'd tried to call back she'd rejected his call.

He pulled up at the Birches' back gate. There were several lights on in the house. He hurried to the door and knocked.

"Mackenna," he called. "Adam?"

There was no answer. He tried the door but it was locked.

"Mackenna?"

He heard a noise then the door opened and Mackenna peered around it. Her eyes were red and a large bruise covered one cheek.

"What's happened?" he asked as she opened the door wider and walked away.

"I've sent Cam packing," she mumbled over her shoulder.

He stepped around a chair leaning against the passage wall and followed her into the kitchen. "Are you alright?"

He stopped in the doorway, surveying the mess. It looked as though there'd been a struggle.

"I'm okay," Mackenna said in a soft voice.

"Did Cam do this?" He put a gentle hand to her cheek.

She winced and shook her head.

"Where's Adam?"

Mackenna's lip wobbled. He opened his arms and she stepped into them. She was shaking. He'd never seen her like this. Why had she been on her own with Cam? Adam should never have left her.

Hugh held her tight until he felt her relax. She eased away from him.

"Sorry," she said. "I'm okay. I've sent Cam packing but I don't know where Adam is." She turned big worried eyes to him. "I think they may have killed him."

Hugh sat her down and took the chair next to her, making sure his feet were clear of the puddle of beer on the floor. "Why would you think that? Where is he?"

"He followed Cam. He's been gone for hours. Then Cam came back. He didn't seem to know Adam was staying here again. Then he said Adam was dead."

Hugh leaned forward and took her cold hands in his. "Why would he say Adam was dead?"

She shook her head. "He didn't exactly say the word dead but he implied it. He said Adam was useless to me."

"Where did Adam go?"

"I don't know." Mackenna sniffed and picked up a mobile phone from the table. "He left his phone behind."

"I tried to ring you."

"Cam switched both phones off." She fiddled with them. "Adam's mum must have tried to ring. What will I tell her if she rings again?"

Both phones jingled to life. Mackenna peered at one then the other.

"Missed call from you." She waggled her phone at him. "Message on Adam's." She held up the other one. "Bet it's from his mum."

"So you have no idea where Adam may have followed Cam?"

Mackenna shook her head. "Cam took my sheep to the abattoir. Because he had the truck we thought he might have been planning another job of his own afterwards. I gave Adam directions to the abattoir. I haven't heard from him since he left here mid-afternoon."

Hugh was worried too. "So we don't even know if he made it to the abattoir or if he did and followed Cam from there." Adam would have contacted Mackenna if he was simply lost, but he didn't want to say that out loud.

"Wait a minute." Mackenna jumped up. "He must have followed Cam. Damn! What was it he said?"

She tapped her finger on her teeth. Hugh watched the frown lift from her face. "Adam must have followed Cam and Cam didn't know who it was. He said something about someone on a bike at the Bennetts' place." She sunk down on her chair again. "I don't know any Bennetts."

"I do," Hugh said. He took his phone from his pocket. "Adrian and Anne. I was there just last week. They were planning to sell some sheep. They live over Millicent way."

"But that's so far away. There could be other Bennetts."

"No harm in trying them." Hugh scrolled through his contact list and selected the number.

Adrian answered straight away and Hugh explained why he was ringing. Adrian sounded upset – there had been an accident. Hugh was at first relieved that the description Adrian gave fitted Adam then worried to hear he was in a bad way. The whole time they were talking Mackenna paced the room around him. He told Adrian he'd call him back later.

"Was Adam there?" she said as soon as he took the phone from his ear.

"Yes, but – "

"We've got to get there." Mackenna snatched up the phones and her car keys. "If Cam has harmed one hair on his head, I'm going to have him for assault."

"Mack." Hugh put a restraining hand on her arm. He saw the fear in her eyes as she returned his gaze.

"Adam's been taken to hospital. The ambulance has only just left the Bennetts'."

"What happened?" Mackenna's lip began to quiver.

"Adrian was pretty upset. Evidently his lad was driving the ute and Adam shot out of their driveway across the road in front of him."

"Why would Adam do that?"

"I don't know, but Adrian said Cam had the sheep loaded in the truck and Trevor was in the ute with his lad . . ."

"I don't understand."

"Adrian said Adam had been behaving strangely. He told Trevor he was a friend of the Bennetts. He didn't have any identification on him. Adrian called the ambulance and the police."

Mackenna opened her mouth but no words came out. She continued to stare at Hugh as if he had all the answers.

"Cam and Dingo left with the sheep before the police and ambulance arrived," he said. "Technically neither of them were involved."

"I should never have thought up this stupid scheme." Big tears began to roll down her cheeks. "What if Adam's . . . what if he's . . ."

Hugh gripped her arms. "Adam was unconscious. They called an ambulance and it took them a while to stabilise him, but he's alive."

Hugh felt Mackenna's arms go rigid. She lifted her hands to his elbows and squeezed. They stood for a moment like a pair of wrestlers locked together.

"I've got to get to him," Mackenna said. She stared straight at Hugh. Her tears had dried. "Will you come?"

"Of course," he said. "I'll drive."

They were level with the Gatehouse when Mackenna shot forward in her seat and let fly with a string of such bad language Hugh thought she'd cracked under the pressure.

He braked to a stop. "What's the matter?"

"I've left the lamb shanks in the oven."

She jumped out of the car and ran inside. In seconds she was back beside him. She leant over and kissed him on the cheek. "I don't know what I would have done without your help tonight."

He smiled. "We're mates. That's what mates do," he said.

CHAPTER

46

Mackenna thought they'd never reach the hospital. A part of her wished she'd driven instead of Hugh. Driving would have given her something to focus on instead of all the scenarios of an injured Adam that played in her head.

It was a relief to finally pull into the car park. She was out of the vehicle before Hugh could turn off the engine but he was by her side again when she reached the emergency waiting room. Mackenna peered around calling Adam's name. Several people stared back at her from their seats. A large sign declared police would be called if visitors became aggressive.

A nurse appeared behind the security glass. "What can we do for you?"

"I'm looking for Adam." Mackenna spoke loudly through the gaps in the glass. "Is he here?"

The nurse raised her eyebrows.

Hugh stepped up beside Mackenna. "Our friend has just been brought here in an ambulance." His tone was soothing. "He's been in a motorbike accident."

Mackenna gripped his hand, thankful once again for his steady presence.

"Our no name patient." The nurse shuffled through some clipboards. "You can fill out his information for us."

"How is he?" Hugh asked.

"I can't tell you anything yet." She scowled from one to the other.

Mackenna wanted to slap the woman for her lack of empathy. No wonder there was a glass barrier. Instead, she tightened her grip on Hugh's arm.

He leaned closer to the glass and spoke in a low voice. "His name is Adam Walker. Mackenna is his partner. She wasn't there when he had the accident, so you can understand her distress."

Once again the nurse flicked her stern gaze from Hugh to Mackenna, then her face softened. "He's having tests," she said. "Come through."

She moved out of sight and suddenly a door in the partition wall slid open. She beckoned them through. The badge on her uniform flipped around revealing her name, Coral. "This way," she said.

Mackenna followed her into a large brightly lit room, loosely partitioned by curtains. People sat or lay on beds with a nurse or a visitor beside them. She glanced at each face expectantly and averted her eyes when it wasn't Adam.

"Here we are." Coral indicated an empty bed and straightened the tangled sheet.

Mackenna's heart skipped a beat. Adam's clothes were piled in the corner with his helmet on top. A blood-soaked bandage and assorted medical equipment littered the cupboard beside the bed and an empty wrapper and a disposable glove lay at her feet.

"We're busy tonight," Coral said. "I'll see if I can find you a chair."

Mackenna looked from the debris to Hugh standing at the end of the bed.

"Let's not jump to conclusions," he said. "He's having tests. He'll be back here grinning at you in no time."

"Here you are." Coral carried a plastic chair. "You look like you've been through the wars yourself."

Mackenna frowned at her. A buzzer went and Coral hurried away.

"That bruise on your cheek is a real shiner." Hugh nodded at her.

Mackenna put a hand to her face and winced as her fingers found the spot where she'd connected with the pipe. It seemed so long ago. Had it really been this afternoon?

"I wasn't watching where I was going."

She perched on the chair and looked at the form on the clipboard. There were so many empty boxes. She began to fill it out with a shaky hand, but her mind was mush and she stopped.

"I don't know half of this stuff," she said and looked up at Hugh. "I should ring his mother."

Hugh glanced at his watch. "It's pretty late," he said. "Let's wait and see how he is."

Mackenna put the clipboard on the bed and began to pace. She looked up at every footfall but none of them came as far as their corner. Beyond the curtains she could hear voices and the sounds of activity as other patients and medical staff came and went.

"How about I go and find us a drink?" Hugh said.

She stopped pacing and shook her head. "I'm sorry. You should go home. I'll be alright."

"I'm not leaving you," he said. "But I will get us a coffee. Please sit for a while."

Mackenna let him guide her back to the chair. He kissed the top of her head and left. She wanted to jump up again but forced herself to stay seated. She leaned forward, put her arms on the bed and rested her head on them. It was taking so long Adam must be in a bad way.

Hugh came back with two polystyrene cups and a sandwich. She took a sip of sweet tea and a bite from the sandwich. Her stomach growled. The bread and ham were deliciously fresh. She had eaten half the sandwich and drained the tea when Coral reappeared.

"Your partner has been admitted to a hospital bed."

"How is he?" Mackenna asked, desperate for information.

"Still unconscious, I believe." Coral picked up Adam's things and thrust them into Mackenna's arms. "Doctor's with him now. He's on ward 4B. Take the first turn left after you exit emergency then follow the signs."

Hugh put his hand on Mackenna's shoulder. Coral was already stripping the bed.

They followed her instructions. Two policemen passed them going the other way. Another nurse directed them to 4B. Mackenna's heart was beating fast as she made her way towards the only lit bed in the ward. The curtains were drawn around it and below them she could see three pairs of feet.

She poked her head around the curtain. Adam lay on the bed, his eyes closed. His face was ashen and his left arm was strapped to his naked chest. He was attached to monitors and a drip fed a tube in his free arm.

"Family's here." The young nurse smiled at Mackenna.

A short woman wearing a white coat with a stethoscope hanging around her neck lifted her eyes from the notes she'd been studying.

"Hello, I'm Dr Cheng," she said. "Are you his relatives?"

"Friends," Mackenna said. She was overwhelmed to see Adam lying so deathly still.

"Mackenna's Adam's girlfriend," Hugh said.

"You weren't there when he had the accident?" Dr Cheng asked.

"No," Adam said as Mackenna shook her head, her gaze locked on Adam's face.

"Come in," the young nurse beckoned. "He's doing okay."

Beside her an older male nurse was fiddling with the head of the bed. "We always end up with the dodgy beds," he said.

"There's a trick to it." The other nurse went to his aid. They pulled at something and bumped the bed but Adam didn't move.

"There's no spinal or head injury other than concussion." Dr Cheng checked the bandage around Adam's arm. "He's broken his collarbone and he's got sutures in a wound on his leg and a few other abrasions, but he should be right to go home tomorrow."

"Tomorrow!" Mackenna flicked her eyes to the doctor then back to Adam's lifeless figure.

"He's been awake," the male nurse said, "but it's best he sleeps now."

"The police want to talk to him," Dr Cheng said. "I've sent them away till morning. There doesn't appear to be any drugs or alcohol in his system."

"He's not a criminal," Mackenna gasped. Hugh placed a reassuring hand on her shoulder.

The young nurse took Adam's clothes from her. "Don't think these will be much good to him. I'll find a bag."

"He's lucky his helmet was a good one." Dr Cheng nodded at the helmet as the nurse carried it out. "And he wasn't going too fast, I'm told." She took a pen from her pocket and scribbled something on the notes then handed them back to the nurse. "He's all yours," she said and ducked out through the curtains.

"There's a visitors' lounge just down the corridor." The nurse flicked on the light over Adam's head and turned off the others.

"I'm not leaving him," Mackenna said.

The nurse's face was expressionless but his eyes swept her with a sympathetic look. "The chair's not very comfortable but one of you can stay if you want."

He left them. Mackenna moved along the bed, taking in every part of Adam she could see that wasn't covered up. Then she held his free hand in hers and sat beside him.

"Are you sure you won't rest in the lounge, Mack?" Hugh asked. "There's probably nothing you can do till morning."

"I'm not leaving him." Mackenna gripped Adam's hand tighter and put her other hand on his bare chest. He felt so soft and unresponsive.

"Okay." Hugh said. "I'll go home and come back for you both in the morning. If you need anything you ring me."

"Thanks," she said, without taking her eyes from Adam. She heard Hugh's footsteps as he left. She continued to stare at Adam's face for a long time, willing his eyes to open but they didn't. Slowly the quiet of the hospital ward settled around them. Somewhere she could hear a persistent drip. Behind her, the small sliver of window not covered by the curtain showed water sliding down the outside. It was raining. She lowered her head onto the bed and let sleep take her.

CHAPTER

47

Adam woke to the sound of singing. He had no idea where he was. His eyes took a while to focus. The yellow light creeping around the edge of the blind had the feel of morning but the room was wrong. The wardrobe wasn't his. Then he remembered Mackenna. This was her room at the Gatehouse. She'd brought him home from the hospital yesterday and he'd slept most of the time since. He felt like he'd been hit with a sledgehammer. He put a hand to his head trying to erase the dull ache that throbbed there.

The singing stopped. All was quiet a moment then Mackenna's face popped around the door.

"Good." She grinned. "You're awake."

"I heard a noise."

Mackenna came in carrying a tray. "That was me singing."

"Don't give up your day job, princess."

"I can't." She pulled a quirky face. "My Kiwi warrior isn't much help."

"Ouch," he said. "Guess I deserved that. No more playing detective for me. Both you and my mother have made that quite clear."

He pushed himself up with his good arm.

"Adam, stop," she said and put the tray on the floor. "Let me help you."

Together they juggled pillows and he wriggled up the bed. His shoulder didn't hurt as long as he kept his arm still.

Mackenna put the tray on his lap and he grinned. There was a soft-boiled egg in a shot glass with its top cut off and laid out beside it was toast cut into strips and several rashers of crispy bacon.

"I haven't had this since I was a kid. Egg with toast fingers."

"My mother calls them soldiers." Mackenna leant over and kissed him. "I thought it would be easy to eat with one hand."

"Aren't you going to feed me?"

"I can't. I have sheep to check. I've got a mob just dropping lambs. I'll have to go into town later to pick up the pivot that's been fixed and get some groceries."

Adam rubbed his fingers across his forehead. "Is it today your parents are coming home?"

"Yes. Patrick and Yasmine are driving them this afternoon." Mackenna sat on the bed and placed a gentle hand over his forehead. "Do you still have a headache?"

"It's there but not so bad."

"Maybe you should go back to the doctor."

"They said it could take days to go." He smiled at her. "I need to get up and get moving."

"Eat your breakfast while I check the sheep. If you're feeling up to it, you can come with me into town."

"I have to call in at the police station to sign the statement. Might as well get that over and done with. That poor Bennett lad could have been facing a negligent driving charge."

"He's so young and it was Dingo who told him to block your path."

"No doubt they thought I was trying to rob them or something. I did take a risk saying I knew the Bennetts."

"I'm glad everyone accepted our version of the story. Dingo's playing dumb and Cam's nowhere to be found."

"Good riddance, I say." Adam looked at her cheek. "It didn't do any harm, you having that shiner." After what she'd told him about her run-in with Cam he was sure Cam had hit her, but she insisted it was an accident with a piece of pipe.

"Hugh was here when Cam returned the truck. He left again without a word. I've been into his room. The only stuff he left behind was dirty clothes and some loose change. Not even a toothbrush. I put it all in a garbage bag and left it on the back verandah."

"I don't think he'll be back for it," Adam said.

"Neither do I." She nestled against his good arm. "I've stripped the bed and left all the windows open. Poor you having to share a room with him."

"You're much more fun." Adam eased his arm out from under her and wrapped it around her shoulder. The contents of the breakfast tray wobbled.

She steadied it then slid away from him. "I do have to go," she said. "Alfie will be getting anxious."

"Alfie? Don't tell me you've got another bloke giving you trouble already?"

"No."

Mackenna laughed. He grinned, glad to hear her bubbling with happiness again.

"Alfie's our alpaca. There's a new mob of sheep lambing and he likes to be in charge."

"Of lambing?" Adam shook his head. Meat on his plate he understood, but he didn't really understand much about the business of producing it.

"He's very protective of the sheep and their lambs. Keeps them safe from foxes." Mackenna laughed again. "Midwife Alfie. There's a thought." She picked up her hat, blew him a kiss and left.

Adam smiled. He could hear her laughing as she left the house.

He leant back against the pillows and closed his eyes. When he'd woken in the hospital it was to find Mackenna holding his hand. He remembered riding his bike out the Bennetts' gate and trying to avoid the ute but after that everything was a blur, until he woke to her smile. Gradually the events of the previous day had come back to him. He had no intention of pressing charges against the Bennett lad for reckless driving, and Adrian Bennett had been more than happy to accept his side of events leading up to the accident.

Adam finished the breakfast Mackenna had made him and stretched gingerly. He really did need to get out of bed and start moving around. He had one good arm. At least he could help Mackenna in the kitchen. She was planning a welcome home meal for her parents. He could start the prep.

By the time she came back he'd showered and dressed himself and made quite a mess in her kitchen. She raised an eyebrow but said nothing.

"I've added to your shopping list," he said.

"You should be resting."

"I'm tired of resting." He moved his head from side to side. "And the headache's gone." He did feel a lot better than he had when he woke up. He nodded at the sunlight streaming through the kitchen window. "Did I dream it or has it rained?"

Mackenna frowned at him. "It rained all day yesterday but you slept through it."

"I opened my eyes a few times."

"Beautiful sunshine now."

"I thought you wanted rain?"

"We did. That was a really good soak but now I want a few days of warmth."

Adam shook his head. He didn't get it.

"Off to town we go then." Mackenna swept up the envelope she'd used to jot down her shopping list.

It took them a few hours to get everything done. Adam was feeling weary when they got back in the car to head for home. He dozed off, only waking as the car slowed at the entrance to the property. He studied Mackenna's profile as she concentrated on her driving. Her earlier happy face had been replaced by a thoughtful frown. She was carrying the load of the farm alone. Having to look after him was an extra burden she didn't need.

"What's up?"

"You're good company," she said, not answering his question.

"Just resting my eyes." He patted her leg. "You'll be glad to have your mum and dad home."

"Mmm," she murmured.

"You can't keep managing without any help."

"I know. I want them home . . . Dad anyway."

"You don't get on with your mum?" Adam was surprised. He thought Mackenna got her tenacity and her energy from her mother. Mrs Birch was always going somewhere, doing something, helping someone. They were very similar in that respect.

"I do," she said. "At least I did. After Dad's heart attack she's been different."

"Worried about your dad probably."

"Yeah, I get that but she's been different. I don't know how she'll react to me sending Cam packing."

"Once your Mum hears how he attacked you she'll understand."

"I suppose, but there's more than just Cam's bad behaviour. The bill pile is growing and I've got another crowd booked for Saturday night at the Gatehouse. She was never keen on that idea."

"It's earning money."

"Yes, I suppose there's that."

"At least it's rained," Adam said trying to be reassuring. Mackenna's smile had well and truly slipped.

"Yes," she replied. "At least it's rained."

CHAPTER
48

Louise put her hand over the mail she'd opened and closed her eyes a moment. The holiday had been wonderful. No meals to cook, no meetings to attend, no fundraisers to work on, nothing to clutter her life other than to spend time with her husband and take in some new sights. She tried to hold onto that feeling but the stack of bills and the looming hospital art show had quickly dragged her back to reality. There was a lot to do.

"It's so good to be home."

She snapped her eyes open. She hadn't heard Lyle's approach. He was already in work clothes and they'd only been back five minutes.

"Where are you going?" she asked.

"Mackenna's coming to pick me up. I want to check out a few things that have happened."

"It's after four. Can't it wait until tomorrow?"

He raised his eyebrows at her. "I'm fine, Lou," he said. "I won't be long."

"Mackenna's cooking us dinner."

"She says she's organised. Adam's helping her."

"What's he doing back here?" Louise thought he was well and truly out of the picture.

"Don't know, but they were over at Murphy's place when I rang. Mackenna's had trouble with one of the pivots and – "

"I can see that." Louise picked up a bill she'd opened and handed it to him. "Six thousand dollars' worth of trouble."

"Bloody hell." Lyle sank to a kitchen chair. "It must have been major."

"What's up?" Patrick strolled into the kitchen with Yasmine close behind him.

She was still wearing a loose coat and scarf over several garments of different lengths. Louise thought it would be nice to see her in something more practical for the farm.

"A few bills," Louise said snatching the paper back again.

"Where's Cam?" Patrick asked.

"Working, I suppose," Louise said. A small part of her wished they hadn't taken on a working man so they didn't have to pay the wages and all the other costs that went with employing someone.

"The spare room's been stripped and cleaned. Not a sign of anyone inhabiting it," Patrick said.

Louise frowned. She'd only been as far as her own bedroom to change her clothes and unpack.

"Hello. Welcome home."

They all turned towards the door at Mackenna's call.

Louise felt a wave of alarm at the sight of her daughter's bruised face and Adam following her through the door with his arm in a sling.

Yasmine gasped and Lyle stood up but Patrick was the only one with a voice.

"What happened to you two?" he asked.

"Nothing too much." Mackenna grinned. "It's a long story. We're both fine."

"Nice to see you, Adam." Patrick nodded at the sling. "Bike?"

"Yes," Adam replied. His smile was a little more sheepish.

Louise noticed he slipped his free arm easily around her daughter's waist.

"He's banned." Mackenna chuckled. "We'll tell you all about it over dinner. You ready to go, Dad?"

"Why don't you wait until the morning?" Louise said. "We've only just got in the door."

"I want to check out the lambs." Lyle reached for his hat. "Looks like we've had some good rain. Cam could start seeding that corner paddock first thing."

Louise saw the quick glance between Adam and Mackenna. "Where is Cam?" she asked.

Mackenna sighed. "I asked him to leave."

There was silence for a moment then Yasmine stepped forward. "Okay if I put the kettle on?"

They all ignored her as she moved to the sink.

"Why?" Lyle asked.

"About time," Patrick added.

Louise spoke over them. "You have no right," she snapped at her daughter. "We need him. Your father needs the help."

"Hang on, Lou," Lyle said. "Let's hear what happened."

"He was ripping us off," Mackenna said. "He was using our truck and our diesel to do jobs on the side."

"He didn't always do his work properly," Patrick chipped in.

"And we think he may have been taking small amounts of farm property and selling them for cash," Adam added.

The kettle filled the pause with its loud bubbling and a solid click as it switched itself off.

Lyle sighed. "Perhaps the tour can wait till the morning. You'd better fill us in."

A cup crashed to the floor and Patrick dashed across the room to support Yasmine.

"What happened?" Louise asked.

"I'm okay," Yasmine said in a small voice. "I just felt faint all of a sudden."

"We had an early lunch," Patrick said, his face full of concern. "Have you eaten anything since?"

Yasmine shook her head.

Mackenna pushed a chair towards her and Patrick lowered his girlfriend onto it. The loose jacket she was wearing fell open. Louise took a step towards Yasmine and noticed the round bulge of her abdomen.

"You're pregnant," she gasped.

Yasmine gathered the loose clothing back over her stomach.

"I've been going to tell you," Patrick said. "It was a surprise for us, too."

Louise stared at her son. "This is your baby?"

"Of course it's my baby."

Mackenna put a hand on her brother's shoulder and one on Yasmine's.

"It's great news," she beamed.

"You knew?" Louise couldn't believe such an obviously advanced pregnancy had escaped her notice.

"Not for long," Mackenna said.

Louise continued to stare at her son and his girlfriend in disbelief.

Adam took over making the tea with his one good hand.

Lyle shook Patrick's hand and bestowed a kiss on Yasmine's cheek. "Congratulations. It's what we've wanted for so long." He turned. "Isn't it fantastic, Lou? We're going to be grandparents."

"But . . ."

"It's not very often you're speechless, Mum." Patrick gave her a cheeky grin.

Her heart melted. Her baby was going to be a father. She rushed forward and wrapped them both in her arms. "It's a surprise, that's all. It really is wonderful news. When are you due?"

"A couple of months," Yasmine said.

"A couple of months! Is there time for a wedding?" Louise asked.

"Steady up, Mum," Patrick said.

"Not till after the baby's born." Yasmine's voice was suddenly strong.

Louise was brushed aside as Patrick knelt at Yasmine's feet.

"You mean that?" he said and took her hands in his.

"Yes."

Louise didn't know where to look. She felt like an intruder.

"Looks like you'll have to break out a bottle of bubbly tonight," Adam said.

"Yes." Mackenna helped him carry the cups to the table. "Why don't we leave you guys to chat? It's getting late and the farm can wait till the morning. Dad, what do you say?"

"It can." Lyle put an arm around Louise and kissed her. "Didn't I tell you things would be right as rain?"

"Good," Mackenna said. "We'll go and get dinner underway so we can eat a bit earlier. Can't have you fading away, Yassie."

Patrick drew Yasmine to her feet and shifted her chair closer to the table. "A cup of tea and a biscuit should do the trick till dinner," he said.

Louise watched him fuss over Yasmine and felt a sudden surge of joy. A baby was wonderful news even if was before the wedding. It wasn't unusual these days. She was so glad she'd convinced Lyle to include Patrick in the farm and to leave it to him. If anything were to happen to Lyle, another Birch would run the property.

CHAPTER
49

The table was set and the fire was flickering with enough heat to chase the chill from the room. Mackenna had one more look around then made her way back to the kitchen. Tonight would be a real celebration. Her parents were home and the news of Yasmine and Patrick's baby had deflected the issue of Cam's departure.

Her heart skipped at the sight of Adam, apron on, making his apricot puddings. She no longer pinched herself to accept he was really here. She was so happy she couldn't imagine anything that could spoil it.

"Hey, babe," she said and slid her arms around him.

She felt his sharp intake of breath and stepped back.

"Careful," he said and turned to reveal his hurt arm out of the sling.

"What are you doing?" she cajoled.

"Making dessert."

"I can see that, chef, but where's your sling?"

"Still here." He pulled it from under the apron. "It was annoying me."

She teetered forward on her toes only allowing her lips to touch his. He grabbed her with his good arm and kissed her back. She reached her arms around his neck as they clung to each other. Adam shifted backwards and they jumped apart at the sound of a bowl hitting the floor.

"Arrg!" Mackenna yelped as something wet splattered her legs.

She looked past the skirt she'd recently donned to replace her jeans. Orange splodges trickled down her bare legs to the floor.

"Damn," Adam said. "That was the apricot mixture for my dessert."

"That wasn't quite where I imagined we'd serve it."

"Not to your family anyway."

Mackenna laughed at the sparkle in his eyes.

"Down boy," she said. "I'll wash this off and whiz up to Mum's. She's got jars full of last summer's apricots."

Mackenna was gone before he had a chance to delay her further. She slipped off her heels and put her feet into the old pair of sheepskin boots she kept in the bathroom. Not a fantastic look but it would keep her warm until she got back.

Patrick's car was still at her parents' back gate. She pulled in behind it. She felt a small thrill of pleasure at the thought of the new baby. It had been touch and go when her mum had found out. Mackenna had seen the look of total disbelief on her mother's face but she'd come round as Mackenna had thought she would. Patrick was her golden child and producing a baby would be his trump card. At least it took the pressure off her. She was sure Adam was the one for her but having a baby wasn't quite on her radar yet.

She slipped through the back door of her old family home. At first she heard nothing then came the murmur of voices from the kitchen. She paused at the mention of her name.

"You can't keep Mackenna here." It was her mother speaking.

"She's my right hand, Lou. I can't do without her."

Mackenna sucked in a breath. Why would her father have such a pleading tone?

"What about Patrick?" Louise said.

"You know he's only home because we needed help."

"You're wrong, Lyle. We've talked about it. He wants to stay but he doesn't feel included. He's your son."

"I know that, but he's chosen a different path."

"This property will be his if anything happens to you."

Mackenna blew out the breath she'd been holding and stepped into the kitchen. "What are you talking about?"

She'd said it in a whisper but they both turned to look at her.

"We thought we were having a private conversation." Louise glared at Mackenna.

"Take it easy, Lou." Lyle patted the chair next to him. "Come and sit down, Mack."

"I'd rather stand." Her voice recovered its strength. "What do you mean this property will be Patrick's?"

"He's the male," Louise said.

"So I'm just the woman with no rights?" Mackenna looked from one parent to the other, desperate for them to burst out laughing and say this was only a joke. Her father's expression was sad but her mother's was one of determination.

"That's not it, love," Lyle said.

"We've been working together for years." Mackenna could feel the turmoil in her chest rising. "I love this place like you do."

Her mother's face softened and she stood up. "It's no life for you."

Mackenna backed away. "You want Patrick to take it on."

"It's his right."

The words hammered into her heart. She turned pleading eyes to her father.

"We can work this out," he said.

"Sounds like you already have. I'm the slave labour and Patrick can turn up and reap the rewards."

"There's a lot to talk about." Lyle stood up too and gave Louise a pleading look but Mackenna back-pedalled. She ran to her car and roared back down the driveway to the Gatehouse. She burst through the door to be greeted by Adam's startled expression. Tears of anger began to roll down her cheeks. She batted them away.

"What's happened?" he said.

"I've just found out that my parents' plans for the future of Woolly Swamp don't include me." She tugged on the fridge door, took out two beers and pulled their tops off. "Let's drink a toast," she growled. "To the biggest sucker on the planet, Mackenna Birch."

Adam stared at her as if she'd gone mad. Maybe she had. All kinds of emotions were coursing through her and none of her thoughts made sense.

Adam put down the beer she'd given him without taking a sip. "What's going on, Mackenna? You went to get apricots."

She looked at the concern on the face of the wonderful man she loved. Adam would stick by her no matter what. She fell against him and felt the security of his one-sided embrace and began to sob.

Finally she pulled away from him and swept a tissue from the box.

"Damn!" she muttered. "I seem to be bursting into tears at the drop of a hat lately."

"Don't be too hard on yourself." Adam drew her close again and kissed her forehead. "You've had some tough times these last few weeks."

"That's right. I've run this place single-handed . . . with a bit of help from my friends." She smiled. "I'll be damned if I'm going to give it all up without a fight."

"Are you sure you didn't misunderstand?"

"No. My parents think the place should be Patrick's."

"What does Patrick think?"

"Probably that he's landed on his feet. He'll get a farm for little effort but he won't find it's that easy."

"Your dad's health is good now, isn't it?"

"As far as I know."

"Then aren't we talking about something that won't happen for a long time?"

"Yes, I hope so, but that's not the point. Woolly Swamp is making great improvements and even if money is tight right now, I don't imagine it will always be. I know it sounds like I'm blowing my own trumpet but at least some of it's due to me. If anything happens to Dad, Patrick can walk in and have the lot. I could work half my life and be left with nothing to show for it."

"Patrick's spoken to me about his work and how much he enjoys it. I've never had the feeling he sees a permanent place for himself here."

Mackenna thought about that. She remembered a conversation before her parents went to New Zealand. Patrick had hinted then that Louise had some plan in mind. Sometimes he'd become antsy during the last few months when she'd tried to tell him what to do but he'd never been cocky. Now she'd discovered he'd been blamed for several issues that had turned out to be due to Cam's poor workmanship. She put her hands to her head.

"I don't know," she growled. "Nothing's been the same since I came back from holidays."

A vehicle pulled up. She looked out the door and came back.

"It's Patrick and Yasmine."

"I don't think he knows any more about this than you did." Adam put a hand on her shoulder. "You've prepared a great meal," he said. "Let's enjoy it and worry about what might be tomorrow."

"You sound so like my dad."

"Lyle's a good bloke." Adam went back to his mixing bowl. "I guess I'm not making apricot puddings," he said.

Mackenna gave him a coy smile. "I've got frozen berries."

"They'll do," he said.

CHAPTER
50

"Open it up, please." Yasmine hopped from one leg to the other. Her face glowed. There was no sign of her earlier light-headedness.

They were standing around Mackenna's kitchen table and in the centre lay a large, paper wrapped parcel tied with a bow. Patrick had carried it in and set it down carefully.

Mackenna studied the gift. It had to be some kind of picture. Adam had encouraged her to make the best of the evening and that's what she'd determined to do but it wasn't so easy with Patrick right beside her.

His eyes were bright like Yasmine's, full of expectation, with no sign of deceit. Perhaps Adam was right. Patrick was unaware of their parents' plans.

She pulled the soft green bow from the paper and began to pick at the sticky tape.

"Just rip it off," Patrick said leaning forward to help her.

"Patrick." Yasmine put a restraining hand on his arm. "This is Mackenna's gift."

"You didn't need . . ." The words dried in her mouth as she slid the framed photograph from its cover. It was a black and white picture of her with her father in the yards. Neither of them was looking at the camera, they were intent on the sheep they were drafting.

"Do you like it?"

"It's . . . when did you . . .?"

Patrick chuckled. "Yasmine's taken hundreds of photos. Sit at the table. She's got something else to show you."

Adam came and stood behind Mackenna. "That's a great photo, Yassie," he said.

"I thought you might like it for your dining room wall." Yasmine smiled at Mackenna.

"It's perfect." Mackenna gave Yasmine a quick hug. "Thanks. I love it."

Patrick opened the laptop and placed it on the table between the two women.

Mackenna was nervous. What were they going to show her now? "I've got food to prepare," she said.

"Everything's done until we're ready to eat." Adam placed a gentle hand on her shoulder.

Yasmine was busy typing. A web browser opened and then a page with the heading *Woolly Swamp Corriedales* across the top. Various photos of their sheep and the farm rolled across the bottom of the page and then some smaller headings and a welcome message.

"What do you think?" Patrick asked.

"It's not finished," Yasmine added. "I can change it any way you like, but Patrick said you need a new web presence."

"What are you all looking at?"

Mackenna glanced up as her mother came through the door, closely followed by Lyle carrying a shopping bag.

"The new Woolly Swamp website," Patrick said.

A frown creased Louise's face. "I thought we agreed it was too expensive to get one made." She glared at Mackenna.

"There's no cost except the hosting," Yasmine said. "I make them for people but for family it's free."

"That's very generous," Lyle said. "I'd like to look at it."

Louise shivered and rubbed her hands together.

"Why don't you head into the dining room?" Mackenna said. "Take the laptop with you. Adam and I will bring down the soup."

"I've got parcels for everyone from New Zealand," Louise said. "Don't be long with the soup. Yasmine needs feeding up."

Mackenna clenched her nails into her palms as she watched her mother herd the others towards the dining room.

"Breathe," Adam whispered in her ear.

"I'm determined not to let her get under my skin."

"Your lamb and barley soup will be a hit."

"I think we'll need more than that." Mackenna glanced from the soup she was serving to Adam. "You make sure their glasses are topped up . . . and mine."

Adam was right about the soup. By the time everyone had emptied their bowls and had some wine the conversation flowed easily. Louise and Lyle were full of holiday stories and they handed out small gifts for everyone.

Mackenna and Yasmine got jade bracelets. Patrick and Adam had wool and possum blend socks.

"You've probably got several pairs already but you might need them for our winter if you're planning to stay," Louise said.

"Thank you," he replied and winked at Mackenna. "I'm planning to make Mackenna's home my home."

Mackenna felt her knees tremble. How had she lived without him? "I'm not sure where that home might be, though." She looked at her mother.

"You've always got a home here," Lyle said.

"As have you and Yasmine," Louise said, nodding at Patrick.

"Right." Adam jumped up. "Pass those plates and I'll get the next course."

"I'll help you," Mackenna said.

"No. My treat. You spend time with your family. Everything's ready, I just have to cook the lamb chops."

"Let me carry something," Yasmine said. "You've only got one arm."

"It's amazing how much I've learnt to do that way."

Their voices faded away down the passage. Mackenna got up to put more wood on the fire.

"Perhaps you can tell us why you needed to fire our working man," Louise said as Mackenna came back to the table.

Instantly the tension was back in her chest. "He was stealing from us."

"Taking the odd extra run in the truck," Louise said.

"You're the one counting the money," Mackenna snapped.

They glared at each other.

"He did disappear from time to time," Lyle said.

"He blamed me for jobs he messed up." Patrick poured them all more wine. Mackenna took a big mouthful.

"I agree that wasn't very sensible but not a sackable offence," Louise said. "Anyway, we've got everyone here now. In some ways it's good not to have to pay that extra wage with money being a bit tight."

"Well if I'm not here you might need to." Mackenna pushed back her chair.

"That's enough." Lyle barked. "Sit down, Mackenna. We need to sort this out once and for all."

"Not now, Lyle," Louise said. "Don't get yourself worked up."

"Yes, now." He picked up his wife's hand. "I know we thought we were doing the right thing back when I was sick . . ." His voice trailed off.

"What's going on?" Patrick asked. He screwed up his face and sent a pleading look to Mackenna.

"We need to make some decisions about the future of Woolly Swamp, should anything happen to me," Lyle finished.

"But you're much better, Dad," Patrick said.

"Yes, and I hope to be around to watch you all go grey, but we still need a plan for the future. You both need security."

"And they've got it," Louise warned.

"Wait a minute," Patrick said. "This isn't still about me having a piece of Woolly Swamp, is it?"

"You're entitled." Louise said.

A surge of anger coursed through Mackenna.

"I thought you were just being generous because I'd helped out a bit." Patrick looked at his father. "I'm happy to help and I'm grateful for the support with the car but I'm not a farmer, Dad. You know that."

"You haven't had the opportunity, Patrick." Louise's tone had softened.

"I don't get it." Patrick shook his head.

"Oh for goodness sake." Mackenna thumped the table. "They're leaving everything to you – the farm, the whole kit and caboodle." She stood up again.

"You can't be serious?"

"Nothing's set in concrete," Lyle said quietly.

"I could do with a bigger income," Patrick said with a smirk.

"Good luck with that," Mackenna snarled. "The only thing they can't leave you is my slave labour. From now on I want to earn a decent wage for all I do."

Mackenna glared from her mother's stony face to the shocked faces of her brother and father. There was a tiny sound from the doorway.

"The dinner is ready." Yasmine came through carrying plates of lamb cutlets and steaming vegetables.

Mackenna stepped round her and out the door.

"Wait, Mackenna."

She ignored Patrick's call and stormed into the kitchen, where Adam was serving up the last of the plates. He looked up.

"What's happened?"

"They've finally admitted it."

"Who? What?"

"My parents are giving Patrick the farm and he thinks it's a good idea."

"Mackenna, I was joking." Patrick had followed her. He stood framed in the doorway, hands on hips, his face in a worried smile.

"I don't find it funny," she snapped.

"You've never had much of a sense of humour. Work's the only thing that makes you happy."

She opened her mouth to retort but nothing came to mind. Was that how he saw her – a humourless workaholic?

"Can't we just enjoy our food?" Adam said. He passed them a plate each and picked up the last one for himself. "It's a welcome home dinner. Maybe you should have your business meeting tomorrow and Yas and I will disappear for a while."

Mackenna could have hugged him. It felt so good to have someone watching her back. He brushed his lips across her cheek as he passed.

"Food's getting cold, guys."

She followed him to the dining room, Patrick's footsteps echoing behind her.

Adam put another log on the fire. As family dinners went it had been stiff and stilted. He was proud of the way Mackenna had held it together in the end. He knew how much she loved Woolly Swamp and the turmoil she was going through.

Louise and Lyle had left as soon as they'd eaten their main course. They were both weary and Adam could see the extra distress the family argument had put on them. Patrick had stayed for dessert. It was Yasmine's favourite part of the meal. She still didn't eat much meat.

Since they'd left, Adam and Mackenna had said little to each other. They'd moved in tandem, clearing dishes, stripping the table, cleaning up. He turned as he heard her cross the dining room floor. He held out his good arm and she stepped into it.

"Thank God I have you," she mumbled into his neck.

"Let's sit down," he said. "I'm guessing you want to talk."

Mackenna sank onto the couch and put her head in her hands.

"We could leave them to it," he said. "Make a whole new start somewhere else."

She turned her head. "You're right. Maybe even Mum's right. This is no life for me. You and I could run a restaurant together instead, maybe in New Zealand. As long as I'm with you I don't care."

Adam studied her face. He'd never wanted the tie or responsibility of running his own place before, but maybe together they could make a go of it. She cuddled in. He ran his fingers over her curls and stared into the fire. He'd never had a lot of ambition. He'd gone where life had taken him. Happy to work and travel, try different places, meet new people, but when he met Mackenna he knew that she was where he wanted to be, regardless of wherever that was.

He liked being at Woolly Swamp and he'd enjoyed sharing the Gatehouse tasting room concept with her. For the first time in a long time he felt real pleasure in creating food for people. If they left here, they might be able to find something similar they could do together.

"What about your family?" he said. "I know this has been a tough time but you're close. If we move away you'll miss them."

"You've moved away."

"Mum and I catch up on the phone most of the time. I spent time with her while Grandpa was sick. My step-dad couldn't be there until the funeral."

"I feel so selfish."

"Why?"

"I've hardly asked you about your family and you know all the ins and outs of mine, warts and all."

"There's nothing much to tell. I'm an only child. My parents divorced when I was young. I don't see my dad much. We've nothing in common and I haven't lived at Mum's for a long time."

She shivered even though the room was warm. He pulled her closer and they were silent again.

Finally she slid from his arm and sat up holding her hands towards the flames.

"I love what I do here. I love my family, as hurtful as this has been." She turned her face to his. The green of her eyes was deeper in the firelight. "And I love Woolly Swamp. If I'm being truly honest, I don't want to be anywhere else."

He reached for her hand. "Then stay."

CHAPTER
51

The kitchen was warm and smelled of baking. Louise cast her eyes around. The table was laid for morning tea and a plate of freshly baked biscuits sat in the centre. It had to be Yasmine's doing. She was such a thoughtful young woman and very proud of her developing baking skills. Louise could hear the shower and assumed that's where Yasmine was now.

Mackenna had rung early asking for a family meeting. Lyle and Patrick had gone off to work not long afterwards. Yasmine hadn't appeared at that stage and Louise had been restless. She walked down to collect the paper. There was no sign of life at the Gatehouse. No doubt Mackenna would be off working somewhere. Perhaps Adam was with her.

Louise felt fidgety so she kept walking. She replayed the events of the past few months over and over in her head. The thought of everything finally being laid on the table when they all gathered for morning tea had brought her back to the house. It would be a relief to get everything into the open and sort things out.

Now there was nothing for her to do and she felt edgy. She glanced at the clock. They'd agreed to meet at ten thirty and it was nearly that now. Perhaps she could have a quick cup of tea to settle her nerves.

"Good morning."

"Hello, Yasmine." Louise smiled. Today the young woman was wearing a long loose red top over jeans. At last something more suited to farm life, and the baby bulge was clearly visible. "You've been baking."

"I hope you don't mind? I made us almond biscuits and then some little cakes. I promised Garry Finn I'd decorate some for his son's birthday. The party's tomorrow."

"I don't mind at all. I'm used to sharing my kitchen. Mackenna's been cooking since she was quite small. We used to make lots of things together." Louise felt a pang of sadness at the loss of those days. Their cooking adventures had been happy times and as Mackenna grew older they'd experimented together, trying out new dishes. Louise always felt she was a good cook but Mackenna had more flair.

Stomping footsteps echoed from outside – Lyle and Patrick getting mud from their boots.

"I've got computer work to do." Yasmine said.

"I'd like you to stay," Patrick said, cutting her off at the kitchen door. "Mackenna and Adam are on their way."

Louise busied herself with the cups. She really wanted this conversation to be without Yasmine and Adam but it appeared that was not to be.

"Let me do this." Yasmine gave her a gentle smile and took over making the tea.

Louise took her seat at the table beside Lyle as Mackenna and Adam came in. Greetings were murmured all around. The cosy feeling Louise had when she'd come back into the kitchen after her walk had dissipated. Now the air was full of tension as they sat around the table fidgeting with their cups. Where should they begin?

"I'm glad you're all here," she said.

"Yes," Lyle took her hand under the table and held it firmly. "We should have had this discussion a long time ago."

"So it's to be a discussion?" Mackenna's tone was sharp. Louise noticed Adam raise his eyebrows at her.

"I . . ." Louise hesitated as Lyle gripped her hand tighter.

"Yes," he said, "it is, but first I want to say something."

He didn't look at Louise. What was he up to?

"I want you all to have a chance to have your say, one at a time, without being interrupted. Whatever is decided here today needs to be by mutual agreement."

"It's your property," Mackenna said.

Louise tensed.

"It's your mother's and mine at the moment but we need to plan for the future."

Louise watched him nod first to Mackenna and then to Patrick.

"We want you to be involved in whatever way you want."

Once again Louise went to speak but Lyle silenced her with another squeeze of her hand.

"You first, Mackenna. If you could have your dream, what would it be?"

Mackenna looked at her mother. There was a moment's hesitation before she spoke.

"I want to remain here at Woolly Swamp doing what I've been doing."

Louise felt the pressure of Lyle's hand on hers.

"Fair enough," he said. "What do you imagine that would look like into the future?"

Once again Mackenna paused.

"Woolly Swamp Corriedales would be a breed with well-developed management to make them the best they can be. We would be producing top-quality meat which we'd be showcasing at the Gatehouse and selling direct to restaurants." Mackenna sat back in her chair. "We're on the way already," she said softly. "You started it Dad, and we've worked together to make improvements. I want to keep doing that with you." Mackenna looked at her brother. "And with you Patrick, if that's what you want, but you have to share the work."

"He has been," Louise cut in.

"Lou." Lyle frowned at her. "No interruptions. You can have your say later."

Louise withdrew her hand from his. She took a mouthful of tea. This wasn't how she'd imagined the family meeting would go.

"Do you want to say any more, Mack?" Lyle asked.

Mackenna looked around the table at each of them. Louise could see the determination in her eyes. She wanted to jump up from the table and wrap her daughter in her arms but she remained where she was.

"No." Mackenna leant towards Adam. He was the one to put an arm around her.

"Okay then." Lyle nodded at Patrick. "Your turn."

Louise turned her attention to her son. He clasped his cup in his hands. His eyes were lowered studying something on the table.

"I love Woolly Swamp, too. It's where I grew up."

Patrick twisted the cup round and round in his hands. Yasmine fidgeted with hers as well. Louise wanted to reach out and stop them both.

"I'm not a farmer, unlike Mackenna. I don't know what she knows."

"This is not a competition, son," Lyle said. "What is it you want to do?"

Patrick looked at his father then at Louise.

"My job," he blurted. "Marketing is what I love. My boss has been fantastic letting me help out here but I had to pass up an opportunity in Sydney."

Louise could hold her tongue no longer. "You wouldn't have left Yasmine."

"It was only for two months. I'd have been back by now."

"Your father had a heart attack," Louise said.

"I know, Mum, and I was happy to help out." He looked her in the eye. "But you want me to stay on and it's not what I want. I like the work I do. I'm not a farmer. Never was one. Mackenna's got those genes, not me."

"But . . ." Louise didn't know what to say. She had everything planned out and none of it was going as she'd hoped. Everyone around the table was silent. Anger rose in her chest. It was all very well to say what your dream was but reality was often a different thing.

"Okay, Lou. Your turn."

She locked eyes with the man she'd married and stood by through thick and thin. He was good natured, gentle and hard working. They'd had a good life and she didn't regret a moment of it, but his heart attack had been a warning that it could all be over in an instant. Things had to change.

"Lyle, you cannot work at the rate you were before your heart attack. We no longer have a working man and it sounds like Patrick is leaving. There's the Gatehouse now. Mackenna can't do everything. I find keeping on top of the paperwork is a huge job and it's only getting bigger with all the extra things we're taking on. The tax rules keep changing and I'm fed up with it. You and I aren't getting any younger. I want us to take more holidays while we can still enjoy ourselves. That's my dream, but it doesn't match anyone else's so what are we going to do?"

"Surely we're all on the same page, Mum," Mackenna said. "Each in our own way love the life we've had at Woolly Swamp."

"Yes, but you can't manage all the work *and* this tasting room you've spent money putting together."

Adam cleared his throat. "I hope it's okay for me to speak? I know I'm not officially family but I'd like to stay and manage the Gatehouse. I enjoy the concept of taking what you produce and showcasing it. There's a lot this region has to offer. I've discovered all kinds of food and beverages on my travels around the district." He squeezed Mackenna. "I'd like to stay on if you'll have me."

Mackenna beamed at him then looked back at her mother.

"I've done the paperwork for restaurants before," Adam continued. "I can make sure the Gatehouse paperwork is in order."

"I've been looking at what Mackenna's tallied so far," Patrick said. "The Gatehouse is making a good go of paying back what it owes."

"Can I say something?" Yasmine asked.

"Of course," Lyle said.

"I've really enjoyed creating the website for Woolly Swamp," she said. "You should also have a Facebook page and maybe a Twitter account. I can look after that side of things for you. I can do that from wherever we live."

Lyle was beaming from ear to ear. He's just loving this, thought Louise, but everyone having their say was all well and good. Putting it into practise was the hard part. There was so much more to plan and organise.

"There's all this extra land we've bought that has to pay for itself," she said. "And these breeding programs you're so keen on, Mackenna. They take work and money."

"A lot of the extra work is data input," Patrick said. "I've been having a look at it on your computer. I'd be happy to help with that and turning out reports. It's what I do and as Yassie said, I can do it from anywhere."

"What about the day-to-day work? Managing stock, putting in pasture, feeding, irrigating." Louise was getting more and more irritated. Was she the only one without the clouds in her eyes?

"That's what I'll be doing," Mackenna said.

"On your own?" Louise snapped. "You'll work yourself to the bone before you're forty. Look at your father."

"Yes, look at me." Lyle said. "I've lived a good life doing what I love. I've helped raise two great kids who've found two equally great partners."

"But, Lyle, you've – "

"It's my turn now," Lyle said. "You've all had your say."

All heads around the table turned in his direction.

"Mackenna won't be on her own. I know I've had a heart attack but I was lucky. I'm not an invalid and the doctor says there's no reason why I can't continue working as I have – "

"He said . . ." Louise cut in but Lyle held up a hand.

"As long as I make some changes, which I have – diet and workload, relax more. I've done what he said and I feel good. Our holiday gave me time away to think about what I want and I know that's working here at Woolly Swamp." He fixed his gaze on Louise. "If I drop dead here, what's the difference between that and on a golf course or overseas somewhere?"

"Dad," Mackenna gasped.

"I don't want to sit around worrying," he said. "I want to be doing things or I may as well not be here. You want to know how Mackenna will manage, Lou? She'll do it with me by her side and with you sometimes, like you've always done when I've needed you, and with Adam when he's not tied up with the Gatehouse. Patrick and Yasmine have offered to do some of the extras that none of us like doing but are necessary. I can't say there'll be much money in it for any of you for a while but with a family like this, working together, the future's looking good." He squeezed her hand. "Wouldn't you agree, Lou?"

Louise considered her husband then glanced around the table at the family she loved. Each of them focused on her expectantly, as if it was her decision. This wasn't how she'd seen the future. They were all so determined to have it their way. She had no say in it at all. She pulled her face into a smile.

"Of course," she said and pushed back from the table. "I don't think anyone's drunk their tea or tried Yasmine's biscuits. I'll put the kettle on for a fresh cup."

"I've had some of mine," Lyle said. "Patrick and I need to get back to that trough we've been fixing."

"I've got some lambs to see to," Mackenna said.

"I'll head back to the Gatehouse then." Adam stood up. "There's a menu to be tweaked."

"I want to get this website finished." Yasmine took another biscuit from the plate. "I'll be in my room if anyone needs me."

Louise watched her children kiss their partners and was surprised by Lyle's peck on her cheek.

"Stop worrying, Lou," he murmured. "Everything will be right as rain. You'll see."

She stood at the sink listening as the sound of their departure faded away with their voices. They thought everything was settled. She knew she should be happy for them but she couldn't shake the worry she felt. She didn't want a different life for herself but she did for her daughter. This family future plan hadn't changed that.

CHAPTER
52

"This has been a great night, Mrs Birch," Adam said. "You must be pleased with the turnout."

"It's better than any of us could have imagined. But please, Adam, call me Louise. I'd much prefer it."

Mackenna could hear the delight in her mother's voice. Adam had worked his magic on her, making food suggestions for the art show opening and then offering to cook. She lifted her hands from the sink then stiffened as her mother's arm went round her shoulders. They'd had an uneasy truce since the family meeting a couple of weeks ago.

"Thanks to both of you for all you've done," Louise said. "Your food was well received and perfect for the occasion. You've both worked so hard."

"No probs, Louise."

Adam was as upbeat as ever. They had been helping with the art show all day, from setting up this morning to preparing and serving the food for supper. Mackenna was exhausted and tomorrow night they were fully booked at the Gatehouse. She was yet to put out her tasting room sign. Bookings for dinner were keeping her busy without casuals dropping in during the weekends.

"We're happy to help," she said, not wanting to admit her degree of fatigue to her mother.

"I thought Daphne and Margaret were doing the dishes?" Louise picked up a tea towel.

"They have been," Mackenna said. "This is just the last of our trays and containers."

"We gave them an early minute," Adam chipped in.

"Yasmine's photo won first prize in the Rural Heart photograph section." Louise beamed with pride.

"I saw that," Mackenna said. "She's got real talent with the camera."

"It deserved to win," Louise said. She stopped her drying and spoke directly to Mackenna. "It captured you and your father so well."

Was this an olive branch? Mackenna didn't know what to say so she went back to scrubbing the oven tray.

"How is Yassie?" Adam asked.

"Doing very well by all accounts. The doctor told her it's going to be a big baby. I don't know how they can tell. You can hardly believe she's got a baby there at all. I think it's a girl but Lyle says a boy. One of us will be right." Louise chuckled.

"Where is Dad?" Mackenna asked.

"Deep in conversation with your uncle Alfred. I don't know whether to rescue him or not." She chuckled again. "I shouldn't be so uncharitable. Alfred and Marion have bought several pieces of art tonight. And the friends they brought with them did as well." She stacked the last of the trays and added her tea towel to the top of the soggy pile in the full bag. "I'll wash all these tomorrow. Did you get a chance to talk to Mary McDonald?"

"Only a quick hello while I was passing around the food," Mackenna said.

"They've heard from Hugh. He's settling in okay."

"Yes," Mackenna said. "I've had an email from him. He sounds busy and happy."

"Such a shame he left . . ." Louise's voice trailed away. "Mary will miss him."

Mackenna studied her mother's face. Surely after getting to know Adam she wasn't still harbouring an idea that Hugh would make a good son-in-law?

"Why don't you two have a cuppa and put your feet up for a moment," Adam said.

Mackenna flopped onto a chair. "I'd much rather have a glass of wine."

"So would I," her mother said as she sat down beside her. "I haven't had a chance to have a drop all night."

"Coming right up, ladies." Adam went out to the hall.

"Adam's made a good recovery," Louise said.

"Thank goodness." It still worried Mackenna to think how close he'd come to permanent damage from playing detective for her.

"You work well together."

Adam came back with two glasses and a bottle of sauvignon blanc.

"Where's yours?" Mackenna asked.

"I'm going to join the blokes for a beer." He poured the wine. "That guy Rory's still here and he's settled in to tell a few stories. He's a funny bloke."

Mackenna felt a pang of nerves as he left. She hadn't spent time alone with her mother since the big family meeting weeks ago.

"He's a wonderful young man," Louise said, nodding towards the door. "People have been telling me all night how lucky I am to have such a talented family."

They each took a sip of their wine.

Louise put her glass on the table and fiddled with the stem. "Life might have been a bit easier for you marrying into Hugh's family, though."

"Mum," Mackenna growled. She knew there was something brewing.

"I just want you to be sure. If you stay on at the farm and continue as you have, one day you'll be doing it alone. Your father won't last forever, as much as he thinks he can. I want him to cut back so we can have more time together travelling, even if it's only around Australia. There's so much we haven't seen."

"I won't be alone. I know we're not married but Adam's made it clear he wants to stay, and I'll keep an eye on Dad. Make sure he's not overdoing it."

Mackenna got up and restacked the empty containers into a more stable pile. She didn't want to have this conversation again.

"What about children?" Louise asked.

"What about them?"

"Do you think you might have them, because even superwomen need a bit of time off to adjust to babies?"

"Patrick and Yas are having a baby. Be happy with that for now."

"I want you to be sure running the farm is what you really want."

"For goodness sake, Mum. We've had this conversation. Why are you bringing it up again?"

Mackenna began shoving the containers and trays into bags.

"Just like your father," Louise snapped. "You throw yourself into work when there's something you don't want to face. We can never have a proper conversation."

"There's nothing to discuss." Mackenna glared at her mother. They held each other's stare until finally Louise spoke.

"Four miscarriages, I had, between you and your brother." She held up her hand with only her thumb tucked into the palm. "It was a terrible time, and I didn't have to keep running a farm."

The anger whooshed from Mackenna's body like air from a deflating balloon. "Mum, I never knew."

"You were a little girl. There was no need for you to know."

"Patrick must have seemed so precious."

"He was." Louise reached across and grasped Mackenna's hand. "But so were you. I vowed after the last miscarriage, when I left you with friends for the night and drove myself to the hospital, that no daughter of mine would have that same lonely life."

Mackenna was shocked. "I've never thought Dad wouldn't care."

"It wasn't that he didn't care. He just didn't know about the last one till it was all over. He was helping someone else who'd had a fire on their property. I couldn't call him away from that. Anyway, I knew the routine by the fourth time."

"Mum." Mackenna put her hand over her mother's.

"Your dad cared but in a different way. His answer to the pain was to work. I didn't want that life for you."

"Mum – "

"Hear me out. When you trained to be a chef, I was so pleased. Then you came back home and started working with your father. I thought it was temporary, a healing time after Carol's death but you made it permanent. At least if you married Hugh, the worry of running the property wouldn't be yours alone and you would still be on a farm."

"You like Adam."

"I do. But he's not a farmer."

"Hugh and I are good mates but we wouldn't have been happy together. Surely you want me to be with the right person and be happy."

"That's all I want."

"Being a farmer makes me happy and I think I can bring a diversity to Woolly Swamp that will only make it better. Adam might not be a farmer but he understands. The time could come when we have to get help but we'll manage for now."

"I just want you to be sure."

Mackenna came around the table and sat beside her mother again. She looked directly into the eyes that mirrored the colour of her own. "I am sure, Mum. As sure as I can be about anything. I know we had a rocky start but since I've been with Adam I feel settled. This is where I want to be and who I want to be with. I hope you can understand that, because I don't want to fight you all the way."

Louise held her gaze then hugged her close.

"I love you, Mackenna. If it's what you really want then I'll be there to help you as well."

"Thanks, Mum."

When her mother sat back Mackenna could see the moisture in her eyes. "Let's finish this wine," she said.

"Let's," her mother responded.

They both kicked off their shoes and settled back in their chairs.

"Did you see that skirt Mavis Pritchard was wearing?" Louise asked.

"I did notice it had very bright stripes."

"Bright!" Louise snorted. "They were like fluorescent GT stripes. I hope she didn't pay a lot for it. If it was any shorter we would have been able to see what she had for breakfast."

"Mum!" Mackenna's glass wobbled, threatening to spill her wine.

Adam and Lyle came in to find them giggling together.

"What are you two up to?" Lyle asked.

"Girl talk," Louise said with a straight face and Mackenna started to laugh.

"What happened to Rory and his stories?" Mackenna asked.

"He was winding up by the time I joined them." Adam said. "I did hear one bit of gossip, though."

"Really?" Louise said. "Only been here five minutes and picking up gossip already."

"Seems Cam has left town owing quite a few people money. He must have been a real con artist. That Dingo guy has left town as well."

"He'll be back when the dust settles," Lyle said. "He'll find a new bloke to take the fall."

"He's obviously smart enough to keep his nose out of trouble," Mackenna said. "The police told me they had a good look around after Adam's accident but they couldn't pin anything on him."

"We'll have something to remember Cam by for a while," Lyle said.

"What else has he done?" Mackenna asked.

"Have you seen that paddock he put in? He must have had a few blocked seeder hoses. There're a couple of long strips around the paddock with no shoots. We'll be reminded of him every time we look at that pasture."

"Stripes," Louise said.

"Like a GT," Mackenna added and they both began to giggle again.

"Time we took you two home, I think," Lyle said. "All this work's gone to your heads."

Mackenna slid her arm through Adam's. He gave her a funny grin.

"Home sounds good," he said.

CHAPTER
53

"You're so clever, Yasmine." Louise looked down at her new grandson and felt a surge of love well up inside her. "He's so perfect."

"Surprised us, that's for sure," Lyle said, reaching a hand round to tuck the blanket under the baby's chin.

"You were surprised," Patrick said. "What about me thinking I was going to deliver our baby on the bathroom floor."

"I think it was actually me doing the work," Yasmine chided him.

"You know what I mean." Patrick smiled at her. "I was relieved when the ambulance arrived."

"And I was relieved we made it to the hospital in time," Yasmine said.

"Well you both did a fantastic job." Lyle slid his hands under the baby. "My turn."

"He's a good size for being a few weeks early." Louise watched Lyle closely. "Do you remember what to do?" she asked.

"Like it was yesterday."

She envied his confidence. Holding her tiny grandson for the first time, she'd felt all fingers and thumbs. Coming into a hospital had brought back the fear that had enveloped her after Lyle's heart attack. She felt as if her inner strength had deserted her altogether.

"No name yet?" she asked, willing herself to relax.

Patrick and Yasmine looked at each other and Louise saw the small nod Yasmine gave her son.

"Harrison Patrick Birch."

Louise felt she would burst with pride. "My father would have liked that," she said. "He was so happy when we named you after him."

"I'll text Mackenna later," Patrick said. "We still hadn't decided when she and Adam were here yesterday."

"They've got another full house tonight at the Gatehouse," Lyle said.

"Adam's loving it." Patrick grinned. "You're slipping, Mum. I thought you would have convinced him to propose to my sister by now."

Louise raised her eyebrows. "That's between Adam and Mackenna."

Patrick looked at his father and burst out laughing.

Louise frowned. "What's so funny?"

"Nothing," Patrick said and Lyle just shook his head.

"They're teasing," Yasmine said. "Thank you for all these lovely gifts, Louise. Harrison will be the best-dressed baby in town."

"I had to drag her out of the shops."

Louise shrugged as Lyle put his arm around her.

"Careful," she said.

"Do you think I'd drop something so precious?" Lyle leant his head against hers and together they gazed at the perfect face of their tiny grandson. Only months ago Louise had been terrified they might never share such a moment. Now that Harrison had arrived there would be a wedding to follow. Yasmine had said so. Louise had made her peace with her daughter. Adam had fitted into life at Woolly Swamp so well and he made Mackenna happy. Life might return to some kind of normalcy.

Lyle gave her shoulder a squeeze. "Here you are, Grandma." He passed the sleeping baby back to her. "Don't spoil him too much."

Adam's arm slid around Mackenna's waist as they waved off the last of the guests. A light sprinkling of rain began to fall.

"Your dad said it would rain tonight."

"When did he say that?"

"Last night when we saw them in Adelaide."

They hurried inside as the rain got heavier.

"Can you believe those people came because they'd eaten Woolly Swamp lamb at Simon's restaurant in Melbourne?" Mackenna said.

"Of course, if they're that way inclined."

"But they were on their way to Adelaide."

"So, it's a bonus for the region as well. Now they're staying over-night instead of driving through," Adam said. "That's got to be good for several businesses besides yours."

"Ours," Mackenna said.

"Are you tired?" Adam asked as they went back into the dining room. He'd cleared away the rest of the dishes from the table while she'd been tallying the bill and chatting with the last group in the tasting room.

"Exhausted," she said and flopped onto the couch in front of the fire. "I'm so glad we had the chance to see Patrick and Yas and the baby, but it's made for a tiring weekend. I've got sheep to get in first thing tomorrow and Dad won't be back."

"Isn't that why you have dogs?" Adam fiddled with the fire, which was already heating just fine.

"Yes, but I would have liked to sleep in."

"We'll do it together." Adam turned to her. He had a funny look on his face. "I really need to learn more about this sheep business."

She raised an eyebrow. "You're looking a little sheepish. Does that help?"

"Maybe." He stepped towards her then stumbled.

"Adam," she gasped as he crouched at her feet. She put her hands out to steady him. "Are you alright?"

"Fantastic," he said and grinned at her.

She eyed him suspiciously. "Have you been drinking the red in the kitchen?"

He shuffled about and rested on one knee.

"What . . .?" Her question died on her lips as he placed a finger against them.

"Mackenna." Adam looked so serious she was speechless.

He took her hands in his. "You have made my life complete. I can't imagine living without you. Will you marry me?"

Mackenna stared into his gorgeous brown eyes. In them she saw the love he declared and she knew, as she'd known for months, he was the man for her. She bit her lip and hoped with all her heart she wasn't dreaming.

"Yes," she said.

He flung his arms around her.

"Yes, yes, yes," she cried and covered his lips with her own.

When they finally came up for air he took her hands again and she laughed.

"What?" he asked.

"Mum's got her wish. A grandchild and a wedding, maybe two if Patrick and Yasmine get their act together."

"Patrick thought we could have a double wedding."

"How did he know?"

"I asked your dad's permission when we met at Patrick's flat last night. There wasn't much opportunity to speak to him and Patrick was there."

"Where was I?"

"Talking with your mum in the kitchen."

"So she doesn't know?"

"Not yet, unless your dad or Patrick have spilled the beans."

"They won't." Mackenna laughed. "Mum will be annoyed at being the last to know."

Adam kissed her then she sat back and held his face in her hands. Rain pounded on the roof.

"What did Dad say when you asked him?"

Adam grinned. "He said I'd be right as rain."

Mackenna groaned. "That's Dad's answer to everything." She looked over Adam's shoulder at the photograph above the fireplace. There was her dad beside her as they drafted the sheep between them. Yasmine had captured an image Mackenna knew she'd always cherish.

Adam climbed up onto the couch next to her. He took her hand in his and slid a solitary diamond ring onto her finger.

"I hope you like it?" he said.

Mackenna held her fingers up so the diamond sparkled in the firelight. "It's beautiful."

The noise overhead grew louder.

"Right as rain," Adam murmured in her ear.

"I'll give you right as rain," she said and pulled his face to hers.

Tricia Stringer grew up on a farm in country South Australia and has spent most of her life in rural communities, which is where she loves to be. She is the mother of three wonderful children and their partners and is lucky enough to be a nanna. Tricia has filled various roles in her local community, owned a post office and bookshop and spent many years in education. She and her husband, Daryl, currently live in the beautiful Copper Coast region where by day she is a teacher and librarian, and by night a writer. Tricia loves to walk on the beach and travel to and across Australia's vast array of communities and landscapes. To date she has written five books for adults and three for children.

In 2013 she won the Romance Writers of Australia (RWA) Romantic Book of the Year Award.

www.triciastringer.com

talk about it

Let's talk about *Right as Rain*.

Join the conversation:

on Facebook.com/harlequinaustralia

on Twitter: @harlequinaus

#rightasrain

Tricia's website: www.triciastringer.com

If there's something you really want to tell Tricia, or

have a question you want answered,

then let's talk about it.

Loved this book?

Turn over for a sample of
Tricia Stringer's stunning new novel,
Riverboat Point!

harlequinbooks.com.au

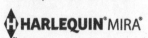

CHAPTER

1

A tapping sound penetrated Savannah's dream. Something jabbed into her back and her hip was wedged firmly. She flung out an arm and hit the steering wheel. She was in a car. Her heart lurched. The car crash! A dog barked. It was loud and close. Her eyes flew open. A huge woolly head, mouth open, teeth exposed, was right in her face.

She jerked backwards. The gear stick dug deeper into her left thigh as she twisted out from under the steering wheel. There was a mist on the driver's side glass between her and the dog.

"Down, Jasper," a male voice commanded, then, "Are you all right?"

Savannah gasped. The dog was replaced by a man's face; unshaven, frowning. She glanced around. The grey light of early morning revealed the interior of her car. Not her parents' car, there had been no crash. She'd pulled over last night, lost and too tired to drive any further.

The dog barked. The man tapped on the window again.

"Are you all right?" he repeated.

Savannah straightened stiffened limbs and felt for the lever to raise her seat.

"Yes, I'm fine," she snapped, glad the closed window separated her from the large German Shepherd.

"Not a good place to stop," the man said. "Just around a bend."

Savannah ignored him. She had completely lost her bearings last night when she'd pulled to the edge of the dirt road. It had been pointless to keep driving.

The man walked on, the dog leading the way, eager to be off. She looked in the rear-view mirror but the back window was covered in mist, like the rest of the windows. She gathered up the towel she'd pulled over her as an extra layer against the cold and used it to wipe the windscreen. A stab of pain shot down her arm. Definitely not a good idea to sleep in her car overnight. She would be stiff and sore all day.

"Bloody Jaxon and his schemes," Savannah muttered. Her brother's desperate phone call the day before had enticed her out of the city to this shack of his, kilometres away from civilisation, on the banks of the Murray River. Trouble was, she'd only been to visit once before to check what she was going guarantor for when he'd bought the place. That had been a year ago and in daylight. Last night it was as if it had disappeared off the map.

She turned the key with stiff fingers. The engine roared to life. She lowered her window and stuck her head out. The crisp chill of early morning air flowed over her. She was parked just around a bend, the stranger had been right. Ahead the road was straight, bordered by wire fences on either side. It stretched on towards some tall gums and ...

"Damn it!" Savannah slapped the steering wheel. She could see Jaxon's distinctive letterbox. The frame of an old pushbike with a box balanced on the handlebars. His idea of a joke. The only bike he ever rode was a Harley-Davidson. She pulled out and drove forward. She had been so close, yet last night in the dark she hadn't realised. Hopelessly lost once she'd left the main highway, she'd driven around for ages. There were no streetlights and not even any moon. When she'd tried ringing Jaxon, his mobile had gone straight to message bank and his landline was answered by his recorded message.

Now, as she approached his driveway, she didn't know whether to be angry or worried. She pulled up in front of the solid mesh gate. On it hung a large blue sign with navy-blue writing declaring "J&S Houseboats". The gate was latched with a chain and a locked padlock. She pulled a set of keys from her console. Jaxon had given her a spare of every key. "You're my guarantor," he'd said with that cheeky grin of his. "Everything here is yours until I can pay it off."

She tested half the keys before she found the one that opened the padlock. The gate swung free, shuddered against the fence then stopped. She drove through and on past the workshop and sheds to Jaxon's shack, perched high above the river. It surprised her now as it had the first time she'd come. The drive through the bush to get here gave no indication of the existence of the wide river flowing past Jaxon's door.

She pulled up under the carport at the side of the shack. There was no sign of Jaxon's bike. She climbed out, stretched her stiff body then stood still, listening. She heard nothing. How he could stand the isolation and silence she didn't know. Give her the sounds of the city any day.

She walked around her car to the verandah that ran the full length of the shack facing the river. All the blinds were closed and the middle section, which was once a wall with two small windows and a rotting wooden door, had been replaced by some kind of panelling, floor-to-ceiling windows and a large sliding glass door. She remembered Jaxon telling her on one of his visits to the city that he'd met someone who had a salvage yard and someone else who was a carpenter and he'd replaced the front of the shack. She tugged on the door handle but it didn't budge. She didn't have the keys for the new door. She knocked on the glass.

"Jaxon!" she called. "Hello!"

She listened but there was no response. She retraced her steps, past her car to the back. Once again the verandah stretched along the length of the shack but this time it ended in a room which was the laundry. The screen door was old and creaked open at her twist of the handle. The door beyond it was also old and weathered but solid. She hoped one of the keys in her hand would open it.

The first key she chose turned the lock. She had to give the door a shove to get it open. The handle slipped from her fingers and the door flung back, slamming into the wall.

Savannah paused on the doorstep and peered into the gloomy interior. The laundry window was filled in with cardboard. The only light came from the doorway and illuminated a large automatic washing machine that took up most of the small space.

"Jaxon?" she called again but with less confidence. Had something happened to him and she was about to find his body?

There was a faint rustle from inside the shack.

She pursed her lips and stepped through the doorway.

"Bloody hell, Jaxon, if you're playing tricks I'll throttle you," Savannah called as she turned right and went up a step, past the toilet and bathroom and into the kitchen.

With every blind closed it was gloomy inside. She wrinkled her nose. There was a smell of something musty. She reached out a hand to find the light switch and flicked it on. Where once there'd been a few old cupboards, a stove and a sink that served as a kitchen there was now a large U-shaped bench. In one corner of the U was a pantry cupboard with open benches joining it at right angles. Under the window a new sink gleamed along with an oven and cooktop. Jaxon had been busy. There must be a lot of work for electricians around the area. From what he'd told her the houseboat side of things ate money rather than made it.

She stepped further into the room but pulled up at a rustling sound. She spun and studied the pantry. It went from the floor nearly to the ceiling, the angled space between the two benches filled by a louvre door. She approached it carefully, her feet silent on the linoleum floor. At the door she stopped, carefully grasped the round handle and tugged. The door swung back, a light came on and a grey blur whizzed along a shelf close to her face. She shrieked and slammed the door shut. Not quick enough to contain the smell of mice.

Savannah clasped a hand over her mouth and hurried to inspect the bedrooms. The house was a rectangle. The kitchen and living area formed an open space in the middle. Jaxon's bedroom was the largest, taking up the side of the house in front of the laundry and bathroom. The bedclothes were pulled up, shoes filled a basket and scattered the floor around it. From the open wardrobe door she could see there were more clothes jumbled in a heap at the base than hanging from hangers. She walked around his double bed. The bedside table was covered in a layer of dust, coins and paper receipts but nothing to indicate Jaxon's whereabouts. Just a faint male smell remained. Better than mice at least, and hopefully it meant they weren't in here.

A picture frame had fallen to the floor. She picked it up. It was one of the last family photos they'd had taken. Their mother had displayed it on the small mantelpiece in their lounge room.

Savannah grew to hate the picture. Their faces smiling on a rare holiday at the beach, all she could see was her large body. How had her mother ever allowed her to wear two-piece bathers, the rolls of fat unrestrained by fabric? Puppy fat her mother had told her, but that's not what the kids at high school had called it. Savannah had hidden the photo. She wondered how Jaxon ended up with it. And where was he now? She put the picture facedown on his bedside table and continued her search.

Across the living room in the opposite wall were two more doors. The front one revealed a double bed and wardrobe and the room behind it was stacked with boxes and electrical gear. In one corner was a desk. Above it hung a pin board with papers clipped in rows and a calendar with an all but naked brunette astride a bike. Files were neatly stacked on the desk alongside the flashing answering machine. That was the house all checked; unless he was in a cupboard or under a bed, Jaxon wasn't here.

Savannah sighed.

"Where are you?" she murmured.

Suddenly desperate to use the bathroom, she went back across the living room. Beyond her the screen door swung open. Savannah turned to see the dog with the large woolly head. It bared its teeth in a snarl. She froze. A man stuck his head round the door. The same bloke she'd seen out on the road.

"Who the hell are you?" he growled.

"None of your business. Get your dog and yourself off my property."

The man's face relaxed into a confident smile. "Your property? You picked the wrong place to break into and tell that lie, sweetheart. This place belongs to my mate."

"Jaxon?" she said ignoring the "sweetheart".

His smile faltered.

She nodded at the keys still hanging from the lock. "They're my keys and I own half this place with my brother, Jaxon Smith."

This time his smile showed relief. "Savannah?"

"Yes but …" She shuffled her feet. The dog snarled again.

"It's okay, Jasper. The lady's a friend." He pushed the dog back and stepped inside, pulling the screen door closed between him and the animal. The dog barked.

"Sit, Jasper," the man commanded and turned back to her with a smile. "I'm Ethan Daly," he said. "Jaxon's neighbour. I've been expecting you. You're just not …"

Ethan put his head to one side and swept his dark brown eyes over her. Savannah felt naked. She wrapped her arms around her waist, ignoring his outstretched hand. He'd looked older out on the road. Now she thought he was a little older than her, perhaps not much more than thirty. The smile softened his features.

He grinned at her and used the hand to bat away a loose lock of dark hair that had fallen over his eyes. "You're not quite what I was expecting." He glanced over her shoulder. "I thought I heard a scream."

"I got a surprise. There's a mouse in the pantry."

"More than one by the smell. I can give you a hand if you like?"

He went to step past her. She pressed a firm hand against his chest. He stopped.

She dropped her hand. "I don't need help," she said.

His smile faded.

"Thanks anyway," she added.

He made a move for the door.

"Do you know where my brother is?" she asked.

"Gone on a holiday."

"A holiday?" That's not what he'd told her when he'd rung.

"I was expecting you days ago. Jaxon said you'd be up to take care of business."

"Business?"

"The houseboat bookings mainly. His other customers know he's away."

"Other customers?"

"His electrical business." A small frown crossed Ethan's face. "You don't know much about your brother, do you? Maybe I should see some ID."

Savannah drew herself up. "My brother's six foot – he got the tall gene. Blue eyes like mine, fair wavy hair – I dye mine – charming smile."

"You dye that too?"

Savannah ignored his dig.

"Jaxon rang me two days ago," she said. "He reckoned he needed my help urgently. I wasn't going to come at all but he sounded desperate and I'm … well, I'm between jobs."

Ethan raised an eyebrow. The dog gave a small whine.

"I don't know why he only rang you recently. He's been gone for over a week."

"A week?"

"Longer. I was beginning to worry. I know he's got a couple of bookings next week."

"Bookings?" Savannah rubbed at her forehead. She had so many questions. Ethan was right to some extent. She knew her brother but nothing about his life since he'd moved to this isolated piece of river. "There must be some mix-up," she said. "Are you sure you're his neighbour? Maybe I should be the one checking ID or perhaps ringing the police."

Savannah stared him in the eye. He looked down.

Guilty, she thought.

He reached around and drew a wallet from his pocket. He flicked it open in front of her to reveal a wild-looking likeness to his face on a driver's licence with the same street address as Jaxon's.

"You can ring the police if you like but as I told you, Jaxon's on holidays. I don't think the police will want to go look for him." He slipped the wallet back in his pocket. "I'll leave you to it. I'm just over the fence that way." He jerked his thumb over his shoulder. "Give me a shout if you need anything."

"I'll be fine," Savannah said. She was already digging her phone from her pocket as Ethan let himself out. She tried not to notice the firm hug of his jeans. Damn it, he was a good-looking guy. And he was fit and well toned, as if he worked out. She'd felt the strength of his chest under her fingers when she'd stopped him from going further into the house.

With her spare hand she tugged the keys from the door and shut it firmly on the nosy neighbour. There would be no chance to find out what was under that shirt. She'd track down Jaxon and hightail it back to the city. She wasn't going to stay in this backwater any longer than she had to. She scrolled down the screen and selected Jaxon's number.

CHAPTER

2

"She's here but I don't think she's going to go for it, mate."

Ethan pressed the phone firmly to his ear as he flicked on the kettle. The voice on the other end of the phone was breaking up.

"Okay." Ethan sighed. "I'll try, but don't blame me if it all blows up in your face." The voice crackled and the call dropped out.

He tossed the handset onto the bench and busied himself making some breakfast. He hadn't wanted to be a part of his mate's plan. Normally Ethan liked to mind his own business. It had worked for him this last year and he'd never had any trouble. Jaxon's houseboat trade had brought a lot more people to this quiet patch of river. Ethan had hoped his friend would lose interest in it and concentrate on the electrical business. But Jaxon had wanted his sister's involvement, said she needed a change of pace.

Savannah Smith was not what Ethan had expected. She had the same angular features as her brother but the feisty temperament was a total reversal of her brother's easygoing persona. Jaxon had had his fingers burnt a few times with his trusting nature. Savannah wasn't going to have the wool pulled over her eyes easily.

It had been stupid blundering into the place thinking she'd broken in. A year ago that could have got him killed. He was getting soft. From the start he'd been on the back foot. He should have realised it was her when he found her parked up the road. The photo he'd been shown had her with longer black hair not the short white spikes she sported now, but those piercing blue eyes were the same and the cute little nose. He shook his head. She could be trouble and this could all blow up in Jaxon's face.

Ethan carried his bowl of cereal and his coffee out to the front deck and settled at the outside table. Jasper padded after him and flopped to the wooden floor. Ethan drew in a breath, closed his eyes then opened them again as he slowly exhaled. The river stretched out before him. The mist that had clung to it when he'd woken was all but gone. The water looked flat and serene, belying the strength of its flow. Shadows turned it to deep green close to his bank but over the other side was the grey-brown of water in full sun. Birds of varying descriptions flew, swam, fished and sang. It was going to be a glorious day on the river.

He thanked his lucky stars again for the day he'd found this place. He'd bought it just before his last deployment. Having a place to call home had helped him settle. The only thing that disturbed his patch of the river was the houseboats coming and going from next door. He twisted to look at his neighbour's river frontage, where he could see glimpses of deck and glass. Four of the tourist attractions were moored there. He was getting used to them.

Ethan finished his cereal and settled back to watch the water as he drank his coffee. The peace of his surroundings had helped him relax. Without realising it, life almost felt normal again. The broken sleep bothered him less often. He thought about the little white pills in the bathroom cabinet. Perhaps the day wasn't far off when he wouldn't need them.

A bang, followed by another loud thud and a muffled yell brought a low growl from Jasper.

"Easy boy," Ethan said and reached down to ruffle the top of the dog's head. "Just our new neighbour chasing a few mice."

Jaxon's shack was separated from Ethan's pole house by only a few metres and a boundary fence. Ethan was glad to discover a good bloke like Jaxon had bought the place next door. They got on well. It had only ever been the two of them in the ten or eleven months since Jaxon had moved in. Now there was Savannah.

Jaxon had said his sister was a city girl. Ethan had imagined a high-heeled, lipstick-wearing office type who'd be pestering him for help at every turn in case she broke a fingernail. He chuckled. Perhaps it wouldn't be so bad having Savannah next door while Jax was away. As long as she minded her own business he'd mind his and they'd get along fine.

"Mr Daly?"

Jasper growled.

Ethan put down his cup.

"Mr Daly!"

Jasper raced to the end of the deck, barking as he went.

"Damn!" Ethan pushed back his chair and strolled after him.

Savannah stood below on her side of the fence, waist high in weeds. Jaxon really should have cleaned them up before he'd gone. It was coming into snake season.

"Sit, Jasper," Ethan said. He placed two hands on the railing and leaned forward. "We're not formal around here. You can call me Ethan."

She put her hands on her hips, tipped back her head and locked her steely gaze on him.

Ethan held her stare. She certainly wasn't the retiring type. "What can I do for you?"

"I wondered if you knew anything about hot water?"

He tried not to smile. "Depends on what kind of hot water."

"The kind that comes out of a tap when you turn it on. I don't seem to have any."

"Jaxon probably turned it off before he left."

"Off?"

"Saves electricity. There'll be a switch in the meter box under the carport. Would you like me to check it?"

"No." She put up a hand. "No need. I'll find it, thanks."

Ethan watched her wade through the long grass until she was out of sight around the corner of the shack. Then he allowed the grin to spread across his face. No, Jaxon's sister was certainly not what he'd been expecting. Damn Jaxon for involving him.

Ethan rubbed at the stubbly skin of his jaw, the smile dropping from his face. He went back to his coffee. He wanted as little to do with Jaxon's scheme as possible and that meant steering clear of his sister. He had promised to help if she had mechanical problems with the houseboats, that was all. Today he would work on his bike and maybe go fishing in the late afternoon, catch something for dinner.

Jasper sat up, ears pricked.

"Mr Daly?"

The dog growled. For a brief moment his deep brown eyes met Ethan's then he lowered himself to the deck and dropped his head on to his outstretched legs.

"Thanks for your support, mate," Ethan said. He stepped around the dog and walked to the railing again. There she was, hands on hips, looking up at him with that piercing stare of hers.

"Ms Smith." He raised his eyebrows.

"I found the switch but it doesn't seem to be working. Do you have any other ideas?"

"I'll come down."

He turned, ignoring her protest. "Stay, Jasper," he said as the dog got to his feet. "You only complicate matters."

Ethan walked through his house and padded down the stairs, hoping he hadn't been wrong about Savannah. Perhaps she was going to be the needy type after all. There was no way he wanted any involvement with her, no matter that she had a pretty face and if her shape under the clothes was anything to go by, a toned body. He needed no complications in his life right now.

He met her under the carport, where she was studying the open meter box.

"It's on," she said turning to look at him. Her eyes defied him to say otherwise but she didn't look too scary with a smudge of dirt on the tip of her nose.

"Yep," he agreed. "It's on." Annoyed now that his morning breakfast ritual had been disrupted.

"Well, it's not working." Her hands were on her hips again.

"What do you mean?"

"There's no hot water. I've checked the kitchen, bathroom and laundry. All cold."

He shook his head, not sure whether to smile or frown. "It's not instant," he said. "It heats up overnight."

"You're kidding?"

He stepped around her. "I can flick it over to heat now but it will take a while."

"What kind of place doesn't have instant hot water?" she snapped.

"I gather you have gas at home?"

"Yes."

"This is an old electric hot water service. It's set to heat at night when power's cheaper. Normally you wouldn't notice." He shut the meter box and turned back to her. "It'll take an hour or so then you should switch it back to night rate."

She glanced from Ethan to the meter box and back then let out a sigh.

He hesitated. For a moment she looked vulnerable. He felt bad about his churlish behaviour. It was obvious she didn't want to be here. This could well blow up in Jaxon's face.

"Thanks ... Ethan."

"No probs, Savannah." He gave her the briefest of smiles. "Call me anytime," he said, but not too enthusiastically.

He saw the steely look return to her eyes.

Good, he thought. Hopefully this had been a call for help out of desperation and she wouldn't do it again in a hurry.

Ethan returned to his house, disposed of the remains of the cold coffee and rinsed his few dishes. Keeping busy didn't banish the picture in his head of his new neighbour. His mobile phone rang. He tensed at the name that glowed on the screen and Savannah was forgotten in an instant. He thought about ignoring the call but it was such a rare occurrence perhaps there was something wrong.

He pressed accept and put the phone to his ear. "Mal," he said, trying to inject a casual tone into his voice. "What's up?"